The House on the Cliff

Belinda G. Buchanan

Copyright © 2024 Belinda G. Buchanan

The House on the Cliff is a work of fiction, a product of the author's imagination. Any resemblance or similarity to any actual events or persons, living or dead, is purely coincidental and not intended by the author.

All rights reserved. In accordance of the U.S. Copyright Act of 1976, the scanning uploading and electronic sharing of any part of this book without the written permission of the author is unlawful piracy and theft of the author's intellectual property. No part of this book may be reproduced, stored in a retrieval system, or transmitted in any form or by any means, without the prior permission in writing of the author. Thank you for respecting the hard work of this author.

Cover design by Staci Troilo

Chapter 1

One hundred feet below the craggy cliffside, the sun's reflection glinted off the dorsal fin of a great white as it broke the surface of the water. Perched atop the jagged bluff, House watched the dark shape swim deliberately toward the outcropping of rocks a few yards from shore, where several elephant seals had gathered. A young pup, lying near the edge beside its sleeping mother, curiously eyed the creature moving beneath the current.

The bitter February wind that had been ravaging House throughout the morning abruptly changed direction, forming choppy whitecaps on the crest of the waves.

The mother seal lifted her head, and—upon catching the scent of danger in the foamy spray—rose from the rock and began maneuvering her bulky frame across the uneven stones. Spotting the giant fin, the tip of which towered nearly half a fathom above the water, she nudged her pup backward and began to bark. Within moments, a dozen blubbery necks were bobbing up and down in unison, each one emitting the same panicked alarm.

Undeterred, the shark continued to circle the rocks in the hopes that its favorite meal would enter the water out of fear...yet driven solely by hunger, its patience soon gave out, and with a flick of its massive tail, turned and began swimming north toward the pier that lay a mile up the coast, for this time of day the ocean churning beneath it would be teeming with chum-laced hooks from eager fishermen, providing far easier prey for the shark to catch.

As the fin disappeared into the depths, the sun's rays fell across House's siding, causing the nest of yellowjackets that had taken refuge for the winter under its weathered clapboards to begin to stir. With a constant hum, the workers' mandibles incessantly scraped back and forth along the wood, irritating House to the point that it found itself wishing it could crush every single one of them, or—at the very least—separate their wings from their jerky little bodies.

Incapable of doing either, however, House

sullenly returned its attention to the sea.

The mother seal was now sprawled out on the rock; sporting deep, jagged scars that marred her sleek brown skin, she held her pup tight against her as it nursed. This was her fifteenth visit in as many years to Echo Point, but her first as a mother, and although most of the colony had already departed, she seemed reluctant to leave...for doing so meant abandoning her baby, who had been born without a right front flipper.

House let go of a small sigh, sending a cloud of soot rolling out of its crumbling chimney. There were times that the magnificence of nature could be overshadowed by its cruelty. After protecting, caring for, and feeding their newborns, the elephant seals would rise from the narrow strip of beach which had served as their home for the past four weeks and begin making their way back to the sea, leaving their pups—who were yet unable to swim—to fend for themselves.

House watched the waves as they crashed against the rocky shoreline. It was desolate—except for the half-eaten corpse of the pup who had frantically followed its mother into the ocean yesterday. Crying after her in a high-pitched bawl, House could still see its tiny flippers flailing helplessly about as the swells washed over its head.

The sound of hammering, mixed with low voices, sent House's gaze swerving to the Victorian next door. Nestled on a grassy knoll near the cliff's edge, construction workers were crawling all over it like ants as they rushed to finish putting up the vinyl siding on its south side. A stocky foreman with a grizzled beard stood on the ground below, restlessly shifting his weight from one foot to the other as he spoke with a young couple.

"How much longer?" the woman asked, her tone as demanding as the expression carved into her face.

"Well, it's like I explained to you over the phone, ma'am. We fell behind because of all the rain, but now that the weather's clear, it shouldn't take long for us to get back on schedule."

The woman's hands shot to her hips, causing her husband, who was standing beside her, to cringe. "That's not an answer," she snapped, her long blonde hair whipping across her shoulders as she shook her head. "Our condo is in escrow, and the buyers want to take possession at the end of the month, which means we need to move out before then. So what I need from you, *Tom*, is a date—no 'maybe this week or next week'—but an actual, certifiable date to go off of."

Lifting his chin, the foreman scratched his neck, leaving a trail of red along his throat. When he had finished, he glanced down at the clipboard he was clutching and slowly parted the two rigid lines serving as his lips. "I've got the cabinet installers, plumber, and tile guys all coming this week. The interior should be finished by next Monday, but keep in mind that there's still a lot to do on the outside. You'll have to put up with the noise while we work."

A lively melody sprang from the woman's yoga pants, momentarily interrupting her condescending glare. "Well, that's not an ideal situation," she said, yanking her cell phone from her flowery waistband, "but I guess we don't have much of a choice, do we?"

The foreman opened his mouth to reply, but she silenced him with a finger before pressing the phone to her ear. "Marcus, hi! ... Thanks for calling me back," she said, swatting at a fly as she started down the hill toward her SUV. "Did you get the pics I sent of the house?"

Mumbling a hurried goodbye to the foreman, the husband picked up his feet and trotted after her like an obedient puppy.

"Yeah, it really is a blank canvas for you to landscape," the woman continued, plucking her sunglasses from the top of her head as she descended the embankment. "But my main concern..." Slipping the shades over a set of cheekbones that jutted from her pale skin like shards of glass, she paused to throw a sideways glance at House. "...is that you do something to hide that monstrosity of an eyesore next door."

A surge of heat swept through House's ducts, crowding its gaze with a reddish-brown hue as particles of dust and grit escaped from its rusted vents.

"Listen, Marcus," she continued, opening the door to her SUV, "I've got to run. Just email me your plans, and I'll call you later."

House watched the woman and her man-pet pull out onto the road before looking back at the Victorian. The workers had finished the side and were in the process of moving the scaffolding to the front, giving House an unobstructed view of its new neighbor.

Pushing itself up on its sinking foundation, House sucked in a breath of salty air through the gap underneath its backdoor. "Good morning," it uttered, then waited. Although they were only separated by thirty yards and a wrought-iron fence, House repeated the greeting just in case...yet the bright yellow dwelling with its ornate wooden carvings and white wraparound porch remained silent.

House's floorboards creaked as it sank back against the cornerstone. There were two other homes within shouting distance on the other side of the small inlet, yet it saw no point in trying to engage them, for the result was always the same. Although House had no recollection of the exact moment it had come into being, it had existed on this ever-changing landscape of rock for more years than it cared to remember, and during that time, had stubbornly come to the slow and painful realization that they were never going to answer.

Approaching footsteps interrupted House's thoughts. Pushing its misery aside, it looked toward the front yard. A man House had never seen before came bounding up its porch steps. He crossed over the water-logged planks, each one groaning beneath his weight, and wrapped a set of thick knuckles around the handle of its door.

House began to tremble with excitement, making the windowpane beneath its gable vibrate.

The man twisted the knob back and forth. When that failed to produce any results, he shoved the tip of his loafer against the tarnished kickplate, causing House to grimace as the door's steel latch slammed against the brittle casing surrounding it.

Appearing satisfied, the man reached into his pocket and retrieved a key; it was the color of dull copper and bent at the tip...and for just the briefest of moments, House ceased to breathe as it anticipated feeling the familiar metal grooves slip inside its lock. As the seconds ticked by, House took the opportunity to study its new owner. Average in height, the man had a full head of thick dark hair combed neatly into place, a close-shaven beard covering a rounded chin, and a pair of eyes that looked like a couple of chestnuts floating in a black pond, yet it was the small titanium band circling his finger that garnered House's interest, for it brought with it the promise of another, not to mention the thrilling possibility of children.

It had been years since tiny voices had echoed throughout House's walls, and it found itself yearning to hear the pitter-patter of bare feet running across its floo—a click followed by a jerk made House look down. A long black box with a keypad was now firmly locked around the handle of its door.

Whistling under his breath, the man stepped off the porch and made his way over to his car, where he popped open the trunk. House watched in bitter silence as he drove a large For Sale/Rent sign into the ground. After pausing to wipe the tops of his shoes, the man slipped behind the leather steering wheel of his shiny BMW and gunned the engine, sending up a spray of muddy gravel as he peeled away.

Chapter 2

The heat that had built up inside House began to dissipate as it stared longingly at the Victorian. The construction workers had gone for the day, and despite having left the front yard littered with sandwich wrappers, cigarette butts, and half-empty cans of energy drinks, the abode stood tall and proud amongst a colorful patch of wild poppies, which had somehow managed to avoid being trampled.

Breathing in the mildew lurking behind its dank, plastered walls, House flexed the southeast corner of its wooden frame, generating just enough movement for the window at the bottom of its staircase to cast the reflection of the setting sun in the direction of the Victorian. "Goodnight," it whispered, watching the light dance along the new dwelling's brilliant canary-colored siding.

After a period of forlorn silence, House glumly turned its attention inward, where its gaze wandered aimlessly from one empty room to the next—only to falter when it fell across the blackened stain embedded in the hardwood that lay just outside the threshold of its main bedroom.

Unable to move past it, House's thoughts became consumed. Not all humans were bad, yet it had stopped being surprised by their behavior long ago, finding that when push came to shove, their very nature tended to run as dark as the blood that coursed through their veins…

House was roused from a deep slumber by the distinct sound of tires crunching on gravel, and upon hearing the familiar sputter of a flathead V8, glanced eagerly toward the drive. A moment later, a pair of bouncing headlights appeared and swept across the walls of its living room, illuminating the cluster of cobwebs hanging from the corner of the staircase.

The brakes squeaked in protest as the tires ground to a stop, and House watched a man cloaked in a heavy black peacoat emerge from the driver's side. Grabbing a burlap bag from the bed of the truck, he started toward House, his footsteps sure and steady as they navigated their way along the darkened cobblestone path.

A blast of air, followed by the foul stench of stale tobacco, days old sweat, and dead fish engulfed House as the door swung open. A cold hand, carved from calluses, began feeling its way along the wall in search of the switch plate.

A jolt of electricity surged through House's frayed knob and tube wiring, flooding the small entryway with light.

Magnus Quinn dropped his bag on the floor and let out a weary sigh. Closing the door behind him, his attention gravitated to the empty wall above the staircase, and as he stood staring at the faded rectangle burned in the plaster, absently reached up and removed his wool cap, allowing his dark locks to fall around his ears.

Finding this weekly ritual of his to be as uncomfortable as it was depressing, House shifted its weight, causing the floorboard in front of its owner's feet to creak.

Magnus' gaze shot to the floor.

Amused by his reaction, House did it again.

Pursing his lips, Magnus turned on his heel and made his way into the living room, where he wasted no time in shedding himself of his coat and boots before indulging in what had become another weekly ritual for him: downing a full glass of whiskey in one swallow.

House increased the flame in its boiler and quickly ushered the water through its pipes in an effort to comfort its owner the only way it could. As the radiator in the living room began emanating heat, Magnus settled back against the worn leather sofa and contentedly licked the whiskey from his lips, while his fingers disappeared into the folds of the thick black whiskers covering his neck.

A low wail, as brazen as it was mournful, sounded in the distance.

Magnus, seeming unconcerned by the noise, propped his feet upon the coffee table and closed his eyes.

Another wail sounded; starting off high and then dropping an octave, it rattled the dishes in the kitchen sink.

House looked outside in time to see a heavy gray mist rolling in from the sea. Long, wispy fingers, dripping with moisture, extended from the moving mass in eerie silence; curling and uncurling, they motioned at House in a beckoning manner as they slithered across the rocks.

A young seagull, disoriented by the encroaching fog, landed on the south peak of its roof. Soon after, House felt something warm drop onto its shingles. As white goop, mixed with rotting chunks of fish, began to slide down the front of its gable, House shook the asphalt squares beneath the gull's webbed feet. Flapping its wings in annoyance, it flew away with a squawk.

House looked in the direction of the jagged bluff that sat near the mouth of the inlet and could just make out the conical-shaped silhouette of the lighthouse. Seconds later, a bright yellow beam shot sideways out of the concrete structure. Cutting through the shroud of white, it lit up the sky and surrounding ocean as the horn lodged in its tower gave off another somber blast, warning passing ships of the impending danger.

The fog, as well as the night, stubbornly dragged on, and as the clock above the mantel struck midnight, House watched the glass that Magnus had been clutching begin to slip from his grasp; tumbling out of his hand, it dropped silently onto the cushion as his breathing fell into a deep and steady rhythm.

Then it happened.

Somewhere amidst the dense shadows, and beyond the bleating horn, House heard the faintest of voices. "Hello?" it shouted in return, its gaze flitting about in the murky haze. "Can you hear me?"

It was answered by a lilting moan that seemed to move effortlessly through the mist.

"Hello?" House called out again, its breath jerking with anticipation.

The moan suddenly shifted direction and began traveling upwards at a rapid pace, breaching the water on the other side of the inlet, and—as what could only be the fluke of a large humpback whale crashed down into the sea, House felt its hope fade into the darkness.

Chapter 3

"In his State of the Union address Thursday night, President Eisenhower said he would be stepping up long-range missile programs and using nuclear submarines to patrol the seas, stressing that it was vital for America to maintain its retaliatory power..."

Magnus yawned and scratched his backside with a spatula as he stood over the stove, waiting for the edges of the bubbling white rings surrounding the yolks to turn brown. Grabbing the handle of the cast-iron skillet, he flicked it upwards, tossing the flattened eggs high into the air, where they did a perfect half-somersault before returning to the pan with a hiss.

"...president also expressed the need for adapting educational programs to match national defense requirements and called on the federal government to provide the funding. In other news, Governor Knight announced that California's unemployment rate has increased by—"

Switching off the radio, Magnus snatched a fork from the drawer beside him and made his way over to the sink, where he promptly hoisted the skillet to his chin and began shoveling its contents into his mouth. When he had finished, he used the sleeve of his shirt to wipe the remnants from his beard, then picking up his mug stepped out onto the deck.

A brisk wind was blowing in from the east, and as the salt air washed over House, it could feel the abrasive granules eating away at its pilings that had been built into the side of the cliff.

Magnus, whose coat was still lying in a heap on the living room floor, seemed unaffected by the cold as he leaned against the railing, drinking his coffee.

As House watched, it couldn't help noticing its owner's relaxed stance was in direct contrast to his gaze, which was skipping nervously about—nearly floundering at times—as it darted from place to place in desperate search of a foothold. After several agonizing moments, Magnus gripped the edge of the rail and heaved his gaze toward the ocean as though he were casting a net. His eyes instantly grew still…as if they'd fallen under the spell of a siren.

House bitterly looked away.

Minutes later, the sound of an approaching car piqued its interest enough to glance toward the gravel drive. A light blue Skylark with white-wall tires rolled to a stop behind Quinn's truck, and an older gentleman with a hardened set of eyes roosting beneath the brim of a gray fedora slid out from the driver's seat and strode to the front door.

When his knocking went unanswered, he jammed his hands into the pockets of his coat and started around the side of the yard. Upon spotting Magnus, the scowl embedded between his brows repositioned itself to his lips as he stared at the set of steps that had been crudely attached to House's southwest corner in order to gain entry to the deck.

The climb, although short, wasn't for the faint of heart — due to the fact that the ground fell away after the first two steps.

Wrapping his fingers around the weathered rail, the man pressed his shoulder against House's clapboards and bolted up the stairs.

Magnus turned at the noise. "John," he exclaimed.

Acknowledging Magnus with a dip of his head, the man's mouth opened and closed like a fish gasping for air as he paused to catch his breath.

"What brings you by?" asked Magnus, his deep voice laced with bewilderment as he let go of the rail.

The man straightened, then forging a tentative smile, crossed over to where Magnus stood. "There's...a matter I need to discuss with you."

House saw its owner's neck stiffen. "And what matter would that be?"

A brown pelican being chased from its intended breakfast by two smaller birds cried out in noisy protest as it swooped overhead, causing the older man to glance up as if he were happy for the distraction.

The disgruntled pelican eventually abandoned its mission and headed out to sea, leaving an awkward silence in its wake.

Magnus cleared his throat, drawing the man's attention. "*What* matter?"

The corners of the man's mouth began to twitch as if they were having trouble staying upright. "Got any more of that?" he asked, gesturing at the mug in his hand.

Magnus eyed him for a moment and then gave a

wary nod. "Aye...come on inside."

House watched the interloper follow its owner through the door and into the kitchen, where he sat down at the small table tucked in the corner.

"Is black okay?" asked Magnus, pulling another mug from the cabinet.

"As long as it's got whiskey in it."

Magnus walked into the living room and retrieved the bottle of Calvert's from the coffee table.

Sitting unnaturally erect, as though his spine were made from a steel pipe, the man removed his hat and placed it on the ball of his knee. "So..." he said, as Magnus returned to the kitchen, "how'd you fair this week?"

Magnus set the bottle on the counter and grasped the handle of the dented percolator. "I can't complain."

"I'm sure you've heard about the *Island Lady*?"

"Aye," answered Magnus, his thick fingers fumbling slightly as they unscrewed the cap on the whiskey.

"Well, as I understand it, there was some chatter on the wharf this morning when the *Fitzgerald* limped into port."

Magnus' jaw tightened beneath his beard, yet he kept silent.

"Several of her crew said they'd seen debris floating in the channel near Settlers Point, but couldn't stop because they were leaking fuel." The man paused to scratch the side of his head, sending a swarm of tiny white flakes raining down upon his shoulders. "They said they'd been trying to outrun

Thursday's storm when a thirty-foot wave nearly capsized them, taking out their—"

"I'm going to repeat my original question to you, John," said Magnus in a clipped tone. "What brings you by?"

The man's pasty face turned crimson, highlighting the deep crevices entrenched in it. "I apologize," he said after a moment. "This matter I need to discuss with you is…difficult to say the least, and I honestly don't know how to begin."

Magnus placed the coffee on the table and sat in the chair across from him. "It's been my experience," he said, matching the man's posture, "that it's best to just get on with it."

John took an ambitious swallow from the cup and let out a stiff cough. "It's about my daughter…Audrey."

A look of confusion consumed Magnus' impatient expression. "What about her?"

"She's gone and gotten herself into trouble."

House heard Magnus take in the smallest of breaths. "I'm sorry, John," he said, sweeping his finger across his brow. "I truly am, but what's this got to do with—"

"I want you to marry her."

The water running through House's pipes came to an abrupt halt.

"I don't understand," said Magnus, narrowing his eyes. "What about the—"

"The *father*?" The redness in John's complexion faded, restoring it to its bloodless pallor. "My best guess is that his body—or what's left of it—is lying at the bottom of the Pacific, somewhere between Settlers Point and wherever the hell the current dragged it."

A deafening silence filled the room, and House didn't know if it was John's words, or the callous manner in which he'd spoken them, that had caused Magnus to clench his fists. "Who was it?" he asked in a hoarse whisper.

"The Killam boy."

Magnus pushed his chair away from the table and got to his feet.

"That's why I need you to marry her."

"Look, John," said Magnus, shaking his head, "I understand the spot you're in, but I cannot do what you're asking of me."

The man sprang from his seat. "Just hear me out," he pleaded, holding up his hands.

"It won't do you any good."

"She can't do this by herself," said John, watching Magnus empty the remains of the percolator into his mug.

"But she *won't* be by herself. She has you," Magnus stated, yet when no verbal confirmation followed, he set his mug on the counter and turned around. "*Doesn't* she?"

The light streaming through the window bounced off the bald spot on the top of John's head as he hung it between his shoulders.

Magnus walked over and picked up his fedora from off the floor. "I hope everything works out for Audrey," he said, thrusting it at him.

House was perplexed by his anger, as it saw the

man's proposition as the perfect means to bring about an end to both its *and* Magnus' loneliness.

John crumpled the edges of his hat as Magnus brushed past him. "You at least *owe* me the courtesy of listening to what I have to say."

Magnus stopped and turned. "I know *exactly* what I owe you, John, but what you're trying to do here has nothing to do with that."

"Now, you see, *that's* where you're wrong." His footsteps echoed off the walls as he made his way across the hardwood and over to Magnus, who was standing in the middle of the living room with his fists—which were still tightly wound—pressed against his sides. "I didn't just give you *money* to buy the *Gwendolyn,* I gave you back your *pride.*" Unfurling a bony finger from the crushed brim of his hat, John stabbed the air in front of Magnus' face. "Because if it weren't for me, you—and that lazy brother of yours—would still be sweeping fish guts from off the cannery floor!"

Magnus closed the gap between them, his imposing six-foot-two frame looking as if it could snap the man in half. "I'll never forget what you did for me, John," he said in an uneven voice. "You changed my life for the better, and I'll always be indebted to you…but I can't marry Audrey."

The sliver of hope clinging to John's face plummeted to the floor with an audible thud, rendering his expression blank. Lifting his chin, he tugged at the collar of his shirt and then reached into the breast pocket of his coat. "Well…perhaps this will help you see things differently."

Magnus eyed the folded paper being offered to him. "What is it?"

John shrugged. "Times are tough. Pacific sardines have all but disappeared off the coast, and I know that each time you go out, you have to waste at least two days travel just to haul in a decent catch."

"That doesn't answer my question."

"Why don't you read it?" said John, stuffing it into his hands. "It's self-explanatory."

Keeping his gaze tethered to his, Magnus made no motion to do so.

A tired-sounding sigh escaped from the older man's lips. "You're barely keeping your head above water, Quinn. And with the proposed fishing sanctions, as well as union rumors on the dock—"

"A *union* that you're in support of," Magnus grumbled.

"Regardless..." John paused to push his glasses back up the bridge of his nose. "Things aren't looking too good for you."

House saw its owner's nostrils flare, causing the unruly nest of hair lining his top lip to flutter wildly about. "What does any of that have to do with—"

"I'm forgiving your loan," said John, tapping the paper with smug desperation. "The *Gwendolyn* is yours free and clear."

Magnus glanced down at the document and then shoved it against John's chest. "I don't want any part of this."

"Quinn, listen—"

"And if you care for your daughter at *all*," he continued, moving toward the door, "you'll stop this nonsense."

"Do you know why I came to you with this, Quinn? Because you're a good man—honest, hardworking, respected by the community. And your crew…" John let out a despondent laugh that seemed to border on jealousy. "Well, they would follow you to hell and back without question."

Magnus wrenched open the door. "Goodbye, John."

Rubbing the edge of his jaw, John tossed the paper on the coffee table and started across the floor. Upon reaching the threshold, he stopped and raised his tiny, asymmetrical eyes. "I love my daughter, Quinn. I wouldn't have asked you otherwise."

"And what about Audrey?" countered Magnus. "Did you ask her what she wanted?"

"What she *wants* is irrelevant."

Magnus began to shake his head.

"I know that may sound cold-hearted to you, but my only concern is finding someone to take care of her."

"Are you sure that's your *only* concern, John? And not the fact that you're running for city commissioner?"

Clearing his throat, the man ran a rigid thumb and forefinger over his mustache as if Magnus' words had somehow wrinkled it. "You *do* realize that I can change that document from paid in full…to balance of loan due upon receipt with just a flick of my pen."

Magnus' knuckles grew white as they tightened around the knob. "Don't blackmail me, John. I promise that it will not end well for you."

The spidery blue vein that had been pulsating off and on behind the man's left temple began to throb. "I meant what I said about you being a good man, Quinn," he replied, yet House noticed his tone was sorely lacking the same enthusiasm as before. "And I also know that you would never do anything to hurt Audrey."

As both men stood unflinching, House saw a flicker of emotion move across its owner's otherwise stoic face.

Seeming to notice it as well, John gave him a contrived smile, followed by a friendly slap on the shoulder. "This is a good offer, Quinn. It's good for you, and it's good for Audrey."

Magnus pushed his hand away. "And good for *you*."

Still smiling, John cocked his head to the side. "Well, like I said," he replied, nodding at the paper lying on the table, "it's a good offer."

The hinges on the door groaned as Magnus pulled it farther open. "You know what you can do with your offer."

The pleased look sitting on John's face disintegrated. Smashing his hat over his ears, he muttered something inaudible and stormed out.

House heard a second set of footsteps in the distance and glanced to its right to find Callum Quinn strolling up the path.

Upon spotting John, Callum's feet faltered slightly. "Morning," he said, forging a taut smile.

John pushed past him with his shoulder and kept going.

Slipping his hands in his pockets, Callum watched him turn his car around in the driveway and gun the engine. It shot forward like a rocket, leaving a trail of dust as wide as it was tall behind. "What's stuck in *his* craw?" he asked, jogging up the steps.

"It doesn't matter," Magnus snapped, shutting the door with what House felt was more force than necessary.

Callum eyed him curiously for a moment and then shrugged. "If you say so," he said, then started toward the kitchen. "Got any coffee left?"

Magnus pinched the bridge of his nose and let out a heavy sigh. "No."

"I brought you your mail." Callum held up the thick bundle for him to see and dropped it on the counter before picking up the percolator and shaking it.

"Are you deaf?" asked Magnus, coming up behind him. "I just told you there wasn't any."

"Just double-checking—ah..." Setting the pot down, Callum's fingers curled around the neck of the bottle of whiskey. "This'll do."

Magnus clamped his mouth closed, making it disappear into the folds of his beard as he slid the rubber band off the mail.

As Callum stood at the counter, draining the amber-colored liquid from its glass container, House watched his gaze subtly shift from the ceiling to Magnus, who was eagerly thumbing through the stack of envelopes. Setting the bottle down, Callum wiped the drops of whiskey from the thick patch of black fuzz nestled under his bottom lip—which resembled a sleeping woolly worm—and turned toward his brother. "She didn't write you."

Magnus' cheeks flushed.

Callum suddenly became preoccupied with a dime-sized scab on the back of his knuckle. "It's a damn shame about Renshaw and his crew," he said, picking at the edges of it.

Magnus lifted his head, but kept his face hidden from Callum. "Has any news come over the scanner?"

"The Coast Guard announced a little while ago that they're calling off the search for today," Callum answered in a quiet voice. "There's another storm moving in." Fresh blood began to ooze from his knuckle, drawing the corners of his mouth farther down. "St. Anthony's is going to be holding a special prayer service this evening."

Magnus returned his attention to the mail, yet House noticed his eyes were far from focused.

"I'll pick you up around seven," said Callum, leaning against the counter.

"I've got things to do."

"Like what?"

"I'm not going, Cal," Magnus replied in a weary tone.

"Oh, come on. When was the last time you went and did anything fun?"

Magnus glanced sharply at his brother. "I didn't realize going to church to pray for men's souls that have been swallowed by the sea was *fun*." Grabbing the newspaper from underneath the stack of mail, he started out of the kitchen. "Not to mention," he continued, snatching his cup of coffee along the way, "having to go up to their families, who are clinging to the belief that their husbands and sons are still alive, and offer them a hope that's never going to come."

Callum's ruddy complexion darkened, leaving it mottled. "That's not what I meant."

"No? What *did* you mean then?" asked Magnus in a disinterested-sounding tone as he sank into the sofa.

"I meant that *after* the service, we could stop by *Gallagher's* and knock back a pint or two."

Magnus licked his thumb and opened the newspaper.

House watched Callum as he stood there waiting for an answer, yet when it became clear that he wasn't going to get one, lifted the bottle of whiskey to his lips once more and took several long swallows. When he had finished, he made his way into the living room and flopped down in a green chair beside the sofa.

The clock above the mantel clicked, and House heard its chimes spooling up.

Callum drummed his fingers against the crumpled piping lining the arm of the chair as the melody began to play. When the last chord had faded into the background, he fastened his eyes on Magnus. "So," he said, blowing out his breath, "when was the last time you sunk your log?"

Magnus dropped the corner of the newspaper.

"Well?" said Callum, arching his brows.

"I think it's time you left."

Callum stood and stretched his lanky arms over his head. "You know, we don't have to go to *Gallagher's*. If you'd rather, we can drive across the Bixby and drown our sorrows at *The Flaming Frog*. It's frequented by women who'll be...sympathetic to your cause."

"You mean whores," Magnus said flatly.

Callum shrugged. "You say tomato, I say tomahto."

Magnus tossed the newspaper aside and got to his feet.

"Where are you going?"

"To take a shower." Walking around the sofa, he grabbed hold of the large wooden post of the staircase and started up, the tips of his shoes banging against each riser as he ascended the narrow steps.

"John McCord is giving you the *Gwendolyn*?"

Both Magnus and House looked down to find Callum standing over the coffee table, the crinkled paper John had thrown on top of it was now clutched tightly between his fingers.

"Not exactly," Magnus answered.

Callum scrunched his eyebrows together. "What the hell does *that* mean?"

"It's a long story," said Magnus, shaking his head, "and a private one at that."

"Well, I'm not in any hurry...and the lines of privacy don't extend to family. So tell me," said Callum, swinging himself around the post and hopping onto the landing, "what's all this about?"

Resting his hand against the railing, Magnus searched his brother's face for the longest time, then looked away.

"Oh, come on," said Callum, giving him a playful nudge. "You can tell m—"

"He wants me to marry Audrey," Magnus blurted.

A roar of laughter flooded the staircase, turning Magnus' complexion dark.

"That's a good one," said Callum, slapping his knee.

"I'm being serious, Cal."

"Okay," Callum replied, still laughing, "I'll bite. Why on earth would John—" He suddenly stopped and jammed his tongue against his cheek.

Magnus sat down on the steps and slumped forward.

Callum scratched at the thin goatee lining his chin for several moments and then stooped to catch his brother's gaze. "Well, one thing's for sure."

"What's that?"

A wry smile broke across his face. "We both know that you're not the one responsible for her...delicate condition."

Magnus let go of a stilted breath and nodded. "Aye."

"Then tell John to bug off," said Callum, straightening.

"I did."

The smile Callum was wearing flattened into a grim line. "But you're still thinking about it," he said, tilting his head, "*aren't* you?"

A low rumble sounded in the distance as Magnus looked in any direction but his brother's.

"For Christ's sake, Magnus," he said, throwing his arms up in the air. "Why?"

"Because Hugh Killam can't."

"Hugh Killa—" Callum's expression shifted from exasperation to rage, as one turbulent wave after another surged behind his eyes. Casting his gaze to the floor, he placed his hands on his hips and slowly shook his head. "This isn't your problem," he said in a low voice.

Black clouds, their bellies swollen with rain, gathered above House, devouring Callum's shadow as he stood on the landing.

Magnus took hold of the railing and hauled himself to his feet. "It won't be long before the storm hits. You need to get back to the lighthouse."

"Did you *hear* me?" asked Callum, his dark hair falling across his brows as he slowly lifted his head.

"Lock the door on your way out."

"Listen," Callum pleaded, "I know these past few months have been rough on you—and God knows that I'm all in favor of you getting some female companionship. But if you do this...you'll just be going from one hopeless situation to another."

"*Lighthouse*, Cal," Magnus snapped, giving him a dismissive wave as he turned to go up the stairs.

"You *don't* love this girl, Magnus!" he called after him. "Hell—you barely even know her! And you're just gonna up and marry her? And then what? Be a daddy to someone else's bastar—"

The rest of Callum's words came out in a breathless grunt as Magnus shoved him against the wall. "Go do your goddamned job!" he yelled, holding him by the collar of his coat. "Because we don't need to lose any *more* brothers to the sea!"

The surprised look on Callum's face was quickly consumed by his anger. Gritting his teeth, he pushed Magnus backward. "So you want me to flip a switch and save the day, is that it?" he asked, a chunk of plaster falling to the floor as he stumbled away from the wall. "Well, I hate to disappoint you, but…" He held up his left hand and uncurled his fist. "Two fingers don't exactly make a hero."

Setting his jaw, Magnus glanced at the mangled nubs of skin where three of Callum's fingers used to sit.

"Aww, don't look so upset, big brother," he said, offering him a bitter grin. "We can't *all* be saviors now…can we?"

Thunder shook the rafters in House's attic, rattling the glass inserts of the light that hung from a chain above the landing.

"What's that?" asked Callum, cupping his ears. "You've nothing left to say?"

Magnus remained silent, except for his chest, which made a crackling noise as it rose and fell.

"Okay then," Callum chirped, stepping down from the landing. "I guess I'm off to do my job, and after that *Gallagher's*—oh, sorry…" Snapping the fingers on his good hand, he stopped and looked back at Magnus. "I mean *church*."

Horizontal drops of freezing rain pelted House's floor as Callum opened the door and ambled out.

Magnus turned and stomped up the stairs—slamming the side of his fist hard against the wall along the way.

Bristling, House sank into its foundation, then attaching its gaze to the back of Callum, sullenly watched him clamber up the moss-covered rocks jutting from the hillside until he was nothing more than a tiny speck of black moving across the slippery terrain.

Chapter 4

"*B*e thou my vision, O Lord of my heart, naught be all else to me, save that thou art..."

House listened to the hauntingly evocative words as they were carried out to sea on the feeble waves of an exhausted ocean. The storm had lasted throughout the day, leaving one of the clapboards under House's front gable dangling, the white pine beams in its attic damp, and its sludge-filled gutters overflowing.

"*...my wisdom and thou my true Word,
I ever with thee, and thou with me, Lord...*"

As the remaining clouds gave way to the darkening horizon, House could just make out the lights dotting the bottom of the valley to its north. It was there that mostly Irish-laden voices, as somber as they were broken, and accompanied by a single weeping violin, had gathered to sing a hymn that House was, unfortunately, all too familiar with.

"*...my great Father, and I thy true son,
Thou in me dwelling, and I with thee one,
High King of heaven, my victory won,
May I reach heaven's joys,*

O bright heaven's Sun!
Heart of my own heart, whatever befall,
Still be my vision, O ruler of all."

Moments later, the stoic bell of St. Anthony's began to toll. Cries of anguish went up as the heavy iron ball struck the inside of the bell six separate times...one for each crewmember of the *Island Lady*.

Not wishing to listen any longer, House turned inward and reluctantly sought its owner.

Straddling the seat of a rusty stool in the cellar, Magnus sat hunched over a crude workbench that had been made from scraps of wood, while a bare light bulb, its thin white shell littered with insect remains, faintly illuminated his fingers as they worked to repair the holes in the fishing net spread out in front of him.

House observed his mending efforts for several minutes before arriving at two conclusions: The first being that even though it was a daunting task, the job probably would've been completed by now if Magnus hadn't kept pausing after each knot he tied to take a drink from the bottle beside his elbow, and the second was the manner in which he slammed it down every time he did, suggested that he had not gotten over his anger toward Callum.

An unnecessary hour passed...followed by another.

The crescent-shaped moon looming in the sky started pulling the tide out to sea, and as the foamy spray rolled backward across the wet sand, Magnus finished off the bottle of Calvert's and got to his feet—but after poorly navigating the amount of space there was between the workbench and wall, staggered to a halt.

A pale sliver of light shone down through the crevices in the floorboards above him as he leaned against the cinderblock, drawing his attention to an elaborately carved picture frame that had been stuffed behind a wooden crate.

House heard a jagged breath fall from its owner's lips as he dropped to his knees. As he sat there, slumped over in a pitiful manner on the floor, he reached out and clumsily ran his finger along the oil painted canvas that was tucked inside the frame.

House watched as Quinn's memories of his wife began to trickle down his cheeks; starting off slow, they quickly gained momentum, cutting a trench through his beard.

It wasn't long before the pilot light in House's boiler began to flicker as its own memories of her began to stir.

Tall, with flowing locks of golden hair that curled around her shoulders, shifting, cat-like eyes the color of the sea, and a perfect set of teeth that were as blinding as the diamond perched atop her finger, Evy Rutherford appeared in House's entryway on a warm summer's day draped across Magnus' arm like the silk curtains that used to hang from its windows when it was younger.

Where Quinn had met her or how long he'd known her remained a mystery to House, yet it found itself happily trading its misgivings for the lively conversation and laughter that now flowed throughout its rooms — not to mention the fresh coat of paint on its outside and new floral wallpaper in its kitchen. House likened it to putting a small bandage on a gaping wound, yet it felt wonderful, nonetheless.

Evy harbored a deep passion for decorating, and during the days Magnus was gone, kept herself busy by scouring through store catalogs, arranging — and rearranging — the furniture, and shopping. She seemed to immensely enjoy the latter, and before long, House's insides were filled with oddities and objects that she lovingly called antiques.

When the weather turned cooler, she commissioned a portrait of herself to be painted. But what started out as something to occupy her time grew into an ugly obsession. Two tense-filled months and three frustrated artists later, it was finally finished, and she proudly mounted the enormous canvas above the staircase. House thought the sheer scale, as well as the gold-leaf frame surrounding it, was a bit much, but then again, it was also nice to have something other than cracks and cobwebs adorning its wall.

By the time December rolled around, House sparkled from top to bottom like the red and green Christmas lights nestled in the branches of the giant evergreen that stood in the corner of its living room.

Although House was extremely fond of Evy, it had picked up on the fact that she seemed to have two very distinct personalities: One was kind, generous, and possessed a type of frenetic energy that kept her from sleeping. The other, which seemed to be the most dominant, was short-tempered, manipulative...and accusatory.

The first snow Echo Point had seen in more than a decade arrived later that winter, and as the newlyweds sat cuddled in front of the fireplace, it occurred to House as it watched Evy run her fingers through Magnus' hair, and playfully giggle before kissing him on his cheek, that she loved him almost as much as he loved her.

Almost...because House saw everything, and as the months fell away, it quickly came to realize that something was horribly wrong.

The sound of Quinn's boots climbing the steps jarred House back to the present. Shoving its memories aside, it waited for its owner to emerge from the cellar.

Glassy-eyed and disheveled, Magnus stumbled into the kitchen, where he snatched the telephone receiver off its cradle and started dialing—only to stop and hang up.

Bowing his head, he took in a breath that was as unsteady as the rest of him and reached for the phone once more, and this time, as the clear plastic dial spun backward, House felt the wire behind its wall begin to hum.

Three evenly spaced rings were followed by a faint click.

"Hello?" croaked a man's voice.

Quinn tightened his grip around the mouthpiece. "John, it's Magnus..."

Chapter 5

House was jolted awake by the sound of relentless knocking. Peering outside, it saw a woman bundled in a red coat pounding on its front door with a pair of tiny fists.

Turning back, House ushered its gaze up the stairs, where it found its owner lying sprawled across the bed; his left leg was sticking out over one side, while his right arm dangled lifelessly over the other.

The knocking grew louder and more determined, eliciting a low groan from the underside of the pillow. Magnus slowly dragged his head out from beneath it and squinted open one eye. As House watched him trying to focus his bloodshot orb, the pounding stopped. Letting out a grunt of relief, Magnus dropped his head onto the pillow.

Small waves of electricity—one right after the other—traveled upwards through House's entryway, setting off an unending series of *dingdongs* as the sparks triggered its doorbell.

"*Christ*, Callum, use your key!" Magnus shouted, but the words came out garbled because of the way his cheek and lips were smashed against the pillow.

The clanging continued, prompting him to curse as he threw the covers back and got to his feet. Using the wall for balance, he jerked on his pants and shirt from last night, then clumsily made his way down the stairs and across the floor. "What do you want, Cal?" he yelled, twisting the lock on the door before yanking it open.

The woman took her finger off the bell. "About time."

Magnus held his hand in front of his face in an effort to shield his eyes from the piercing sunlight. "Can I help you?" he asked, his voice plummeting to a raspy whisper.

"Listen to me very carefully," the woman said, jabbing her forefinger, which was still pointed, in his direction. "I know all about my father's ridiculous plan—and I don't care if he offered you the *moon* in exchange, I want you to tell him no."

Magnus lowered his hand and grimaced. "Audrey."

The woman tilted her head and sarcastically blinked her big green eyes. "*Magnus.*"

A cold silence settled between them.

"So have I made myself clear, or do you need me to repeat it?"

Magnus pushed his shoulder away from the doorjamb he'd been leaning against and stared down at her. "You're a little late with your demands," he said in a clipped tone. "I called John last night and told him I'd do it."

House watched the woman's lips fold in on themselves. "Really?" she said flatly. "Well, tell me…was that before or *after* you got drunk?"

The skin lining the edges of Magnus' beard turned crimson.

"Well?"

Magnus rubbed his whiskers as if he were trying to wipe away his embarrassment. "It's cold," he finally said. "Why don't you come inside where we can discuss this?"

Crossing her arms tight against her, Audrey gave him a guarded look as she stepped into the entryway.

"Sit down," said Magnus, gesturing at the sofa as he walked past her. "I'll make some coffee."

"I prefer tea," she called after him, glancing around the living room with what House could only determine to be disdain, "with two sugars."

"I don't have any."

"Any *what*? Tea? Or sugar?"

Magnus winced as the shrillness of her voice followed him into the kitchen.

"Because if you're out of sugar, I can take it with hone—"

"I have *coffee* and *whiskey*," he snapped, then pausing to sweep his bleary gaze over the counter, glanced woefully at the cellar door and frowned. "Make that just coffee."

With an impatient sigh, Audrey unbuttoned her coat and sat down on the edge of the cushion.

Magnus dumped a heaping spoonful of ground coffee into the percolator's metal basket and set it on the burner, momentarily squashing the flickering ring of blue and orange flames.

Audrey watched him yank two mugs from the cabinet beside the stove. "So I want to know," she said in a voice that was at least two octaves higher than before, "what sort of deal my father struck with you. I asked him outright, but he refused to—"

"Can you *please*"—Magnus dropped the spoon onto the counter and closed his eyes—"just...not talk for a minute?"

Audrey's upper lip expanded outward, distorting the freckles splayed across her nose, as she shoved her tongue between it and her front teeth.

The water sputtering inside the clear globe on top of the percolator turned dark, but instead of letting the coffee continue to brew, Magnus grabbed the handle and poured the steaming liquid into the jade-colored mugs, then turning from the counter, walked back into the living room and sat down in the chair next to the sofa.

"I don't like coffee," Audrey said, giving a dismissive wave at the mug he'd placed on the table for her.

"Then don't drink it," he retorted, taking an eager sip of his own.

Crossing her legs, she began to bounce her foot as she glared in Magnus' direction.

Several swallows later, he lowered his mug and let out a satisfied breath.

"Are you finished?"

His eyes flickered. "For now."

"What was the deal you made with my father?"

Magnus involuntarily glanced at the wrinkled paper lying on the coffee table. "It doesn't matter," he answered, shifting in the sagging chair.

"*Doesn't* matter?" Audrey leaned forward. "It most certainly *does* matter! I'm not some piece of property that can just be traded aw—"

"It doesn't *matter*," said Magnus, talking over her, "because I turned him down."

The indignation circling Audrey's face faded, leaving behind a swirl of confusion. "Why?"

Magnus shifted his weight in the chair again, and House surmised that the comfort he was seeking wasn't about to be found as long as he remained as rigid as a piece of driftwood.

"Why?" she repeated, digging her nails into the arm of the sofa.

"Because it wouldn't have been right."

"Oh...I see," she said, giving him a crooked nod. "So you're marrying me out of pity."

"No—"

"Yes, you are."

"No, I'm—"

"You just said—"

"Don't go twisting my words around, *Audrey!*" he yelled. "I *know* what I said!"

A prickly silence that seemed to House to be as familiar to them as it was stifling descended from the rafters.

Audrey sat back against the cushion in frustration, inadvertently drawing Magnus' attention to the medium-sized bump protruding from her stomach. She watched him, her eyes narrowing until they were just two green slits, and then pretentiously cleared her throat.

Magnus dropped his head.

"If you're not doing it out of pity," she said, giving him a disbelieving glance, "then why are you—"

"I'm sorry about Hugh."

Whatever else Audrey was intending to say died on her lips.

Magnus lifted his gaze, which was suddenly swimming in grief, to meet hers. "He was a good lad."

Audrey's face grew pale, rendering her hardened features blank. Knotting her fingers together, she looked toward the window on the other side of the room.

"I hired him on as a deckhand last summer," Magnus continued. "He was a bit of a greenhorn, but a quick learner."

"Then why was he on the *Island Lady*?" she asked in a tone that sounded as harsh as it was accusing.

Magnus took in a small breath. "I had to let him go after a few months," he said, his voice cracking with guilt, "because I couldn't afford to keep him on."

House noticed a subtle change in her expression, yet she kept her focus on the window.

"Audrey…I'm not going to sit here and try and pretend to understand what you must be going through right now," Magnus said softly, "and I know this isn't how you expected your life to turn out, but—"

"I want you to call my father and tell him that you've had a change of heart about marrying me."

Magnus blinked, then solemnly shook his head. "I can't do that."

"Why not?" she asked, cutting her eyes back to him. "Don't you *have* one?"

The knot in Magnus' jaw grew more pronounced. Setting his mug down, he got to his feet.

"*Well?*" Audrey's left eyebrow disappeared beneath her fiery-red bangs. "*Do* you?"

"You know," said Magnus, gingerly rubbing his temple, "you're making it really hard to like you right now."

"You *used* to do more than just like me," she countered, batting her eyes at him.

Magnus stopped rubbing his temple and looked down at her. "That was a long time ago, Audrey," he said, lowering his hand. "We were just kids."

House saw the carefully crafted smile she was wearing dip ever so slightly. "That's true. A lot has happened since then."

He gave a weary nod. "Aye."

Flipping her hair over her shoulder, Audrey settled back into the cushion. "I heard you'd gotten married."

"That's right," he said, avoiding her penetrating gaze as he bent down to retrieve his coffee.

"Why did she leave you?"

Magnus gripped the mug so tightly that House thought it was going to shatter in his palm. "That's no one's business but mine."

"Well, the rumor in town was that she just up and left you one day," Audrey said, watching him closely. "Were you messing around on her?"

Her words washed over Magnus like jagged slivers of glass, leaving his face riddled with hurt.

House's boiler fluctuated, causing the radiator in the living room beside Audrey to hiss, and as a burst of steam erupted through the valve, it began to chastise itself for ever thinking that this union was a good idea.

Magnus set his mug down hard—splashing the table with coffee—and started toward the front door.

"Are we done?" Audrey asked innocently.

"You know…" he said, glancing back at her, "no one is forcing you to marry me."

"Oh, thank the Lord!" she exclaimed, lifting her hands toward the ceiling. When she had finished her gesture of exaggerated praise, she got up and made her way over to where he was standing. "Because— aside from the fact that you *look* like a member of the Donner Party—you *smell* like a distillery."

Magnus reached around her, purposefully letting the ends of his beard graze her cheek as he jerked opened the door.

She snapped her head back. "Why do you want to marry me?" she demanded, kicking the door shut with her foot.

"Well," he said, reaching for the knob once more, "it's certainly not for your charming personality."

Audrey stepped to the left to block him, sending his hand into the curve of her waist. "I'm not leaving until you tell me."

He recoiled his fingers and dropped his hand to his side, yet his eyes remained locked with hers.

"*Well?*" she prompted.

In one swift motion, Magnus picked her up by her shoulders, causing her lips to part as her feet left the floor. Swinging her around like a crane, he set her down on the braided rug that haphazardly graced the entryway and wrenched open the door. "I *wanted* to marry you," he said, ushering her out, "because every child needs a father…and that wee one you're carryin' is *no* different."

Audrey stood on the porch—red hair flailing in the wind and mouth still agape—as he slammed the door in her face.

Chapter 6

House took in a breath of damp air from its flue, then after straightening itself up on its foundation, yawned and stretched, pulling its plastered walls farther away from their studs, which in turn, widened the crack in the ceiling above the staircase. Indifferent to the damage its actions had caused, however, House fell back against its cornerstone and sullenly watched its owner as he moved about in the dimly lit bedroom.

As Magnus grabbed a change of clothes from the dresser and tossed them into a bag, House tried to discern if it was because of the events that had transpired over the weekend, or his excitement of heading back to sea, that had gotten him up at four o'clock this morning. Whichever the reason, House accepted the return to normalcy with ambivalence...as it wasn't at all looking forward to the loneliness the next several days would bring.

Slinging the bag over his shoulder, Magnus turned off the light and made his way downstairs to the kitchen, and as he filled his thermos, the sound of an approaching vehicle sent House's gaze careening outside.

It was still too dark to identify the person getting out of the car, but as they crossed in front of the headlights, House caught a glimpse of red hair and cringed.

"What are you doing here, Audrey?" Quinn's voice boomed from the porch.

"I need to talk to you."

Tightening his fingers around the strap of his bag, he stepped off the porch and started down the stone path. "I've got to get to the harbor."

Audrey reached out and grabbed him by his coat. "What did you mean yesterday when you said wanted?"

His eyebrows slanted downward as he impatiently shook his head. "*What?*"

"Yesterday, at the door, you told me you *wanted*—past tense—to marry me, because every child needs a father." Audrey's breath transformed the air in front of her lips into a quivering cloud of white. "Does that mean you no longer want to marry me?" she asked, searching his face.

Magnus' jaw stiffened. "What do you want me to say, Audrey?"

"The truth."

Something that sounded like a disgruntled snort came from the back of his throat. "I already gave you the truth. I laid it all out there in the open for you yesterday—only to have *each* and *every* one of my words met with resentment."

A single blink released Audrey's tears.

Magnus looked away. "I have to go," he muttered. With his long stride carrying him swiftly down the path, he threw his bag in the bed of the truck and jerked open the door. A moment later, the pickup's dull black fenders began to shake as the engine roared to life.

Audrey bowed her head and wiped at her cheeks with the palms of her hands, making House wonder where the abrasive disposition she had so proudly displayed the previous morning had disappeared to.

Keenly aware that the sputtering flathead hadn't shifted into reverse, House peered through the truck's windshield and saw Magnus' knuckles wrapped around the steering wheel, and although it couldn't hear any of the heated conversation that he was having with himself in the cab, it was able to lip-read the single profanity that he kept uttering over and over…and over.

Shoving his shoulder against the driver's side door, Magnus got out of the truck and strode back to Audrey, stopping just inches from her face.

Startled by his actions, her hands shot up between them and landed against his chest—where they promptly curled into fists.

"What is it that you want me to do?" he asked her in a hoarse whisper.

She shook her head, sending a ragged sob tumbling from her lips. "I don't know," she answered, clenching the folds of his coat between her fingers.

Both of Quinn's arms twitched, yet remained at his sides. "Well, when you figure it out," he said, taking a step back, "you let me know."

She reached out for him only to grasp the chilly air. "Where are you going?"

"I *told* you I have to get to the harbor. My men are waiting."

Audrey's open hand went to her hip. "You're the captain of the bloody boat," she snapped. "I'm pretty sure they're not going to leave without you!"

Ah, there it is, House thought to itself.

"Time is money," Magnus countered, climbing into his truck, "and right now…I don't have a lot of either." Closing his door, he backed up into the grass next to her and rolled down his window, where his eyes seemed to hesitate before fastening themselves onto hers. "Goodbye, Audrey."

She stared at the cloud of exhaust as he drove away, then taking in a decisive breath, got in her car and started the engine. Shifting into reverse, she turned around—giving little regard to the shrubbery in her path—and took off after him with her horn blaring.

The front of Quinn's truck suddenly dipped down, its brake lights flooding the gravel beneath it a bright red.

Flinging open her door, Audrey scrambled out from behind the wheel and began running toward him.

House tipped its weight forward as it strained to hear what she was saying, but a subtle movement on the outskirts of its vision caused its concentration to falter. Looking back at the lighthouse, it conducted a quick search of the darkened tower—and saw the unmistakable glow of Callum's cigarette.

Chapter 7

Something wiry, quivering, and coated in cobwebs brushed against the wooden laths behind the kitchen wall, causing House to stir. Looking inward, it saw a plump gray rat go scurrying across the slats.

House gave a conflicted sigh as it watched the creature scale the tiny space behind the plaster with timid agility, for there was a time not so long ago that it would have done everything in its power to scare it off…yet after five days of unmitigated silence, it found its company welcoming.

"Hello, Mr. Rat," House said in a soft voice. "What brings you by on this fine afternoon?"

The rodent's ears twitched, but its only response was to begin gnawing on the insulation surrounding the wiring with its long yellow teeth.

House grimaced. "Please don't do that."

Unfazed, the rodent continued to blissfully chew through the insulation, eventually exposing the old copper wiring.

"Please don't," House repeated in a stern manner.

The rat stopped, yet House doubted that it was because it had heard its plea and knew it was more likely due to the fact that the creature's efforts had yielded nothing edible.

The fellowship ended as quickly as it had begun, and as the furry visitor squeezed its body through a tiny opening in the attic eaves, House grudgingly returned its attention to the sea, where the giant swells on the horizon lulled it into a deep, dream-filled sleep.

The suspension beneath Callum's rusted Dodge pickup creaked as it bounced along the driveway before coming to a stop, and as Magnus got out and walked around to the driver's side, House found itself both relieved and terrified to see him.

"Thanks for the lift," said Magnus, grabbing his bag from the back. "Do you wanna come in for a drink?"

Callum took a long drag off his cigarette and nodded. "Sounds good," he said, sending a plume of smoke rolling out of his nostrils as he reached for the handle.

House suddenly felt the latch on its front door begin to scrape against the wood casing. It hurriedly threw all its weight against the top corner – but was unable to prevent it from swinging open. House sank back in defeat as Evy Quinn walked stoically to the edge of the porch and aimed an icy glare in Magnus' direction.

"Uh...you know on second thought," said Callum, releasing his grip on the handle, "I think I'm just gonna head home and grab a quick shower. I'm meeting the guys at Gallagher's in a little bit."

House watched Magnus slip his hands, which had grown stiff, into his pockets.

"Listen," said Callum, stealing a sideways glance at Evy, "why don't you come with me?"

"Maybe next time," Magnus replied, shaking his head.

Callum tossed his cigarette out the window. "It's your funeral," he mumbled, starting the engine.

Slinging his bag over his shoulder, Magnus waited for Callum to turn his pickup around before making his way to the porch. "Hi, love," he said, leaning in to give Evy a kiss on her cheek.

She moved her head out of his reach. "Where have you been?"

Magnus straightened. "You know where I've been," he said, brushing past her.

Wracked with fear and shame, House could not look at its owner as he walked into the small foyer.

"I know you came into the harbor four hours ago," said Evy, following on his heels. "But what I want to know is what have you been doing since?"

"We've been through this," he replied, starting into the kitchen. "When we dock, we have to secure the Gwendolyn, offload our catch, get in line to have it weighed, haggle over a fair price, and get paid. Then I have to pay my crew for the week, along with everyone else I owe money to. All of that takes time."

"I don't believe you – "

Magnus coughed and cursed, forcing House to lift its gaze. Its owner was standing in the middle of the kitchen with the back of his wrist pressed tight against his nose and mouth. After a moment, he took his hand away, allowing House to see his face, which aside from being dotted with five days' worth of stubble, was lean, haggard – and filled with disquiet as he stared at the maggots feasting off the rotting meat on the counter.

"Did you hear me?" asked Evy, stepping in his line of sight. "I said I don't believe you – "

"My God, Evy…" Cupping her chin in his hand, the apprehension in Magnus' eyes narrowed as they zeroed in on the left side of her head. "What the devil have you done to yourself?"

"Answer my fucking question," she said, wriggling out of his grasp.

Clenching his jaw, Magnus walked over to the sink and pulled a brown paper bag out from underneath it. "I've answered it," he said, raking the mess on the counter into the sack.

Evy grabbed the percolator off the stove and hurled it at him — where it just missed hitting his left ear before slamming into the cabinet.

"What the hell was that for?" he yelled, turning around.

Evy picked up the glass ashtray in response and threw it, this time successfully striking him on the right side of his forehead. "I'm not an idiot, Magnus! I hear what people are saying about you!"

Magnus snatched the dishtowel off the counter and pressed it against the gash above his eyebrow. "What people, Evy! Tell me!" he said, moving toward her. "What people?"

She gave him an incredulous look. "You know what people," she said in a loud whisper.

House heard Magnus' breath tremble as he took it in. "No," he said, shaking his head.

"They're the ones that —"

"Evy —"

" — live in the rocks below the cliff," she said, pointing toward the window.

Magnus' face grew taut. "There's nobody down there, Evy."

"Yes, there is!"

"No—"

"I hear them at night," she yelled. "The women can levitate. They float right outside our bedroom window, mocking me."

Magnus tossed the bloodied dishtowel in the sink and sighed. "Evy—"

"And you know what else? They don't even try to keep their voices down when they're talking about you and your whore—and all those explicit things you're doing to her!"

"Listen to me," said Magnus, taking her by the shoulders. "I'm not doing anything with anyone."

Her chin began to quiver. "But I heard them."

"There is no them, Evy. There's no one out there."

"You don't believe me," she said, her eyes welling with tears. "You think I'm just making all this up for attention."

"No, that's not what I think," he said, catching her tears with his thumb. "I believe you...but what I'm trying to make you understand is that what you're seeing isn't real."

She snapped her head back to look at him. "You think I'm crazy, don't you?"

"What I think," he said in a soft voice, "is that we need to call Dr. Greenberg."

Evy's body grew rigid. "No."

"Evy—"

"No," she repeated, pushing against him.

Magnus held her tighter. "You're not getting any better, and—"

"Any better? Let me tell you something," she said, jabbing her finger against his chest. "You try being strapped down to a table with wires stuck to your head— while they shock you over and over until you piss yourself— and see if you get any better!"

Silence, wrapped in guilt, followed her words.

"I won't let them do that to you again," said Magnus, his voice coming out in a rough whisper. "I promise."

Evy wiped her eyes. "You're only doing this because you hate me."

"No," he said, shaking his head.

"Just admit it. You hate me, and you're never going to forgive me for what I did."

Magnus gave her a weary look. "I don't hate you."

Her hand fell hard across his face. "Liar!"

Magnus' expression darkened. "I don't hate you," he said, pulling her closer, "but you need help."

"I'm not going," said Evy, digging her nails into the skin on his forearms.

Turning her loose with a sigh, Magnus started for the stairs.

"Where are you going?"

He stopped and swung an unsteady gaze in her direction. "To pack you some clothes."

As he disappeared into the bedroom, Evy's eyes went from blue to gray...to distant, and as she sank to the floor in the doorway of the kitchen, House began to shudder when she resumed what she'd been doing for the past hour and a half: pulling her hair out by the roots— one bloody fistful at a time— while muttering incoherently.

No longer able to watch, House moved its attention upstairs, where it found its owner kneeling beside the bed. After retrieving a small suitcase out from under it, he crossed over to the dresser and slid open the top drawer.

"Magnus?"

He turned and took an uneven step backward as Evy rushed into his arms.

"Please don't do this..." she begged, burying her face in his shirt.

"I'm sorry," he replied in a stilted voice as he tenderly stroked what was left of her hair.

Sniffing, she looked up at him and laid the palm of her hand against his reddened cheek. "Don't you love me?"

A wounded expression stung his eyes. "You know I do."

She undid the sash on her robe and let the ends of it fall open. "Don't you want me?" she asked, grazing his chin with her teeth.

Magnus' breath rushed out of him. "Always," he murmured.

"Then show me." Grasping the back of his neck, Evy closed her mouth over his and began grinding her hips hard against him.

Magnus suddenly pulled away with a yelp. Touching his fingers to his bottom lip, his gaze went from the blood running down them to Evy.

Grinning back at him, she licked the red droplets from the corner of her mouth...then in one swift motion pulled her right hand out of the pocket of her robe and raised it high above her head.

House caught a glimpse of steel — yet could only look on in horror as she sank the butcher knife deep into Magnus' chest.

The feeling of its owner's hand on its doorknob startled House awake. Straightening, it hastily took in its breath, inadvertently sucking a chunk of creosote farther down its chimney. After several moments of struggling, it finally managed to get the nightmare stuffed back into the dark crevice it had slithered out of and swung its gaze toward the clock on the mantel.

Surprised to learn it was just after three, House glanced curiously at Magnus who, instead of flopping back against the sofa to drown his sorrows, hurried up the stairs and jumped into the shower.

As a vast cloud of steam began to rise above the curtain, the first explanation that came to House regarding why Magnus was home half a day early was because something that hadn't occurred in months must have happened: he had hauled in a good catch. Overjoyed that its owner's luck had changed, a surge of ecstasy swept through House's wires running behind the bathroom wall, causing the light over the vanity to flicker.

The water shut off with a clunk, and as Magnus stepped out of the tub and began wiping away the condensation on the mirror, House's elation quickly vanished upon seeing that his reflection did not share in its enthusiasm.

Drying his hands off on the towel that was wrapped around his waist, Magnus stared solemnly at the bleary-eyed individual looking back at him.

After a moment, he let out a miserable sigh and pulled open the drawer beside him, where he began rifling through it until his hand closed around a pair of silver shears.

~

Half an hour later, what looked to be the hacked-up remains of a grizzly bear lay in a heap at the bottom of the sink.

"*Son-of-a—*"

House turned its attention back to the main bedroom, where for the past five minutes, Magnus—donning a crisp white shirt and pair of navy trousers—had been wrestling with a burgundy tie that he'd looped around his neck.

"Helloooo...Magnus?"

House saw its owner flinch upon hearing Callum's voice. "Up here," he called, raising his chin as he stuffed the front of his tie through the crooked knot he'd made.

The sound of Callum climbing the stairs filled the small room—followed by a whooping howl. "*Holy shit!* What did you do?"

Magnus turned from the mirror that was attached to the dresser and jabbed a finger in his brother's direction. "Not another word," he warned.

"No—I mean, seriously..." Holding his stomach, Callum doubled over. "What...did you...do?" he asked, croaking out the words between breathless fits of laughter.

Scowling, Magnus turned back to the mirror.

"Here," said Callum, wiping his eyes, "let me help you with that."

Magnus shook his head. "I've got it."

"No—really, I can help." Taking him by the shoulders, Callum spun him around—and started laughing all over again.

"Just get out," said Magnus, shoving him.

"Okay, okay…I promise, I'll stop. Just let me help."

Magnus glanced down at his tie and then lowered his arms in defeat.

Plucking it from his chest, Callum got to work, and although he didn't come right out and say it, House knew that this small act was his way of apologizing for his behavior the other day. House *also* knew that Magnus would accept it—because he always did.

"So, why didn't you just swing by *O'Malley's* for a shave and…um…" Callum's lips transformed into a tight smirk as his gaze swept over the dark and uneven sprigs of hair that were sticking up all over his brother's head. "…haircut."

"Because I'm pressed for time."

Callum folded his collar down and took a step back. "There," he said proudly, "all done."

Magnus turned to the mirror. Grunting his approval, he set about removing the half-dozen or so tiny pieces of bloodied toilet paper that dotted his face and chin.

Callum leaned against the dresser, watching. "You know the funeral for Renshaw and his crew isn't until seven, right?"

House saw Magnus hesitate before pulling off the last bit of tissue stuck to his jaw. "Aye, but there's somewhere else I have to be first."

"Where do you have to go?" asked Callum, scrunching his eyebrows together. "Especially dressed like that?"

Magnus turned from the mirror and widened his stance, looking as if he were preparing to do battle. "To the courthouse in Monterey."

Several seconds ticked by, and then Callum's good mood disintegrated. "Does this have anything to do with the pre-dawn visit Audrey McCord paid you the other day?"

The muscle in Magnus' jaw flexed as he involuntarily glanced at the lighthouse through the window.

"Christ, Magnus!" Callum pushed himself away from the dresser, sending the back of the mirror slamming into the wall. "Tell me, what did she do to make you change your mind—huh? Did she cry?" Thrusting his bottom lip out, he twisted his knuckles back and forth against his cheeks. "Did she go all *boo-hoo* on you?"

Magnus snatched his jacket off the bed and started toward the door. "This is none of your concern, Cal."

Callum stepped in front of him, blocking his exit. Placing a hand against his chest, the corners of his mouth curled into a snarl as he leaned in. "It's not yours either," he said in a gritted whisper.

Magnus knocked his hand out of the way. "Why does this bother you so much?"

"Because I can't just stand by and watch you throw your life away over some girl you barely know."

"This isn't just *some girl*," he countered, shoving him aside.

"Oh, my mistake," said Callum, bowing sarcastically. "*Some girl* you had a thing with *ten* years ago."

Magnus stopped at the threshold. Grasping the wooden casing surrounding the door, he looked over his shoulder at Callum, enabling House to see that his clean-shaven face, while pale and nicked, was filled with hopeless exasperation. "I don't expect you to understand my reasons for doing this, but a little support from my family would be nice."

Callum's eyes flickered. "Don't worry, big brother," he said with a passive smile. "I'll be here to help you pick up the pieces when it's over, just like I did with Evy—who, if I'm not mistaken…" He paused and tilted his head in a condescending manner. "I *also* told you not to marry."

Magnus tightened his grip on the casing. "I want you gone by the time I get back."

His face still twisted in a sneer, Callum placed his right hand over his heart and pretentiously raised the other. "You have my word," he said, holding up his misshapen nubs. "Scout's honor."

Seeming less than satisfied that he'd made his point, Magnus turned and walked out.

"Wait," called Callum, trotting after him. "There's something I need to ask you."

Magnus paused beside the banister and sighed. "What?"

A cynical grin pushed against the inside edges of Callum's goatee. "Do you want me to turn down the bed before I go?"

Fueled by the intake of a sharp breath, Magnus' exasperation morphed into anger. Balling the fingers on his right hand into a fist, he pivoted on his heel and lurched down the stairs.

Callum remained at the top of the landing, his face half-sorry, half-sullen as he watched him leave. He then made good on his promise…but not before helping himself to the bottle of vodka that was stashed under the kitchen sink.

~

Night had fallen by the time Magnus returned with his new bride, and as he carried Audrey's things up to the spare bedroom at the end of the hall, House attributed their silence to the fact that they both appeared physically and emotionally drained.

Magnus placed her suitcases on the floor and straightened. "I know it's a little cramped," he said, offering her an apologetic shrug, "but you can't beat the view." Skirting around the foot of the bed, he eagerly drew back the heavy toile curtains and waited.

"It's nice," Audrey replied, throwing little more than a passing glance at the glimmering ocean on the other side of the bay window as she removed her coat.

Magnus dropped his arms and wiped his palms against his trousers. Taking in a shallow breath, his gaze began to wander aimlessly around the room, jumping from one object to the next in what seemed to House to be a desperate attempt to find something to say, yet when the porcelain lamp that had been molded into the shape of a voluptuous mermaid—and had a brass rod jutting out of the top of her head—failed to yield any results, he reluctantly returned his attention to Audrey. "You looked very pretty today," he finally offered.

A swath of red shot up from Audrey's neck, engulfing her face. "Well, I'm probably the only bride that ever wore black to her wedding," she muttered, lifting the smallest of the two suitcases onto the bed.

House saw the smile that was perched precariously on its owner's lips topple to the floor.

Shifting his weight from one foot to the other, Magnus watched her pull several articles of clothing out of the satin-lined box. "Do you need any help?"

"No, thank you," she replied, her words nearly eclipsing his as she leaned over the bed.

He reached up to stroke his beard, only to have his fingers slide down the edge of a razor-burnt jaw. "Can I get you anything?" he asked. "I...um, don't have any tea, but—"

"Thanks, but I think I'd just like to get unpacked."

"Are you sure?"

Audrey stopped what she was doing and looked up. "You know...it's been a long day," she said in a polite voice that seemed to House to be as forced as the smile accompanying it. "I just want to unpack and settle in."

"Well, I'll let you get to it, then," he said, backing out of the room. "Make yourself at home, and if you need anything, just let me know."

"I will," she said, nodding. "Thanks."

Magnus reached for his beard again, but caught himself and awkwardly ran his hand through his uneven locks instead. "Well, goodnig—"

"Goodnight," she answered, giving him another hurried nod.

He closed his mouth and, with his lips stretching into a thin line, turned from the doorway.

House—its opinion of Audrey in complete and perfect agreement with Callum's—gratefully followed.

Its owner had only gotten a few steps down the hall, however, when a muffled sob penetrated House's interior wall.

Magnus stopped in his tracks and glanced back, giving House no choice but to do the same.

Audrey was standing at the window with her chin tucked into her chest. The nightgown she'd been holding was pressed tight against her mouth while her shoulders shook beneath a straggle of red tresses.

Magnus' breath quickened as a steady stream of tears started down her cheek, yet he made no effort to go in and comfort her. Cloaked by the darkness, he watched her from the shadows for the longest time—before lowering his gaze and walking away.

Chapter 8

The bottom of the sun shimmered as it dipped below the horizon, coloring the sea with its warmth.

House felt movement in its cellar, but having no desire to see what its owner was up to, chose instead to watch the last rays of light fade from the marbled sky, for even though today had been the start of a brand-new day, it had merely brought more of the same. Magnus and his ambiguous bride had left out early this morning only to return separately a few hours later; Magnus toting three bags of groceries and a bottle of Calvert's, Audrey with the rest of her things and her car. And aside from Magnus carrying the boxes upstairs for her, there had been no interaction between them…or conversation.

The strong smell of fish began to permeate its walls.

Turning its attention to the kitchen, House found Audrey crouched in front of the oven, her long locks draped across her shoulders as she patiently drizzled lemon juice over the large, headless creature that lay simmering in the roasting pan.

"That smells good."

Both Audrey and House looked up to discover Magnus standing in the doorway of the cellar.

"Thanks," Audrey mumbled, bumping the oven door closed with her hip. "It just needs a few more minutes."

"Is there anything I can do to help?" he asked, flashing her an eager smile—which sailed right into the back of her head as she turned away.

"No, I've got it," she said, rinsing her fingers in the sink.

House watched Magnus restlessly shift his feet. He seemed determined to prove his brother wrong, yet clueless as to how to go about it. Slumping his shoulders in defeat, he walked into the living room and bent down to stoke the fire.

"You've certainly collected a lot of...*things*."

Magnus glanced behind him. Audrey had entered the living room and was busily running the tips of her fingers along the edge of a cluttered bookcase. "Thanks," he answered, "but I'd be lying if I said they were mine."

"Oh, that's right..." She paused to look at him. "You don't lie, *do* you?"

Magnus shook his head. "I've never seen the point," he said, making House wonder if he was choosing to ignore her condescending tone—or just oblivious to it.

"So...*that*," she continued, pointing at a bronze statue of a monkey smoking a cigarette, "along with everything else in here, is your ex-wife's?"

Magnus leaned the poker against the stone hearth and straightened. "Aye."

House didn't know if it was its owner's delayed response or the edge in his voice that caused

Audrey's gaze to swerve back to him—where it teetered for a few moments before hurriedly drifting past his shoulder. "I'd forgotten how much you look like your father," she said, awkwardly reaching around him to pick up a silver frame from off the mantel.

"Do you think so?"

She wiped the layer of dust off the glass with her thumb and nodded. "You have the same build," she explained, holding it up for him to see. "Your eyes are the same...and you have the same dimpled chin."

While its owner's cheeks were busy turning pink, House studied the black and white photo for itself. It had been placed on the mantel by Evy around the same time the monkey had shown up. A tall, slender, broad-chested man dressed in a worn Guernsey sweater and oilskin pants was standing on a dock in front of a ship that appeared to have seen better days. Holding onto the ends of a thick rope that was coiled around his shoulder, his sun-weathered face was aimed in the general direction of the camera lens, while the curved handle of a wooden pipe dangled from his lips.

"How old was he here?"

Magnus scratched the back of his neck. "Thirty-five, I think."

"The same age as you are now."

"Aye."

Audrey's expression grew solemn. "Don't you ever worry that you'll end up like him?"

"You mean bald?" Magnus laughed. "I hope not."

"No..." she said, returning the frame to the mantel. "I mean taken by the sea."

The grin sitting above Magnus' new-found dimple crumbled. Several agonizing seconds went by, and then a cheerful-sounding bell went off in the kitchen, prompting Audrey to walk away.

Magnus waited for her to fill the plates and set them on the table before taking the seat across from her. "This looks delicious," he said, enthusiastically plunging his fork into the flaked white meat.

Unfolding her napkin, Audrey watched him shovel a large portion into his mouth. "Magnus? I'm sorry for what I just said."

He shook his head and swallowed, forcing the chunk of fish down his throat. "There's no need for you to be sorry."

"*Are* you worried, though?"

His lips stretched into a bleak smile. "In light of what's happened...I understand your fears, but I learned a long time ago that nothing can be gained by worrying over things that are out of my control. The sea is one of them."

Acknowledging his words with a half-hearted nod, Audrey's eyelashes grazed her cheeks as she returned her attention to her plate.

Magnus continued to stare at her, his gaze, unencumbered for the first time, thirstily drank her in, sweeping over every line, curve, and freckle her delicate face held; when it seemed close to overflowing, he swallowed and let it fall to the table, where it settled upon her wrist.

Curious as to why he'd stopped there, House followed suit and noticed a tiny rose engraved on the inside of her forearm. House had never seen a woman with a tattoo before, yet found the exquisitely formed, vibrant red petals to be a striking contrast to the dull blue nautical star that was sprawled across its owner's right shoulder.

"It's in memory of my mother."

Magnus looked up to find Audrey's eyes fixed on his. He dipped his head apologetically. "I was…very sorry to hear of her passing."

Audrey tugged at the sleeve of her sweater, pulling it over the colorful ink. "Thank you."

"She was one of the sweetest women I've ever had the fortune to know, and she never passed up an opportunity to brag to me about your accomplishments," said Magnus with a small chuckle.

"You know…" Audrey said, tucking a wisp of hair behind her ear, "I looked for you at the funeral."

Finding her statement ridiculously hard to believe, House scoffed, making the floorboards beneath her feet creak.

Magnus leaned back in his chair and plucked the bottle of Calvert's from off the counter. "Well," he replied, breaking the seal, "I didn't want to upset you any further by being there."

Audrey put her fork down. "Why would you think that would upset me?"

"Because the last time we spoke," he said, pouring the whiskey into his glass, "you called me a pig-headed bastard."

She gave him an exaggerated, single blink. "Funny. I don't remember that."

"That's not surprising," he said flatly.

"What's that supposed to mean?"

"Nothing," he replied, raising the glass to his lips.

Audrey tilted her head, making the blood rush to one side of her face. "Are you implying that I don't remember that day?"

"No, I'm simply—"

"Because I do. I remember *exactly* where we were. I remember what time it was. I remember the rain coming down around us...and I remember every ugly word you—"

Magnus brought his glass down hard against the table, sending the amber-colored liquid sloshing over the side. "Can we *please* change the subject?"

"Why?" she asked, giving him a shrug that was just as—if not more—sarcastic than her previous gesture. "*You're* the one that brought it up."

"I only wanted to tell you how sorry I was about your mother—not rehash the bloody past!"

Crossing her arms, Audrey sat back, her jade-colored eyes boring a hole into the center of Magnus' skull as he picked up his glass and drained it of its contents.

A long and painful silence followed.

It was eventually broken by the sound of Magnus' fork hitting the plate as he rammed the tines of it into his fish.

House cast an expectant glance at the plate to see if it had cracked, only to catch sight of its owner's nostrils flaring outward as his breath noisily exited through them.

After several moments, Magnus reached for the bottle again. "Did you like living in San Francisco?" he asked, the low inflection in his voice suggesting to House that he was struggling to let go of his anger.

"Yes."

Magnus waited for Audrey to expound upon her answer, but when it became clear that she wasn't about to, he refilled his glass and took another swallow. When he'd finished, he grudgingly looked across the table at her. "Did you enjoy teaching there?"

Sitting forward, Audrey lowered her arms and gripped the linen napkin that was lying in her lap. "I adored it," she finally said, a small smile digging at the corners of her downturned mouth. "There's not a better place in the world to teach art to a group of inquisitive eleven-year-olds than The Golden City." She absently began twisting the napkin around the tips of her fingers. "All you had to do to be inspired was look out the window..."

As she went on, House realized that her voice, which seemed to be virulent by nature, had grown soft, almost dulcet—and judging by the serene expression that had settled upon its owner's face—guessed that he'd noticed it as well.

"...was always something to do there, along with plenty of friends to do it with."

The fire in the hearth crackled and hissed, drawing attention to the fact that she'd stopped talking.

Startled by the silence, Magnus' eyes slowly found their way to hers. "It sounds like you had a nice life there."

"I did," she replied, holding his gaze. "In fact, I wish I'd never come back."

Her remark left the edge of Magnus' jaw swimming in a sea of crimson. "Why *did* you then?" he asked, shoving his plate away.

Audrey pursed her lips. "Because last month, the school board saw fit to dismiss me."

Magnus' brows knotted together, momentarily disrupting their downward slant. "Why?"

"Are you seriou—?" Audrey got to her feet. "Why do you *think*?" she yelled, gesturing at her stomach. "Apparently, this made me a bad role model for young girls, who are—according to the principal—'very impressionable at that age.'"

The muscles running along the back of Magnus' hand rose like strands of rope as he gripped his glass.

"What's the matter?" she asked, leaning over the table. "Are you all out of questions?"

Magnus stared at her for the longest time, his expression unreadable. "Did Hugh know that you were pregnant?"

Audrey's face darkened. Throwing her napkin on the table, she grabbed her plate and stalked over to the sink.

Magnus rose stiffly from his chair. "*Did* he?"

"Why should it matter to you?"

"It's a fair question," he said, walking up behind her, "and one that I deserve an answer to."

"Why?" She whirled around. "Are you trying to do the math?"

"My God, woman!" he said, throwing his head back. "Why do you have to be so spiteful? Would it kill you to just talk to me? Or would that be considered too much work for that barbed tongue of yours?"

"You want an answer?" Audrey folded her arms against her chest. "Okay. Here it is. I met Hugh the night after my mother's funeral. I was at *Gallagher's* catching up with a few of my girlfriends from high school, when I noticed him smiling at me from the other end of the bar. He was sweet. I was lonely. And we were *both* just a little bit drunk," she said, matter of fact, yet House could see the tears pooling in her eyes. "I was already back teaching when I found out that I was..." She turned from Magnus and wrapped her fingers around the edge of the sink. "I was planning on telling him last week."

Magnus' gaze softened. "I'm sorry."

"You know," she said, shaking her head, "I was perfectly prepared to raise this baby on my own — but with no job, no income in the foreseeable future, and no family other than my father, it didn't leave me much of a choice."

Reaching into his pocket, Magnus pulled out a neatly folded handkerchief and offered it to her. "Do you want to know what I think?" he asked, placing his other hand on her shoulder. "I think that principal of yours is a bloody stook."

She shrugged him off. "I don't need or *want* your pity."

Magnus dropped the handkerchief on the counter and rubbed his jaw.

"Knock knock..."

House looked toward the front door in time to see Callum walking through it with one hand behind his back and the other covering his eyes. "I hope you two lovebirds are decent."

Snatching the handkerchief off the counter, Audrey raked it across her eyelids.

Magnus went to the threshold of the kitchen and stopped. "What are you doing here, Cal?"

"What do you mean, what am I doing here?" he asked, lowering his hand. "I came to welcome Audrey to the family. So..." He craned his neck trying to peer around him. "Where *is* my new sister-in-law?"

Magnus stepped in his line of sight. "This isn't a good time."

Undeterred, Callum looked past his brother's shoulder. "Ah, there she is. Hi, Audrey," he sang out.

Taking in a deep breath, she turned from the sink and acknowledged Callum with a curt nod.

"Geez, Magnus," he said, throwing up his arm. "You haven't even been married twenty-four hours and you've already made her cry."

Magnus sighed. "I *said* this isn't a good time."

"But I come bearing gifts," Callum replied, whipping a bottle of wine out from behind his back. "After the funeral, I didn't even get a chance to offer my congratulations, because the two of you hurried out of the church like you'd been shot out of a cannon. I'm guessing you were both just anxious to get on with your honeymoon." He waggled his eyebrows and grinned. "Am I right?"

An uncomfortable silence erupted.

"Oh, come on," said Callum, making a face. "Can't you take a joke?"

"Cal, this isn't—"

"Here," he said, thrusting the bottle at Magnus. "I promise, just one toast and I'm gone—hey, is that perch?" Traipsing across the floor, he plopped down in Magnus' chair and helped himself to his plate.

House felt a vibration beginning to stir behind its kitchen wall. Seconds later the phone let out a shrill yell.

Magnus walked around the table and yanked the receiver off its cradle. "Hello?" he grumbled into the yellow mouthpiece. "Amos? ... No, sorry, it's all right. What's wrong?"

"*Well*, love?"

Audrey's gaze traveled from Magnus to Callum.

Bits of fish clung to his chin as he leaned over and patted the chair beside him. "Don't be shy."

"...sorry to hear that," said Magnus, pressing his knuckles hard against the wallpaper's peeling seam. "Do you know for how long?"

With Magnus' back still turned, Audrey walked up to the table—and promptly snatched the plate away from Callum.

"...don't worry about it," Magnus continued, "and be sure and let me know if you need anything..."

As Audrey marched toward the sink, House noticed Callum leering at her backside. Watching her intently, his tongue slithered out from between his lips and slowly began to lick the grease off his thumb as he adjusted his crotch with his good hand.

"Aye...take care."

"So," chirped Callum, cutting his eyes to his brother as he hung up the phone, "who died?"

The frown Magnus was sporting turned into a scowl.

"Oh—sorry," Callum replied in a tone that was anything but. "Bad choice of words."

Shaking his head in a dismissive manner, Magnus placed the bottle on the table and sat down. "Amos Balfour broke his leg this afternoon."

"How the hell did he do that?"

"He fell off a ladder while trying to patch a hole in his roof."

Callum laughed. "What a feckin' eejit."

A clattering noise filled the kitchen as Audrey dropped the plate in the sink.

"Eejit or not," said Magnus, rubbing his eyes, "I'm out a deckhand for the next six weeks."

"Well, if you're short a hand..." With mock enthusiasm, Callum placed his elbows on the table and propped his chin on his nubbed fingers.

"I'm being serious, Cal."

"So am I," he said innocently.

House sighed. The hurt expression Callum had meticulously plastered to his face was as fake as it was over the top, and yet Magnus fell for it every—single—time.

"Aww, come on, Magnus. Things could be a lot worse."

"How so?"

Callum picked up the butter knife beside him and began turning it end over end while aiming a set of piercing—though somewhat glazed—brown eyes at his brother. "At least Amos' accident wasn't your fault."

House saw its owner's jaw tighten.

"Tell me something," said Callum, pressing his shoulder blades against the wooden slats of the chair. "Does what happened to me ever keep you awake at night?"

The echo of Audrey's footsteps only served to magnify the tension that was circling the room.

Callum watched her place the wine glasses on the table and return to her seat before looking back at Magnus. "Did you tell her about that day?"

"No."

"Why not?"

"Because contrary to the popular opinion you have of yourself," Magnus answered in a tired voice, "the subject of you never came up."

"Well," said Callum, slapping his knee, "let me rectify that."

"Cal—"

"It was just after dawn," he started, "and there was a storm brewing a few miles to the east of us. You could see the lightning in the distance, as well as the cold black swells surging below." Callum paused to glance at Audrey. "Have you ever been on a ship during a storm, love?"

Audrey answered him with a cold stare.

"Well," Callum continued, "there's nothing to compare it to. You're standing on the deck trying to do your job while twenty-foot waves are crashing against it, and the rain coming at you is so hard it feels like your face is being pelted with glass." He stopped and shook his head. "Anyway, the eight hundred feet of net we'd put out was already roiling with fish. I hit the lever on the winch to start bringing it up, but after a few revolutions it stopped. That was when Magnus gave the order to roundhaul..."

Having the ability to repeat Callum's sea-faring tale verbatim, House looked at Audrey. She was sitting in the chair with her hands and legs crossed; her right foot, which was dangling just above her left ankle, impatiently swung back and forth as she listened to him prattle on.

"...deck of the *Gwendolyn* was pitching at a forty-five-degree angle as we started pulling the net in by hand. Within seconds, we were knee-deep in net and sardines. Now, we didn't say it out loud, but we could feel the excitement coursing through us each time we pulled." Callum paused—right on cue—and grinned. "We knew it was going to be a great day. But just then, the wind changed direction, and the net started to go under the ship," he said, making a furious downward gesture with his fingers. "Magnus brought her about, and it was all hands on deck to pull it in. We had maybe two hundred feet of net left when the deck pitched again, throwing me forward against the winch—which suddenly started turning. Before I could get my feet under me, it caught the tip of my glove and jerked my fingers into the capstan as it began winding the cable."

The clock on the mantel in the living room clicked and began playing a buoyant melody.

"You can't possibly know what real pain is, Audrey," said Callum, raising his voice to be heard, "until you've had your fingers wedged between a rotating drum and steel cable. The tension on it was so tight that it broke every one of my knuckles before ripping off the skin and slicing through the muscle and bone." Letting out a quivering breath, Callum grimaced and closed his eyes. When he opened them again, they were looking straight at Magnus. "If it hadn't been for the quick actions of a greenhorn, I would've lost more than my fingers that morning."

Magnus stared back at him, his lips pulled tight across his face in a grim line, as his fists rested uneasily in his lap.

"Why didn't you turn off the winch?"

Callum's damning gaze faltered. "*What?*" he asked, jerking his head toward Audrey.

"You said that you hit the lever on the winch to bring up the net. When it quit, why didn't you turn it off?"

Something that sounded like a breathless laugh tumbled from the back of Callum's throat. "Between the ship thrashing about and trying to save our catch...it was absolute chaos. There was no time to think—just react."

"Well," said Audrey, uncrossing her legs, "perhaps if you'd been—shall we say—*sober* that morning, your brain would've been able to recall the safety measures associated with operating something so dangerous."

Placing his hands flat on the table, Callum leaned forward. "Listen—"

"My father told me what happened to you," she continued, talking over him. "He said you were so drunk that morning you could barely stand."

The dark abyss serving as Callum's eyes narrowed. Sitting back, his upper lip twisted into an odd shape, exposing his teeth. "Well, your father wasn't there, *was* he?"

Magnus cleared his throat. "It's getting late, Cal. Why don't you head on back to the lighthouse, and I'll talk to you tomorrow?"

"Not until I make a toast," he said, keeping his eyes on Audrey.

"Let's save it for another night."

"No, no...I've got this," insisted Callum. Picking up the bottle of wine before Magnus could, he started to pour it, yet noticed that Audrey had only placed two glasses on the table. "Won't you be having any?"

"No," she replied in a clipped tone.

"Oh, that's right," he said, smacking his forehead with the heel of his palm. "I forgot about you being in the... *family* way."

Audrey's eyes shot from Callum to Magnus—whose face flooded with guilt.

"Well, don't you worry," Callum said, tilting the bottle on its side, which House noticed was half-empty, "I'll drink your share." When the glass was close to spilling over, he slid his chair back and stood up. "To my brother Magnus and his beautiful bride." Raising his glass, the corners of his mouth twitched before forming a smug grin that was as lopsided as his stance. "May you always be in love with each other as much as you are at this very moment."

Magnus left his glass on the table as he watched Callum empty the contents of his in one swallow.

"Now...what shall we toast to next?"

Magnus shook his head. "It's getting late."

"Nonsense," said Callum, refilling his glass. "The night is still young."

Magnus got to his feet. "We're *done*," he said, snatching the bottle out of his grasp. "I have to make some calls."

Callum shooed him away with his arm. "Go ahead. I'll keep Audrey company for you. It'll give us a chance to catch up. So tell me, love," he said, turning his attention to her, "what have you been up to? I mean — well, besides the obvious — "

Magnus' knuckles slammed into Callum's mouth, knocking him — and the chair he was standing in front of — to the floor. "That's enough!"

Callum's locks clung to his blood-red cheeks as he worked to untangle his foot from the chair leg. Using the table for leverage, he pulled himself up. "I never thought I'd see the day," he said, clenching his fists, "when you'd choose a whore over your own brother. I just hope you had enough sense in that do-gooder brain of yours to take McCord up on his offer." Glancing at Audrey, he let his gaze travel the length of her body and paused to force his rapidly swelling upper lip into the shape of a smirk. "At least that would give you *something* of value."

"Get out," said Magnus, moving toward him.

Callum's hand suddenly shot out from his side; grabbing the bottle of wine off the table, he turned and hurled it across the room.

House winced as it exploded against its far wall.

As the burgundy liquid mixed with bits of green glass slid down the floral wallpaper and dropped onto the floor, Callum slowly turned back to Magnus. Holding up his right hand, he bent his fingers—except for the middle one—toward his palm. "Fuck you," he said in a voice choked with rage.

The hardwood in the living room shuddered beneath Callum's boots as he stormed out of the kitchen and jerked open the front door.

Magnus watched him stumble down the steps and into the darkness before turning to Audrey, who'd retreated to the corner of the kitchen. He sighed and shook his head. "I'm sorry."

"For what?" she snapped. "Your brother's behavior—or yours?"

His face took on a bewildered expression. "I was just—"

"You were just *what*? Protecting me? Being my knight in shining armor?" She looked at him with a semblance of disgust. "I don't need you to be *either*!"

"Audrey..."

Shoving the fallen chair out of her way, she marched past him—and his outstretched hand—and started up the stairs.

Chapter 9

The smell of burning ammonia, wrapped inside ringlets of thick white smoke, floated up and over House's sagging gutters before vanishing into a backdrop of blue.

Leaning against the railing, Magnus, who'd been up since dawn, returned the cigar to his lips, and as his cheeks caved inward, House listened to the tip of the brown leafy paper crackle in protest as the fiery orange embers consumed it.

A cool breeze began to stir, sending an unexpected shiver across his shoulders—yet it didn't appear to House that its owner possessed any desire to go back inside. Instead, after having stared morosely at the ocean for the past two and a half hours, Magnus reluctantly untethered his gaze from the pair of steel moorings that held it there and dragged it over to the lighthouse.

Squinting into the sun, House looked over as well, but saw no signs of life coming from it.

The collar of Magnus' shirt started to flap as the wind increased. He reached up to turn it down, then slipped his fingers inside the gap between the top two buttons, where they instinctively began feeling their way along his left collarbone.

House stiffened, causing the lower windowpane in the kitchen to clank against its sill. Why its owner continued to torture himself was something it would never understand, and yet as his fingertips touched upon the scar embedded in his chest, it watched his face succumb to the memory. House's gaze darted in all directions, trying to outrun what was coming, but—being linked to Magnus in ways it could not explain—was unsuccessful in keeping the images of that night from forming...

The engorged veins in Magnus' neck crawled across his throat as he pinched the top of the gaping wound closed and inserted the needle into the flap of skin. A breathless groan spilled from his lips as he pushed it farther in.

After pausing to take a swallow of whiskey, he grabbed hold of the tip of the needle and pulled it — along with the blood-soaked fishing line that he'd looped around the eye — the rest of the way through.

Seven profanity-filled passes later, the blood flowing down his chest eased to a trickle and stopped. Grasping a small pair of scissors, he managed to tie a double — albeit sloppy — turle knot in the line and snipped off the end.

He took another swig from the bottle of Calvert's, then pushed himself to his feet and made his way out of the cellar. Holding onto the banister for support, his face was pale and devoid of emotion as he started up the stairs.

"Evy?" he said in a low voice, poking his head inside their darkened bedroom.

Having earlier felt its floor beneath the old clawfoot tub grow heavy as Evy filled it with water, House absently turned its attention to the bathroom—and began to shudder so violently, the drinking glass toppled off the vanity.

Upon hearing the noise, Magnus hurried down the hall and knocked. "Evy?" he called, trying the knob. When no answer came, he pounded on the door with his fist. "Evy!" Raising his leg, he brought his foot down hard against the door, tearing the top of it from its hinges as it swung open and slammed into the wall.

Stepping inside, his eyes widened in horror as they went from the bloodied razor blade lying on the toilet seat to the steady stream of red gushing out of his wife's wrists.

"Evy!" With a guttural cry, Magnus fell to his knees. Lifting her out of the tub, the crimson-colored water sloshed over him and pooled onto the white penny-tiled floor as he cradled her lifeless body against him –

"Magnus?"

House jerked its gaze to the left.

Audrey was standing in the middle of the deck, her eyes fixated on the side of its owner's face as he stared at something she could not see. Tilting her head, she drew closer to him. "Magnus?"

He abruptly straightened at the sound of his name, causing a ragged breath, mixed with a plume of smoke, to come rushing out of his lips.

"Is everything all right?"

"Aye," he answered, keeping his back to her.

"Are you sure?"

Setting his jaw, he turned around. "Did you need something?"

"I thought I could even up your hair for you."

A pinkish hue besieged his cheeks as he glanced at the bed sheet and pair of shears she was holding.

Without waiting for him to answer, Audrey walked over to a metal chair that had been spray painted blue two summers ago — in a poor attempt to hide its rust — and looked at him expectantly.

Begrudgingly knocking the ashes off the end of his cigar, Magnus stamped out the embers on the wooden rail and stuck it in the pocket of his shirt before sitting down.

Audrey draped the sheet over the front of him and tied the corners behind his neck. Using the teeth of the comb, she lifted up a section of his hair, then holding the locks firmly between her fingers, snipped off the jagged sprigs. As she worked, House noticed her hand would occasionally brush against the side of his jaw, sending a wave of goosebumps rolling across the back of his neck.

The wind picked up once more, delivering a spray of salt against House, and as the gritty beads infiltrated the splintered cracks of its clapboards, it began to feel as uncomfortable as its owner looked.

"Audrey," said Magnus in a hesitant voice as she dragged the comb through his hair, "I'm sorry about last night."

"It's all right."

"No — it's *not*," he said, gripping the folds of the sheet. "I shouldn't have lost my temper like that. And I know you don't need protecting, but…" He paused and let out a frustrated-sounding sigh. "Cal just has a way of setting me off."

"Well, if it's any consolation," she replied, leaning in close to trim the hair above his ear, "it's not just you that he does that to — and if he were *my* brother, I would find him an impossible cross to bear."

A long bout of silence followed.

"He hasn't always been like that," Magnus finally said as she stepped behind him.

"Like *what*? A jerk?" She bent down and began cutting the stray hairs at the base of his neck. "*Yes*, he has. If anything, he's turned into an even bigger one. What I don't understand, though, is why you continue to let him blame you for what happened."

"Because it's true," he said in a rigid tone. "I knew the winch wasn't working properly, but couldn't spare the time or money to repair it."

"He was drun—"

"Drunk—aye," said Magnus. "I could smell the liquor on his breath that morning, but let it slide because I needed him." A band of white fell across the knuckles of his left hand as he pressed his fingertips into his palm. "It was the last day of the season, and I had to bring in a decent catch."

"Callum's not a child," Audrey replied, roughly flattening Magnus' cowlick before taking the shears to it. "He's a full-grown man. That accident was due to his own stupidity and nothing else—and I think it's high time you quit tormenting yourself over it. Dwelling on the past only breeds misery, and no matter how much we want it to, it's something that can never be changed."

The curve in Magnus' jaw flexed. "You know..." he said, cutting his eyes behind him, "of all the things I've missed about you, your brutal, quickly formed opinions aren't one of them."

Audrey dug the teeth of the comb into his scalp.

"Ow!"

"Oh, did that hurt?"

He swiveled around to look at her. "*Yes!*"

"Sorry."

"I don't think you are."

Moving to the front of the chair, Audrey slipped her right leg between his knees and bent down. "So," she said, smoothing the strands of hairs along his forehead, "what *did* you miss about me?"

House watched the pinstripes on the sheet jump as Magnus bounced his knee in an obvious attempt to keep his eyes away from her cleavage.

"*Well?*" she prodded.

Magnus' gaze slowly came around to hers. "I suppose...it would be your ability to stop talking when the other person in the conversation is clearly irritated."

A high-pitched cackle started in Audrey's throat only to escape through her nostrils as she placed the shears against his forehead.

"I missed *that*," he said, the gruffness in his voice fading.

"What?"

"That half-giggle, half-snort of yours."

Audrey drew back. "I don't *snort*."

"*Half*-snort," he corrected.

"My...my...the charm just oozes out of you, doesn't it?"

He proudly puffed out his chest. "Well, I try."

"So," she said, trimming the straggles of hair hanging below his right eyebrow, "what is it exactly that you like about this half-giggle...*non*-snort thing I do—" The blades of the shears strayed slightly as they came together. Sucking in her breath, Audrey's hand went to the side of her stomach.

"What's wrong?" asked Magnus, leaning forward.

"It's nothing," she said after a moment. "The baby just kicked really hard." Letting out a wobbly breath, she raised the shears to resume her task.

A few seconds later, he saw her wince again. "I think you've got a wee rugby player in there."

As Magnus' infatuation with her fluttering stomach increased, something that could only be described as a wave of sorrow washed over Audrey's face, draining it of its color.

"Are you sure you're all right?"

Audrey blinked, freeing her eyes from the despair that seemed intent on swallowing them.

"Maybe you should sit down for a minute."

"I'm fine," she said, brushing away Magnus' concern with a shake of her head, then with renewed vigor, placed the edge of the shears against his temple and bent down.

"I could be wrong, though."

"About what?"

"Instead of a rugby player...you could be having a ballerina."

"I suppose so," Audrey murmured, as she worked to repair his self-inflicted atrocity that was dangling between her blades.

"Well, if that turns out to be the case," he continued, arching his brows in order to see her, "I'm sure she's going to be just as beautiful as her mother."

His words were met with an awkward silence, causing both of their cheeks to flush.

"There," said Audrey, straightening, "all finished."

Magnus hurriedly undid the knot from the sheet and went to stand—only to discover Audrey's leg was still firmly planted between his knees. He lifted his head to find her staring at him.

She placed her palm against the side of his face and gave him a pitying smile. "You didn't have to do that, you know," she said, caressing one of the numerous cuts lining his jaw with her thumb.

Magnus let out a small laugh. "I think I *did*."

Audrey stopped moving her thumb, yet her hand remained where it was.

"Now do I look like the Magnus you remember?" he asked, gazing up at her.

She answered him with a hesitant nod. "Yes, only..."

"Only what?"

"Sadder."

House saw its owner's jaw tense beneath her fingertips.

Audrey's expression grew somber, pulling the corners of her mouth down. "Why did your wife leave you?" she asked softly.

The legs on the chair scraped across the deck as Magnus pushed it back and stood. "Why don't you tell me more about San Francisco, instead?" he asked, his arm grazing her stomach as he made his way toward the railing.

Audrey walked over to the edge of the deck and shook out the sheet. When she was done, she folded the corners together and turned around. "Why don't you ever want to talk about her?"

He pulled the half-smoked cigar from his pocket and flipped open his lighter. "It's like you said earlier," he answered, doing a poor job of hiding his grief as he cupped his hand around the flame.

"*What* is?" she asked, watching the end of the cigar begin to burn a bright red.

"Dwelling on the past," he said, looking down at the jagged cliffside below, "…only breeds misery."

Chapter 10

Magnus held his razor under the trickling water and lifted his tired eyes to meet his reflection. As he drew the blade across the bottom of his chin, the distinct smell of coffee began to waft up the stairs. Furrowing his brows, he plowed through the remaining two rows of shaving cream lining the underside of his jaw and rinsed his face, then pulling his arms through a thick navy Guernsey, hurried out of the bathroom.

House gave a stiff yawn and watched its owner as he rushed down the stairs, across the living room floor, and through the open doorway of the kitchen—where he awkwardly stopped to finger-comb his damp hair.

Upon hearing the stutter of footsteps, Audrey turned from the stove.

Magnus' hands fell like dead weight to his sides. "Did I wake you?" he asked in a voice that sounded more excited than contrite.

She returned her attention to the sizzling skillet. "Not at all," she said, grasping the spatula between her thumb and forefinger. "I just wanted to make you breakfast and see you off."

House yawned again, sucking the damp, grease-laden air into its walls. Having watched Audrey toss and turn in bed for most of the night, before letting out a strangled scream that had left her sobbing into her pillow up until an hour ago, House found itself doubting the validity — or sincerity — of her words.

Magnus seemed taken aback by her response as well, and absently scratched the side of his neck as he watched her slip a thick omelet between two slices of bread and wrap it in foil.

"Here you go," she said, holding it out to him.

"Thank you." As he took it from her, she reached up and wiped away a dab of shaving cream that was clinging to his left earlobe.

His eyes, no longer clouded with sleep — but clear and bright — shot to hers.

"I'll walk you out," she said, then picking up his thermos from off the counter, skirted past him.

House saw a faint smile tug at its owner's lips as he pointed his feet toward the living room and followed. "Are you going to be all right while I'm gone?" he asked, pausing in the entryway to put on his coat.

"I think I can manage," said Audrey, sounding offended by his question as she moved to unlock the door.

"I'm only asking because staying in this house by yourself can get pretty lonely at times. The days can be incredibly long, and the nights..." Magnus' words faltered when he noticed that Audrey was staring at him over her shoulder, a curious look perched upon her face. "Or — at least that's what I've been told," he mumbled.

"Told by *whom*?"

House watched Magnus' cheeks flush as he grappled for an answer.

Audrey let him flounder for a moment and then dismissed her question with a shake of her head. "Truthfully, after everything that's happened this week—not to mention all the stares and whispers that were being hurled in my direction at the funeral—I welcome the solitude."

"I understand," said Magnus, picking up his bag from off the floor, "but if you should need anything, you can call Callum. I left his number by the phone."

"I don't think I'll be calling your brother for anything," she replied, following him out the door.

Magnus turned around. "Listen, I know that he—"

"I'll be fine," she said, thrusting the thermos into his hand.

Despite the approaching dawn, House noticed that the moon appeared to be in no hurry to go to sleep; lingering just above the century-old oak beside the porch, it shone through its naked branches, framing Audrey in a silky light. House watched its owner absently stuff the sandwich in the pocket of his coat as he stood there seemingly admiring the way her scarlet tresses hung in slight disarray across the front of her robe.

Audrey folded her arms, sending Magnus' enamored gaze crashing to his feet.

House couldn't tell by her gesture if she was angry, flattered, or simply amused...but the one thing it *was* certain of was that she took great delight in seeing him squirm, as indicated by the slight upturn in the corners of her mouth.

"Well, I better get to it," said Magnus, pressing the thermos against his leg, then mumbling an awkward goodbye, started down the path to his truck.

"Magnus?"

He stopped and turned. "You'll catch your death out here," he said, motioning for her to go back inside as she picked her way across the dew-covered stones.

"Please...this isn't the eighteenth century," she retorted.

"No, but it's cold and —" A heavy sigh cut him off, making him scowl.

"Oh, did I do that out loud?" asked Audrey, batting her lashes at him. "Sorry. Please continue."

Magnus scratched at his jaw. "Did you want something?"

Audrey pulled a small sprig of leaves from the pocket of her robe. "For luck," she said, slipping the stem of it through the frayed buttonhole on the lapel of his coat. "I know it's not from a furze, but it's all I could find."

Magnus looked down at the half-dead oak leaf sticking out of his lapel and smirked.

"What? Aren't you as superstitious as the rest of the fishermen in this town?"

"If I believed in such nonsense, my luck would *already* be doomed for encountering a redhaired lass on the way to the boat." He paused and cocked his right brow. "Especially a barefoot one."

"Fine," snapped Audrey, grasping the top of the sprig, "you don't have to—"

Magnus closed his hand around hers. "I didn't say that I didn't like it."

She looked up at him, enabling House to see that aside from the dark circles under her eyes, the cheerless expression she seemed so fond of wearing had returned. "Promise me something."

"What?"

"That you'll be careful."

He lowered his hand. "Aye," he said, giving her a reassuring nod, "I promise." As the sky above them began to lighten, Magnus' gaze drifted from Audrey to her fingers, which were still gripping his coat. "Anything els—"

Audrey pulled him toward her, then standing on the tips of her toes, kissed the side of his cheek. "No, that's it," she said, patting him on his chest as if she were petting a large, dumb dog. "I'll see you Friday."

She offered up a wave with the back of her hand and started down the path, leaving Magnus to scratch his head as he watched her trot up the steps and disappear through the front door.

"You havin' fun playin' house?" said a voice in the darkness.

The baffled look on Magnus' face fell away. Taking in a stilted breath, he pressed his lips together and turned around. "How long have you been standing there?"

Callum emerged from the shadows and lifted his shoulders in a half shrug. "Long enough," he replied, flicking his cigarette into the air with his thumb and middle finger.

House heard Magnus grind his jaw as he made his way down the path and over to his truck where Callum was waiting. "It's kind of early for you to be awake, isn't it?"

"On the contrary," replied Callum, his curly locks flopping across his forehead as he leaned against the truck's left front fender. "I haven't been to bed yet."

"And why's that?" asked Magnus, tossing his bag into the back of the truck. "Your conscience bothering you?"

When Callum didn't answer, Magnus turned to find a bottle of beer pressed against his lips. After several swallows, Callum lowered the bottle and forged a smile that was as cold and dark as his eyes. "No. Is *yours*?"

Magnus jerked open the driver's side door, making his brother scramble to get out of the way as it swung around. "If you've come here looking for an apology, you're not going to get one. You were out of line the other night."

"*I* was out of line?" Callum jammed his nubbed fingers against his chest. "*You* were the one being rude, telling me to leave before I'd even sat down."

"You and I both know why you were there," said Magnus, climbing into the seat, "and it *wasn't* to wish us well. It's high time you stopped acting like a pathetic, put-upon child and started taking responsibility for your actions. Because the sooner you do, the better off we'll all be."

Callum's lips flattened as he cut his gaze to the front door. "Did Audrey put those big words in your mouth?"

House watched the hopeful look lurking behind Magnus' face yield to anger, staining his cheeks.

"Well?" Callum held his arms out from his sides, spilling beer down the back of his wrist. "*Did* she?"

Flexing his jaw, Magnus reached for the door.

Callum grabbed hold of it, refusing to let it close. "Because that sounds *exactly* like something she would say."

Magnus dropped his hand into his lap. "Cal, I don't have time—"

"Would you have married Audrey if she wasn't pregnant?"

"That's a pointless question," he snapped, jamming the key in the ignition.

The engine turned over, sputtered—and promptly died.

Gripping the steering wheel, Magnus swore and tried again.

"Let me put it to you a different way," said Callum, raising his voice to be heard over the lethargic *ruh...ruh...ruh* sound the engine was making. "If Audrey was no longer pregnant, would you stay married to her?"

The air around them grew still.

"What the hell kind of question is that?" asked Magnus, jerking his head toward his brother.

Callum stared back at him, yet his hardened expression remained unchanged. "I'm talking about a year from now, when that little bastard of hers is runnin' around, and you come home after a long week at sea — smellin' like somethin' that crawled out of a whale's ass — do you honestly think she's gonna want you the way you want her? Because I've seen the way you look at her...and I've seen the way she looks at you." Narrowing his eyes, the right side of Callum's mouth lifted ever so slightly. "It's not the same."

Magnus yanked the door out of Callum's grasp, making him stumble forward. As it slammed closed with a clunk, he turned the key in the ignition again...and again.

"You're flooding it — "

"I know how to start my own goddamn truck, Callum!" He turned the key a fourth time, and then — amidst the foul stench of gasoline fumes — tossed his head back in frustration.

Callum took another swig of his beer and bent down. "Listen, Magpie," he said, hunching his shoulders as he rested his elbows on the open window frame, "the only thing I want is for you to be happy, because God knows after everything you've been through, you deserve it. But this...what you're doing here..." He paused and shook his head. "You're just setting yourself up for more heartache — "

The V8 came to life with a throaty roar.

Cupping his hand around the gear knob, Magnus shifted the long metal stick coming out of the floorboard and looked expectantly at Callum, who grudgingly pushed himself away from the door.

The engine rumbled beneath the hood as Magnus began backing up. Moments later, the truck lurched forward, slinging gravel from its rear tires as it took off down the drive.

~

House sighed contentedly as it soaked in the warmth of the sunlight streaming through its spotless windows. Much to its delight, Audrey had spent the last few days cleaning. Starting with the kitchen, she'd organized the cupboards, scrubbed every inch of the countertops, and mopped the floor before moving on to the living room, where she'd swiftly relegated the cigarette-smoking monkey — along with several other relics belonging to Evy — to the cellar.

House's gaze traveled easily across the uncluttered bookcase and end tables, and although it found it somewhat freeing not to have constant reminders of Evy lurking about, it also knew that Magnus wasn't going to share in the same opinion.

Not wishing to dwell upon what was to come, however, House shifted its attention to the main bedroom, where Audrey was ironing the shirt Magnus had worn to their supposedly voluntary wedding. As the iron glided over the cotton fabric, Audrey began to hum, and even though House didn't recognize the tune that had been caressing its walls all week, it discerned that she had not only welcomed the solitude awaiting her, but was also thriving in it.

Setting the iron upright, Audrey made her way over to the faded chifforobe squatting on the floor beside the bed. As she opened its door, the harmonious melody emanating from her throat stumbled, skipped — and then stopped altogether.

House peered over her shoulder and saw that she was staring at the multitude of dresses crammed between the cabinet's cedar walls. Halfheartedly running the back of her hand across their sleeves, it came upon a strapless red dress hanging in the center. As her finger followed the outline of the accentuated dip in the front, House recalled it as being one of Evy's — and Magnus' — favorites.

Dropping her gaze, Audrey blinked back tears as she surveyed her own prominent feature protruding beneath a rumpled, untucked blouse.

After a moment, she shoved the garment aside and jammed Magnus' shirt next to it on the metal pipe serving as the rod, yet as she went to close the door, her eyes were drawn to a wooden box nestled in the bottom of the cabinet. As House watched her carry it over to the bed, it knew with absolute certainty that in the next few seconds her misery was about to be compounded exponentially.

Sitting on the freshly washed bed cover, Audrey pried open the lid to the box, and as her gaze fell upon a small silver rattle, the sound of crunching gravel pulled House's attention outside — where it was dismayed to see John McCord's car coming up the drive.

Hurriedly shifting its focus back to Audrey, it found her holding the rattle in one hand and clutching a black-and-white Polaroid of Evy in the other. Resting its weight against its foundation, House stared at the photo, vividly remembering the day Magnus had taken it. It had been a good day.

"*Magnus, please…*" *Evy's hesitant laughter echoed throughout the bedroom.* "*I look hideous.*"

"*You couldn't look hideous if you tried,*" *he said, loading the square pack of film into the camera.* "*In fact, I think you look positively radiating.*"

"*Do you?*" *she asked, her blonde hair spilling across the pillow as she arched her back and stretched.*

"*I do.*" *Lowering the camera, Magnus leaned over the bed and kissed her hard on the lips.* "*And you know what else?*" *he said, pulling away.* "*It's taking every ounce of self-control I have to keep from ravishing your body right now.*"

"*Well…*" *said Evy, playing with the chest hairs that were peeking out of his shirt,* "*why don't you just tell that self-control of yours to get lost and kiss me again?*"

"*Oh, I intend to,*" *he replied, arching his brows,* "*but first, let me see that beautiful smile of yours.*"

Evy's blue eyes danced as he straightened, and with the afternoon sun settling in around her, rested her hand atop her swollen belly and smiled.

"*Okay,*" *said Magnus, squinting through the tiny window of the camera,* "*one…two…three —*"

A short burst of electrical current coursed through House's wall, vanquishing its memory.

Audrey's posture stiffened upon hearing the bell. Carefully returning the items to the box, she swept a knuckle across her cheeks and hurried downstairs, where she cautiously peeped through the lace curtains in the foyer before unlocking the door.

"Dad," she said in a less-than-enthusiastic tone.

"Hello, sweetheart."

"What are you doing here?"

Her father removed his hat and let out a raspy chuckle. "Do I need a reason?" he asked, walking inside.

"Well, quite frankly," she replied, blocking his path with a well-placed elbow as her hand traveled to her hip, "yes."

"Everything happened so quickly last week," said her father, stepping around her blockade, "that you and I never really got a chance to talk."

Audrey's face twisted into a scowl. "We had plenty of chances *before* then," she said, crossing her arms.

McCord's jaw flexed as he set the package that he'd carried in with him on top of the teardrop-shaped coffee table—another of Evy's purchases that reminded House of a giant planchette, which was a device one of its previous owner's used on something called a Ouija board that they swore was a portal to commune with the dead.

"Well, I'm here now," he answered, tossing his hat beside it.

With her arms still folded, Audrey came around the sofa and plopped herself down on the opposite end.

"So," he said, stealing a sideways glance at her stomach as he leaned back against the cushion, "how have you been?"

She uncrossed her arms long enough to place one of Evy's garish throw pillows over her enlarged midriff. "Fine."

"And Magnus?"

"Fine."

Letting out his breath, her father awkwardly shuffled his gaze around the living room. "It looks like you've been doing some cleaning."

"Yes."

McCord's frustration began to bleed through on his lips, pulling them taut. "Listen," he said, scratching his temple, "I'm sorry for my initial reaction when I found out that you were..."

Audrey's eyes narrowed. "*Pregnant.* You can say it, Dad. We're both adults. And it's not just your initial reaction that you should be apologizing for. It's the way you handled the whole bloody thing."

Her father crossed his bony ankle over his knee. "I'm sorry that you think what I did was wrong," he said, dismissing her words with his hand as if he were swatting away a fly. "But doing what was best for you was my only concern."

The radiator in the living room clanked and groaned, temporarily interrupting the silence that had planted itself between them.

"Oh, before I forget..." Uncrossing his legs, her father sat forward and picked up the package from off the table. "I brought you a present."

Audrey rose staunchly from the sofa. "I don't think my marriage to Magnus constitutes a wedding gift—especially one coming from you." She turned, sending her hair whipping around her shoulders, and marched into the kitchen.

Her father ran his fingers back and forth along the creases in his forehead and sighed as he listened to the cabinets open and slam. After a moment, he reluctantly stood and started across the floor.

Audrey was standing over the stove, glaring at the blue flame licking the underside of the kettle.

With an expression that was as sullen as his eyes, McCord walked up behind her and held out the package. "It's from your mother," he said softly.

A wave of grief surged through Audrey's face, leaving the skin surrounding her cheeks mottled. Turning from the stove, she took the medium-sized parcel from her father without looking at him and slid her fingernail down the seam of the brown butcher paper. A small white gown trimmed in lace appeared.

"You were christened in that," he said proudly. "Your mother saved it all these years with the hope of giving it to her first grandchild."

House watched Audrey knot her fingers together, as if she were trying to hold in the sob that her uneven breaths were determined to expel. "Thank you," she whispered, giving him a jerky nod.

Her father took the package from her and placed it on the counter. "Your mother loved you so very much, and even though I can't change what's happened, I want you to know—"

The kettle opened its hinged mouth, flooding the tiny kitchen with a shrill scream.

McCord's eyes filled with disappointment as Audrey turned away. "I...just want you to know that I will always be here for you," he continued, talking loud enough to be heard over the dying whistle.

House watched the side of Audrey's face as she opened the tin of tea. "Would you like some?" she asked after a moment, her half-wavering, half-brusque tone indicating to House that she was skeptical of her father's declaration.

"I'd love some."

A small but guarded smile found its way onto Audrey's lips as she pulled another mug from the cabinet.

"So," he said, leaning against the counter, "have you thought of any names?"

"Not yet."

"You know, when you were born, I wanted to name you Maureen—after my great-grandmother. It was a good Irish name, but..." McCord paused and shook his head. "Your mother was having none of it. She insisted on naming you after the nurse that helped deliver you."

Audrey looked over her shoulder at her father, and House saw her jaw grow lax as the ambivalence in it faded. "I've never heard that story before."

"Well, if you and Magnus would care to join me for dinner this Sunday, I'm sure I can come up with a few more."

Absently setting the kettle on the stove, Audrey beamed back at him. "I'd like that," she said, picking up the mugs.

As they started toward the table, House saw her

father glance at his watch as he followed along behind her.

"Can I bring anything?" asked Audrey, dipping a spoon into the blue and white porcelain sugar bowl that House had not seen since before the turn of the century—yet fondly remembered the family it belonged to. Audrey had discovered the hand-painted floral vessel while cleaning out the back of the cabinet under the sink. Elated with her find, she'd washed it, filled it with sugar, and had gleefully placed it in the center of the barren table.

"Just your appetites," McCord replied. The women's auxiliary is taking care of everything."

Audrey slipped her father a curious glance as he sat down across from her. "Why is the women's auxiliary cooking dinner for you?"

"It's not so much a dinner, as a function."

"So this is a campaign thing," Audrey said flatly, dumping the sugar she'd piled on the spoon into her tea.

"It is, which is why I want you there." Pausing to clear his throat, her father leaned across the table and placed his hand over hers. "As you well know, I'm not very good at discussing my feelings, but I'm very proud of the woman you've become…and my only desire is for us to be a family again."

Audrey's gaze shot to her hand as it lay coiled beneath her father's…yet House noticed she made no motion to pull it away.

As an awkward silence moved in, McCord sat back in his chair.

"Dad," said Audrey, tucking a strand of hair behind her ear, "did you know Magnus' wife?"

He shrugged and threw his right arm over the back of the chair. "No, I remember hearing that he'd taken one, but I never saw her in town, and Magnus never spoke of her. Why?"

"No reason," she said, picking up her mug. "I was just curious."

Stretching his legs under the table, Audrey's father began to stroke the edges of his mustache with his thumb and forefinger. "Speaking of Magnus…" he said, eyeing her closely as she took a sip of tea, "there is one thing I'd like you to do for me before you come."

"What's that?"

"Talk to him about backing me in the election."

Audrey set her mug down.

"He holds a lot of sway with the men on the dock," her father rushed to explain, "and a public show of support from him would go a long way."

"Well, Magnus may have some pull when it comes to others," said Audrey, picking up her mug again, "but I certainly don't have any pull over *him*."

"Now, don't sell yourself short," McCord replied in a condescending tone that was eerily reminiscent of his daughter's. "If a husband wants a happy life, he must listen to his wife."

Shifting in her seat, Audrey pressed the mug to her lips.

"So," he said, arching his brows expectantly, "will you talk to him?"

Audrey stared at her father over the rim of her cup. "I'll do my best," she answered, yet House noted her words came out sounding as conflicted as the look on her face.

A triumphant grin pushed against McCord's cheeks. "Aye, that's my girl."

The sunlight that was pouring into the kitchen swiftly faded as dark clouds began to gather outside.

"Is there something wrong with your tea?" asked Audrey, noticing that he hadn't touched it.

McCord shook his head. "No, it's fine, but—gah!" he exclaimed, doing a poor job of pretending to notice the time on his watch. "I have to be going." Getting to his feet, he came around the table and bent down to give Audrey a kiss on the cheek. "Slán."

"Slán leat," she answered, offering him the customary—albeit wooden sounding—reply from the one staying behind.

"Oh, and promise me that you'll wear your heavy coat when you come," he said, avoiding her gaze as he straightened. "We'll be eating outside, and I don't want you catching cold."

Audrey remained at the table as her father made his way into the living room—and yet, before the front door had even closed, House saw that her eyes were brimming with tears.

Chapter 11

Thunder ricocheted through the canyon like little pops of fireworks before cracking so loud overhead that it sounded to House as if it had torn a hole in the sky.

A flash of lightning, as brilliant as it was blinding, illuminated the swells surging below; massive and dark, they rose up out of the sea like a giant wall, where they hovered in the air under their own momentum before free-falling thirty feet—engulfing the narrow strip of shore, as they slammed one after the other into the craggy cliffside.

"...three inches of rain has already fallen in parts of Big Sur and the surrounding valleys. We have reports coming in of wide-spread flooding and power outages up and down the coast from Carmel to Lucia, where at least one person has died..."

House's gaze fell upon Audrey as it tried with unavailing success to shield its attic eaves from the blowing rain. Magnus' bride was standing in front of the television, her eyes fixated on its rounded screen, as she absently chewed her thumbnail.

"...producing numerous squalls along the coast." The weatherman turned from the map and held up his hands. "Folks, this is going to get worse before it gets better. If you're near a river, lake, stream, or along the coast, you need to be on the lookout for flooding. It can happen in an instan—" The weatherman's face was abruptly funneled into a shrinking black hole.

Darkness enveloped House, leaving it momentarily stunned. As it struggled to see, the bottoms of Audrey's bare feet began groping their way across its hardwood floors. After a few moments, her fingertips touched upon the drawer next to the stove and started rifling through it.

House felt something rake against its counter, followed by the pungent smell of sulfur. There was a tiny flickering light, and then Audrey's troubled face appeared.

The battering wind suddenly changed direction and—with a shrieking howl—ripped the shingles above House's gable clean off, sending its asphalt tiles skipping across the roof like a hooked fish before vanishing into the rain-filled sky.

Scavenging through the rest of the cabinets, Audrey lit every candle she could find and placed them throughout the kitchen and living room, using empty glasses and whiskey bottles to hold them upright.

As she bent down to place one on the coffee table, the distinct sound of a key turning in the lock made her stop. Cupping her hand around the flame, she hurried to the front door. "Magnu—" Audrey's relieved expression faltered.

"Guess again."

"What are you doing here?" she asked, watching Callum slip the key to the door inside the pocket of his rainslicker.

He cocked his head and smiled. "Is that any way to greet your brother-in-law?"

Audrey gripped the candle tighter. "Answer my question."

Sighing, Callum switched his flashlight to his other hand as he wiped the rain from his forehead. "I came to check on you."

"Well, as you can see," she said, arching her eyebrows as she swung the door toward his face, "I'm fine—"

He jammed his foot up against the kickplate. "You know, I just risked my life—and what's left of my limbs—to get here," he said, nodding in the direction of the lighthouse. "The least you could do is let me come inside and get warm." Before Audrey could say anything else, he squeezed past her and walked into the living room, where he paused to hold his hand over the radiator. "It's getting cold in here. Let me get a fire going."

"That won't be necessary."

Removing his rainslicker, Callum bent down and pulled a log out of the woodbin. "Here," he said, waving his flashlight at her, "hold this for me."

Audrey squinted against the beam, yet remained by the door, causing his jaw to tighten.

Setting the flashlight down, he grabbed the candle off the mantel and shoved a piece of crumpled newspaper under the log.

"Have you heard from Magnus?" she asked, watching him hold the flame under the paper until it caught fire.

"About half-a-dozen ships made it in ahead of the storm, but the *Gwendolyn* wasn't one of them," he replied, kneeling between the gargoyle-shaped andirons. "It's no cause for alarm, though. Magnus likes to sail her past Settler's Point, which is a full day's travel — in *good* weather. I wouldn't expect him until sometime tomorrow night."

As the smoky scent of burning hickory began to fill the living room, Callum picked up his flashlight and returned to the entryway. "There's nothing for you to worry your pretty little head about," he continued, stopping in front of Audrey, who was still standing by the door with her right hand clutching the candle, the other wrapped around the knob. "Magnus knows what he's doing." Leaning in close, Callum lightly ran the back of his knuckle along the sleeve of her blouse. "He's probably just anchored offshore somewhere riding it ou —"

"Don't touch me!" she said, slapping his hand away.

The black fuzz lying dormant above Callum's chin widened as a whiskey-soaked grin spread across his lips.

"I want you to leave," she demanded, the flame on the candle fluttering beneath her breath as her fingers fumbled to turn the knob.

"I will, but *first*" – grabbing her by the wrist, he jerked her toward him, sending the candlestick clattering to the floor — "we're going to talk —"

The rest of Callum's words were drowned out by an ear-splitting crack. Before House could determine the source of the noise, the window in its living room imploded, and as shards of glass flew everywhere, it felt its porch being wrenched from its clapboards. Huge chunks of wood and water began to rain down as a large tree branch from the oak in the front yard smashed through the roof—the force of impact nearly knocking House off its foundation.

When the shaking had stopped, Callum let go of Audrey and opened the door. "Jesus, Mary, and Joseph," he muttered, clasping his hand on top of his head. Holding his flashlight in front of him, he went outside to survey the damage.

As House fought to recover its breath, it felt Audrey take a step backward and dart up the stairs.

Unfortunately for her, the sound of her feet—as they came down against the treads—garnered Callum's attention as well. He shoved the tangle of limbs out of his way and started after her. Taking the steps two at a time, he caught her roughly by the arm and spun her around.

"Let me *go*!"

"You know Magnus doesn't love you," he said, staring down at her as she tried to pry his hand loose. "And the truth is…he never will." He pushed himself hard against her, pinning her to the rail. "You want to know why?"

"Callum," she pleaded, the panic in her voice rising, "please go home."

He bent down and put his lips close to her ear. "Because the only woman he's ever going to love is Evy."

Audrey stopped struggling, and House didn't know if it was because she was unable to move, or what Callum had said, that forced her eyes upward.

"That's right." Locking his disjointed gaze with hers, Callum nodded and feigned a sigh. "My brother's a hopeless masochist."

Audrey remained still for another moment and then resumed her attempts to free herself from his grasp.

"What?" he said, giving her a playful shrug. "You mean you don't know?"

"Know *what*? she asked, the rims of her eyes flooding as she tried to pull away from him.

Callum's breath came rushing out. "About Evy being a *feckin'* loon! About all the terrible things she said and did to him. About one night absolutely losing it and stabbing him in his chest before..." His voice trailed off. "Oh, now...don't cry," he said, drawing his head back. "I just figured he'd told you about her, seeing as how the two of you are *married* and all." Letting go of her arm, he reached up and wiped at her tears, making her flinch. "But to be fair, you haven't exactly been honest with him, either." The insolent smirk affixed to his mouth twitched as his eyes narrowed. "*Have you?*"

Audrey didn't answer, but House thought the dagger-like expression forming beneath the scarlet swirls that were busily dancing across her cheeks spoke volumes.

Callum held the flashlight so that the beam shone on both their faces. "This is what's going to happen. Tomorrow morning, I'm taking you to see a guy I know in Monterey, and then when Magnus gets home," he said, his upper lip twisting into a snarl, "you're going to tell him that you lost the baby—because there's no way in hell I'm going to just stand by and let my own *kid* call me Uncle."

A deafening silence followed.

"You're wrong," said Audrey in a choked whisper. "Hugh Killam is the baby's father."

Callum's nostrils flared. "You didn't even *know* Hugh Killam—let alone *spread* your legs for him!"

Audrey's hand hurtled at Callum. "You bastard!"

Moving his face out of the line of fire, he caught her by the wrist.

Her other hand shot up, poised to strike.

"Go ahead," he taunted, jerking her closer. "You know how much it turns me on when you fight back. Or don't you remember?"

Her palm came down hard against his jaw, the force of the blow making him turn his head. "I remember *everything* about that night"—her voice shook—"I begged you to stop!"

Callum grinned and rubbed his cheek. "Well, that's not how I remember it…but I guess we'll just have to agree to disagree, won't we?" He lowered his flashlight and started down the stairs. "I'll see you in the morning, *love*."

"No…you won't," said Audrey, hesitantly drawing herself up to her full—albeit—unremarkable stature, "and when Magnus gets home, I'm telling him everything!"

Something in Callum's eyes flashed, igniting the black tar-like substance lurking behind them.

Whirling around, he jammed his hand under the trembling curve of her chin. "Who do you think he's going to believe?" he asked, eliciting a sharp cry from her as he dug his thumb and mutilated nubs into her cheeks. "Me? Or someone who's done nothing but lie to him since the day she got here!"

Half-formed sobs mixed with gasping pleas tumbled from Audrey's pinched lips as he began pushing her backward up the steps.

Upon reaching the top of the landing, Callum slid his hand around to the back of her neck. "There are other ways to get rid of it," he said, pointing the beam of his flashlight down the darkened stairs. "Accidents like this happen all the time. And after that, it won't matter to Magnus who the father is, because this ridiculous responsibility he feels toward you will be over."

"Please, Callum," she begged, clawing at the banister, "don't do this!"

Drawing a panicked breath filled with fire and ash, House tried to twist itself on its foundation in the hopes that the sudden movement would be enough to knock Callum off balance—but the massive branch of the oak tree held its frame immobile.

"*Callum!*"

House sent its gaze flailing about the room in a desperate bid to find its owner—for it was *his* voice that had pierced the darkness.

A bolt of lightning zigzagged across the sky, lighting up the entryway. Magnus was standing in front of the door, his face and fists wet and clenched in fury.

"Magnus..." said Callum, "we were just—"

"Get your hands off her!"

Callum let Audrey go and killed the flashlight. "She's been lying to you," he said, firing his words rapidly into the darkness as the sound of heavy footsteps barreled toward him. "You can't believe anything she—"

House heard Callum's breath being forced out of him as both men fell against the landing. Moments later, something hard and inflexible struck the floor. A low grown sounded, and House felt the object being lifted.

A sudden surge of electricity coursed through the wiring in House's walls, causing the lights to flicker on. Squinting against the brightness, House saw Callum lying beneath his brother; his eyes—half-closed and disoriented—were struggling to focus, while the back of his head dangled just above the floor, held there by Magnus as he clutched the collar of his shirt. House shifted its gaze to its owner and realized that if it hadn't been for the scar above his right eyebrow, he would've been unrecognizable, for his expression was as black as the night, and harbored a rage that surpassed all understanding as he slammed Callum's head into the floor again—and again.

"Magnus!" screamed Audrey, yanking on his arm. "Stop it!"

As Audrey tried to pull him off of Callum, House felt its knob and tube wiring behind the outlet in the living room begin to grow hot; within seconds, the metal ribbon inside the ceramic fuse melted, propelling House into darkness once more.

"Magnus...*stop!*"

There was a sickening crack—and then nothing.

In the moments that followed, a small circle of light bounced off the ceiling and swept along the upstairs wall in wild, quivering arcs until it stumbled across Magnus. His head and shoulders were pitched forward, pulled down by his heaving chest, which violently jerked and crackled with every spasm of breath that fell from his lips. Straining to see beyond the outer realm of the flashlight as it traveled from Magnus to Callum, House saw that its owner's fists were no longer wound around Callum's shirt, but coiled instead against his upper thighs—each knuckle bone-white and trembling—as he straddled his brother, whose eyes were open...but no longer moving; brownish-red blood seeped from his right ear and trickled down his neck, while a mass of dark liquid pooled around his now misshapen head.

With a jagged sob, Audrey dropped the flashlight and sank to the steps.

~

House's breath drifted in and out of its walls, turning the air in its darkened living room into swirling vapors of white as it stared into the blackness. The roaring fire inside its giant hearth had been reduced to a single glowing ember, and apart from the dying light of the candle in the kitchen, there was no movement or sound of any kind.

Although House couldn't see its occupants, it knew exactly where they were. Audrey was sitting in the middle of its stairs, her head and dampened cheeks resting against its balusters. Magnus' arms were curled tightly beneath him, his knees and forehead dug into the floor next to Callum, whose body still lay sprawled at the top of the landing.

As another round of thunder shook its windowpanes, it felt the unrelenting rain beginning to work its way under the flashing surrounding its chimney, where it ran along the ceiling before pooling in the plaster above the fireplace. A few minutes later, it started to drip onto the hardwood, joining the ever-growing puddle of water by the window…yet House was too cold and stiff to care.

The darkness in the upstairs hall suddenly stirred.

House swerved its gaze in time to see its owner's boots fall in front of the feeble beam of the flashlight as they started down the steps.

Audrey lifted her head. "Where are you going?"

"To start a fire," he said hoarsely, "and then get the sheriff."

"What are you going to tell him?"

"The truth," he answered, his footsteps heavy and labored as they descended the stairs.

"No, Magnus!" Grabbing the flashlight off the tread, Audrey pulled herself to her feet. "You can't!"

House watched the tiny beam gallop past Magnus and then cut in front of him.

"Don't do this," Audrey begged, her eyes swollen to mere slits as she pushed against his chest. "You'll go to jail for the rest of your life!"

Through the dim glow of the flashlight, House saw that its owner's cheeks were ashen, taut, and streaked with red. His lips, dry and cracked, slowly parted, allowing a shallow breath to escape. "Aye...it's what I deserve."

"No," she said in a strained hiss, "you don't!"

Magnus wearily untangled her fingers from his coat and stepped around her.

"For just once in your *bloody* life..." Audrey said, grasping him by his elbow, "why can't you *lie*?"

He jerked his arm away with such force that she had to grab hold of the banister to keep her balance. "Your lying is what *got* us here!" he yelled, his words coming out in a low growl as his fists began to shake. Pressing them against his sides, he turned his back on her and resumed his descent.

The faint circle of light bobbed up and down as Audrey trailed after him. "Magnus, wait—"

"Why did you say that Hugh Killam was the father?" he asked, the harshness in his voice slicing through the darkness as his feet came to a stop at the base of the stairs.

In the silence that followed, a slant of moonlight found its way around the clouds and crept through the window above the landing, bathing the stairwell and its beleaguered inhabitants in a mournful glow.

Magnus' chest rose sharply as he inhaled. "*Tell me!*"

House watched the tears that had collected at the bottom of Audrey's chin begin to drop one by one onto the floor as her mouth twisted open. "Because the dead can't speak."

Magnus' jaw twitched. "You should've told me the truth from the beginning," he said, walking away.

"Hugh *was* at the bar that night!" Audrey called out to him as he started for the door. "But so was your brother."

Magnus stopped in the entryway, but made no motion to turn the knob.

Wiping her inflamed cheeks, Audrey let the small beam guide her down the remaining stairs and over to where Magnus stood. "After my friends left, Callum came over to the table and sat down. He bought me a drink and we talked, and then we drank and talked some more. When it was closing time, he offered to drive me home." Her face took on an unnatural shape as it contorted. "We'd only gone a mile or two down the road when he pulled off to the side…"

Magnus bowed his head, the anger in his jaw giving way to unmitigated grief, as the rest of her account lurched from her lips with a stuttering sob. "I'm sorry," he said, taking her in his arms.

Audrey's tiny frame convulsed as she buried her face in his chest. "I begged him to stop, but he wouldn't listen…"

House lowered its gaze to its damp, glass-strewn floor. Although Callum was not without his faults, they were a far cry from the man Audrey had just described, and House doubted that it could ever think of him in the same way again.

"I lied to you about it," Audrey said, clutching the back of Magnus' shoulders, "because believing in the fantasy that Hugh was the baby's father was easier than reliving what Callum had done."

House heard a creak and then felt something give along its northeast corner. It glanced outside in time to see its downspout by the driveway go toppling to the ground, taking part of the gutter with it.

House's owner turned at the noise, but Audrey refused to let him go. "Magnus," she said, "please say it was an accident."

Glancing back at her, he tenderly pushed her matted hair away from her face and drew a constricted-sounding breath. "Audrey—"

She grabbed his hand and placed it against her stomach.

There was a moment of confusion, and then House saw Magnus' fingers flex as they lay splayed across her belly.

"See?" Audrey whispered through her tears. "She knows the sound of your voice."

Magnus looked down as an involuntary smile began to bleed onto the corners of his lips—yet before it could fully form, he yanked back his hand.

Audrey clasped her fingers over her mouth and shuddered as he turned and slammed his fist into the wall with a garbled yell.

House grimaced as bits of its plaster buckled and then crumbled around its owner's knuckles.

Wrenching the door open, Magnus stumbled out into the rain.

"Magnus, wait!" called Audrey, cutting her feet on the snarl of limbs as she ran after him. "Magnus!"

The shrillness of her cries pierced the night air, causing the shutter dangling beneath House's gable to quiver as they echoed across the broken sky.

Chapter 12

*T*he sound of Magnus' truck coming up the driveway gave House reason to let out its breath, and yet as the burst of stale air — wrapped tightly in the form of a relieved sigh — went sailing out of its flue, it kept its exhausted gaze fixed on Evy.

As it listened intently for the loose board on the porch to creak beneath the weight of its owner's feet, yellow light spilled in a diagonal slant from a brass floor lamp, illuminating the darkened corner of the drawing room. It was there that Evy sat slumped against the wall; her knees drawn to her chest, the thin lace strap of her nightgown hung partly off her left shoulder, while the bottom of it, as well as her feet, were drenched in blood.

House felt the lock at its front entrance begin to turn and then the heavy mahogany door swung open.

"Hello...Evy?" Magnus called, his deep voice filled with apprehension, as his footsteps echoed across the floor. "Evy—"

House heard its owner's breath catch in his throat, followed by his boots pounding against its hardwood, before bursting into its line of sight.

"Evy..." said Magnus, kneeling on the clay tiles in front of her.

Lifting her head, Evy's damp locks clung to her cheeks as she turned her sunken eyes toward him. "I'm sorry," she said in a listless whisper. "I tried to stop it from happening...but couldn't."

Magnus' face grew pale as his attention stumbled from her bloodstained hands to the wadded robe they were clutching. "But you weren't due for another three weeks," he murmured.

A single tear slid down Evy's cheek as she watched his trembling fingers struggle to peel back the satin edge of the robe. "I know..."

A tiny pair of deep brown eyes peered up at Magnus — and blinked, wresting a half-cry, half-laugh from his chest.

"...but he just couldn't wait."

Magnus looked at Evy through his tears. "It's a boy?"

"Yes," she answered, giving him a tired smile.

"And he's okay?"

"It would appear so."

Leaning forward, Magnus cupped her chin in his hand and tenderly kissed her on the lips. "I'm so sorry you had to do this by yourself."

Evy let out a long, contented sigh. "I don't know."

"What don't you know?" he asked, closing his eyes as he rested his forehead against hers.

"Orla is asking me what we're going to name him."

House saw Magnus' jaw stiffen as he drew back. "Who's Orla?"

"One of the women in the colony, silly. She showed me how to cut the umbilical cord..."

An all too familiar expression consumed Magnus' face as his gaze went from the bloodied shears lying on the tiles to the darkness lurking on the other side of the glass door.

"She's telling me that we need to name him something special," she continued. "What do you think about Ezra?"

"I don't know," he replied, wiping his cheek on his shoulder.

"Well, I like it, and so does Orla."

"Evy, listen to me," said Magnus, shifting his weight to his other knee in order to catch her gaze, which had grown distant. "We can talk about names in a minute, but right now I need to go call for help."

"Mags?" she said, reaching for him.

"I'm right here," he answered, wrapping his hand around hers.

The iridescent blue in Evy's eyes flickered at him – and then returned to their absent state. "What's a good middle name for Ezra?"

Magnus swallowed and shook his head. "Just stay right here. I'll be right back." Getting to his feet, he hurried into the kitchen and yanked the phone off its cradle.

As the wire behind House's wall began to tingle, Evy resumed her unintelligible conversation with her invisible friend Orla.

"Yeah?" answered Callum, his usual irritated-sounding tone seeping through the receiver.

"Cal, I need you over here right now!"

"What's wron –"

"Evy's had the baby. She's lost a lot of blood…"

Using the wall for support, Evy gradually stood and opened the door that led out to the deck, causing House to suck in a panic-stricken breath.

"…need to get her and the baby to the hospital."

"I'm on my way," replied Callum, sounding more sober than House had ever heard him.

"Just hurr –" Magnus glanced over his shoulder and dropped the phone.

The infant mewed softly as Evy walked to the edge of the deck. Lifting him to her lips, she lovingly kissed the side of his face — then let him go.

"No!"

What little breath remained in House fell away as Magnus' chest slammed against its wooden balusters. Leaning hard into its foundation, House braced itself, digging its pilings deeper into the rain-soaked cliff as Magnus threw his upper body over the railing; with his shoulder and arm outstretched, the tips of his fingers closed around a piece of the robe as it plunged toward the rocks below.

A raw howl of grief suddenly went up, piercing the deafening silence as Magnus fell to his knees.

"It's all right, darling," Evy cooed, stroking the back of his head. "Orla has him. See?" Smiling brightly, she pointed into the blackness. "He's just fine. Now he'll never know any pain."

Burying his face in the bloodied garment, Magnus' entire body began to shake as one violent sob after another tore through it.

"Magnus?"

House woke gasping for air at the sound of Audrey's voice. Disoriented, it tried to straighten — only to find that it was still pinned by the debris on its front porch. Reluctantly conceding to the fact that it was stuck, House concentrated its efforts instead on freeing itself from the lingering images of the nightmare. As it struggled to let them go, it saw Audrey leave the bottom step of the cellar and make her way over to Magnus, whose head and torso were slumped across his workbench, an empty bottle of Calvert's beside his elbow.

Placing her hand on his shoulder, she bent down next to his ear. "Magnus?"

"No!" he shouted, rearing his head up.

Rainwater spilled from House's gutters and slid down its clapboards like tears as it solemnly watched its owner's flailing arms reach again and again for what wasn't there.

Amidst the commotion, the whiskey bottle rolled off the edge of the bench, and as the sound of shattering glass reverberated off the cinderblock walls, Magnus' tortured expression began to fade. Pressing the heels of his hands against his eyes, he swallowed the bulge of tears in his throat and let out a labored breath.

"Magnus," repeated Audrey in a tone that bordered on impatient.

He lowered his hands and forced his gaze upward.

Audrey nervously glanced behind her. When she turned back to him, her face was filled with apprehension. "Donagh is here."

Shuttling its attention upstairs, House discovered a heavyset man, wearing a wrinkled shirt and khakis that were half-stuffed into a pair of rubber boots, standing in its entryway.

Upon hearing the clatter of footsteps, the man stopped studying the fist-sized hole in the wall next to him and turned, allowing House to see the six-pointed gold star that was pinned to his chest.

Magnus offered him a stiff nod as he drew near. "Donagh."

"Quinn," he said in a gravelly voice. "Ah need tae talk to ya…" Placing a set of meaty hands on his hips, he cut his eyes to Audrey, who had come up behind him. "…outside."

Without argument, Magnus slid his now wooden-like arms through the sleeves of his coat before following him out the door.

"Hell o' a storm last night," said Donagh in his thick, Irish brogue as he used what was left of the porch rail for balance in order to navigate his legs over the tree branch.

Keeping silent, Magnus' left foot landed awkwardly on the step as he brought it down.

The swollen earth sloshed beneath the soles of the two men's boots as they began walking across the yard.

"Ah don't know about ya," said Donagh, rubbing the back of his neck, "but Ah could sure use a cup o' coffee. Ah've been puttin' out fires all night. There were downed trees, power lines, and debris flying at me in every direction…"

House saw Magnus briefly close his eyes as Donagh prattled on.

"…flooded roads—oh, and…" Donagh paused to clear his throat and spit, sending a wad of phlegm hurtling toward the ground. "…not tae mention the half-dozen calls Ah got from Mary O'Brien about seein' a banshee roamin' the woods near the back o' her hou—"

"Why are you here, Donagh?" blurted Magnus, stopping at the edge of the yard.

House found its owner's question, as well as his demanding demeanor, more than a little odd considering the fact that he knew — without a bloody doubt — what the answer was going to be.

Donagh turned around, then letting go of a heavy sigh that reeked of cigarettes, removed his hat and ran his fingers through the greasy strands of reddish-blonde hair clinging to his scalp. "There's uh...no easy way tae say this, Quinn," he said, scratching at his grizzled jaw, "but earlier this mornin', a fisherman found yar brother's body floatin' on the other side of the point..."

Dropping his gaze, Magnus sank his chin deep into his chest. House knew it was a forced — if not quickly improvised — reaction in an effort to hide his shame, and yet as Donagh went on, it couldn't help noticing its owner's grief-stricken face seemed to be as genuine as the unbridled sorrow that was clouding his eyes.

"...smelled o' alcohol." Donagh ran his tongue over his tobacco-stained teeth and dipped his head toward the lighthouse. "Ah found a half-empty bottle o' whiskey sittin' beside the rail..."

House's sight grew dim as the memory of Magnus carrying Callum up the slippery terrain flooded its senses. For hours, Magnus had knelt outside on the parapet in the pouring rain, his dark silhouette hunched over his brother's body as the tower's yellow beacon swept across the raging sea below. Then, with the twilight rapidly fading, Magnus dragged him over to the railing and, cradling his neck in the crook of his arm, stood him up. Drawing an uneven breath, House shifted its gaze to the sun in the hopes that its blinding rays would vanquish what followed—yet the image of Callum's head smashing against the rocks came anyway.

"Quinn?"

House and its owner both blinked.

Magnus lifted his eyes and aimed them in Donagh's general direction—who was watching him with an expectant look perched upon his rounded face. "Sorry. What?"

"When did ya last see him?"

"Nearly a week ago," replied Magnus with a feeble shrug.

Donagh tugged at the waistband of his khakis, pulling them up and over his bulging midsection. "Did he seem upset about anythin'?"

The skin surrounding Magnus' eyes bunched. "You're not about to stand there and tell me that you think he jumped, are you, Donagh? Because I know my brother, and he sure as hell wouldn't—"

"No," said Donagh, raising his hands, which in turn caused the top of his pants to disappear beneath his stomach once more, "that's not what Ah'm sayin' at all. Ah'm just tryin' tae piece together what happened."

"Well, if he was drunk like you think," countered Magnus, "my guess is that he lost his footing and fell."

House saw Donagh casually glance at the abrasions running across the backs of Magnus' knuckles.

His subtlety wasn't lost on Magnus, who stuck his hands in the pockets of his coat.

The leather holster strapped to Donagh's hip creaked as he shifted his weight. After several moments, he shook his head and sighed. "Yeah," he said, pulling out a pack of Camels, "that's what Ah figure happened too."

House saw Magnus' shoulders visibly relax.

"Ah'm sorry, Quinn," mumbled Donagh, holding the flame of his lighter underneath his cigarette. "Ah know your brother was a bit of a scut, but all in all he was a good lad." He stuffed the lighter into his pocket and let out a wheezy chuckle. "And a hell o' a poker player."

"Aye," said Magnus, his relief giving way to guilt—which promptly settled in his jaw, "that he was."

Donagh pushed the right side of his bottom lip out and exhaled a stream of smoke. "Ah really hate tae do this tae ya now, Quinn, but Ah'm going tae need you tae come down tae the station and fill out some paperwork." He paused and nodded toward the porch. "Ah'll wait if ya want tae tell yar...uh...bride that."

"Let's just get on with it," said Magnus, shouldering past him.

Donagh took a final drag from his cigarette and tossed it in the grass before turning to follow.

The balding tires on the patrol car spun against the wet gravel as they started down the drive. House watched the car until it disappeared from its sight, then slowly hauled its gaze back across the yard, over the tree branch and chunks of roof lying on its porch, and into the foyer, where it found Audrey standing in front of the broken window, her lifeless eyes transfixed on something it could not see.

House felt the water running through its pipes beginning to warm, and as the liquid wound its way through the coils of its radiators, the one in the living room let out a cacophony of banging and clanking sounds, startling Audrey.

She rubbed her forehead for a moment, then carefully picking her way around the shards of glass, went into the kitchen where she filled a bucket with soapy water and carried it upstairs.

The foaming bubbles beneath the brush turned a pale pink as Audrey furiously dragged its bristles across the bloodstained floor. While observing the erratic—almost frantic—movements of Audrey's arm, House saw her chin flatten, causing the determined expression she was wearing to waver, and as the tears began to slide down her cheeks, her lips twisted open, allowing a breathless cry to escape.

Rocking back on her heels, she bowed her head and clasped her hands over her mouth as one anguish-filled sob after another tumbled out.

~

Magnus returned three hours later, looking to House—if possible—worse than he had before he'd left.

Upon hearing the door open, Audrey, who'd been lying on her bed with her knees drawn to her chest, bolted upright and hurried out into the hallway. "Magnus?" she called to him from the top of the stairs.

He stopped in the middle of the living room and swung his beleaguered gaze toward hers.

"Did…" She absently curled her fingers around the banister. "…everything go…all right?"

The expression on Magnus' face shifted, causing her to grip the rail tighter. Lowering his eyes, he pulled a brown paper bag from the pocket of his coat and disappeared into the cellar.

Chapter 13

A warm breeze, peppered with the scent of lilacs, swirled around House, flooding its senses. Inhaling deeply, it pulled the sweet fragrance through its flue and open windows, while a raucous chorus of squeaks and croaks rose up from the jagged rocks below. Perched atop their oddly shaped mud nests—that had been painstakingly built into the face of the rock—were hundreds of male cliff swallows, their square chestnut-colored tails keeping perfect time with each guttural note sung in the hopes of attracting a mate.

House listened intently, letting the racket drown out the faint but angry chanting coming from the mouths of even angrier men at the harbor.

Magnus had refused to back Audrey's father in the primary election, which had resulted in a landslide victory for his opponent. Determined not to give up on his ideals, however, an embattled John McCord had brought in a union representative and had held meeting after meeting with the dockworkers until they'd agreed to join. The grumblings over pay had started almost immediately, and three weeks later, the newly formed ILWU Local 173 went on strike, turning brother against brother…and father against son.

In the days that followed, Magnus lost half his crew — as they'd refused to cross the picket line. He'd taken the *Gwendolyn* out anyway, only to return a week later with a nearly empty cargo hold and a face grimmer than House had ever seen.

As thunder boomed in the distance, a rhythmic creak drew House's attention to its front. Audrey was sitting in the middle of the swing on the porch, the bottoms of her feet carelessly brushing against the dirt-laden floorboards as it lazily swung back and forth.

House sighed as it looked around. Although Magnus had repaired the damage, the posts holding up the new porch roof had not been painted as of yet, and that — combined with the scraps of wood, dented gutter, and mismatched shingles he'd used — made House's outward appearance look shoddier than ever.

The sun's light began to fade, putting an end to the cliff swallows' grating melody.

Audrey sucked in her breath, as if she'd been awakened from a deep sleep, and dug her heels into the planks, bringing the swing to a crooked stop. After a moment, she stood and went inside — yet unable to see her feet over her engorged belly, her footsteps were heavy and awkward as they started up the stairs.

It was an agonizingly slow ascent, and after reaching the top of the landing, she pressed her hand to her side and bent over as she waited for her breath to catch up to her. The sound of running water caused her to shift her winded gaze toward the bathroom. Letting go of her side, she straightened and with her open mouth still pleading for air, continued on.

As she walked into her bedroom, House saw her expression of indifference—which seemed to have taken up permanent residence in her face—waver when she noticed the cradle sitting in front of the window.

House's owner had spent the last few days in the cellar doing what he seemed to do best as of late, but during the small moments in-between, when his eyes were clear and his hands were steady, he managed to finish building the cradle that was intended for his and Evy's child.

Walking around the foot of the bed, Audrey ran her hand across the cradle's wooden headboard, letting her fingertips trace over the image of the teddy bear that had been carved into it.

As House watched her admiring the cradle, it felt a trickle of current enter into its walls on each side, followed closely by the jarring clang of the telephone.

Audrey stepped out into the hall and tossed a weary glance downstairs. As the ringing persisted, she sighed and started toward Magnus' bedroom, her bare feet instinctively avoiding the floorboards beside the landing, which despite the endless scrubbings, had permeated the hardwood, turning the planks a brownish crimson.

She reached for the phone on the nightstand and pressed it to her ear. "Hello?" she panted into the mouthpiece.

"Audrey?" asked a woman's voice.
"Yes?"
"This is Janet."
"Janet!" she exclaimed. "How are you?"
"I'm fine. I just wanted to call and tell you that the girl..."

House heard the water in the bathroom shut off.

"...was supposed to move into the apartment changed her mind. So if you're still wanting to come, I'd be happy to have you as a roommate."

Relief washed over Audrey's face, bringing a tired smile to her lips. "That's great news," she said, twisting the cord around her fingers. "Thank you—" A shadow fell across the wall in front of her, making her whirl around.

Magnus, damp and shirtless, was standing in the doorway watching her.

"I'm going to have to call you back," said Audrey in a low voice.

"Okay, but—"

The woman's voice ended in a click as Audrey dropped the receiver onto its base. "Sorry," she said to Magnus, gesturing at the phone in an apologetic manner, "this one was closer."

He eyed her curiously as he walked into the room. "Who was that?"

"Just a friend," she murmured, her startled gaze straying to the raised one-inch scar sitting just below his left collarbone.

House saw the side of Magnus' jaw flex as he picked up his shirt from off the bed.

"Thank you for the cradle," she said, plucking a strand of hair from her reddened cheek.

"Well," Magnus replied, pulling his arms through the sleeves, "the wee one's got to have a place to sleep."

"It's beautiful."

"I suppose it'll do," he said, crossing over to the dresser.

Several moments passed as she watched him rifle through the top drawer for a pair of socks without holes in them, and then her lips slowly parted. "Magnus…"

"Aye?"

Audrey glanced down at her stomach and swallowed hard. "Has Evy ever let you see your child?"

He stopped ransacking the drawer and turned around. "*What?*"

She shrank back at his tone. "I…found a picture of Evy in a box that—"

Magnus shoved the drawer closed. "You had no right to go through my things!" he yelled, moving toward her. "No right, whatsoever!"

"I'm sorry," she said in a broken whisper as she hurried past him and out of the room.

The top of the sun sank beneath the ocean, paving the way for the darkness, and as it slithered through the windows, devouring most of the light that the tiny lamp on the dresser was giving off, Magnus turned and started after her.

His footsteps faltered upon reaching the doorway of her bedroom. "What are you doing?"

"The person on the phone was a teacher friend of mine," Audrey said, tossing two armfuls of clothes into her suitcase that lay open on the bed. "She said I could come room with her."

"And do *what*?"

Audrey made her way back to the armoire and yanked several blouses from their hangers.

Magnus strode over to the foot of the bed, blocking her return path. "I asked you what you were going to—"

"I don't know!" she shouted, trying to go around him. "All I know is that I can't live here!"

"Audrey—"

"This semblance of a marriage is never going to work."

"It will," he said, grasping her by the shoulders, "but I just need some time."

"Time?" Audrey threw the garments on the bed. "It's been *five* months since that night, Magnus, and you can't even *look* at me! If I stay, the baby and I would be a constant reminder—and all the whiskey in the world won't wash away the guilt that's coursing through your veins. It will eat away at you, bit by bit, until there's nothing left inside of you but bitterness and hatred for me."

Magnus pulled her closer. "That's not true."

"You deserve to be happy, Magnus. And you and I both know that it's not going to be with me."

"Audrey—"

"Look me in the eyes and tell me that you're not still in love with Evy."

In the silence that followed, House watched Audrey's face become streaked with tears as Magnus—clearly caught off guard—struggled to give her an answer.

She pushed hard against his chest, making him drop his hands. "Never mind."

Magnus clenched his jaw. "Audrey, would you just listen to me for one feckin' minute?"

"There's nothing you can say," she said, picking up one of her blouses from off the bed, "that's going to convince me—"

Magnus sent the mermaid lamp on the nightstand crashing to the floor. "My son was just hours old when Evy killed him!" he shouted, his face twisting in agony. "And six months later, she tried to kill herself!"

The clothing slipped from Audrey's fingers.

Magnus' entire body shook. "That's why I don't want to talk about Evy—and that's why...I don't..." His voice grew still at the sound of gushing water. He looked down, only to have his breath seize in his throat.

Following his gaze, House saw that the tops of Audrey's feet were wet, while the bottom of her sundress clung to her legs and thighs.

Audrey's eyes grew wide with terror. "Magnus—" Clutching her stomach, she let out a cry and doubled over.

Stumbling forward, he scooped her into his arms, and after using his foot to shove the suitcase out of his way, eased her down onto the bed. "Audrey," he said, touching her cheek with his knuckles, "I need to call for help."

"Hurry," she pleaded, her legs writhing back and forth on the mattress.

He rushed out of the room, and a few seconds later, House felt a familiar crackle behind its wall, and although it could hear its owner speaking loudly into the phone, it could not discern what he was saying because of Audrey's cries.

Lying on her side with her eyes squeezed shut, she held her hands tight against her stomach as one painful sounding sob after another tore itself from her throat.

Magnus returned to the room, breathing heavily. "Just hold on," he said, dropping to his knees beside her. "An ambulance is on the way."

"Something's wrong..."

"Everything's going to be all right. Help is comi—"

Audrey reached out and grabbed Magnus by his shirt. "*Something's wrong!*" she repeated, then rolling over onto her back, dug her shoulder blades into the mattress as another wave of pain hit. "You have to help it!"

Magnus' panicked expression turned to apprehension as he moved to the end of the bed. Reaching under the drenched folds of her sundress, he pulled her underwear down and over her trembling legs.

A tiny foot, purplish and tinged with blue appeared.

"It's coming out breech," he said in a half-whisper.

House stared somberly at the foot dangling from the birth canal. It was a sobering reminder that life was as fragile as it was precious, and could be taken away before it ever began—as evidenced by the small set of bones lying tucked behind a loose cinderblock in its cellar. Others were scattered across its property, put there in the dirt by grieving fathers, their simple wooden markers having washed away over the years.

Clasping her knees, Audrey cried out again.

As the faint wail of a siren sounded in the distance, a second foot descended, bearing the same mottled hue as the other one.

"Audrey," said Magnus, gently grasping the baby's feet, "I need you to push."

"I can't..."

"*Yes*, you can. Come on...just one big push."

Audrey's hair, damp and matted with sweat, spilled around her shoulders as she lifted her head off the pillow; spreading her hands across her swollen stomach, the veins in her throat bulged beneath her skin as she gritted her teeth and pushed.

An umbilical cord wrapped around a mass of still gray flesh slid out.

A sob cut off Audrey's breath as she strained to see. "Why isn't it crying?"

Tears crowded Magnus' eyes as he frantically removed the cord from around the baby's neck and covered its tiny mouth with his.

The light above the bed flickered as House tried to will its own life into the infant's as it lay motionless in the crook of its owner's arm.

As moment after agonizing moment passed, House felt the air in the room, thick, clammy, and suspended in a deafening quiet start to grow heavy as a steady rain began to fall on its roof.

There was a crack of thunder—and then a feeble cry sounded.

Relief, in the form of a solemn grin, found its way onto Magnus' lips as he gazed down at the squalling bundle. "It's a girl," he said, coming around the edge of the bed. He leaned down to place the baby in Audrey's arms, only to find them limp at her sides. "Audrey?"

Peering over its owner's shoulder, House saw that her head was listed to one side and her eyes were closed.

"Audrey!" yelled Magnus, shaking her.

House's gaze went from the tears streaked across her ashen, unmoving face to the dark red blood seeping into the mattress between her legs.

Chapter 14

The ocean churned and thrashed, heaving its crooked waves against the jagged outcropping near the shore. House watched the white spray shoot high into the air and then break up into a thousand tiny droplets before returning to the agitated sea.

Black clouds began to gather overhead, making House cast a sidelong glance at its owner.

Magnus was slumped in a chair in the corner of the room with his head propped against his fist as he stared out the window. He'd been like that for hours, but House could tell by the way his eyes followed the waves, as they rose to meet the darkening sky, that his soul was restless.

The baby suddenly stirred, drawing Magnus to his feet. As he made his way over to the cradle, House studied his face carefully, searching for the smallest inflection—a glimmer in his eye, or a tug of his lips—that would indicate joy. The only movement it saw, however, was in his jaw; no longer slack, the skin surrounding it was stretched so tight that House thought the bone was going to pierce it.

"What was his name?"

House shifted its attention to Audrey. She was lying in the bed, a pile of blankets covering her frail-looking body, and although the color had returned to her cheeks, House suspected it was only because her chin was trembling.

Scratching at the stubble on his neck, Magnus took in an uneven breath. "I didn't get a chance to give him one," he replied, keeping his gaze locked inside the confines of the cradle.

As Audrey continued to stare at the side of his tortured face, her impending tears began to fall; slipping from the corners of her eyes, they rolled down and dropped one by one onto the pillow beneath her. "I'm sorry," she said in a fractured whisper.

Magnus wrapped his fingers around the edge of the cradle.

"Where is Evy now?"

"The state mental hospital in Santa Clara or…" He paused and shook his head. "That's where she was. The last time I went to visit, they informed me that Evy's mother—whom Evy told me had died in a fire when she was twelve—had signed her out. Three weeks later, I was served divorce papers by an attorney in Monterrey. That was a year and a half ago…and I haven't heard from her since."

The sound of an approaching car made House glance toward the driveway. Magnus must have picked up on it as well because he turned and walked out of Audrey's room without saying another word.

He hurried down the stairs and looked out the window—where he promptly balled his hand into a fist. Crossing over to the entryway, he jerked open the door, startling John McCord, whose finger was poised to ring the bell.

Standing on opposites sides of the threshold, neither of the two men seemed to possess the desire to acknowledge the other one's presence.

"What can I do for you, John?" Magnus finally asked, his voice laced with restraint.

"I called the hospital this morning to check on Audrey and my granddaughter, and the nurse on the phone said that they'd been discharged."

"Aye. I brought them home this morning."

John shifted his feet. "Well, can I see them?"

"Audrey's not up for having visitors just yet."

"You know," said McCord, removing his hat, "I've had a rough couple of weeks. Perhaps you and I could talk over a cup of coffee while I wait."

Magnus blocked the doorway with his arm. "Those rough couple of weeks you've had were *self-inflicted*...and as far as you and I go, we have nothing further to discuss."

John's complexion darkened. "*You* may not, but there's plenty I have to say to you. And I'd like to start," he said, waving a piece of paper at him that he'd pulled from the breast pocket of his suit, "by asking why I received this from you in the mail?"

"It's what I owe you on the *Gwendolyn*—down to the last penny."

"I didn't ask you what it was," John said, folding the check. "I asked you why? You're in no position financially to do that, and with the strike showing no end in sight, you're going to end up in the poorhouse, taking my daughter and grandchild with you."

"I'd rather end up destitute than be indebted to you for another minute."

"Don't be stupid, Quinn. Take your money and take the *Gwendolyn* like I originally offered." McCord looked away and sucked in his breath, highlighting the bags under his eyes. When he returned his gaze to Magnus, his expression seemed—at best—ambiguously pleasant. "Besides, you're part of the family now."

A small cry came from upstairs, making Magnus grip the edge of the door. "Would this be the same family that you tried to barter away?"

McCord's right eyelid twitched. "I understand how difficult it is for a man to swallow his pride," he said, holding the check out to him, "so let me make this easy on you—"

"Here's an idea," said Magnus, raising his voice. "Why don't you swallow your *own* feckin' pride and get your arse down to the docks to fix that mess you made?" Taking a step back, he slammed the door in McCord's face with such force that the heavy brass ring of the knocker swung straight out—just narrowly missing his nose.

As Magnus turned and started up the stairs, House's gaze hurried ahead of him.

Audrey was sitting on the window seat, a small smile perched on her face as she cradled the baby against her left breast. The sound of footsteps made her glance at the doorway.

"I'm sorry," said Magnus, averting his eyes.

"It's all right," she replied, rushing to cover herself with the blanket.

"That was your father."

"I gathered."

A sandpapery sound filled the room as Magnus scratched at his unshaven jaw. "How are you feeling?"

"Better."

Magnus hesitated and then stepped inside. "Can I get you anything?" he asked, making his way toward her.

"No, I'm fine."

Audrey's words seemed to neutralize him, causing his footsteps to falter. "Well…let me know if you do."

"I will," she said, glancing in any direction but his.

He lingered by the bed for a moment and then reluctantly started for the door.

"Magnus?"

He stopped and eagerly glanced back.

"Try and get some sleep," she said in a voice etched with concern as her eyes briefly locked with his.

In the disappointing silence that followed, House watched its owner start once more for the door. He hadn't gotten very far—when he suddenly reached out and grabbed hold of the bedpost. The buttons on his shirt pulled against their slots as he took in his breath. "I don't love Evy," he said, looking back at Audrey. "Not anymore. But there's a part of me that will always care for her, in spite of what she did."

Audrey reached for his hand. "I'm so sorry, Magnus," she whispered, blinking back her tears. "You have every right to feel the way you feel. And I had no business asking you what I did that night. I just didn't know."

He pulled his hand from her grasp. "No one knew..." he said, wearily sitting down beside her, "except for Callum."

House saw Audrey stiffen at the mention of his name, making it realize that although her tormentor was dead and buried, the memory of what he'd done that night would never leave her. The same went for Magnus who, aside from the scars that marked his heart, would never be able to forgive himself. For these two, in spite of the fact that their battles were over, there would be no respite, no celebration, no victory dance...and as they sat side by side on the window seat, bodies close, but not touching, House was overcome with grief in knowing that neither of them would ever find peace.

The baby began to fuss and then cry.

"May I?" asked Magnus, holding out his hands.

House felt a trickle of excitement beginning to coarse through its walls as Audrey placed the squalling infant in its owner's waiting arms.

"There, there..." Speaking in a hushed tone, his massive fingers covered most of the baby's head and neck as he gently swayed her back and forth. "...it's all right." Her cries soon diminished. "So, what are you going to name this pretty little lass?"

"I was thinking of calling her Delia, after my mother."

"Delia," he repeated. "A beautiful name for a beautiful girl." Magnus gently stroked the strands of red hair peeking out of the top of the blanket with his fingertips and smiled. "You know, I think she looks just like you."

Audrey clasped her hands tightly together.

"She's got your eyes, and she's got your—"

"Magnus, when I'm able…I'm still going to San Francisco."

House's elation sank behind its walls, where it was left to languish beneath a pile of rat droppings.

Magnus' mouth drew into a thin, hard line as he stood from the window seat.

Audrey brushed away her tears. "I'm sorry," she said, watching him place the baby in the cradle. "I never meant to hurt you—"

"I sold the *Gwendolyn* to Owen Connelly."

House felt its foundation begin to tremble.

"What?" Audrey's eyes swirled with confusion—then widened. "No, Magnus," she said, getting to her feet. "I can't let you do this."

"It's done."

She shook her head, sending her tangled tresses flying. "Well—*undo* it."

"I've lived and worked in this town my whole life, and the only thing I have to show for it is this cursed house," he said bitterly. "I'm no better off now than the day I was born."

"Magnus," Audrey said in a warning tone, drawing closer to him, "you need to think about what you're doing."

"That's *all* I've done for the past five days, Audrey," he said, turning from the cradle. "And while I was sitting beside your hospital bed, praying for you to wake up, I realized that I'd made a lot of mistakes over the years. But the one I regret the most..." His breath quivered as the rims of his eyes began to water. "...is having ever let you go."

A conflicted smile crowded Audrey's lips. "What are you saying?"

"I'm saying that I want to spend the rest of my life with you," he replied, his dark locks falling across his brows as he looked down at her. "And I don't care if that happens to be in San Francisco or the other side of the world, because I know it's going to be all right as long as you and this wee one are with me."

House's anger surged, shattering the lightbulb that was suspended above the workbench in the cellar.

Reaching into his pocket, Magnus pulled out a small gold band, encrusted with a tiny diamond, and dropped to one knee. "So...Audrina Lynn McCord Quinn, will you do me the honor of staying married to me?"

Audrey's face flooded with tears as he slipped the ring onto her finger. "Magnus..." She paused and took in an uneven breath.

The lines in Magnus' forehead deepened as he gazed up at her, waiting.

Angling her head downward, Audrey swallowed hard. "With everything—that's happened," she said, the words jerking out of her, "do you think you can ever learn to love me again?"

Magnus stood, and with his tall frame towering over hers, bent down and tenderly kissed her on the lips. It lasted only a moment, and then he drew back. "I never stopped," he whispered.

The clouds opened up, sending a deluge of rain falling upon House's roof.

"*Well*, woman?" said Magnus, cocking his brow. "I need an answer."

Audrey laughed and tearfully threw her arms around his neck. "Yes! Oh, Magnus—yes!"

Chapter 15

House stared dismally into the horizon, trying to see past the thick blanket of fog that was covering the ocean. The sun had been up for hours, yet House's thoughts were still firmly entrenched in darkness, and although it had no desire to hold onto its memories of Magnus—who'd left for a new life with Audrey less than two weeks after redeclaring his love for her—found that it couldn't exactly let them go either. What bothered House the most was the fact that its owner hadn't looked back…and that was far more hurtful than any blow his fist had ever landed on its walls.

As the fog began to lift, House involuntarily glanced in the direction of the lighthouse. After Callum's death, the Coast Guard—spouting rhetoric about the high costs of manning it, as well as the need for efficiency—had come in and automated it.

In the years following, House had watched the beacon turn on faithfully at dusk, where its unwavering light would sweep across the dark waters, guiding passing ships away from the rocky shoals…until one day it didn't.

It was on a cold and drizzly February morning—two families and a decade later—that House had been awakened by a barking dog, and as it sat there listening, it slowly came to realize that it wasn't the dog that had interrupted its sleep, but rather the eerie silence surrounding it.

Seconds later, the ground beneath House began to shake. The stone foundation it was anchored on suddenly shifted, and House felt itself being pulled apart. Dirt bubbled up from below, making House gasp for air as the damp earth engulfed the jagged space where there used to be concrete. The tremendous pressure blew out its front windows and sent a spiderweb of fractures running through its plastered walls.

As House's right side sank deeper into the mud, it saw the tower of the lighthouse start to sway as if it were a leaf blowing in the wind. There was a loud boom—and then a huge cloud of white powdery smoke filled the sky as it crumbled into the sea.

By the time the ground had grown still, the only thing left standing of the lighthouse was its spiral staircase that led to the parapet, and the tiny, one-room cottage near the front, which had served as Callum's living quarters.

The sun's rays strengthened, burning off the remaining fog, and as the dense gray mist vanished into a backdrop of blue, House found itself staring at the dwelling that had been built on top of the lighthouse's ashes. Made entirely of glass and steel, the perfectly square foundation was rooted deep in the soil, while its sleek, angular roof jutted out over the point.

House remembered its excitement upon learning that the odd-looking structure was going to be a residence; unfortunately, it hadn't taken long for its enthusiasm to wane, when—after many days of prodding and pleading—it determined that the effervescent home was just as cold and unaware as the man who'd moved into it.

The shrill whine of a table saw cut into House's thoughts, sending them scurrying back into the dank, dark, gaping hole from which they'd crawled out of. Letting go of a deep sigh, House bitterly turned its attention to the Victorian, whose front yard was bustling with activity.

One worker was skillfully forming and bending gutters with the help of an elaborate machine, while another was standing on a ladder, his left arm hooked around the top rung, as he painted the columns on the porch, and still two more were in the process of unloading a heavy box from a truck that had the words *A&P Plumbing* stenciled on its side. As House watched the men struggling to carry the box through the front entrance, it heard an engine shut off, followed by the sound of a car door opening.

Looking past the truck, House found the woman from yesterday getting out of her SUV. With her tiny arms swinging back and forth like a pair of angry pistons, she marched toward the foreman, who—upon noticing her—promptly stiffened.

"How's it going, Tom?" she asked, taking off her sunglasses. "Are we still on schedule to move in next week?"

Squaring his shoulders, the foreman stuck the grease pencil he'd been using to mark trim behind his ear and cleared his throat. "You can move in, but you won't have full use of your master bath."

The woman tilted her head, exposing the pulsing, rope-like vein in her neck. "Why not?"

"I was told that the tile you wanted for the shower and floor is on backorder. It'll be another four weeks at least."

"Is the tile guy here?" she asked, scanning the half-dozen vehicles lining the driveway.

House saw the foreman's posture relax after realizing that someone other than himself was about to experience her wrath. "Yeah," he answered, gleefully jerking his thumb toward the front door, "he's upstairs."

As the woman strode past him, House noticed her man-pet standing near the SUV. Balancing one little girl on his hip, and holding the hand of another, he kept shifting his feet as if he were trying to decide whether or not to follow his wife inside. House's gaze drifted from the man's embattled expression to the toddler in his arms; wearing a pink coat, the side of her head lay nestled against his shoulder, while a small blanket, covered in polka-dots and crumbs, twisted slowly in the breeze as it dangled from her fingertips.

"Daddy?" The little girl beside him squeezed his hand excitedly. "Can we go in and see our rooms?"

The man looked down and shook his head. "Not today, sweetheart," he said, plucking a strand of hair from her cheek. "I don't think it's safe."

Her face filled with disappointment, but she didn't say anything, reminding House of another flaxen-haired girl it used to know.

That thought, while innocent, brought with it the familiar smell of lavender and incense, and as the unwanted fragrance began drifting through its walls, House became saturated in trepidation, because it knew that before it could draw its next breath, the thick, acrid smell of smoke was going to swoop in—and it did, right on cue.

Although House fought desperately to remain in the present, it felt the sights and sounds in front of it beginning to slip away as its gaze fell upon the blackened floorboards that lay charred and crumbling beneath the filthy, mildewed carpet in its living room...

"You have always done what you were told. You are kind...responsible...and patient to a fault."

By the light of the candle, House watched its occupant, Maura Litsey, as she studied the palm of the woman sitting across from her. "You have suffered a loss recently…someone you loved very much."

The woman lifted her amber-colored eyes. "My father. He'd been sick for a long time. I quit work to care for him."

"Let me see your other hand," Maura said in a voice that held more indifference than it did compassion.

The woman hesitated and then slowly extended her right arm.

"Ah…" The beads of Maura's turquoise necklace clacked against the table as she leaned forward. "You have good health, and a long life in front of you."

The orange flame flickered beneath Maura's breath as she spoke, illuminating the younger woman's face, whose delicate features seemed shrouded in sadness.

"Do you have a particular question that you want the answer to?"

The woman swallowed, and then, with a pair of lips that barely moved, asked the question that House had heard nearly every woman who had come to see Maura ask. "Will I ever be married?"

Maura gave her a knowing smile and glanced down. "I see two men in your life," she replied after a moment. "One you like…and one whom you've loved from a distance since you were a girl."

The woman hooked her feet around the back legs of her chair as though Maura's words were going to cause her to take flight.

"What's going on?"

"Shh!"

"But I can't hear."

House absently flicked its gaze to the top of the stairs, where its two young masters sat perched on the landing.

"What did she say—"

Charlie Montgomery put her hand over her brother's mouth. "Stop talking," she said in a hissy whisper. "If Grams hears you, she's gonna get mad."

Travis looked at his sister and narrowed his eyes. Seconds later, Charlie yanked her hand back, eliciting a giggle from him.

"You're so gross," she said, wiping her palm on her corduroys.

"Because of your generous nature, you are taken advantage of easily…"

House returned its attention to the corner of the living room, where it watched Maura run her fingernail across one of the lines etched in the woman's palm and tap it. "*Especially* by the man you like."

The woman's shoulders drooped, pulling her head down with them.

"When the first leaf falls, the man your heart has been pining for will notice you." Maura let go of the woman's hand and looked directly at her. "Before that happens, you must decide what you want."

House waited for her to go on, but the woman—appearing oddly satisfied—slid her chair back and stood. "Thank you," she said, offering Maura a folded five-dollar bill.

Acknowledging her with a deep nod that highlighted the blue eyeshadow caked in the creases of her lids, Maura rose and escorted her to the entryway, which had been walled up with sheets of dark paneling in order to separate it from the living room. "Good luck to you," she said, stuffing the money down the left side of her brassiere, "and have a blessed day."

As she opened the hollow-core door, a man, whom House had come to know quite well, eagerly got up from the cracked vinyl chair that sat along the far wall and took a step forward. "Ma'am," he said, touching his thumb and forefinger to the gray cap that was pulled low across his brow.

Averting her eyes, the woman hurried past him and slipped through the front door that led outside.

Maura waited until the woman was out of earshot and then looked at the man. "No," she said, swatting at the folded newspaper he was clutching.

"But, Maura," he pleaded, "this time is different. I got a hot tip about Darling Donnager in the third. I just need you to tell me if he's gonna place."

Maura shook her head as she began pushing him toward the door.

"But he's 50-1 odds," he protested, holding the racing form out to her as he shuffled backward.

"*Goodbye*, Ed."

With a sigh, Ed turned and started down the porch steps—but after getting halfway across the yard, stopped and looked back. "Are we still on for Friday night?"

House saw the lines around Maura's eyes soften. "Pick me up at seven—and don't be late this time."

Ed's grin widened, propelling his cheeks into his jaws. "I won't."

"Where are you taking me?"

"*Burger Wagon.* I've got a coupon."

Maura arched her brows in disdain.

"You know, if you would just help me out," he said, waving the racing form in the air as he walked around his car's front bumper, which House noticed was being held in place by baling wire, "I'd be able to spring for a bottle of champagne at *Giovanni's*—and I'm not talking about the cheap stuff."

Folding her arms, Maura leaned against the doorjamb and smiled. "I prefer gin."

"Well…I guess it's *your* loss." Ed's lopsided gaze lingered in her direction for a moment, then turning away, he gave another sigh—which House couldn't tell stemmed from frustration or adoration—and got in his car.

As the engine coughed and sputtered to life, Maura flipped the sign that was hanging beside her to CLOSED and went back inside. "Okay, you two," she called, yanking the purple scarf off her head, "get down here and help Grams with dinner."

House's stairs shook as its young masters ran down them.

Travis paused at the bottom of the staircase to bend his knees and then jumped. "What are we having?" he asked, sticking his landing on the living room floor.

"Tuna casserole."

Travis scrunched up his face. "But Billy doesn't like tuna."

"Then Billy can go hungry," said Maura, pinching out the flame of the candle.

As Charlie went to squeeze past her brother, he held his arms out from his sides and spread his feet, blocking her. "What's the password?"

"Move it, creep," she replied, shoving him out of her way.

Travis fell to the floor in spectacular fashion. "Ow," he said, letting out an equally dramatic groan.

Rolling her eyes, Charlie stepped over him and followed Maura into the kitchen. "Grams," she said, shimmying open the drawer beside the stove, "do you like Mr. Ratner?"

A surge of heat bounced off House's ceiling as Maura lowered the oven door. "Of course I do."

"Then why won't you ever pick the horses for him?"

"Yeah," Travis chimed in, bounding up behind her. "Then we'd be rich."

"No, *we* wouldn't. And neither would Ed." Setting the bubbling casserole on the stove, Maura pointed an oven-mitt-clad hand at Travis. "He'd just find something else to gamble away his winnings on."

Charlie turned from the drawer. "But how do you know if you don't try?"

"Because I've known men like Ed my entire life," she answered, the impatience in her voice rising. "They're all the same."

"Then why do you keep going out on dates with him—"

"Travis," said Maura, her mouth twisting to one side as she flung the mitt down, "please, just go set the table."

"Fine," he mumbled, turning away. "Come on, Billy."

"And don't you dare drop those plates."

"But, Grams…" Travis stopped and put his hands on his hips. "That was Billy, and I told you he didn't drop them on purpo—"

"Travis Michael, I'm too tired to argue with you," Maura snapped. "Do what I said."

The sound of the front door opening and closing sent House's gaze swerving to the living room, where it found its main occupant, Shay Montgomery, leaning against the paneled wall as she took off her shoes.

"No one in this family ever believes me," House heard Travis say.

"And why do you suppose that is?" countered Maura.

Letting her purse fall from her shoulder, Shay slowly made her way across the slanted floor, then pausing to forge a weary smile, stepped into the kitchen.

"Hi, Mom," said Travis, arranging a set of chipped, mismatched plates on the table.

"Hello, sweetheart," she replied, trying in vain to smooth his sprawling cowlick before stooping to kiss him on the cheek. "How was school?"

"Good," he answered, giving her a gap-toothed grin.

Shay sat down in the chair and placed her left ankle on top of her knee. "And, Charlie," she said, the slender muscle in her forearm flexing as she massaged the ball of her stockinged foot, "how was *your* day?"

"It was okay."

Shay tilted her head, sending her blonde ponytail sliding across the back of her white polyester smock. "*Just* okay?"

"As okay as eighth grade can be," Charlie answered, plucking a fork from the drawer.

Maura set the casserole on the table. "How was work?"

"Long," Shay replied, returning her foot to the peeling linoleum. "A woman was admitted this afternoon with—"

"Hey, Mom, guess what?"

Shay sighed and pursed her lips. "What, Travis?"

"We had a fire drill today, and we all had to go outside in the rain."

House watched Shay widen her eyes in mock enthusiasm. "I bet that was fun."

"It was, but a lot of the girls didn't like getting wet. Some of them cried."

"Well, I'd probably cry too if I got wet," said Shay, letting go of a clipped laugh that House noticed seemed to be specifically reserved for Travis.

"But they didn't even care about getting to see the fire truck—"

Maura cleared her throat, the rigidness of which caused Travis to fall silent.

Charlie finished setting the table and took the seat next to her mother.

Travis sat with his hands folded in his lap as Maura spooned the casserole onto his plate. "What about Billy?"

"You told me he didn't like tuna casserole."

"He doesn't, but he says he'll try it anyway."

"Then he can share yours," said Maura, picking up the pitcher of Kool-Aid.

Travis' gaze went from his grandmother to Shay. "Mom," he whined, drawing out the word.

With Maura looking on, Shay leaned across the table and reached for the empty plate Travis had placed beside him.

"Billy says thanks," Travis chirped.

Shay offered a curt smile in return. "Tell Billy he's welcome."

Shaking her head, Maura filled the glasses with the watery red liquid and sat down.

"So, Charlie," said Shay, deliberately turning to her daughter, "are you excited for Saturday?"

"I guess," she answered, pushing the food around on her plate.

"How many girls are coming? I need to put in the order for the cake tomorrow."

"I didn't invite any."

"Why on earth not?" asked Maura.

Charlie looked up. "Because I'm turning thirteen, Grams—not six. I'm too old for birthday parties."

"Well, what about Missy and Tonya?" Shay prompted. "You invited *them*, didn't you?"

"No."

The narrow space between Shay's eyebrows crinkled. "But I thought they were going to sleep over."

"Missy has to go see her dad this weekend, and ever since Tonya got a boyfriend, he's all she talks about. I don't want to spend my birthday listening to her go on and on about him." And with that, Charlie shoved her fork—its tines loaded with tuna and noodles—into her mouth and began to chew.

Shay exchanged a pointed glance with her mother, but neither seemed to know what to say.

"Mom, can Billy have some Kool-Aid?"

"He can have water," Shay answered, rubbing her forehead, "and *you* can get it for him."

"Guess what else happened today?" asked Travis on his way to the sink.

His question was met with silence.

Undeterred, he launched into his story, which involved a boy named Matt, a blackboard, and a red magic marker.

When dinner—and Travis' meaningless tale—were over, Charlie cleared the table and headed upstairs, where she swiftly disappeared into the bedroom that she shared with him.

~

As evening settled in, House found itself dividing its time between watching a cartoon with Travis, who was sitting cross-legged on the living room floor—his nose inches from the TV, and Shay and her mother, who were engaged in quiet conversation as they stood side by side at the kitchen sink.

"You know, last week Charlie was so excited about her birthday and slumber party," said Shay, absently running a dishtowel over a plate. "What do you think made her change her mind?"

A gentle breeze floated through the window that was being kept propped open with a paint stirrer, ruffling Maura's blouse as she rinsed the pan she'd been scrubbing. "Who knows with that girl?"

"Maybe I should go and talk to her."

"She's not the one you need to talk to."

The worried expression that was ever-present on Shay's face deepened. "What happened?"

Maura let the pan slip back into the soapy water. "Travis' teacher called me this morning. They didn't have a fire drill. He pulled the alarm and blamed it on Billy."

The grating sound effects coming from the TV grew louder.

"Well?" said Maura, turning from the sink. "Aren't you going to say anything?"

Shay threw the towel on the counter. "We've been over this, Mom. It's just a phase he's going through."

"That *phase* almost got him suspended, and I had to cancel two readings because of having to go down to the school and convince his principal otherwise."

"I'm sorry you had to do that," Shay replied, yet House couldn't help noticing the lack of remorse in her voice.

"Travis is the one who should be sorry," Maura said, jerking her head toward the living room. "You need to make him understand that what he did was wrong."

"Fine, I'll talk to him—"

"*And* you need to quit indulging him when it comes to Billy. It's time to stop all that nonsense."

Shay's lips tightened. "I told you that Billy is a coping mechanism for him."

"It's an excuse for bad behavior."

"I talked to a psychiatrist, and he said that—"

"*Psychiatrist?* You mean that intern you share cigarettes with behind the back stairwell of the hospital?"

The skin beneath Shay's cheeks turned crimson. "You know how hard it is for Travis to make friends," she stated, hiding her face behind the cabinet door as she stacked the plate on the shelf.

"Yes, I *do* know. And I also know that he's never going to have *any* as long as you keep enabling him to play with some made up one."

The raw sound of artillery fire, coupled with the roaring whine of a helicopter, suddenly engulfed the kitchen.

House's gaze shot back to the TV, where a chaotic scene was unfolding.

"...ended with sixteen wounded men on the ground. The medivac—"

Walter Cronkite's voice and the bloody soldiers being carried across an open field on stretchers abruptly vanished.

Travis looked up in surprise. Shay was standing over him, the heel of her hand — stiff and trembling — pressed tight against the silver knob on the console.

"Sorry," he said, his chin flattening, "I changed the channel, and it was just on."

House watched Shay straighten as she struggled to draw her emotions back inside her. "Let's talk for a minute," she said, making her way over to the couch.

The denim patches that had been sewn over the knees of Travis' jeans scraped across the matted fibers of the carpet as he got to his feet.

Shay pulled him into her lap and wrapped her arms around his. "Grams told me what really happened today," she said, resting her cheek on the top of his head. "Why did you do it?"

"I didn't," he said, picking at the black letters on her nametag. "*Billy* did."

"I need you to listen to me, Travis. I know how much you miss Tyler…" Shay's mouth quivered as she spoke, causing her words to come out uneven. "And it's perfectly okay to have an imaginary friend…but it's not okay for you to do bad things and then blame it on them." She paused and took in a stilted-sounding breath. "So, no TV and no playing outside for the rest of the week."

Travis raised his head. "But, Mom…" His eyes began to well with a mix of panic and anger. "Billy really did pull the fire alarm."

Shay stood up, dumping him off her lap. "Go to your room," she said, aiming him toward the stairs.

"And while you're there, I want you to write a letter to your principal, telling him how sorry you are."

"Mom—"

"*Now*, Travis. I'll be up in a little while to check it."

House silently absorbed the tiny blows of wrath coming from Travis' feet as he stomped up the steps.

After the bedroom door had closed—loudly, Shay's gaze went from the landing at the top of the stairs to the television's olive-gray screen; from there, it slowly drifted to the picture housed in the large wooden frame hanging on the wall above it.

The stoic face of a boy clothed in a man's uniform stared back at her.

As Shay's sunken eyes pierced the glass, House awkwardly shifted its weight, causing the radiator in the living room to clank against its ill-fitting, spray-painted cover.

The saloon doors, which had been added to the kitchen entrance by the previous owner—around the same time as all the paneling, banged open.

"It's time for *MacMillan and Wife*," said Maura, stepping in front of Shay's line of sight to turn on the TV.

As the screen crackled and came to life, House saw Maura steal a sideways glance at the picture, then walking around the coffee table, took Shay by the arm and pulled her down onto the couch, seeming determined to distract her from her impending tears.

~

House rested against its listing foundation as it watched a brown pelican circle the sky high above the ocean. Folding its wings, it dove headfirst into the water—only to surface with its beak empty. It rode the swells for several moments before wearily taking flight again, eliciting an anxious sigh from House. The juvenile bird had been searching for a meal for over two hours, and as darkness surrounded the inlet, House knew the chances of it falling prey to what lurked in the depths greatly increased with each futile dive.

Having no wish to see the pelican's fate unfold, House turned its attention inward to its young master...and found that her troubled face far outweighed its concern for the bird.

Charlie was sitting on the window seat, her left shoulder and side of her head slumped against the thick pane of glass. Moonlight spilled across her blonde locks, bathing their ends in a warm glow, as she hugged her knees to her chest.

"I can't wait for my birthday."

Charlie stirred slightly at her brother's voice. "You just *had* a birthday."

"I mean my *next* birthday."

House glanced at its littlest master. Travis was lying in bed with his head propped upon his hand. "You know what I want?"

"What?"

Travis blew out his breath. "A baseball," he said, watching the folds of the sheet Shay had strung between their beds flutter in the darkness. "That way, when Tyler comes home, we can play catch."

"You already have a baseball."

"It's Tyler's ball. I found it in his room...but I lost it."

The fabric of Charlie's nightgown rustled softly as she folded her arms across her stomach. "Well, I'm sure you'll find it."

"No...it's gone forever," he muttered. "Probably in Timbuktu by now."

"Why do you say that?"

"Because me and Billy were playing with it outside, and he threw it too far, and it went over the cliff."

"Travis"—Charlie turned from the window—"you know you're not allowed to even go *near* the back of the house."

"That's what I told Billy, but he wouldn't listen." Travis dug his elbow into the mattress, pushing himself up. "You're not going to tell Mom, are you?" he pleaded, his eyes straining to see past the floral sheet.

Letting out a long and frustrated-sounding sigh, Charlie returned her gaze to the window. "No."

Relieved, House's young master flopped over onto his back. "Do you think Tyler's gonna be mad at me when he comes home?" he asked, holding up the first two fingers of his right hand.

"No...I think he's just going to be happy to be home."

"Well, I know *I'll* be happy," said Travis, watching the bunny shadow puppet he'd made hop across the makeshift curtain.

"Me too."

A single knock on the door startled the both of them.

"That's enough talking," Shay called. "Go to sleep." When no response came, she pressed her ear to the door. "Do you hear me?"

Travis, who was apparently still mad over losing his TV privileges, as well as having to write a three-paragraph apology to his principal, kept silent.

"Sorry, Mom," said Charlie.

Travis waited for his mother's silhouette to disappear from the crack beneath the door before resuming his puppet show. "Charlie," he said in a loud whisper, "can I ask you something?"

"What?"

"Why don't you really want to have any of your friends come to your birthday party?"

"Because."

"Because why?"

"Just because," she snapped.

"That's *not* an answer."

Charlie's eyes flickered, filling their rims with tears. "Because I overheard one of them saying that Grams is nothing but a money-grubbing charlatan."

Travis stopped his bunny in mid-hop and lowered his hand. "What does that mean?"

Staring out at the night sky, Charlie swallowed and wiped her cheek on her shoulder. "A fake."

Chapter 16

"*W*hen did you get so tall?"

Tyler Montgomery looked down at his mother with eyes that were the color of the sea and laughed. "I don't know."

Shay reached up to sweep one of his curls from off his forehead, yet his graduation cap held it firmly in place.

As the two of them stood in the middle of the cellar — the cinderblock walls of which had been painted a light blue — House was unexpectedly struck by Shay's beauty. Her slight figure, normally covered by her nurse's uniform, or oversized sweater and jeans, was now clothed in a tight, knee-length black dress that was cut low across the shoulders, while her long golden locks hung in soft ringlets down her back.

Tyler shifted his feet as she fussed with his tie. "Do you think Dad's coming?"

"I don't know," she said, avoiding his gaze.

Tyler's lips filled with disappointment, pulling them taut.

"But if he doesn't," Shay added quickly, "it's important to remember that it's not because he doesn't love you —"

"Come on, Mom..." Tyler shook his head, causing the red tassel dangling from the corner of his cap to swing back and forth. "I'm not a kid."

"Oh, that's right," said Shay, letting go of his tie. "I forgot, you're a man now — and you know everything."

Tyler drew back and scowled. "That's not what I meant."

The sound of heavy footsteps, followed by Maura yelling at Travis to get dressed, trickled down the concrete steps.

As particles of dust rained from the floor joists above, Shay took Tyler by the hand and led him over to the small cot in the corner.

"What?" he grumbled, plopping down beside her.

House watched her retrieve the velvet black box she'd hidden underneath his pillow when he'd gone upstairs to shower.

"I got you something," she said, turning back to him.

When Tyler saw the box, his irritation morphed into shame, leaving his eyes downcast.

"Well," said Shay, waving it under his nose, "aren't you going to open it?"

As he took the box, Shay clasped her hands together excitedly.

Peering over Tyler's shoulder as he lifted the hinged lid, House saw a stainless-steel watch with a large black face nestled in the felt lining.

"Do you like it?"

Tyler ran his thumb over the silver links and nodded. "I do," he replied in a soft whisper.

"It shows the day and month," Shay explained, pointing at the small, rectangular window on the watch's face, "and you never have to wind it or put batteries in it."

Tyler eagerly pulled it out and fastened it to his wrist. "What do you think?" he asked, holding up his arm.

"I think it looks great."

"I'm leaving in five minutes!" yelled Maura from upstairs. "Those of you who are going had better get in the car, and that includes you, Tyler — unless you're planning on walking!"

Shay sighed. "We better go," she said, getting to her feet. "You know how Grams gets when we're running late—"

Tyler suddenly threw his arms around her with such force that she had to take a step back to keep her balance. "Thank you, Mom," he said, hugging her tight, "and not just for the watch."

The curves of Shay's mouth began to take shape, revealing a wavering dimple on each side. "You're welcome."

"Three minutes!" shouted Maura.

Shay reluctantly pulled away from his embrace. "You know," she said, doing her best to hold back her tears. "I can't believe my baby boy is graduating from high school."

"Me neither," he answered, lowering his arms, "and you wanna know what the best part about that is?"

Shay quickly wiped her eyes as he turned away. "What?"

"I don't become an official member of the International Brotherhood of Painters, Local 32", until the first of the month." Tyler glanced back at his mother and grinned. "That means I've got two whole weeks to loaf."

The sound of Maura's station wagon returning jostled House awake. Letting out a stale breath, it tried to hold onto the dream, yet it faded—like always—leaving behind a terrible silence.

As Maura started up the path, House sullenly stared at the empty cot sitting against the far wall; a stained pillow with gray stripes and no slip was propped on top of a red wool blanket that had been pulled neatly across the thin mattress. Dozens of baseball cards were taped to the wall above it, along with a cover page from *Life* magazine that featured a photograph of Don Drysdale throwing a pitch.

A chest of drawers missing most of its knobs stood beside the cot, while a lamp with a broken shade, tattered baseball glove, and a half-empty bottle of Aqua Velva adorned its top.

On the wall opposite the bed was a Pink Floyd poster, which House had gathered was a band, based on the fact that its young master had constantly listened to an album touting the same name. Below the poster were two wire milk crates that had been turned on their sides and stacked together to provide a tabletop for his record player, as well as storage for his cherished collection of LPs.

House looked down at the large oval rug sprawled across its concrete floor and smiled inwardly, remembering the day that Tyler had come carrying it in, absolutely elated with his side-of-the-road find. He would crank up the volume on the record player and sit for hours in the middle of that rug—its braided crevices lined with dirt—while strumming his guitar.

Several cardboard boxes, a mustard-yellow washing machine with a matching—but non-working—dryer, a stop sign peppered with holes, and a grungy longboard standing in the corner rounded out the rest of the room.

An overwhelming and aching desire to see its young master began to stir deep within House, causing the shutters beneath its front gable to shake.

Five days after graduating, Tyler had received a letter from the Selective Service…three weeks after that, he'd been inducted into the United States Army.

The front door opened and closed. Pushing its misery aside, House's gaze slowly climbed the cellar steps, where it met Maura in the kitchen.

"I swear those kids are going to be the death of me," she muttered, flinging her purse on the counter. Grabbing her mug out of the sink, she poured the last of the coffee into it and then topped it off with gin.

House had found mornings with its family to be fairly hectic, and as it watched Maura take three long, uninhibited sips of her concoction, gathered that this particular morning, the drive to school must have been worse than usual.

Most days, Shay typically left early to start her shift at the hospital, leaving Maura to get Travis and Charlie ready by herself. The main problem was that it always took a good amount of time for Charlie to spool up, making Travis—who ran full throttle the moment his eyes opened—that much more irritating to her, which almost always resulted in an eruption of bickering and name-calling over the use of the bathroom, who ate all the Count Chocula, and who was going to ride shotgun with Grams.

A knock on the entryway door interrupted Maura mid-swallow. Folding her lips, she set the mug on the counter and walked out of the kitchen.

The knocking grew louder and more impatient.

"Coming," she called, the square heels of her shoes thumping across the carpet as she quickened her pace. Hurrying past the table, she grabbed her pre-tied scarf off the back of the chair and paused to slip it on before opening the door to the entryway.

A tall man with broad shoulders, stuffed inside a cream-colored polyester sport coat, appeared.

"Welcome," said Maura, tilting her head in his direction. "Please, come in."

As the man stepped through the door, House noticed his eyes, which were bulbous and dull—and lodged on either side of a nose that had been broken at least once in its lifetime—begin to scan the room.

"This way," she continued, showing him to the table. "I'm Madam Maura."

The man, whose shirt was unbuttoned all the way down to his mid-section—exposing a heavy gold chain that weaved in and out of a thick black carpeting of chest hairs—watched her light the small incense cone and candle, but said nothing in return.

"Please," she said, blowing out the match, "sit down."

House saw the man throw a casual glance toward the doorway that was framed in green curtains at the opposite end of the living room before taking the seat across from her.

"So..." Maura smiled at the man in what House believed to be an effort to put him at ease. "What can I do for you?"

The cuckoo clock on the wall chimed, causing his gaze to swerve past Maura's shoulder as the little yellow bird popped out of its tiny door.

"Would you like me to tell you your fortune?"

Looking down, the man saw Maura's hands reaching for his and shook his head. "No," he said in a gravelly pitch.

Maura stopped and lifted her pencil-drawn brows. "*No*? Then what do you wan—"

The man suddenly wrapped his enormous fingers around Maura's wrists and yanked them across the table, eliciting a breathless yelp from her lips.

House sat straight up, causing the bulbs in the wagon wheel light hanging above the couch to rattle against their glass covers.

The man's eyes—which were now very much alive—narrowed. "I'm going to tell you *your* fortune."

"Let me go," demanded Maura in a panicked whisper.

"I predict," he said, a lock of hair falling in a greasy clump along his left brow as he leaned forward, "that you're going to tell Iris you made a terrible mistake."

Maura shook her head, unleashing her tears. "I don't know any Iris."

"Don't fucking lie to me!" he yelled, jerking her closer. "I know she was here!"

The candle toppled onto its side, spilling wax over the tablecloth as Maura struggled to break free of his grasp. "I never take names—*ever*!"

The man's mouth twisted farther open, revealing a crooked set of teeth that looked like old Chiclets. "Well, let me refresh your memory," he said, tightening his grip on her wrists. "She came to see you yesterday, and you—taking her for an easy mark—started spouting some mumbo-jumbo bullshit about love, and told her to dump me."

Maura stopped struggling. "That's not what I said."

The man stared at her for a moment, then clenching his massive jaw, picked up her wrists and brought them down hard against the table.

Maura cried out in pain, and House—propelled by both anger and fear—threw all its weight forward, making its floor joist beneath the entryway groan.

The man's head spun toward the door.

In one swift motion, Maura yanked her right forearm from his distracted grasp and reached under the table.

Seconds later, a single click echoed throughout the room.

The man turned back to Maura...and slowly raised his hands.

"That's not what I said," she repeated, pointing a .38 snub nose revolver at the oily space between his eyes. "Well—not exactly." Shrugging, she jammed the barrel under his chin, bringing him to his feet. "But I think she made the right choice."

With his hands still raised, the man, whose pockmarked face was now a dark crimson, began walking backward.

Aided by the gun, Maura and her five-and-a-half-foot frame guided him through the doorway and across the wooden floor of the tiny waiting room.

As his feet stumbled over the threshold of the front door, the man dropped his hands and balled his fingers into two tightly wound fists. "I'll be back," he said, staring down at her with his bulging eyes.

Maura lowered the revolver and pointed it directly at his hairy, heaving chest. "Not unless you want six holes put in you, you won't."

Flaring his nostrils, the man took a step forward, causing Maura's finger to flinch as it sat curled around the trigger. "This isn't over," he said in a snarled whisper.

Readjusting her grip on the gun, Maura leveled her gaze at him. "Get out of here before I call the police."

House watched the man rigidly tilt his head to the right until the bones in his neck cracked...then giving a sharp tug to the bottom of his sport coat with the pair of meat hooks serving as his hands, turned and strode down the steps.

Maura remained at the threshold, with the gun still raised, until he had driven away. When his car was no longer in sight, she let out a trembling breath—that rapidly evolved into a series of sobs—as she slid to the floor.

~

The shadows from the setting sun inched their way across the carpet, turning an already dark space—thanks to the wood paneling that had been nailed into the walls—even darker.

From drawing room, to sunroom, to storage room; over the years this space had served many different purposes, but had never been utilized as a bedroom—until now.

House glanced at the heavy green drapes that hung near the top of the ceiling; held up by a single curtain rod, they had been pulled across the room's wide entrance in order to separate it from the living room.

As the shadows grew longer, House turned its attention back to Maura. She sat unmoving in front of a waterfall vanity, staring blankly at her mirrored reflection.

"Grams? Can we come in?"

The vacant expression behind Maura's eyes flickered. Taking in an uneven breath, she pulled the sleeves of her dress down over her wrists, which House noticed were starting to show signs of bruising, then reached for a tube of lipstick. "If you have to," she replied in a disgruntled tone.

A skinned elbow materialized between the slit in the curtains, followed closely by Travis, and then Charlie.

House watched its youngest master forge a straight path to the bed, where he flopped on top of its stark white coverlet.

"Why can't we stay here by ourselves tonight?" Charlie asked, coming around the side of the vanity.

Maura glanced at her granddaughter's sulking face as she fumbled with the cap. "Because your mom had to work a double shift."

"I've babysat Travis before."

"Not at night, you haven't," she answered, leaning in close to the mirror as she slid the red pigment over her lips.

"But, Grams…"

House felt its wall by the stairs begin to tingle. Moments later the doorbell sounded.

"I'll get it," said Travis, jumping off the bed.

"No"—Maura leapt from her chair and grabbed him by his arm—"*I'll* get it."

The water that had been refilling the tank of the toilet above them for the past five minutes finally shut off, ushering in a jarring silence.

Turning loose of Travis' arm, Maura shouldered past Charlie, ignoring the surprised look on her face, and darted through the curtains. After making her way across the living room in a hurried, worried trot, she cautiously peered out the window in the foyer.

"You're late," she said, unlocking the front door.

Ed raised his left eyebrow. "Well, *sorry*. I got held up at *Angelos*." The smell of cheap cologne and anchovies preceded him as he walked inside.

"Mr. Ratner!" said Travis, running to greet him.

"Hey, sport! Put it there!"

Travis placed his hand in Ed's and shook it.

"Is that the best you can do? You got a spaghetti noodle for an arm or somethin'?"

Accepting the challenge with a Kool-Aid-stained grin, Travis' thumbnail turned white as he squeezed.

"Ow—ow—ow," Ed groaned, dropping to one knee.

Travis giggled. "I *told* you I was strong."

"Here," said Ed, handing him a thin, square, white box with a grease stain on top, "take this into the kitchen for me."

As Travis did what he was told, Ed pushed himself to his feet and turned back to Maura. "Is everything okay?" he asked, eyeing her curiously as he watched her twist the lock on the front door.

"Yes, why?"

"Because you sounded strange on the phone, and looking at you now…it just seems like there's something bothering you."

Maura turned from the door. "Everything's fine," she said, scratching the back of her right ear lobe.

House saw Ed's gaze narrow slightly at her answer.

Smoothing her dress, Maura placed her hand on Ed's shoulder and gave him a warm smile. "Thank you for being so understanding about tonight."

"You know what?" he said, slipping his arm around her waist. "You look absolutely ravishing. What do you say we ditch these ankle biters and go sit in the backseat of my car for a bit?"

"Ed…"

"I've got gin," he sang in a low voice, kissing the side of her neck. "It's from—"

"There's dead minnows on my pizza!"

Ed's lips folded inward. "That's my half," he called. "Yours and Charlie's half is pepperoni!"

Straightening, he returned his attention to Maura. "Now, where was I?"

"I believe you were propositioning me."

"Oh, right," he said, staring into her eyes. "So, how about it?"

Travis made a gagging noise. "But the whole pizza smells like fish!"

Maura sighed and shook her head. "You have no idea what you'd be in for if we did—because *that*," she said, pointing toward the kitchen, "is just the tip of the iceberg with him."

"I'm only talking twenty minutes. What's the worst that could happen? I mean—there's no fire alarm for him to pull."

Maura's smile evaporated.

"Oh, come on," said Ed, filling the room with his raspy laugh, "I'm just kidding."

"Well, it wasn't funny."

"Yes, it was."

Turning away from him, Maura started for the kitchen.

"You know what?" Ed mused, falling into step with her.

She stopped and gave him a peevish look. "What?"

Ed's mustache spread across his face, causing the lines around his eyes to crinkle. "You're even more beautiful when you're angry."

A flurry of pink engulfed Maura's cheeks, neutralizing whatever biting remark was perched and waiting on the tip of her tongue.

"Come on," he said, patting her affectionately on the bottom, "I'm starving."

They walked into the kitchen, where Charlie was doing her best to convince her brother that his slice of pizza was not going to taste like dead fish.

"So..." Ed sat down at the table and rubbed his hands together. "What do you say we have some fun while we eat, huh?" Reaching into his coat pocket, he retrieved a worn deck of cards. "Anyone up for a little five-card stud?"

"*I* am," answered Travis.

Charlie glared at him. "You don't even know what that *is*."

"I do *too*."

"Then sit down and eat this pizza that cost me five bucks," Ed said flatly. He then pulled Maura's chair out for her and glanced at Charlie, who was standing by the table with her arms crossed. "You wanna play?"

She gave an indifferent shrug. "I guess."

"Okay, then. I'm gonna spot you both fifty cents." Taking a bite of his pizza, Ed leaned back and began digging in his pants pocket. "Now, the object of the game is to try and get the highest hand."

"Can Billy play?" asked Travis, picking a piece of lint off of one of the coins Ed had put in front of him.

"No, I don't play poker with people I can't see."

"Why not?"

"Because it's bad for my wallet."

Travis shoved a pepperoni in his mouth as Ed dealt the cards, one facedown and one up, to each of them. "Can Billy *watch*?"

"As long as he keeps quiet."
"He says he will."
"Okay everyone, ante up."
"How much?" asked Charlie.
"Ten cents—come on, Travis," Ed said, snapping his fingers to get his attention, which had wandered to the headless anchovy on Maura's plate, "put your dime in."
Travis folded his legs under him as he began picking through his change. "This is fun."
"Now…" Ed paused to lick the pizza sauce from the corner of his mouth. "Charlie, you got the highest card, so you get to bet first…"
While Travis and Charlie concentrated on what Ed was telling them, House noticed Maura holding her slice of pizza limply between her fingers as she gazed across the table at him.

Chapter 17

"Open mine next!" said Travis, making the springs beneath the couch creak as he bounced up and down on his knees.

Charlie took the present from him and began tearing at the wrapping paper, the seams—and non-seams—of which had been heavily taped. After a lot of pulling and tugging, the blue foil finally relented, revealing a small package containing a red rubber ball, and a dozen curious-shaped pieces of metal. "Jacks," said Charlie, arching her brows. "Thanks, Travis."

"They're from Billy, too."

Charlie nodded at the empty cushion beside him. "Thanks, Billy."

"See, Grams?" Travis stopped bouncing and flashed a triumphant grin at his grandmother. "I *told* you she'd like them."

"Yes, you did," Maura answered, giving him a tired smile in return.

House noticed the dark circles staining the skin beneath her eyes and let out a stilted sigh, sending a coarse-sounding whistle running through its ducts, which had been added a few years ago by one of its previous owners.

After Ed had gone home last night, Maura had nervously paced the floor while waiting up for Shay, then—ushering her inside with a hurried greeting—promptly locked the door behind her and went to bed. She eventually drifted off, but had slept fitfully, waking every few minutes to the tiniest of sounds.

"Open the one from Mom," said Travis, gesturing excitedly at the remaining present on the coffee table.

House glanced across the living room and saw Shay, who was curled up in the chair—using her elbow for a pillow—rouse slightly as Charlie set the jacks aside and reached for the neatly wrapped box.

Clawing at the paper, Charlie's generally insolent features lit up the instant she removed the box's cardboard lid. "Mom...thank you!"

Shay's eyes sparkled, deepening their aquamarine color. "You're welcome, sweetheart."

House studied the pair of jeans Charlie was now clutching to her chest. They were blue with brown suede pockets; several patches of umber in varying lengths were stitched to the thighs, while each leg from the knee down was a soft olive green that flared sharply at the bottom.

As Charlie ran upstairs to try them on, Shay headed into the kitchen and pulled the cake from *Wilson's Bakery* out of the fridge.

"How long did you have those jeans on layaway?" asked Maura, coming up behind her.

Shay tilted her head. "Four months," she answered, placing the cake on the counter. She then sank thirteen candles into the icing and set their tips ablaze with her lighter.

"You kids better hurry!" called Maura, grabbing the camera from off the table.

Charlie, her elusive smile, and her jeans of many colors came bounding into the kitchen with Travis on her heels. "What do you think?"

Shay's disheveled ponytail fell across the front of her shoulder as she turned around. "They look great on you!"

"Grams?"

Maura stopped fiddling with the cubed-shaped flashbulb on top of the camera and glanced up. "Well, you certainly won't have to worry about finding a shirt to matc—"

"All right," said Shay, holding the cake out to Charlie, "let's sing."

"*Happy birthday to you...*"

"*Happy birthday to you...*"

Maura took the picture and then joined in with Shay and Travis—who was half a stanza ahead and off key.

House, priding itself on knowing all the words, gleefully sang along with its family.

"Make a wish!" said Travis.

Charlie closed her eyes, and as her breath fell across the flickering candles, House felt its driveway begin to rumble.

It looked outside in time to see a sleek black car with a busted headlight come barreling to a stop behind Shay's white Pontiac. The driver's side door swung open and a man with dark hair, layered down to his shoulders, got out. Placing a cigarette between his lips, he started across the yard with a decided swagger.

House watched the man, wearing creased jeans, a faded blue t-shirt, and brown leather jacket stop when he got to the life-size wooden palm jutting out of the ground. The giant sign, which bore the words "Madame Maura's Palm Readings $5" in large block print, was fastened to a two by four that had been set in concrete.

"What'd you wish for?" asked Travis.

"If I tell you, it won't come true," Charlie replied, licking the icing off one of the candles as her mother drew a knife through the cake.

Although House was keenly aware of the conversation and actions taking place in the kitchen, its focus remained on the stranger as he swiped a match across the palm, scoring the painted letters in the middle, and lit his cigarette. His meticulously bronzed cheeks caved inward as he inhaled, pulling his shirt snug against his chest. With smoke pouring from his nostrils, he flicked the half-smoked cigarette into the grass and started up the porch steps.

"Mom," said Shay, slipping a piece of cake onto a paper plate, "can you get the ice cream out of the freezer?"

The man twisted the knob on the front door and—despite House's efforts—shoved it open. "Hello?" he called, walking through the open door in the entryway.

Maura jumped at the sound of the man's voice, sending the forks in her hand clattering to the floor.

Travis' eyes widened as he turned to his sister. "Maybe it's the mailman bringing you something for your birthday!" Ducking under her arm, he pushed past the saloon doors and ran into the living room.

Charlie seemed doubtful, but followed her brother anyway, catching the doors before they swung closed.

"Wait, you two!" Maura said, kicking the forks across the linoleum as she skirted around the table.

Shay stepped in front of her, blocking her path. "You told me you weren't going to schedule any readings today," she said in an accusing tone.

The apprehension burrowed between the lines in Maura's forehead morphed into a scowl as she bent down to pick up the forks. "I didn't—"

"Dad!"

Shay and her mother locked eyes.

"Hey, kiddo!" boomed the man's voice.

Plunging the knife into the cake, Shay stalked out of the kitchen.

House watched Travis bury his face in the man's shirt. "I missed you," he said, throwing his arms around his waist.

"I missed you too, buddy." After a moment, he glanced over at Charlie, who was standing stoically beside the couch, and smiled—causing the velvety black mustache that extended all the way down his chin to lift slightly. "What about you, Charlie-girl? You got a hug for your old man?"

Releasing the top of the cushion from her grip, Charlie walked up to her father and gave him a side hug.

"That's my girl," he said, drawing her against his chest.

"Is there something wrong with the doorbell?"

The man dropped his arms to his sides and looked across the room. "It's nice to see you too, Shay."

She answered him with an icy glare.

Tilting his head to the right, he peered around her shoulder and nodded. "Maura."

House glanced at the saloon doors. Shay's mother was standing between them with her tongue jammed against her cheek. "*Rom*," she replied, spitting out the word as if it tasted bitter.

"Guess what, Dad?" said Travis, resting his chin on his belt buckle. "It's Charlie's birthday."

An awkward silence followed his announcement.

Charlie's face filled with hurt, causing her blonde locks to fall across her cheeks as she dropped her gaze to the floor.

"I'm so sorry, Charlie-girl. You must think I'm a real jerk, showing up on today of all days without a present, don't you?"

"It's okay."

"Let me see if I have anything." Rom began searching through his pockets. "There has to be something—wait—what's this?" he said, producing a small box. "Now, how do you suppose *that* got in there?"

Charlie took the box from him and opened it. An oval-shaped stone, golden-yellow in color with a rich black line cutting through its middle, sat atop a thin band of gold.

"What is it?" asked Travis, pulling on Charlie's wrist to see.

"It's a tiger's eye," she said, running the tip of her fingernail along its quartz edge.

"What do you think, Charlie-girl?"

"I love it. Thanks, Dad." She hugged him tightly — with both arms this time, yet the rigidity in her movements made House wonder if her affection was being given out of gratitude — or obligation.

"Hey, Dad?" said Travis.

"What?"

"We're having cake and ice cream. Do you want some?"

House heard Shay suck in her breath.

The corner of Rom's mouth twitched. "I'd love some."

"Come on, then," said Travis, slipping his hand in his.

Strutting across the floor, Rom smugly cut his eyes at Shay as Travis led him past her and into the kitchen.

Pivoting on her heel, Shay muttered a faint obscenity, then shoved the saloon doors out of her way. By the time she reached the table, Rom had seated himself in her chair, with Charlie and Travis flanking him.

"First piece goes to the birthday girl," said Shay in an overly chipper tone, yet House noticed the tips of her knuckles were white as she set the paper plate in front of her daughter.

"Thanks, Mom."

"You're welcome," she replied, forming a smile that never quite reached its potential.

"Mmm, this looks good, doesn't it, Trav?" said Rom, watching Shay dole out the rest of the slices.

"It sure does."

"One scoop or two?" asked Maura, trailing behind Shay with the carton of ice cream.

"Three," answered Travis. "And can Billy have some too, please?"

Maura, appearing to House to be too exasperated to argue, plopped a small scoop of the frozen treat onto the empty plate next to him and moved on.

"Who's Billy?" asked Rom, using the side of his fork to scrape the pink icing off his cake.

"My best friend."

Rom shoved the mangled bite into his mouth and glanced around the kitchen. "Well, where the hell is he?"

"He's right here," replied Travis, putting his arm across the back of the chair beside him. "He says hi."

Flexing his jaw, Rom set his fork down and leveled the pair of smooth brown pebbles serving as his eyes at Shay.

"How long are you going to be in town for, Dad?" blurted Charlie.

Keeping his gaze locked on Shay, he slowly parted his thin lips. "What would you say if I told you indefinitely?"

Travis licked the ice cream that was running down his hand. "Does that mean a long time?"

"It does. I'm renting a house from a buddy of mine on the other side of the Bixby."

"What's it like?" asked Travis, helping himself to the ice cream on Billy's plate.

"Well, it doesn't have as much...wallpaper or paneling as yours," he said with a smirk, "but it's got a fantastic view of the ocean *and* a swimming pool. What do you say to that?"

Maura flicked her wrist, sending the scoop of ice cream meant for Rom's plate onto his crotch.

"Son-of-a-bitch!" he said, leaping out of his chair.

"Oh, silly me," Maura replied sweetly. Setting the carton on the table, she reached for the dishtowel and began wiping the seat of his chair. "You better go wash that off. I wouldn't want those expensive jeans of yours to stain...especially *there*."

A swarm of dark red swirls infiltrated Rom's cheeks, leaving them stiff and ruddy. "Where's the bathroom?"

Shay gestured with her arm. "At the top of the stairs."

Refusing to respect the bounds of privacy, House followed Rom into the bathroom and watched him as he wet a washcloth and began rubbing the melted chocolate off the front of his jeans.

When he had finished, several obscenities rushed from his downturned lips as he stared at the large, damp spot circling the bottom of his zipper. Flinging the rag in the sink, he untucked his shirt and glanced at the mirrored medicine cabinet above the vanity. Jerking it open, his fingers began crawling along the shelves' contents like a spider, stopping occasionally to inspect the insides of a pill box or medicine bottle.

It wasn't long before they came across a prescription for Shay that was hidden behind a jar of cold cream. Twisting off the cap, Rom tossed two of the white tablets into his mouth and swallowed, then sticking the bottle in his pocket, opened the door—only to find Shay waiting on the other side. "Your mother did that on purpose," he grumbled, marching past her.

"Were you telling the truth down there? About staying indefinitely?"

"Why would I lie about something like that?"

"What about the band you were touring with?"

"We had a falling out."

"A falling out," Shay repeated. "Over what?"

Rom sighed and turned around. "Artistic differences."

House saw the vein in Shay's temple begin to throb. "So, in other words…you were fired."

"*No*, I chose to walk away."

"You chose to walk away from the only steady paycheck you've had in months—over artistic differences?"

"That's right."

Shay took a deep breath, pulling her lips in with it. "Do you have another job lined up?"

"I made some calls."

"*And*?"

"Jesus, Shay…" said Rom, rubbing his forehead. "In case you've forgotten, we're not married anymore."

"No, but you're still Travis' and Charlie's father," she countered, keeping her voice low, "and I haven't gotten a dime of child support from you in over a *year*. I'm just wondering when you're going to grow up and start *acting* like one."

"First of all," he said, holding up his finger, "the pay wasn't that great. And second, I'm not about to compromise my music—especially for those assholes in *Bad Persuasion*. If I don't stand up for what I believe in, I'm never going to get where I want to be, and if that means not getting to play with them in one shitty bar after another, then that's just another sacrifice—in a long line of sacrifices—I'm willing to make."

"Sacrifice?" Shay's hands flew to her hips. "What would you know about *sacrifice*? Or are you talking about when you have to choose between doing lines of cocaine and strung-out whores over basic necessities for your children—like food and clothing?"

The edge of Rom's jaw hardened, making it look as if the bone was going to pierce his skin.

House felt a familiar buzzing in its walls, followed by the grating ring of the telephone.

"Shay," yelled Maura, her voice cutting through the silence that had descended upon the hallway, "it's the hospital."

"I'll take it up here," she called down, then turning back to Rom, gave him an expectant look. "You know where the door is."

His eyebrows came together in an angry V. "I'm done here anyway," he said, then cracking his knuckles one at a time beneath his thumb, turned and started down the stairs.

Shay remained in the hall until he'd reached the bottom landing before walking into her bedroom and grabbing the phone off the nightstand. "This is Shay," she said, sighing the words into the receiver.

"Dad," said Travis, running out of the kitchen, "where're you going?"

"I've got to get home."

"Can't you stay and play with me?"

"Not this time."

"Then can me and Billy spend the night with you?" he asked, clutching his hand. "Please?"

"Listen, buddy," said Rom, squatting in front of him, "I've got a lot to do this weekend. I have to unpack and get settled in. But *next* weekend, you can come for sure, okay?"

Travis' chin quivered as he nodded.

Rom reached out and tousled Travis' hair, which House noticed was the same dark color as his. "That's my boy," he said, either oblivious to the tears that were currently cutting a clean swath through the dried chocolate surrounding his mouth…or just indifferent to it.

Rom stood and gave Charlie, who was watching him from the doorway of the kitchen alongside Maura, a rigid wave. "Happy birthday, Charlie-girl."

Offering him a small smile in return, she edged past her grandmother and disappeared into the kitchen.

As he headed out the door, House saw Shay hurrying down the stairs. "Rom?"

He kept walking in his arrogant gait, further provoking Shay's anger.

"Rom!" she yelled, following him outside, where dark clouds were busy gathering.

He stopped in the middle of the gravel drive and wheeled around. "*What?*"

"You should've checked with me before telling Travis he could spend the night with you next weekend," she said, her bare feet coming to a halt at the edge of the grass.

"Well, I've already done it, so if you want to break his heart and tell him that he can't…go right ahead."

Crossing her arms, Shay jammed her fists under her armpits. "I'll agree to let him spend Friday night with you," she said in a clipped tone, "but *I'm* taking him and picking him up."

"Whatever makes you happy," he replied, shoving a cigarette between his lips.

Shay's eyes flickered as she watched him light the tip. "I need your address."

Rom pulled a pen from his jacket and scribbled something on the matchbook. "Here," he said, ripping off the cover.

As Shay reached out to take it, her fingers inadvertently grazed his, causing both of their indignant expressions to falter.

"Have you heard from Ty?" he asked, taking the cigarette out of his mouth.

Shay looked at the ground. "Not since June. That's when he wrote to tell me that he and his unit were waiting for transportation to an area just north of Saigon."

"How did he sound?"

She abruptly lifted her head. "How the fuck do you *think* he sounded, Rom?"

"You know, Shay..." he said, a steady stream of smoke swirling from his knuckles as he rubbed the bridge of his nose with his thumbnail. "I'm doing the best I can here, and I would really appreciate it if you could cut me some slack."

"Cut you some slack?" Shay's voice rose sharply. "I'll cut you some slack when you start paying me the child support you owe."

House watched Rom's upper lip twist into a snarl as he started around his car.

"Oh—and, Rom?"

Resting a clenched hand on the hood, he looked back at her.

Shay picked her way across the gravel and came to stand directly in front of him. "The next time you decide to just drop by, use the goddamn doorbell."

Rom flung his cigarette at her feet. "Fuck you, Shay," he said, jerking open the door.

Moments later, the engine bellowed to life; the rear tires kicked up gravel as they spun backward into the grass, then—amidst a popping muffler and vibrating spoiler that was cracked in the middle—shot crookedly down the driveway.

Shay stared after him, her eyes floundering in the sea of darkness that had engulfed them, as he vanished into a cloud of dust.

Chapter 18

House let out a contented sigh and stretched as the sun's rays began to warm the roof, making its wet, stiff shingles much more pliable.

It had been a troubling and turbulent past two days for House's family, and it selfishly took advantage of the momentary respite, while watching the sea's turquoise-colored waves crash against the shore—regurgitating what last night's storm had dumped into it.

A tree, enormous in both girth and stature, floated helplessly on its side, its vast tangle of roots caught in the outcropping of rocks a few yards from shore. One wave after another rolled over the trunk, stripping it of its bark each time it was flung into the sharp reef.

Amidst the chattering seagulls flying overhead, House could faintly hear the bell of St. Anthony's ringing in the distance, its mournful clang beckoning for those who remained in the nearly vacant town to come inside for worship. As the eleventh and final toll sounded, a heavy set of knuckles rapped on House's front door, sending a startled shiver rolling through its overflowing gutters.

Drawing in a dank breath of air from its eaves, House shifted its attention inward as Maura unlocked the door and cracked it open.

A short man with thinning hair and thick glasses—and whose circumference rivaled the tree's—appeared on the other side. "Madam Maura?"

"Yes?"

"I heard you could help me."

"I'm sorry, I don't do readings on Sunday. Come back tomorr—"

"Please," he said, holding his hand against the door, "I've driven over two hours to get here."

Maura eyed him warily, then took a resigned step back. "Come in."

House felt its floorboards in the entryway dip beneath the man's weight as he followed her into the living room and sat down at the table. He nervously wiped a bead of sweat from his brow, allowing House to see the diamond ring wrapped around his pinky, as well as the gold watch affixed to his wrist.

While Maura lit the candle, House took quick stock of the rest of its family's whereabouts. Shay was asleep in her bedroom with the curtains drawn tight; having departed for the hospital shortly after her confrontation with Rom yesterday, she'd come straggling back in just before dawn. Charlie was sitting at the kitchen table with her cheeks propped on her fists as she read the funnies in the Sunday paper. And Travis—

House's gaze zeroed in on its young master. He was squatting in the side yard holding something in his hands. Upon closer inspection, House realized it was a box of matches—and felt its clapboards grow rigid as Travis tried repeatedly to set the clump of grass in front of him on fire. With his tongue pressed against his lower lip, he held one lit match after another to the wet blades before dropping the charred stick on the ground.

"You have been struggling with a decision."

Determining that its lawn was temporarily safe from being engulfed in flames, House returned its attention to Maura and her client.

"A big change has come into your life involving work."

"Yes," said the man, the anxious expression residing in the folds of his round, sweaty face urging her to go on.

Maura ran her finger along the broken line arcing across his left palm. "It would mean lots of travel and a move to Denver."

"Yes...yes, that's exactly right." The man's lips fluttered furiously as he spoke, like a butterfly with a broken wing.

Maura's gaze shifted to his right palm and then back to his left. "This job is particularly important to you, and one that you have worked your entire life for...but you are racked with indecision because of your feelings for someone. Your wife—no..." Maura slowly lifted her head, locking eyes with his. "Someone *else's* wife."

In the corner of its peripheral vision, House saw Charlie drop the chocolate chip cookie she'd been eating and tiptoe across the kitchen, where she promptly pressed her ear against the slats of the saloon doors.

"What can I say? She makes me feel young," the man replied with an unapologetic shrug, "and I'm ready to leave my wife and make a fresh start with her in Denver. The problem is..." He paused to let out a hurried sigh, filling the space with the smell of stale coffee and nicotine. "She told me she needs time to think it over—but *time* isn't a luxury I have."

Maura shook her head. "You don't love this woman."

"No," he said, giving her an absurd look, "but we have a good time together, and when I'm with my wife, she's all I can think about." The man shifted in his seat. "Madame Maura, it is absolutely imperative that you tell me if she's going to come with me, so I'll know whether or not to file for divorce. My new job is very lucrative—and if I end up having to give half my assets to my wife, I'd much rather do it now when I don't stand as much to lose."

House watched the stunned expression on Maura's face transform into what could only be called disgust.

"Now, I have a long drive back," he continued, "and as I've already stated, time is of the essence, so please..."

Pursing her lips, Maura returned her attention to his palm. "While this woman is very fond of you *and* your money, she's happy with the existing arrangement. She will never leave her husband and children for you."

Disappointment hugged the man's mouth, causing the corners of it to descend into his sagging jowls.

"And your wife, whom you think you are deceiving," Maura went on, "is well aware of your indiscretions and is in the process of making plans to leave you."

An assortment of emotions surged behind the man's eyes, leaving them crestfallen. "But I...I *can't* be alone." His Adam's apple, barely visible under the mound of flesh covering his neck, struggled to go down as he swallowed.

With a gaze that held little empathy for him, Maura watched as he slumped back in his chair. "Is there anything else you want to know?"

The man stared at his lap. "Will my wife forgive me?"

"No," she said in a clipped tone. "The pain you have caused her over the course of your marriage is too great."

House felt the heel of the man's shoe tapping against its carpeted floor, which seemed to be in an alternating rhythm with the rapid, jerky breaths falling out of his pig-like nostrils.

Maura raised an impatient brow. "Is there anything els—"

The man suddenly sat forward, bumping his enormous stomach against the table. "What does my future hold for me?" he demanded, thrusting his hands in front of her. "Will I find someone else to be with?"

Maura steadied the candle, and as she took hold of his palms once more, House saw an almost imperceptible wince cross her face. A full minute passed before she spoke. "I see you in Denver...and your heart is happy."

The devastation lining the man's lips dissolved. "So, you're saying I won't be alone?"

"Yes."

"When will I meet her? Two months...six months?"

Maura withdrew her hands. "Soon."

Letting out something that sounded like a whoop, the man stood up, nearly knocking over his chair.

"Is there anything else you wish to know?"

"No, you've been more than helpful," he said, handing her a twenty-dollar bill.

Maura nodded. "Have a blessed day," she said, leading him toward the door.

The man stopped in the middle of the entryway. "Before I go, could I trouble you for a glass of water? I'm parched."

"Of course," she replied in a stilted voice as she turned toward the kitchen. "I'll be right ba—"

"I've got it, Grams." Charlie burst through the saloon doors carrying the proffered water.

As the man began to drink, House noticed Charlie purposefully avoiding her grandmother's piercing scowl.

The man smacked his lips. "That hit the spot. Thank you."

Charlie smiled back at him, ignorant of the fact that he was subtly ogling her budding breasts, and reached for the glass. "You're welco—"

House heard its young master sharply inhale. Swerving its gaze, it saw the blood draining from her face as her mouth twisted in agony—yet before it could discern what was happening, a dozen needle-like shards dug into its oak planks as the glass exploded around her feet.

"I'm sorry," said the man, taking an awkward step to the right. "I thought you had a grip on it."

Maura slid her hand around the crook of the man's arm. "Let me show you out."

"Oh..." he said, as she began pulling him across the entryway. "Well, let me at least pay for the glass."

"That isn't necessary."

"Are you certain? Because it's no trouble."

Maura wrenched open the front door. "I'm positive," she replied, shoving him through it sideways. "Thank you for coming."

The man stumbled over the threshold and turned. "Well...thank you for the readi—"

"My pleasure," said Maura, closing the door on him. She then made her way back into the living room to find that Charlie had already retrieved a broom and dustpan from the kitchen.

"Sorry, Grams."

"Here, give me that." Maura took the broom and shooed her away. "You're going to cut your feet."

Charlie lowered her hands to her sides, and although the color had returned to her face, House noticed her lips—while now closed—were trembling.

"What happened?"

House looked upstairs and saw Shay glowering at her mother from the top of the landing.

"It's just some broken glass," she replied, giving her a dismissive wave. "Go back to bed."

Folding her arms, Shay's bloodshot eyes scanned the living room. "Where's Travis?"

"Outside."

Her brows came together. "He's grounded, or did you forget?"

"I didn't forget," countered Maura, placing her hand on her hip. "But what was I supposed to do? He can't watch TV, and if I'd made him stay in his room, there was no way you were going to get any sleep."

"Well, I'm up *now*," Shay snapped, dropping her arms.

"I'll go get him, Grams." Charlie's voice was quiet as she stepped over the glistening pieces of glass in the foyer.

Maura watched her slip out the door before looking back at Shay. "Why don't you try and get some more sleep? I know we'll *all* be better off if you do."

Shay's lips formed a rigid line across her face. Pivoting on her heels, she made her way into the bathroom and yanked open the medicine cabinet, yet after a moment of searching, returned to the landing. "What did you do with my sleeping pills?"

A heavy sigh rolled out of Maura's nostrils. "I haven't touched them."

"Well, they were there yesterd—" Shay stopped midsentence. House saw her face grow dark as she jammed her tongue against the inside of her cheek, then turning from the landing, stalked back to her bedroom and slammed the door.

~

Charlie's steps were slow and deliberate as she walked across the wet grass. "Travis?" she called out.

House's youngest master jerked his head up. His eyes wide with fear, he brought the burning match to his lips to blow out—just as his sister rounded the corner.

"What are you doing?" she said, snatching the box from his fingers.

Travis shrugged innocently. "Just playing with Billy."

Charlie glanced at the pile of blackened matches at his feet as she yanked him up by his arm. "Get in the house. Mom wants you inside."

"I *hate* being grounded," he huffed, twisting out of her grasp. "What am I supposed to do for fun?"

Charlie gave him an incredulous look. "Well, not burn the *house* down, idiot!"

A clinking sound, followed by footsteps made them both turn around.

Moments later, their grandmother appeared, prompting Charlie to hide the box of matches behind her back.

"Travis, your mom is in the shower," said Maura, lifting the lid off the dented trashcan that sat against House's wooden clapboards. "You better be inside by the time she gets out."

Travis saw Charlie adjust her grip on the box and shot her a pleading look.

Charlie stared back at him and then tilted her head toward the front yard. "Go on. I'll be there in a minute, and we'll play jacks if you want," she said, although her tone seemed less-than-enthusiastic.

"Thanks. Come on, Billy!"

After Travis had vanished from her sight, Charlie rigidly shifted her attention to Maura. "Grams?" she said, watching the chunks of glass slide from the dustpan into the garbage pail.

"*What?*" she grumbled, trying to get the lid to close around the can's bent edges.

"Never mind. Here, let me do it." Reaching out, she took the lid from her grandmother, and when she had turned away, hurriedly tossed the box of matches into the can before smashing the lid down.

"I'm sorry," Maura said, looking back at her. "I didn't mean to snap at you. It's just been one of those days."

"That's okay."

Maura glanced at Charlie as she fell into step with her. "Is there something wrong?"

"No, why?"

"You seem awfully quiet…even for you."

"I'm fine."

Maura frowned at her answer, but kept walking. "Come on," she said with a sigh, "let's go see what we can rustle up for lunch—"

"Why did you lie to that man about him not being alone?"

Maura shook her head as she climbed the steps to the porch. "Because when it comes to certain things, most people don't want to hear the truth. They'd rather hear a—" The rickety boards beneath her feet wobbled as she came to an abrupt stop. Clutching the dustpan between her fingers, Maura spun around. "How did you know I was lying?"

Charlie looked solemnly at her grandmother and then blinked, unleashing a force of tears that surged down her reddened cheeks. "Because I saw him die," she said in a ragged whisper.

The dustpan cartwheeled down the steps and clattered against the broken sidewalk as Maura made her way back to Charlie. Without speaking, she took her hands in hers and closed her eyes.

House heard an audible hitch in Maura's breath—followed by the roar of an engine. Glancing toward the driveway, it saw a silver Cadillac roll up behind Shay's car and stop. The driver's side door swung open, and then the mild-mannered woman from the other day scrambled out from behind the wheel.

"Madam Maura," she called, hurrying across the crushed gravel.

Maura let go of Charlie's hands. "Get inside."

"But, Grams…" A small sob escaped from the back of Charlie's throat.

"It's going to be all right, child," she said, wiping away her tears. "We'll talk in a little while, I promise. But right now, I need you to get in the house."

"Madam Maura!"

Charlie gave her grandmother a half-nod and swallowed, further deepening the swath of dimples that had embedded themselves in her chin, then stealing a sideways glance at the woman—who was approaching at a rapid pace—dragged the back of her knuckles across her eyelids and ran inside.

When the front door had closed, Maura turned her full attention to the woman. "Stop right there," she commanded, holding up her hand.

The woman, appearing somewhat baffled by the greeting, slowed, but continued advancing in her direction. "Please, I need your help."

"I can't help you," Maura replied, looking nervously down the driveway.

"My boyfriend said he came to see you the other day and that you told him I was going to marry him." The woman reached for Maura as if she were grasping at a life preserver. "I need to know if that's true."

Maura took a step back, refusing to let her touch her. "If you drove all the way here to ask me that, I think you know the truth."

A cool breeze began to swirl around them, rustling the leaves on the sycamore that stood in the middle of the yard.

House watched the woman absently shift her attention to the tree's vibrant yellow foliage fluttering about on the low-hanging branches—only to look back at Maura with a panicked expression. "Please, I'm begging you…just tell me."

"I'm sorry," said Maura, starting for the porch. "I can't."

The woman ran after her. "Has my future changed?"

Maura stopped and turned around. "What I told you still remains true, but your future can and *will* change depending upon the choice—or choices—you make. Now, your boyfriend, if that's what you want to call him, did come by the other day, but his version of what happened and mine are not the same. Do you understand what I'm saying?"

The woman's hollowed out cheeks turned a striking color of red—but whether it had been born out of embarrassment or anger, House did not know.

Maura stooped to pick up the dustpan and straightened. "I can't see you again," she said, casting another anxious glance toward the drive.

A single tear began to trickle down the woman's face.

House saw the harsh lines surrounding Maura's lips soften ever so slightly as they parted. "*You* have the power to decide what you want. It's not up to him," she said, then pivoting on her heel, hurriedly scaled the steps to the porch and disappeared through the front door.

Chapter 19

The smell of fried bologna lingered in the kitchen as House watched its family eat in silence. The lack of conversation was as odd as it was unbearable, and House found itself wishing there was something it could do to end it. Even Billy—it seemed—had nothing to say.

Shifting its weight, House leaned against its front cornerstone, making the floor joist beside it groan in protest.

Charlie responded by flicking her sullen gaze toward the living room—only to return it to her plate seconds later.

"Who was that woman in the driveway?" asked Shay, rolling the piece of crust she'd picked off her sandwich between her thumb and forefinger.

Maura took a long sip from her glass, which House noticed she'd filled with gin, and swallowed. "No one."

"Well, she was obviously *someone*," Shay retorted, "because I saw you talking with her."

Maura's cheeks turned pink. "She wanted a reading. I told her to come back tomorrow."

Shay stared at her mother for several moments, then stoically went back to picking at her bread.

Maura set her glass down and stood, garnering everyone's attention. "I was going to wait until after lunch to give you this," she said, walking around the table, "but I think now's as good a time as any." Reaching into the drawer beside the fridge, she held up an envelope that had colorful red and blue stripes bordering its edges.

The rankled expression lurking on Shay's face crumbled.

"The mailman delivered it yesterday after you'd gone to work."

"Is it money?" asked Travis, stuffing the last bite of bologna in his mouth.

"No, it's…" Shay paused to clear her throat. "It's a letter from your brother."

The sounds of scooting chairs and running feet filled the kitchen.

As Travis and Charlie jockeyed for position, Shay slit the envelope open with her thumbnail and pulled out a single piece of paper…then after taking extreme care in unfolding it, began to read out loud. "Hi, Mom. I'm sorry it's been so long since I've written. My unit's been on the move, and we haven't stayed in one place for very long. We had to go through a jungle that took us four days to get through because we could only travel at night. I'd heard about the jungle being hot from some of the other guys, but that doesn't even begin to describe it. The sweat just pours out of you, and it doesn't matter if you're walking, sitting, sleeping, or just breathing. We finally made camp yesterday not far from a small lake and got to go swimming. We had to do it with our clothes and boots on, but it was nice to feel the cool water on my skin. We were supposed to get a week's R and R, but it got cancelled, so for now we're trying to make the best of what some of the guys are calling Lake Gonorrhea. Ha-Ha."

"What's gonorrhea?"

"Something that you'll learn about when you're older," Maura said to Travis, "but for now, that word doesn't need to be repeated."

Shay returned her attention to the letter, and after finding her place, continued reading. "But enough about me. How is everyone there? I hope this reaches you by the twentieth, because I wanted to wish Charlie a happy thirteenth birthday. I've got something for her…"

House saw Maura place her hand on the top of Charlie's shoulder—which she promptly rebuffed.

"…but don't know when I'll be able to mail it. And tell Travis I can't wait to play catch with him…"

Reaching down, Maura curled her fingers around her glass and took a long drink.

"…a new game to teach him when I come home."

"What's it called?" asked Travis, using his elbow to cut in front of his sister.

"Stop it, Travis!" said Charlie, shoving him out of her way.

"Ow!"

With her free hand, Maura grabbed the back of Travis' shirt and dragged him over to stand beside her.

"But I didn't do anything!" he howled.

"Do you want to hear the rest of your brother's letter?"

"Yes."

"Then stand here and be quiet!"

Jutting out his lower lip, Travis folded his arms and glared at Charlie.

Shay sighed and rubbed her forehead. "I miss you all, and I especially miss Grams' cooking. Tell her that I can't wait to taste her meatloaf and mashed potatoes, and don't even get me started on her homemade biscuits..."

House looked at Maura, but any hint of a smile had left her face.

"All we have to eat here are K rations, which I've grown sick of—" Shay suddenly fell silent, yet her eyes continued to move across the paper.

"Go on, Mom," demanded Charlie.

Shay stopped reading and looked up. "I'll be home soon. Only one hundred sixty-three more days to go. Love you all, Tyler," she said, the words rushing out of her as she folded the letter.

"Well, that was nice," said Maura, giving Shay's arm a gentle pat before leaning around her to pick up her plate. "Who wants birthday cake?"

"Me and Billy do!"

"Then help me clear the dishes from the table." Maura glanced at Charlie on the way to the sink. "That means you, too."

House's young master, however, remained seated, her gaze steadfastly locked on her mother and the slight tremble in her fingers as she slid the paper back into its envelope.

"Charlene Francis Montgomery, did you hear what I said?"

Answering her grandmother with a roll of her eyes, Charlie grabbed her plate, and as she began making her way to the sink, House saw Shay rise stiffly from her chair and turn away.

~

House stared, utterly mesmerized, at the fluorescent green globs sliding up and down in the cone-shaped glass enclosure that sat on Charlie's nightstand; surrounded by a tranquil sea of bright blue liquid, the globs floated effortlessly about, like jellyfish without their tentacles, continuously colliding, melding, and splitting apart.

A sharp knock sounded. "Charlie?"

"Go away."

House glanced at its young master. She was lying face down on her bed with her hands jammed underneath the pillow.

In spite of the gruff warning, the door opened anyway, and Maura stepped inside. "Don't you want any supper?" she asked, walking around the makeshift curtain.

"No."

Maura's gaze darted restlessly about the room before settling on the glowing green blobs. "The lava lamp looks nice in your room," she said, perching herself on the edge of the bed. "Do you like it?"

"Yes," Charlie mumbled, then taking in a small breath, added, "thank you."

"Do you want to talk about what happened today?"

Silence.

"You know," said Maura, reaching out to stroke the back of her hair, "I wish I could tell you that it won't happen again, but it's going to—and as you grow, you may find that your gift will manifest itself in other ways besides touch."

Charlie jerked her head up. "It's not a *gift*, Grams. It's a curse—and it's all your fault," she said, then pushing her arm away, buried her face in her pillow once more.

Her words and actions elicited a weary sigh from Maura. "Charlie, are you going to listen to me or lay there and pout?"

"Pout," she replied in a muffled voice.

Maura slipped her hand underneath her granddaughter's armpit and pulled her up. "I was exactly thirteen years and ten days old when I had my first vision, and it happened in a very public place along a crowded sidewalk."

Charlie stared stubbornly at the floor.

"I was waiting at the bus stop when a woman carrying a big box with a red bow on it rushed past me, grazing my hand with hers. In less time than it took to blink, I saw her pinned beneath a twisted heap of metal on a train track...her body and face crushed beyond recognition, with the mangled present lying beside her."

House watched its young master's eyes slowly find their way to her grandmother. "What did you do?"

"I let out a bloodcurdling scream, catching the woman's attention—as well as everyone else's on the block. The woman hurried back to me and asked if I was all right. I grabbed her by the sleeve…and in one giant, rambling breath told her what I had seen."

"What happened?"

Maura tilted her head. "She slapped me hard across my cheek and called me—among other things—a no good filthy gypsy, and said that trying to scare her into giving me money was shameful, not to mention a crime. Then she turned and pushed her way through the crowd of onlookers before disappearing."

The tips of Charlie's knuckles grew white as she twisted the rumpled bedspread around her fingers. "I'm sorry she did that to you, Grams."

Maura gave her a bleak smile.

"What happened next?"

"Well, I ran the twelve and a half blocks home, where I proceeded to cry on my mother's shoulder for the better part of two hours. After she'd dried my tears, she told me what I'm about to repeat to you."

"Which is what?" asked Charlie, her expression as curious as it was tentative.

"What happened today is a precursor of things to come. You might have another vision tomorrow—or not for ten years. Whatever the case may be, it's important to remember that you have been blessed with a gift that has existed in our family for five generations. It is not to be toyed with, or exploited, but nurtured and, above all…respected."

House didn't know what its young master was expecting Maura to say, but judging by the look on her face, that wasn't it.

"Then she gave me this." Reaching up, Maura unfastened one of the beaded necklaces that hung around her neck and handed it to Charlie. "These are made from tourmaline."

Charlie turned the strand of polished black stones — made up of varying shapes and sizes — over in her palm.

"Tourmaline possesses the power to protect you from negative energy, and helps ward off evil by sending it back to those who wish you harm."

"Grams?"

Maura looked over her shoulder as Travis poked his head around the sheet. "What is it?"

"Can me and Billy have some ice cream?"

"Yes."

"And can we watch TV?"

Maura rubbed her temples. "Where's your mother?"

"I dunno. Outside, I think." Travis pulled the edge of the sheet around his chin and blinked his painfully innocent — though somewhat calculating — eyes at her, waiting.

Several seconds ticked by.

"So...can we?"

"Fine," said Maura, dropping her hands.

"Yay! Thanks, Grams!" Letting go of the sheet, Travis catapulted himself across his bed and fled the room, as if he were afraid that she was going to change her mind.

"Grams," said Charlie, rolling the beads between her fingers, "do you think you stopped that woman from dying that day?"

Maura turned back to her. "I don't know, but I read the obituary column every single day for a month and never saw her in it, and never heard about any accidents involving a train on the news."

Charlie stopped rolling the beads and looked up. "Then don't you think that man today deserved to know he was going to die?"

"No..." said Maura, shaking her head, "because his death was not imminent."

"I saw him choking on his own *blood*, Grams." Charlie's shoulders shook as she sucked in her breath. "Then I saw maggots eating his flesh as it rotted off his body. How is that not imminent?" she asked, her eyes clouding with tears.

Maura was quiet for several moments, leading House to believe that she was either amazed at the detail with which Charlie had described the man's fate—or horrified for her having seen it at all. "Because when I touched his hands," she finally said, "I felt the blackness moving in his lungs, but I *also* saw the wrinkles in his face, and the streaks of silver in his hair." Maura cupped the side of Charlie's cheek and wiped her tears with her thumb. "Telling him he was going to become sick and then die would have only caused him years of unnecessary torment."

Charlie drew her head back. "But why did you lie to him about not being alone? He died in a big house with no one around. Nobody even came to check on him."

"Listen to me, sweetheart." Wrapping an arm around Charlie's shoulder, the mattress creaked as

Maura leaned over and rested her head on top of hers. "There are two things you need to understand. The first is that a person's life is determined by the choices they make—and those are infinite. Even the smallest decision can alter one's path in a mighty way. And the second and most important thing," said Maura, lifting her brows, "is that sometimes all anyone is looking for is hope."

Charlie sniffed. "Is that why you lied to him?"

"If I told you that you were going to meet the love of your life at Point Lobos State Park one day, where do you think I would find you?"

House saw its young master's mouth twitch. "The park."

"And what do you think your chances of meeting someone there would be?"

Charlie shrugged. "Pretty good, I guess."

"Why?"

"Because I would be looking for him?"

"Exactly," said Maura, pulling her closer. "That's what hope does. It opens us up to a wealth of possibilities—and that man left the house today *full* of it."

Charlie slowly stood and walked over to the window. "Will it always be like this?" she asked, her pale reflection filling with doubt as she stared out into the darkness. "Seeing things that I don't want to...and having to lie to people to keep from hurting them?"

"No...not always," said Maura, pushing herself up from the bed. "I can teach you things to help control the unsolicited ones. And to answer your second question...it's much too late to be having a discussion on ethics. You've got school tomorrow."

Turning from the window with a stifled sigh, Charlie followed her grandmother around the hanging sheet and past Travis' bed.

"Promise me you'll put that man out of your mind and go to sleep," said Maura, stepping into the hallway. "Because nothing was ever solved by worrying."

"I will," replied Charlie, yet House noticed her answer didn't exactly resonate with confidence.

Maura stopped and looked back at her. "And I meant what I said this afternoon...when I told you that you were going to be all right."

Wiping her face with her sleeve, Charlie gave her a small nod.

"I'm sending your brother up in fifteen minutes," Maura said, turning away, "so I suggest you do what you need to do in the bathroom *now* if you want any peace."

Still holding the necklace in her left hand, Charlie placed her other against the wall for balance and leaned out the doorway. "Grams?"

"What?"

House was suddenly jolted by the intense warmth seeping from her fingertips, causing the wooden lath behind its plaster to shudder.

Charlie abruptly yanked her hand back.

Forcing itself to get control, House saw its young master standing in front of its wall, her eyes and mouth wide open.

"What?" Maura repeated.

Charlie tore her attention from the wall, where it eventually found its way to her grandmother. "Thanks for the necklace," she said in an absent, half-whisper.

Maura nodded and started for the stairs. "See you in the morning."

Closing the door, Charlie positioned herself directly in front of the wall once more, and after pausing to slip the necklace over her head, slowly raised her hand.

The anticipation of feeling her touch again sent the water languishing in House's drainage pipe rushing in the opposite direction, making the toilet gurgle and belch as it was forced upwards through the flange. Sensing the heat off her hand as it came closer, House suppressed another shudder and giddily held its breath—only to watch her outstretched fingers curl against her palm.

House's bewildered gaze went from its young master's hand to her face and found that her determined expression was now riddled with fear. Dropping her arm to her side, she jerked open the door and bolted out.

~

The blaring and distinctive call of a killdeer, which sounded to House like an endless loop of frantic chatter, pierced the cool night air as it sat listlessly on its crumbling foundation, watching the smoke from Shay's third cigarette waft across the porch.

"Are you going to tell me what's in the rest of the letter, or make me guess?"

Shay lifted her head upon hearing her mother's voice, but didn't turn around. "Well, with your...*talent*," she said, flicking her ashes over the side of the steps, "I wouldn't think I'd have to do either."

In the pale stream of light emanating from the porch's bare bulb, House saw something flash across Maura's face as she let go of the screen door—which slammed shut with a bang.

Shay briefly closed her eyes at the noise, then taking a long drag off her cigarette, pulled Tyler's letter from the pocket of her cardigan. "Here."

Maura sat down on the step beside her, then unfolding the paper, silently began moving her lips.

Peering over her shoulder, House could just make out its missing young master's scrawled handwriting.

...grown sick of eating K rations. Supplies are hard to come by here, so we're only allowed one meal a day, but they keep saying that's going to change. We're on our 4th straight day of rain, and I'm tired of all the mud. You can't walk without slipping or sinking in it. I haven't gotten much sleep lately. I've had to pull machine gun duty for the past few nights. Screaming mortars and gunfire have become an everyday part of life where we're at. When I do get to sleep, I have to do it with one eye open and my

helmet on because of the rats and spiders. You know how much I hate spiders? Well, the ones here are as big as your hand. Occasionally my body gives out and I fall into a deep sleep, but my dreams are only of this place, this Hell on earth. I wish I could just turn off my brain and unsee what I've seen. Me and some of the other guys had really been looking forward to our R&R next week. Being told it's been cancelled has been a real blow to our morale.

I've got to go. We're packing up to move out in the morning. We were hoping we'd be leaving by chopper, but were just told we'd be going on foot. That means more jungle. I'm not sure the sores on my feet can take it. I miss you all so much, and wish I was home sitting around the table with you eating and laughing, and enjoying Gram's pineapple upside down cake. Only 163 more days to go.

Love you all,
Tyler

Maura took her time folding the letter before handing it back to Shay.

"I—just want him—home," she said in a broken voice.

Maura put her arm around her. "I know you do, sweetheart."

With a breathless sob, Shay pressed the letter to her lips and bowed her head, sending a barrage of tears hurtling down her face.

House stiffly turned its gaze toward the ocean, allowing the hysterical jabber of the killdeer to drown out her cries.

Chapter 20

"Brrrrrt...brrrrrt! Oh, no...fall back! We need to take cover—brrrrrt!"

House yawned and shifted its weight as it listened to Travis making machine gun sounds while playing with his little green army men, who were currently taking refuge from heavy artillery fire behind a bowl of cereal.

"Here they come! Get ready...brrrrrt...brrr—"

Two of the three men were abruptly swallowed by Maura's hand.

"Grams!"

"I told you five minutes ago to stop," she said, tossing the plastic soldiers into the drawer. "You're giving me a headache. Now I want you to sit there quietly, and eat your breakfast."

"But the flakes are soggy."

"That's your own fault, dummy."

Travis scowled at his sister. "I *know* you are, but what am *I*?"

"Clearly...you're a genius," Charlie replied in a sarcastic tone as she reached for the milk.

House felt the worn rubber soles of Shay's shoes descending its stairs in rapid fashion and looked over in time to see her rush through the saloon doors. "Has anyone seen my purse?"

"Over there." Maura pointed.

As Shay turned toward the table, her frenzied gaze fell upon Charlie. "Oh...you look so pretty!"

House studied its young master for a moment. Although she was wearing her new multi-colored jeans—for the third day in a row—she had chosen a slim-fitting navy turtleneck with half zipper for her top, which not only accented her long and slender torso, but also served to highlight her golden locks as they cascaded down her shoulders. The tourmaline necklace Maura had given her rounded out the ensemble nicely.

"Thanks," said Charlie, answering her in the same insecure tone that she'd used last night with her grandmother.

"Me and Billy can't wait until Friday," Travis said, watching his mother reach behind him.

"And why's that?" asked Shay, snatching her purse off the back of his chair.

"I'm spending the night at Dad's, remember?"

Shay's jaw tightened.

Travis stopped dragging his spoon through his disintegrated cornflakes. "I still get to go, don't I?"

"You have to behave these next few days. I don't want to get a call from school like your grandmother got last week," Shay replied, yet House heard the underlying hope in her voice that he would not pass the stipulation.

"Me and Billy are gonna be extra good, I promise."

"You know, Charlie...I was thinking," said Shay, slinging the worn strap over her shoulder, "that you could have your slumber party this weekend. How does that sound?"

Charlie moved her lips sideways, which House had come to learn was her version of a shrug. "I'll think about it."

"All right," Shay replied, doing a poor job of hiding her frustration at her daughter's answer. "I'll see you guys later."

"Mom, wait!" exclaimed Charlie. "We have to turn our lunch money in today."

Stifling the sigh that had filled her chest, Shay pulled out her change purse and retrieved two crumpled dollar bills. "Here," she said, placing them on the table. "Let me see if I have any quarters…"

House saw a trace of red begin to surround Shay's cheeks as she rummaged in the bottom of her bag for enough coins to make up the difference.

"I'll take care of it," Maura said, stepping toward her. "You need to get to work. You know how bad traffic can be in the mornings—especially on a Monday."

Shay's gaze shifted from her purse to her mother…and then to the bologna and cheese sandwich wrapped in plastic that she was holding out to her, along with a brown-speckled banana. Giving her a subtle, yet grateful nod, she took the offered items and turned away. "'Bye, guys," she called over her shoulder as she hurried out of the kitchen. "Have a good day at school."

After hearing the front door close, Maura sent Travis upstairs to brush his teeth, then leaned over the table to gather his dishes. "How'd you sleep last night, Charlie?"

"Okay, I guess," she answered, carrying her bowl to the sink.

"I think your mom had a good idea about the slumber party, don't you?"

"Maybe," she muttered, twisting the knob on the faucet.

Maura's arm shot out in front of her and shut it off, drawing Charlie's startled gaze. "I need you to listen to me," she said, leaning against the gold-flecked countertop. "I know right now you just want to isolate yourself from everything and everyone, but having this gift doesn't mean you have to stop living your life."

"That's really easy for you to say, Grams. You're not in middle school."

"Do you think I was *born* this old?" asked Maura, placing her hands on her hips. "Did you not hear anything I told you last night?"

"I heard *everything*—which is why I don't want anything to do with this stupid gift! The kids at school think I'm weird enough already—sharing a bedroom with Travis and his invisible friend in this rundown house, and having a dad in a rock band that nobody's *ever* heard of, and a grandmother who—"

"A grandmother who *what*?" asked Maura, narrowing her eyes.

Charlie dropped her gaze to the floor.

"Well, I'm sorry that I embarrass you," Maura said in a hurt tone, "but until things like electricity, food, and clothing become free, I'm going to do what I have to do."

"Brrrrrt...brrrrrt!" The bowl in the sink began to rattle as Travis and his lead feet returned to the kitchen. "Ready, Grams."

"Go on and get in the car," she replied, wiping the toothpaste from his mouth. "We'll be there in a second."

As Travis bounded out of the kitchen—with Billy apparently in tow—Charlie fidgeted with the sleeve of her turtleneck. "I'm sorry, Grams. I didn't mean what I said."

Maura tilted her head. "Well, I think you *did*...but I understand."

Fighting back tears, Charlie slowly raised her eyes. "You do?"

"Of *course* I do. You see, aside from not being born old, I was also once a teenager—if you recall my story from last night—and I lived in a tiny apartment above a fish market with my parents, grandparents, and not one—but three very annoying brothers, who seemed to me at the time that their only purpose in life was to embarrass me."

The latter part of her grandmother's statement provoked a disparaging laugh from Charlie.

Maura took her hands in hers and held them tight. "I want you to do something for me."

"What?"

"Have your slumber party."

Charlie shook her head. "Grams—"

"Travis will be spending the night at your dad's, so we'll take down the curtain in your bedroom and erase all evidence of him and Billy. You're going to have lots of fun. I promise."

After a moment, Charlie let out a reluctant sigh. "Okay," she said, wiping at the corners of her eyes.

"Now..." Maura stooped to catch her gaze which had found its way to the floor again. "Let me see that beautiful smile of yours."

To House's amazement, its young master obliged, and the single action illuminated her entire face.

"That's better," said Maura, letting go of her hands. "Come on, we're going to be late for school."

With her newly upturned lips pushing against her cheeks, Charlie's tourmaline beads glinted in the sunlight as she leaned over to retrieve her math book from off the table.

"And don't worry about me come Friday," Maura said, grabbing her keys. "I'll just be a normal, but hip and sexy-looking, grandmother who bakes cookies."

Charlie burst through the saloon doors with a giggle; it was as sweet as it was unguarded...and was something House hadn't heard her do since before Tyler had left for a place called Vietnam.

~

House woke to the jarring feeling that it was being watched. Sitting erect, it rapidly flicked its gaze from room to room as it struggled to get its bearings, but found no movement of any kind. Travis and Charlie were fast asleep, as were Shay and Maura.

Turning its attention outward, House fought to see what lay beyond the front porch, but with heavy clouds covering the crescent-shaped moon, there was only darkness — and a slight, pungent smell.

House shifted its weight, setting off a series of creaks and groans, as it leaned as far forward on its foundation as it could, then swept its restricted gaze across the blackened landscape.

The single, shrill yip of a fox pierced the night air. Several more joined in, each one louder than the other. Their frenzied, high-pitched barks went on for a good minute or so — and then suddenly stopped. It was there, amidst the startled silence, that House heard something.

Straining against the confines of its rebar, House listened intently. In the distance, just beyond the edge of the drive, it picked up on the vague sound of an engine idling.

A forceful wind began to stir, sending dozens of yellowish-brown leaves raining down onto the sidewalk, and as the foul odor seeped inside the slatted eaves under its roof, a sliver of moonlight emerged from behind the clouds. Narrowing its gaze, House peered through the branches of the massive spruce that sat next to the road and could just make out the faint glow of taillights.

A rush of adrenaline coursed through the knob and tube wiring behind House's walls, causing the porch light to flicker. Moments later, it heard the engine begin to rev — followed by the squall of tires.

House's fear subsided as quickly as it had come, shrouding it in darkness once more, and yet before its breathing could return to normal, it was filled with a sense of foreboding as it watched the taillights disappear around the bend in the road.

Chapter 21

"Who would have done something like this?" asked Shay, pushing the bottom of the shovel along the grass with her right hand, while pressing the back of her other against her nose and mouth.

Maura shrugged as she held the brown paper bag at arm's length. "It was probably just some kids."

"Kids *egg* houses and *toilet paper* trees, they don't throw red paint all over a sign and leave a dozen fish heads in front of it," Shay snapped, dumping another one of the bulging eyed, bloody-gilled creatures into the bag.

"Mom?"

Both Maura and Shay peered around the giant palm sticking out of the ground.

"What's going on?" asked Travis, walking to the edge of the porch.

"Nothing," Shay replied, "go back inside."

Travis wrinkled his nose. "What's that smell?"

"A dead possum. Coyotes must've gotten it last night."

"Cool!" he exclaimed, leaping off the porch. "Let me see—"

"Stop right there," said Shay, holding up her hand.

"But I just wanna see it."

"Travis Michael, if you take one more step, you can forget about spending the night with your dad."

House's youngest master stopped…and then cut his eyes to his left. "Billy wants to know why we can't see it?"

Slamming the tip of the shovel into the dirt, Shay came around the side of the palm. "Do you remember our conversation yesterday morning about you staying out of trouble?"

Travis met her question with a silent glare.

"Well, this *right* here is what I'm talking about. Now, I want you to go back inside and eat your breakfast—or you can forget about Friday."

House heard the creak of the screen door and saw Charlie step out onto the porch. "Come on, Travis," she said, holding it open for him. "If you hurry, you'll have time to watch Bullwinkle before school."

Clenching his fists in an air of defiance, Travis pivoted around, and as his feet pounded against the steps, House noticed Charlie's troubled gaze shift from him to the base of the sign, and then over to her grandmother…where it lingered for several moments before she pulled the door closed.

"Mom, are you going to help me or not?"

Maura turned around. "Sorry," she replied, holding out the sack.

After Shay had scooped up the last fish head, she traded her mother the shovel for the bag and set off across the yard, gathering dirt and blades of wet grass on the tops of her white shoes, which she'd spent half an hour polishing the night before.

Maura followed her around the side of the house in an awkward half-run. "Let me take care of that," she said, reaching for the bag. "You're going to be late for wor—"

"Just who exactly did you piss off?" asked Shay, stopping at the edge of the steps that led to the deck.

Maura's chest rose up and down as she paused to scratch the back of her right earlobe. "No one," she said, reaching for the bag once more.

Shay held it from her grasp. "No one," she repeated.

Maura straightened and lowered her hand. "That's right."

As the wind whipped about, Shay's eyes grew dark with anger. "Well, how about we blame this on Billy then," she said, shaking the sack at her mother, "because it couldn't possibly have had anything to do with that woman who came by the other day—*could it?*"

House glanced at Maura, and although her winded expression remained passive, it was fairly certain the circles of red infiltrating her cheeks weren't stemming from the cold.

Gripping the weathered handrail, Shay flung the bag over the side.

House watched it plummet straight down the edge of the cliff before catching on a small ledge and busting open, spilling the fish heads into the crags of rock and swirling surf below.

"What's it going to take for you to stop toying with people's lives?" Shay asked, turning back to her mother. "A brick through our window...having our tires slash—"

"I care about my clients, Shay," said Maura, raising her voice.

"No—if you really cared about them, you'd give them some nice, trite answer when you looked at their palms, then they'd pay you and be on their merry way!"

"I can't do that, and you *know* it."

"Well, given that we just had a dozen fish heads dumped in our front yard, maybe you should *start*!"

Silence, as forceful as it was cutting, anchored itself between them.

"You're going to be late for work," Maura said in a coarse whisper, then taking an uneven step backward, turned and—with a gait that was as stiff as her jaw—began walking away. As she disappeared around the corner, House saw her use her knuckle to brush aside the wounded look that had settled upon her face.

~

The back of the door slapped lazily against House's wooden siding as a gentle, mid-morning breeze drifted across the deck and into Maura's bedroom. The lethargic tapping, combined with the sound of the waves hitting the shore, was enough to lull House to sleep but—harnessed with guilt over slumbering through last night's incident—fought hard to stay awake.

"I'm glad you came over."

Looking inward, House let its gaze settle on Maura, who was twirling Ed's chest hairs around her finger as they lay entwined beneath the sheets.

"Well, I'm glad you called," Ed replied, yet House could hear the edge in his voice.

"Do you still have friends on the force?"

"I do...but they don't have any jurisdiction here. Why don't you let me call the sheriff? At the very least, a report needs to be taken."

Maura lifted her head and snorted. "Because Lester Suggs spends his days with his hands either wrapped around a bottle of whiskey or some young, dumb thing at the bar down by the pier."

"Hmm...some young, dumb thing, you say? What's the name of that bar?"

House saw the sheet billow as Maura swiftly moved her right foot.

"Ow!" Ed exclaimed. "I was just kidding."

"I'm glad you find this so amusing."

Pushing himself up, Ed leaned back against the iron headboard. "I don't find what happened to you amusing at all," he said, staring down at her. "To tell you the truth, I'm mad over the whole goddamned thing."

"Me too," she answered, resting her chin on his torso.

"No—I mean I'm mad at *you*."

Maura blinked and sat up. "Why are you mad at *me*?"

"Because you didn't let me know about that asshole and what he did to you until today. I don't like being lied to—especially by you."

"I didn't lie to you," Maura said, gathering the sheet around her.

Ed's jaw shifted. "When I asked you if everything was all right that night I came over, you looked at me and lied right to my face. You may be a psychic, but I was a detective for thirty-two years. I pick up on things, too—like the way you scratch that spot behind your ear when you're avoiding the truth."

Maura's face pinched in discomfort, making her eyes falter. "I told you everything was all right," she said, forcing herself to look at him, "because I didn't want to worry you."

"Well, you were damn lucky he didn't hurt you."

"Luck had nothing to do with it," she retorted. "I can take care of myself."

"*This* time. Next time, you might not be so fortunate. Those fish heads were a warning."

"Ed, sweetheart," she said, running the tip of her finger along the bottom of his chin, "you don't know for certain he did that. It could've just been some kids who did it on a dare."

He drew his head back. "It was a warning. *But* if you truly believe that, why did you call me?"

"You know what?" Throwing back the sheet, Maura rose from the bed and pulled on her robe. "I'm sorry I did."

House saw Ed watch her disappear through the open door that led to the deck—then with a resigned scowl that merged his thick eyebrows together, untangled his feet from the covers and started after her.

Maura's gaze swept over the deck, which—aside from two half-dead plants languishing in concrete planters—was barren. Eventually, yet somewhat begrudgingly, her eyes settled on Ed as he closed the distance between them. "Let's just say for the sake of argument that you're right."

He stopped, seeming surprised by her words. "Well, for the sake of *argument*," he said, his anger fading as he slipped his arms around her waist, "I agree with your assessment."

Maura turned the side of her face into his chest. "So what do we do?"

"Can you give me a good description of the man?" he asked, kissing her chestnut-colored curls as they sat in disarray on top of her head.

"Right down to the number of hairs lining his nostrils."

"That's good," he said, moving his lips to her neck. "Did you see what kind of car he was driving?"

Maura closed her eyes and sighed. "The only thing I can tell you was that it was dark blue."

"And what about this Iris woman?" Ed murmured, tugging on the sash of her robe. "Did you get her last name?"

"I don't do names," she said flatly, sounding irritated with him for not remembering.

Ed straightened with a sigh and dropped his hands. "Well, what *can* you tell me about her? Other than the fact that she's got a prick for a boyfriend."

"I know she's not from around here."

"Why do you say that?"

"Because people in this town don't have two nickels to rub together, and she had *a lot* of nickels. She was driving a new Cadillac."

"Did you get the plate?"

"Sorry," said Maura, tilting her head in a condescending manner. "I wasn't wearing my detective hat. But after hearing you boast about all your years of experience as one, I'm thinking *you* should've gotten the number—because you parked right beside her that day you showed up begging me to pick the horses for you."

The wind began to stir, ruffling the bushy ring of blackish-gray hair that ran in a perfect semicircle behind Ed's ears. "You know...if I closed my eyes, I would swear that I was standing here listening to my ex-wife."

Maura's tepid gaze narrowed. "Which one?"

Another frustrated-sounding sigh slipped through the small opening between Ed's lips.

A sudden surge of what House determined to be guilt swarmed Maura's cheeks, leaving their edges red. "I'm sorry. I shouldn't have said that. These past few days have been trying...in more ways than one."

Ed scratched the knot that had formed on the side of his jaw. "It's all right."

"But in my defense, it's kind of hard to take you seriously right now," Maura said, gesturing at his lower half.

He looked down at himself. "What? You don't like my boxers?"

"I like your boxers just fine. It's your knobby, scrawny chicken legs stuffed inside those black socks that's making things difficult."

"Well...I can do something about that," he said, an insolent grin spreading across his face as he pulled her tight against him.

Maura batted her eyes sarcastically. "Are you going to take them off?"

"Among other things..." Parting her robe with his fingers, Ed walked her backward over to the bed and eased her down onto the mattress.

Chapter 22

"Who's cuter? David Cassidy or Donny Osmond?"

"Donny for sure," answered Charlie, gazing dreamily into the eyes of a young man with shiny dark hair and dazzling smile.

"Definitely Donny," said Missy, her shoulder wedged against Charlie's as the two of them hovered over the picture in the magazine.

"How could you guys like him better than David?" Tonya angrily flipped the page and pointed to a guy with long chestnut-colored hair, who was wearing a white Henley with brown stitching and tight-fitting bell bottoms. "*Look* at him. He's way cuter."

Missy twirled her raven locks around her fingers as she gave Tonya an emphatic nod. "Yeah, you're right. He *is* cuter."

"I still like Donny better," said Charlie with a shrug.

Looking up from the magazine, Tonya's inky black eyes zeroed in on Charlie's. "I bet you listen to 'Puppy Love' all the time, don't you?"

"Not *all* the time," Charlie answered, as a twinge of red began circling her cheeks.

"God"—Tonya shook her head and sneered—"that's such a dumb song."

"Yeah, it's a really dumb song," chimed Missy.

The saloon doors swung open, drawing their attention.

"Who wants popcorn?" asked Maura, carrying a small pan with yellow and white kernels peeking out of the top of what looked to House to be a crinkled balloon made of aluminum foil.

"Thank you, Mrs. Litsey," said Tonya, as she watched the older woman bend over and place the pan on the floor in front of them.

Charlie got to her feet and stretched. "I'll get us some drinks." As she followed Maura—who was dressed conservatively in black knit pants and matching top—House saw Tonya elbow Missy in the ribs.

"Where do you suppose her crystal ball is?" she asked in a loud whisper.

Missy flashed her a grin. "I don't know. Probably with her tarot cards."

"Yeah, or maybe it's hidden inside that beehive hairdo of hers."

The two girls looked at each other and began to giggle.

House bristled, causing the warped sheet of paneling behind the television to buckle even further, which in turn pushed Tyler's picture off its nail. The frame toppled forward and landed on the console with a thud, bringing the girls' laughter to a swift halt.

Heavy footsteps echoed across the kitchen linoleum.

"We didn't do it," Tonya said to Maura as she burst through the doors, "it just fell."

Maura gave her a disbelieving glance, while Charlie stood looking on behind her, clutching three bottles of Coke between her knuckles.

"Cross our hearts," added Missy, drawing an X on her chest with her finger.

Sucking in her breath, Maura turned and walked back into the kitchen.

Tonya looked at Charlie and held up her hands. "I swear that picture fell off the wall all by itself," she said, letting out a stilted laugh. "I think your house is haunted."

"It isn't haunted," replied Charlie, sitting cross-legged on the floor, "it's just old."

"Clearly," said Tonya, rolling her eyes, "but that doesn't explain why the picture fell."

Charlie, whose cheeks were still stinging from the 'Puppy Love' remark, gave another small, but indecisive shrug. "Well, I don't know what else to tell you," she said, holding out the bottle of Coke to her.

Tonya shook her head. "I never drink from the bottle. You don't know how many lips have touched it."

Missy swallowed and wiped her mouth. "Me neither."

"I'm sure they sterilize them or something before filling them up," said Charlie, arching her brow, which House noticed was eerily reminiscent of her grandmother.

"How would you know? Do you work at the Coke factory?"

Charlie stared at Tonya for a moment and then begrudgingly got up. "I'll get some glasses."

After Charlie had disappeared into the kitchen, Tonya cupped her hand around one side of her mouth. "That picture didn't fall off the wall by itself," she whispered in Missy's ear. "Something pushed it."

Although House was sorry for what had happened to Tyler's picture, it felt a smug sense of satisfaction creeping through its ducts as it looked at the spooked expression hiding behind Tonya's heavily made-up face, and found itself wishing it could do it again, because neither she nor her lackey Missy — whose teeth were covered in metal grids — seemed deserving of the kindness and generosity that its family had bestowed upon them.

In spite of what had happened earlier in the week, Maura had been true to her word in regard to the slumber party, for other than the palm in the front yard — which was still smeared with red paint — there was nothing visible within House's walls to indicate her profession, *or* the fact that Charlie and Travis shared a bedroom. Maura had also carefully counted out several coins from the meager stash she kept hidden in a coffee can beneath her bed and gone to the store, returning an hour later with the popcorn and a carton of Coca-Cola, something House had seen them have only once before.

The front door opened and slammed, startling both girls.

Moments later, a disgruntled-looking Shay walked through the entryway...followed by Travis.

"Hi, Mrs. Montgomery," said Tonya, swiveling around on her bottom.

Shay offered a curt nod in reply. "Are you girls having fun?" she asked, walking past them.

"Yeah," they answered in unison, watching her shove the saloon doors out of her way.

As the doors banged closed, House saw Tonya and Missy exchange glances.

"What are you guys doing?"

The girls shifted their attention from each other to Travis, who was standing beside the coffee table, wearing a forlorn look.

Tossing her hair over her shoulder, Tonya stretched her legs out in front of her and leaned back on her palms. "What's in the bag?" she asked, using her big toe to point at the brown paper sack he was holding.

"My pajamas and stuff."

Missy grabbed a handful of popcorn and shoved it into her mouth. "Aren't you supposed to be staying at your dad's or something?"

"Yeah, but he wasn't home."

"Aww...poor baby," said Tonya, sticking out her lower lip. "Is Barney sad, too?"

"Who's Barney?"

"Your imaginary friend."

Travis placed his hand on his hip. "His name's Billy."

Tonya stifled a giggle. "Oh, sorry."

"That's okay," said Travis, plopping himself down on the edge of the couch. "Billy doesn't mind."

"So, is he here right now?"

"Yeah."

"Where?" asked Missy.

"He's right beside me," Travis answered, seeming delighted by the attention these older girls were paying him.

"Come here," said Tonya, motioning at Travis, "I want to tell you a secret."

He shook his head. "You can say it in front of Billy."

"Well, let me whisper it to you, and then if you want, you can tell Billy."

"Okay."

As Travis hopped off the cushion, House saw Tonya cut her eyes at Missy and grin.

"So, what's the secret?" he asked, coming around the table.

Grabbing Travis by the elbow, Tonya pulled him down and pressed her lips to his ear. "You're an *idiot*."

Missy's shoulders shook as she burst out laughing.

House's littlest master straightened and with his eyes filling with tears, stumbled through the doors of the kitchen, where he promptly bumped into Charlie.

"Watch where you're going," she snapped—yet her voice softened when she saw Travis' face. "What's wrong?"

"Nothing," he said, pushing past her. He ran over to Shay, who was seated at the table talking to Maura, and after climbing into her lap, buried his head against her shoulder.

Tightening her grip on the glasses, Charlie turned and walked into the living room. "What happened?"

With a smile tugging at the corner of her mouth, Tonya gave an innocent blink and shrugged. "Beats me."

~

"Do you have any threes?"

Travis lowered the bottle of Coke he'd been contentedly swigging on and checked his cards. "Go fish," he said, burping the last word.

Repelling slightly at the smell, Shay reached over and drew a card from the deck that sat in the middle of her bed. A squeal of laughter found its way underneath the door, drawing Travis' attention.

"Your turn, Trav."

He looked back at his mother and laid his cards down. "I don't feel like playing anymore."

"But you can't stop now," Shay lamented. "After losing seven hands straight, I'm winning this one."

"Mr. Ratner told me that I should always quit when I'm ahead."

"Oh, he did, did he? Well, remind me to have a little talk with him the next time I see him." Shay gathered the deck of cards and set them on the nightstand. "So, what do you want to beat me at next? Checkers or Battleship?"

"Can we just watch TV?"

Shay gave a faint smile, and although Travis' sullen demeanor hadn't been lost on her, she seemed relieved to not have to play anymore games. "Let me see what I can do."

As she walked across the room and began to fiddle with the rabbit ears attached to the small black and white television sitting on top of her dresser, House saw Travis turn and whisper something to the shadowy space beside the nightstand.

"How's that?" asked Shay.

Travis looked. The snowy image on the screen was now clear and had slowed to just one roll every few seconds instead of ten. "Good."

As the theme song to *The Odd Couple* began to come through the TV's tiny speaker, Travis crawled under the covers. "Mom," he said, pulling the sheet up around his chin, "do you care if Billy sleeps with us?"

"No, just as long as he doesn't kick me."

"He says he won't."

Slipping into bed, Shay held up her arm, inviting Travis to snuggle against her. "I'm sorry you didn't get to spend the night with your dad," she said, kissing his forehead, "but this is nice, isn't it? Having our very own slumber party?"

"Yeah."

Several moments passed as if Shay were waiting for him to expound on his answer, but when he didn't, she turned her gaze to the TV.

"Mom?"

"What, sweetie?"

Travis wiped his nose on the sleeve of his pajamas. "Why did Charlie's friends make fun of me over Billy?"

The muscle in Shay's jaw hardened. "Because they're small-minded."

"What does that mean?"

Shay's eyes grew distant as she tenderly stroked his hair. "It means that they don't have any imagination…so it's easier for them to poke fun at you instead of trying to understand how creative you are."

As an eruption of canned laughter from the TV filled the room, House looked out at the dark waves glinting beneath the moonlight and let go of a miserable sigh as a familiar feeling of apprehension began circling it. Perched high upon this cliff, House had seen its share of strange things, some of which were downright unexplainable, but it never saw Evy's floating people that lived in the rocks…or invisible ones that caused mischief.

Turning back to Travis, House became consumed with worry for its littlest master.

~

One pan of Jiffy Pop, two batches of cookies, three hours, and a stern warning from Maura later, Tonya, Missy, and Charlie had finally quieted down and were watching television.

As the scary show, ridiculous in both concept and special effects, droned on, House couldn't help noticing that Tonya seemed restless. After a few more moments, she reached out and shut off the TV. "This show is boring. Let's play truth or dare."

Neither Missy nor Charlie said anything.

"Oh, come on, are you too scared to play?"

"No, but Charlie is," replied Missy, deflecting the attention off herself.

Charlie looked at Missy and scowled. "No, I'm not."

"Okay then, I'll go first," Tonya said, scooting closer to them. "Ask me something."

Resting her elbows on her legs, Missy leaned forward. "Truth or dare…have you ever French-kissed a boy?"

"Truth. Me and Tim Sterrett made out under the bleachers last Friday."

"That's not really a secret," said Charlie, laughing.

Tonya's gaze shot to Charlie. "Your turn," she said, pulling a flashlight out of her sleeping bag.

"What's that for?"

Tonya held it under her pointy chin. "Because it's more fun playing it in the dark," she said, staring at Charlie with what now looked like two black holes, "so turn off that stupid wagon wheel light."

Her smile fading, Charlie stood and made her way over to the wall behind the couch.

"Hurry up," said Missy.

Charlie flipped the switch, and with the exception of the inverted triangular beam illuminating Tonya's face, the living room was cloaked in darkness.

"Shine the light on the floor so I can see how to get back," Charlie said in a shrill whisper.

Tonya did as she asked, but just as Charlie started toward her, turned it off.

In the disorienting blindness, House felt Charlie's hand fumble along its wall. A searing heat suddenly tore through House, making it let go of a breathless scream. As it searched for the source of the pain, roiling billows of thick black smoke rose from the living room floor and slithered across its ceiling like giant tentacles. Struggling to breathe, House saw that its wall by the stairs was on fire. A series of whistles, pops, and groans sounded as the bright orange flames burned through the paneling and began to devour its wooden laths—causing House to convulse in agony as the blackened slats bubbled and blistered.

Amidst its anguish, House fought to find its family, but could not see beyond the ball of fire. Frantically looking in the direction of the landing at the top of the stairs, it caught sight of a small piece of flickering debris fluttering downward, and as House choked on the hot, acrid smoke seeping into its vents, it helplessly watched the burning fragment fall onto the velvet drapes that separated Maura's bedroom from the living room. There was a deafening whoosh—and then the curtains erupted into flames.

The glass windows in the entryway shattered, and as House felt what little oxygen there was being sucked out of the room, the upstairs began to fill with noxious smoke, making the stairwell impassable.

Gasping for air, House thought it heard Maura's voice screaming for Charlie, but—reeling with panic and confusion—could not see where she was.

As the heat reached intolerable levels, House's panic gave way to terror as it felt the fire spread to its second floor.

House's shutters furiously banged against its clapboards as it struggled to breathe.

"Grams!"

Through the flames, House saw its young master standing outside Maura's room, her blood-red face streaked with tears as she shrieked for her grandmother. Using every ounce of strength it had, House slammed its weight against the front of its foundation in an attempt to move Charlie away from the flames—but the sudden tilt of the floor knocked her off her feet.

The latch on the front door, buckling under the strain, slipped from its strike plate, drawing Charlie's hysterical gaze as it swung open. Feeling its breath leaving it, House's sight began to grow dim as she crawled toward the threshold. The lamp on the end table toppled over, blocking her path. As she scurried around the melted plastic shade, the couch and both chairs simultaneously ignited—engulfing the living room and its young master in a roaring inferno.

"*Charlie!*" Maura's face abruptly appeared.

As the fiery images faded, House instinctively took in a deep breath and swerved its unfocused gaze to Charlie; free from smoke and flames, the veins in her throat looked like braided rope as one scream after another rolled out of it.

"Charlie!" Maura yelled, taking her by the shoulders.

"Grams! The house is on fire!"

"Look at me," Maura said in a harsh voice, shaking her. "There's no fire!"

Charlie's fingers clawed at Maura's nightgown. "But I saw it happen! Don't you understand? I *saw* it!"

Maura's eyes filled with emotion as she cupped the side of Charlie's face in her palm. "It's okay," she whispered.

A creak at the top of the stairs made Maura glance up…and slowly lower her hand.

Following her gaze, House saw Shay standing near the top of the landing, her expression unreadable.

Charlie looked too, and then, as if picking up on the unsettling quiet that had surrounded her, blinked and turned around.

Missy and Tonya were sitting motionless by the TV, with their heads drawn back and mouths twisted in horror.

Chapter 23

"When were you going to tell me?"

"It wasn't my place."

Shay's coffee cup came down hard against the kitchen table. "Since *when*?"

House stared sullenly at the squares of sunlight the window had thrown onto its yellowed linoleum. It had been a long, tense night...and the morning wasn't shaping up to be any better.

Maura sat rigidly in the chair across from Shay with her hands folded around her own cup. "What she saw regarding that man absolutely terrified her. She only told me because she knew I would understand."

The legs of Shay's chair scraped across the floor as she got to her feet. "And *I* wouldn't?"

"I'm not blind, Shay—and neither is Charlie," Maura said, watching her dump the rest of her coffee into the sink. "Because when it comes to what I do, she sees the disapproving glances you hurl in my direction, and hears the patronizing tone in your voice when you speak to me."

Gripping the edge of the sink, Shay bowed her head until her chin nearly touched her chest. Several moments passed, and then her lips slowly parted. "I just want her to have a normal life."

Maura's face became inflamed. "You know," she said, shoving her chair backward, "I have been tiptoeing around you since you were *thirteen* years old—and I don't think this is about Charlie at all. This is about you being jealous over the fact that it skipped you."

House heard Shay take in a small breath. "You're wrong."

"Am I—"

"Yes."

"Then why are you so angry?"

Shay's ponytail whipped around her shoulders as she turned from the sink. "Did you see Tonya and Missy this morning when their mothers came to pick them up?" she asked, stabbing her finger toward the living room. "They wouldn't even *look* at Charlie as they were leaving. I don't want that for her."

"I don't want that for her either," said Maura, shaking her head. "Which is why I'm going to teach her how to control it."

"So she can do *what*?" Shay yelled, holding her arms out from her sides. "Hang a shingle next to yours that reads Madam Maura and Granddaughter?"

House watched the squares of sunlight slither across the floor in silent retreat, casting a long shadow between both women.

The doorbell rang out, making House shiver as the unexpected jolt surged behind its wall.

Dropping her arms, Shay marched into the living room and wrenched open the front door.

Rom Montgomery and his perfectly feathered hair appeared.

"What are you doing here?" she asked, grounding out the words between clenched teeth.

"I wanted to tell you that I'm sorry I wasn't home when you and Travis came by last night. Some guys I know called and asked me to jam with them...and I just lost track of time."

"Well, thanks for driving all the way here to explain yourself," Shay replied, swinging the door around. "I feel much better."

"Why do you always have to be such an unforgiving bit—" Glancing away, Rom took a deep breath and slowly let it out. "Look," he said, cutting his gaze back to her, "I'm here now, and I'd like to make it up to Trav by taking him out for breakfast."

Pushing the screen door out of her way, Shay stepped onto the porch.

Rom shrugged. "So...are you going to go get him?"

"He's not going anywhere with you—ever, and neither is Charlie."

"Why the hell not?"

"Because last night, Travis and I met your *buddy* that you're renting your house from."

Rom's forehead creased, causing his little pebble eyes to narrow. "*What* buddy?"

"Seriously?" Shay glared at him. "She had red hair, big tits...went by the name of Cherry? Oh, and she must *really* like powdered donuts—because she had traces of white all over her nose."

House watched Rom's face go from confusion to anger, leaving it clouded in darkness. "You can't stop me from seeing my kids."

"Well, I have a slip of paper signed by the judge that says I can," Shay replied, giving him a flippant smile.

Rom's hands shot up, grabbing her by the arms. "You try enforcing that and I fucking promise I'll make your life a living hell!"

The screen door creaked.

Glancing over his shoulder, Rom saw Maura standing behind him and promptly let go of Shay.

"I have to run to the store, so you need to move your car," Maura said to him in a tone that House had never heard her use before. Clutching the straps of her purse, she made her way down the steps, and upon reaching the path, turned around and looked expectantly at her former son-in-law. "That means now."

Flicking his gaze from Maura to Shay, whose eyes had filled with tears, Rom took a great deal of time lighting a cigarette before stepping off the porch. "Where're you going?" he said to Maura, the corners of his mouth curving upwards as he ambled past the giant palm. "To buy some *paint*?"

~

House listened to the gentle patter of rain falling on its roof. It was still early in the afternoon, but the dark clouds looming overhead made it seem much later.

Turning its attention inward, House found Shay

sitting at the kitchen table paying bills. Upon further scrutinization, however, it realized that paying was not the correct word. *Staring* seemed to be the more accurate term. With her head down and shoulders slumped forward, her eyes appeared lost in thought as they blankly fixated on the past-due invoice lying in front of her.

House felt movement to its left and looked over to see Charlie standing in front of the saloon-style doors. "Mom?"

Shay glanced up. "What is it, sweetheart?" she replied with a fraught expression that sharply contrasted the eagerness in her voice. "Are you hungry? Do you want me to get dinner started?"

Charlie shifted her feet. "Um, no...I just wanted to ask if you knew how long Grams was going to be at the store?"

Shay's enthusiasm faltered. "She got home a few minutes ago. I think she's in the bathroom."

"Thanks," she said, turning away.

"Charlie?"

House's young master stopped and glanced back. "I'm always here...if you want to talk."

Charlie gave her mother an awkward nod that was accompanied by an equally awkward smile. "Okay," she said, then hurried out of the kitchen, leaving Shay to stare helplessly after her.

Although House was reluctant to abandon Shay as well, the feeling of water rushing through its pipes caused it to shift its attention upstairs.

A cloud of steam rose from the tub, enveloping the mirror in a wet fog, as Maura sprinkled a liberal amount of Calgon—a gift from Ed—into the churning water. Removing her robe, she stepped into the cast-iron tub and wearily slipped beneath the foamy white bubbles.

In spite of having been gone for most of the day, Maura had returned with only a package of toilet paper and bag of Bugles—which Travis had promptly partaken of. As she leaned back, House noticed that her cheeks were extremely flushed, which given the amount of heat coming off the water, wouldn't have been all that concerning if not for the fact that the rest of her face was ashen.

A soft knock sounded.

"Grams?" Charlie's voice came through the door. "Can I come in?"

"You may," answered Maura, sinking deeper into the tub.

House stiffened as its young master walked inside. After last night, it had no desire for her to touch any part of its walls ever again, and judging by the way she kept her hands pressed against her sides as she moved about…guessed she wasn't too keen on it either.

"Can we talk for a minute?" she asked, using her elbow to shut the door.

Maura looked at her granddaughter's despondent expression and offered a sympathetic nod.

Closing the lid on the toilet, Charlie sat down.

Several moments of silence went by.

"I know you're upset over what you saw last night," said Maura, "but not everything you see will come to fruition. With precognition…that's what your gift is called...sometimes these visions are simply a warning so that we can change direction. Remember what I told you about the power of choices?"

Charlie answered her by dropping her gaze to the floor.

"It could also be a metaphor for something else."

"Like what?"

"Like, maybe you're feeling stressed and overwhelmed, because you think you don't have any control."

House saw Charlie's chest rise and fall.

"First thing tomorrow, if you're willing, I'm going to teach you how to quiet your mind. Once you've accomplished that, it will be easier for you to separate your own thoughts from your psychic senses."

Charlie's eyes briefly filled with hope before being consumed by doubt.

"It's going to be all right," said Maura, patting her on the arm. "I promise."

"You keep saying that...but you're wrong." A stray tear slid down Charlie's cheek as the bottom of her chin started to quiver. "Missy and Tonya think I belong in a freak show, and by Monday, all the other kids at school will think that too."

"Charlie..." said Maura, tilting her head, "that's not true."

"Yes, it is," she replied, pulling her arm away.

Maura sat up, sending a wave of suds rolling toward the front of the tub. "I know this is hard for you to believe right now, but in a few years, you're going to be a grown woman out making your way in the world. And what happened when you were in the eighth grade will be nothing but a distant, unremarkable memory. And as far as Missy and Tonya are concerned, those girls are going to be knocked-up and living in some trailer park before they're twenty-one, so I wouldn't put much stock in what they think of you."

Charlie's eyebrows shot up, disappearing beneath a tangle of blonde locks. "Did you *see* that happen?"

"The first part I did," Maura replied, the sternness in her voice fading, "but one doesn't have to be a psychic to see how those girls are going to turn out. Being an imbecile can only get you so far."

Something that sounded to House like a sob being eaten by a hyena erupted from the back of Charlie's throat.

~

The rain had slowed to a steady drizzle as Maura turned out the light in the kitchen before making her way into the living room.

"Goodnight, Grams," said Travis, calling to her from the top of the landing.

"See you in the morning," she replied, stifling a yawn. As she walked by the television, House noticed her gaze being drawn to Tyler's picture, which was still lying on top of it.

Gingerly picking it up, she turned it over in her hands and wiped a trace of dust off the glass. As she stood on her tiptoes to hang it back on its nail, House saw her wince and take in a sharp breath. She clutched at her chest, sending the picture hurtling to the floor. As splinters of glass flew across the room, Maura, whose eyes were now wide open and clouded with fear, reached for the wall with trembling fingers—only to fall forward, striking her right temple against the corner of the television. She collapsed in a sprawling heap in front of the coffee table.

Chapter 24

The bell of St. Anthony's tolled in the distance as Charlie sat on the edge of her window seat, rolling the jacks ball back and forth beneath her palm.

From what House had been able to gather by listening in on the phone calls Shay had made from the hospital, Maura had suffered a heart attack, and the next seventy-two hours for her were critical.

"Charlie?"

She stopped rolling the rubber ball and looked up.

Travis stood beside the foot of her bed. "I'm hungry."

"Mom said Mr. Ratner was bringing over a bucket of chicken."

"Do you think he'll play poker with us?"

"He might," Charlie replied in a quiet voice. "Why don't you go wait outside for him on the porch?"

Travis pivoted around and went to push the makeshift curtain out of his way, but hesitated. Pursing his lips, he glanced back at his sister. "Billy wants to know if Grams is going to die?"

Charlie's eyes wavered. "You know Grams," she said, giving him a bleak smile, "she's too stubborn to do any such thing."

Travis stared at her for a long time, then letting go of an almost imperceptible nod, disappeared behind the sheet.

House watched him trudge down the steps and cross the floor in the living room. Upon reaching the entryway, he stopped and pulled something small from his jeans pocket before heading out the front door. Narrowing its gaze, House quickly came to realize that Travis had somehow come into possession of Shay's disposable lighter.

As Travis repeatedly flicked the little black lever with his thumb, House's memory of him playing with the box of matches, combined with the waking nightmare of itself on fire, sent a shudder rolling across its roof, rattling the vent in Charlie's room — and drawing her eyes upward.

"I know you're here," she said, clutching the ball between her fingers. "I can feel you watching me."

House's breath caught in its damper, making the metal plate clank as it flipped closed.

Charlie rose from the window seat. "Are you a ghost?" she asked in an uneven whisper. "If you *are*...make another noise."

Fairly certain that it wasn't, House stood very, very still.

The back of Charlie's neck prickled with goosebumps. "What are you then?" she pleaded, the fabric of her knit top fluttering erratically as her heart pounded against her chest.

Not wanting to upset her any further, House tried to quell its emotions, but could not stop itself from shaking with glee. For, after all these years...to finally be acknowledged, the feeling was indescribable.

In the midst of its elation, House heard a car door slam. Thinking it was Ed, it absently glanced outside—only to find the man who had hurt Maura making his way up the sidewalk.

"Whatcha doing there?"

Travis stopped flicking the lighter.

The man paused at the bottom step. "Didn't anyone ever tell you that playing with fire is dangerous?" he asked, his gold chain glinting in the afternoon sun as he bent down.

Stuffing the lighter in his pocket, Travis got to his feet.

"What's the matter?" The man laughed. "Cat got your tongue?"

"I'm not s'posed to talk to strangers," he answered.

A shallow, unsettling smile unfurled across the man's lips. "Well, I'm no stranger. I'm a friend of Maura's. Is she home—"

"Who is it, Travis?"

The man straightened. "I'm sorry to bother you," he said, dipping his head in Charlie's direction as she walked across the porch, "but I'm—"

"He's looking for Grams."

House watched Charlie casually grasp Travis by the shoulders and pull him toward her. "She's not here right now."

"Well, that's a shame," the man replied, climbing the steps. "Do you know when she'll be home?"

"No." Charlie began backing up, dragging Travis with her. "But if you want to leave a message," she said, bumping against the screen door, "I'll be sure she gets it." As she fumbled behind her for the handle, the man closed the distance between them with his long stride.

"I already left her a message," he said in a low voice, putting his face close to hers. "Just tell her I'll see her soon." His creepy smile reemerged as he reached out and patted Travis on the head. "Okay, then. You kids have a nice day."

As he turned and started across the porch, Charlie opened the door and jerked her brother inside.

"He was weird."

"I know," said Charlie, shoving the hook on the screen door through its eye-latch.

House clenched and unclenched its shutters, making them bang against its siding as it watched the man, who was whistling a toneless tune, get in his car and drive away.

~

The smell of coffee and burnt toast permeated the fruit-striped wallpaper that had been pasted over the other half-dozen or so layers adorning the kitchen; aside from having been sloppily applied, the recent addition was also terribly thin, allowing the print of copper pans and rolling pins underneath it to bleed through.

As the sun began to fill the small space, House let its attention wander from the papered walls to the top of the refrigerator, where it settled on Maura's bottle of gin that she kept stashed behind a box of cereal. Having no desire to dwell on her noticeable absence, however, it forced its gaze to move on—only to have it slam into Charlie. Standing in front of the sink with her arms folded, House's young master stared out the window, her pale blue eyes as haunted as the expression on her face.

Yesterday afternoon, Charlie had met an unshaven, bleary-eyed Ed at the door, and told him about the strange visit from the man, prompting him to stay until Shay returned from the hospital. After playing an obligatory hand of five-card stud with him and Travis, Charlie had then absconded to her room, yet in spite of House's intentional rattles, groans, and creaks…refused to engage in any further conversations with it.

The sound of footsteps caused House to glance across the room, where it found a haggard-looking Shay coming up the cellar steps carrying a basket of wet clothes.

"Charlie, I need your help."

Turning from the window, Charlie obediently followed her mother out of the kitchen.

"Travis," said Shay, stepping around him as he sat on the floor watching *Underdog*, "I'm going outside to hang laundry, so I need you to listen for the phone."

"Okay."

Shay stopped in the entryway and looked back. "And *answer* it if it rings."

"Okay," he repeated, the dull colors of the cartoon reflecting in his eyes.

Letting out a rankled sigh, Shay stepped through the door and headed around to the side yard.

House saw Charlie shiver in her short-sleeve shirt as her bare feet picked their way across the wet, soggy leaves.

"I don't know how long I'll be," said Shay, setting the basket on the ground, "but while I'm gone, I want you and Travis to stay inside with the door locked. Don't open it for anyone."

"We won't."

"There's a can of tuna in the cabinet—and there should be enough mayonnaise in the fridge to mix it with."

"There's still some chicken left, too," Charlie said, watching her hang a pair of Travis' jeans on the frayed rope serving as the clothesline.

As Shay slid a clothespin over the denim waistband, Charlie plucked one of her tops from the tangle of clothes in the basket. "Mom, can Travis and I please go with you to see Grams?"

"I'm sorry, sweetheart," she said, grabbing the shirt and giving it a vicious snap to rid it of its wrinkles, "but kids aren't allowed in the unit she's in."

Disappointment flooded Charlie's face. Bending down, she picked up a tube sock from the pile.

"Listen, I know how badly you want to see her, and I promise I'll take you just as soon as she gets moved to a private room."

"Is she?"

"Is she *what*?" Shay mumbled around the clothespin she'd stuck between her lips.

"*Is* Grams going to be moved to a private room?"

Fastening the clothespin to the shirt, Shay dropped her gaze and shoved the basket farther down the line with her foot.

"Mom?"

Shay reached for a towel, and then slowly lifted her eyes—which were partially obscured by her puffy, drooping lids—to meet Charlie's. "She's made it through the first thirty-six hours, so that's a really good sign," she said, conjuring a smile that looked to House to be as fake as the optimism in her voice sounded.

Seeming to notice it as well, Charlie hung the sock on the rope and reached for another one.

For the next few minutes they worked in tandem silence until all that was left in the basket was a sheet.

"I'm going to try and get home before dark," said Shay, handing Charlie one of the corners, "but it all depends on when I get to talk to Gram's doctor. So, I need you to make sure Travis takes a shower and that his math is finished, because I know he came home with multiplication problems on Friday."

"All right," said Charlie, pulling the sheet taut.

"We're all going to have to get up earlier than usual tomorrow..." Shay paused to arch her brow at Charlie. "Which means getting out of bed the first time I ask."

"Can't we stay home one more day?"

"No, I can't miss anymore work, and you two have to go back to school."

Charlie's chin flattened and began to quiver like a child's. "Please?" she begged.

"Sweetheart," Shay said, letting go of the sheet, "I know you're embarrassed over what happened the other night, but you can't become a recluse—"

"You don't understand," Charlie snapped. "And you never will!"

Her words left a visible mark on Shay's cheek. Turning away so that her face was hidden, she rigidly bent down to retrieve the basket.

"Mom..." The anger in Charlie's voice changed to alarm as her focus shifted to the front yard.

Silence.

"*Mom.*"

Shay eventually looked up. "What?" Following her daughter's gaze, she saw a black sedan coming up the drive. "Is that the man from yesterday?" she asked, squinting into the sun.

"I don't think so."

The car rolled to a stop behind Maura's station wagon and shut off its engine.

"Stay here," Shay said to Charlie, starting across the yard—but her footsteps faltered when the doors opened, and two men dressed in formal-looking, dark-green uniforms got out. "Oh—God!" The basket fell from her grasp. "N-no!"

Hearing her mother's screams, Charlie sprinted around the wooden laundry post.

Shay staggered forward with a whimper and then her knees buckled, plunging them to the ground. Clutching at the damp earth, her whole body shook as she lifted her head toward the heavens and let out a guttural cry.

Chapter 25

Drops of rain fell upon House's sagging roof and slid down its shingles like dirty tears as it stared at the empty cot sitting against the far wall.

Nine days had passed since House had learned that its young master would never be coming home. Nine exhaustive days filled with darkness, longing…and unmitigated grief. Grief tinged with anger so pervasive it left no room to breathe.

A subtle vibration forced House's despondent gaze upwards, where just below the constant footsteps of strangers, muffled whispers, and faint clinks of forks touching plates…it came across a fly entangled in a web. As the insect's wings became detached from its tiny, flailing body in its attempt to free itself, a large peanut-shaped spider rapidly descended from the exposed floor joists above and, after administering what would be a fatal bite, began to wrap the paralyzed creature in silk with its long, paper-thin legs.

Having little desire to watch the carnage, and even less desire to remain in a space that its young master would never again occupy, House swallowed the bitter rainwater that had pooled in its eaves and slowly turned its gaze to the living room.

Dozens of people, dressed in various shades of black, were milling quietly about…like a fragmented flock of seagulls with no direction. Some of them stood alone, their rigid expressions either fixed on the window beside the fireplace or cup of coffee in their hands, while others were gathered in small clusters, speaking in awkward tones about the weather—yet House noticed most had congregated in the kitchen, where a spread of casseroles, sandwiches, and desserts filled every inch of the rectangular table.

"Excuse me, please..."

Upon hearing a familiar voice, House glanced across the kitchen and saw Ed Ratner; nearly unrecognizable in his dark suit and tie, he patiently weaved his way through the crowd and out the saloon doors, which had been crudely fixed to stay open.

"Here you go," he said, coming around the front of the chair that Maura was sitting in.

As she reached for the cup of coffee he was offering, House was taken aback by how frail she appeared; her eyes were just mere shells, sunk deep into their sockets, and the dark rouge covering her cheeks only emphasized her pallor. She was a far cry from the spry woman who, just a little over two weeks ago, had shoved the barrel of a gun under a man's chin.

Ed bent down and patted the left breast pocket of his suit. "I made it just the way you like it," he said, giving her a wink.

Maura lifted her brow, pulling one side of her lips into a feeble smile.

"Shay...can I bring you a plate of something?"

House looked to its right and saw her sitting on the couch with two women huddled on either side of her, both of whom appeared eager to help.

"No, thank you," Shay answered in a hollow-sounding voice.

The woman on the left, a plump brunette, exchanged a disparaging glance with the other one, a slender redhead with big green eyes and a long, thick braid running down her bumpy spine.

Over the past few days, Shay had rarely spoken and barely eaten; her face was drawn and gaunt, while dark, crescent-shaped circles lined the skin beneath her eyes.

Clearing her throat, the redhead sat forward and reached for Shay's hand. "We wanted to be sure and tell you not to worry about work, because me and Jan," she said, pausing to nod at the brunette, "along with the other girls, are going to cover your shifts for as long as you need."

Shay stared at the woman's fingers as they lay tightly wrapped around her hand, but said nothing.

Heavy footsteps on the porch drew House's attention to the entryway, and as it waited for another mourner to come through the door, its gaze involuntarily drifted to its young masters. Hunkered together on the bottom landing in their Sunday best, their heads were down, and their cheeks notably crusted with dried tears, as Rom, who—other than stealing an occasional glance at Shay—was doing what he could to console them, yet his obvious incompetence only seemed to be making it worse. Travis buried his face between his knees, as hiccupping sobs...one after another, began to rack his small frame.

As the sun sank below the horizon, the clouds opened up the rest of the way, drenching House in a pummeling rain.

~

Night had fallen hard by the time the sea of cars cluttering the drive began to disperse, leaving House's family to grieve alone amongst the deafening quiet once more.

As the last set of tires turned out onto the road, House felt something small and wet fall upon its concrete floor in the cellar, and reluctantly forced its gaze to descend the steps, where it found Shay sitting on the edge of Tyler's cot.

Clutching a rectangular frame to her chest...black tears, breathless and raging, slid down her face as she slowly rocked back and forth.

House heard movement on its steps, and moments later saw Rom appear at the base of the stairwell. Cloaked by the darkness, he stood there watching her—his fingertips dug into the mortared ridge of the cinderblocks—before tenderly calling her name.

Shay stopped rocking, but did not look at him.

"I brought you something," he said, stepping out of the shadows. Making his way over to the cot, Rom held out a glass of water, along with a little white tablet—which House couldn't help noticing was the exact size, shape, and color of the pills he'd stolen from her. "I thought you could use this."

Silence followed his gesture.

"Well, I'll just leave them here," he said, placing both items on the dresser beside her, "in case you change your mind."

A tear beaded on Shay's upper lip as she lowered the picture frame. "Do you remember when this was taken?"

Rom sat down next to her and gave the photo a hesitant glance. "It was just after we brought him home from the hospital," he answered, balling the fingers of his left hand into a fist as if he were fighting to keep his emotions at bay. "It was our first morning as a family."

"I remember holding him in my arms so tight that day, I could feel his little heart beating against mine, and then I promised that I'd always be there for him, and..." Shay's mouth trembled as she shook her head. "That I'd never let anyone hurt him."

Rom's own eyes grew moist, leaving them downcast. "You were a good mother. What happened wasn't your fault."

"Do you think he cried out for me?"

"Shay—"

"It's a question that I keep asking myself over and over."

"Shay..." Rom slowly raised his head. "Please don't do this to yoursel—"

"*Did he?*" Her mouth contorted into an unnatural shape. "Did he cry out for me as he lay scared and dying in that god-forsaken place—wondering why I wasn't there?"

Rom's body gave a visible jerk. "I don't know," he said, his chest heaving as he drew a stuttering breath. "But I do know that he knew you loved him." Clenching his jaw, he swallowed hard several times, before forcing his lips to part again. "I can't say the same about me. I was the one who was never there for him. You were the one that taught him how to tie his shoes, ride a bike...and do a million other amazing things."

"I miss—him—so much," she said in a jagged whisper.

"I know you do," he murmured, using the pad of his thumb to wipe her red and swollen cheeks.

"When I saw him lying in that casket today...I realized that I was never going to see him open his blue eyes again...or hear that shrill fluster in his voice when he gets angry, or see that one unruly blonde curl fall across his forehead when he laughs—" A deep sob replaced the rest of Shay's words.

"It's okay," Rom said, holding her tight.

Turning her face into his neck, Shay's shoulders pitched and bucked as a silent retch fell from the back of her throat...followed by a raw, primal wail.

House shivered—causing the window in the kitchen to rattle—as Shay's inconsolable shriek reverberated off its block walls.

~

Charlie opened the fridge and removed a plate wrapped in tin foil. "Be sure and get some napkins," she said to Travis, shutting the door with her hip.

"Got them," he answered, stuffing them in his pockets before grabbing two bottles of grape Nehi off the counter.

The two of them then made their way into the living room and sat down on the couch beside their grandmother.

Charlie set the plate on the coffee table and peeled back the foil to reveal a dozen or so crustless ham sandwiches. "Would you like one, Grams?" she asked, raising her voice loud enough to be heard over the police sirens on TV.

"No, thank you," she said, keeping her gaze, which House considered to be as distant as it was troubled, semi-aimed in the direction of the chase scene that was currently unfolding on *Adam-12*.

House watched Travis and Charlie devour their sandwiches and reach for more. Neither of them had eaten today, as they'd both seemed reluctant to do so with complete strangers looking on—and even now as they sat there, blissfully chewing, House could see an almost guilt-like expression resonating behind Charlie's face for enjoying her meal amidst the sporadic, muffled cries of her mother that were emanating from the cellar.

"Can you turn it up?" asked Travis, gesturing at the screen. "Billy can't hear."

"If you would stop slurping your Nehi, we could *all* hear," Charlie snapped, yet grabbed the clunky remote off the table anyway. As she pressed the big rocker button on the left, House felt footsteps that were too heavy to be Shay's walking across its linoleum, and glanced over in time to see Rom come through the doorway.

Travis set his Nehi down. "Are you leaving, Dad?"

Rom stopped in front of the television and turned. The rims of his eyelids were red and brimming with tears. "Yeah..." he said, then cleared his throat, as if he were trying to remove the brokenness in his voice. "Can I get a hug before I go?"

House's young masters stood and edged their way around the coffee table.

"When will I see you again?" asked Travis, hugging his waist.

"I don't know, but I need you to promise me something."

Travis drew back and licked the grape soda from his lips. "What?"

Dropping to one knee, Rom wrapped his hands, which House noticed were trembling badly, around their outer wrists and looked up at them. "Promise me that you'll be good for your mom and Grams."

Charlie rolled her shoulder, brushing a rogue tear from her cheek. "I promise."

"So do me and Billy," said Travis.

Rom pulled them tight against him. "I love you...don't ever forget that," he said in a strained whisper. As he got to his feet, his fractured gaze gravitated to his ex-mother-in-law. "Take care."

Maura stared back at him—her own eyes swimming with emotion—and dipped her head. "You too, Rom."

Disappearing through the entryway, Rom slipped out the door and stumbled down the steps. As he hurried along the uneven path, a sliver of moonlight fell around him, allowing House to see that his hardened jaw was now drenched in tears.

His pace—and breath—quickening, the bottoms of his boots slapped against the puddles of water as he unbuttoned his collar and jerked his tie loose. "Fuck!" he screamed, bringing his fists down hard against the roof of his car.

The noise ricocheted through the trees like a gunshot, sending a flock of nesting starlings scattering into the sky.

Wiping his eyes with his knuckles, Rom stared solemnly at the large dent above the driver's side door as he reached into the pocket of his blazer and pulled out a small vial.

Narrowing its gaze, House watched him tap out a white powdery substance along the webbing between his thumb and forefinger…and snort it up his left nostril.

Respite from his grief came four and a half minutes later. Slipping into his car with a glassy, but euphoric expression, Rom started the engine and tore off down the driveway.

Chapter 26

Maura gathered her nightgown around her as she watched Charlie pull the velvet green curtains—serving as her bedroom door—the rest of the way closed. "You don't have to keep doing this," she said, repeating the words she'd stubbornly stated every night for the past three nights. "I'm perfectly capable of staying in my own room by myself."

"I know you are, Grams," Charlie replied in a tired voice, "but if you were to need anything, we wouldn't be able to *hear* you from upstairs. And besides, I really don't mind. Sleeping with you is a nice change from Travis."

Maura let go of a clipped laugh. "Sleeping on a bed of *nails* would be a nice change from Travis."

"Did you take your medication?" asked Charlie, gesturing at the bottle on the nightstand as she leaned over to turn down the bed.

"Yes."

Charlie straightened and gave her grandmother a skeptical look.

"Do you want to check under my tongue?" she asked, arching her brows.

"No, I just want you to get better."

"I know you do." Maura let go of a small sigh as she sat down on the edge of the mattress. "Is your mom still asleep in...the cellar?" she asked, seeming incapable at the moment of speaking Tyler's name.

"Do you want me to wake her?"

"No, just let her be," Maura said, flipping back the corner of the blanket.

Climbing in beside her, Charlie pulled the covers over her and turned out the light.

As darkness fell across the room, House shifted its attention to the dimly lit cellar and saw that the pill Rom had left on the dresser was gone. Curled up on her side, Shay lay unmoving; her eyes were closed, her breathing was deep...and her face was devoid of the unrelenting anguish that had been haunting it for the past nine days.

"Grams, have you ever sensed anything strange inside the house?"

House swerved its gaze back to Maura's darkened bedroom.

"Strange like what? You mean like a presence?"

"I guess," said Charlie.

"In other homes that I've lived in, yes—but not this one," Maura answered. "Why are you asking?"

House heard its young master take in a small breath. "I can't really explain it, but sometimes when I touch the wall...I can feel things. It's like the house is alive."

Pure, unadulterated joy swept through House; crackling and tingling like an electrical spark behind its plaster, the surge was so great, it made the door that led to the deck rattle against its jamb.

Charlie jerked her head up, and House saw the rigid outline of her face as she sat motionless, listening.

"There are things in this world that we may never understand," Maura said softly, "but they do exist — even if we can't see them."

A flash of lightning briefly lit up the bedroom, and House caught the anxiety in its young master's eyes. Knotting her fingers together, Charlie lay back against her pillow. "How do you know if these things are good or evil?"

The sheets rustled as Maura rolled over on her side. "It's been a really long day, sweetheart. Can we talk about this in the morning?"

Thunder rumbled overhead, vibrating the pictures on the wall.

"Grams?"

"What?" answered Maura in a tone that was running thin on patience.

"If your gift is through touch, like mine, why do you read people's palms?"

"Because it's easier for them to believe that their future is coming from the lines in their hands rather than what I see. My mother taught me that."

Rain began to peck at the windows as a jagged bolt of lightning shot out of the clouds, illuminating the sky as its branch-like tethers darted toward the ocean.

"When you were holding Tyler's picture that night...the night you had your heart attack," Charlie said, the low tenor of her voice resonating indifference for the approaching storm, "did you see him die?"

A long bout of silence followed Charlie's question before Maura's voice breached the darkness. "No, the only thing I saw was the floor coming toward me."

As the wind shook through the trees, House picked up on the distinct sound of Maura's fingernails scraping against the skin behind her ear.

~

A deafening crack of thunder jarred House from a deep sleep. In its waking confusion, it was momentarily surrounded by a semblance of peace...but then the memory of the horrific tragedy that had befallen its family came rushing back, flooding its walls with grief. Glancing at the digital clock on Maura's nightstand, it saw that there were still several hours to go before dawn.

Drops of cold, stinging rain began to pelt House's windows in the entryway, making it turn its bleary gaze to the front yard. As it stared into the blackness, it noticed a tiny speck of orange light hovering beside the thick trunk of the sycamore.

Feeling a stab of apprehension, House glanced toward the driveway and saw the Pontiac belonging to Shay, as well as Maura's station wagon, but no other vehicle was in sight.

Sheet lightning suddenly lit up the sky. Swerving its attention back to the tree, House saw a tall, hulking figure standing under it. The cascading darkness quickly engulfed the figure once more, and

House leaned forward as it strained to see beyond the realm of its porch light.

Seconds later, another flash of lightning came, and House caught sight of the figure moving toward its porch. The smell of cigarette smoke and bourbon preceded the figure's footsteps, which were heavy and uneven, as they fell upon its wooden planks — eventually revealing the rain-soaked face of the man who had hurt Maura.

Carrying something in his right hand, he set it down and opened the screen door, which had been left unlocked.

House straightened and centered the mass of its weight on the floor joist in its living room; the sudden shift in pressure caused the front door to twist against its jamb, making it nearly impossible to open. With its breath suspended in its creosote-lined flue, House fought to remain still as it focused on the small crowbar the man had pulled from his coat...yet after a few moments, its termite-riddled joist began to tremble.

The man wedged the flat tip of the bar between the lock and jamb and forced it open, then picking up what looked like a metal can, stepped inside the foyer, where he wasted little effort in gaining entry through its hollow-core door.

House began to rock back and forth on its foundation, doing everything it could to wake its family — but it was the man bumping into the lamp on the end table that made Maura sit up in bed. Clicking on the light beside her, she threw back the covers, and as she started across the room, House felt something wet seeping into its carpet just outside her curtained door.

"Travis," she said in a low hiss, parting the curtains with her arm, "what are you doi—" Maura's hands flew to her mouth as she let out a muffled scream.

Charlie's feet hit the floor with a thud. "Grams?"

Maura held out her arm for Charlie to stop. "What do you want"—her voice shook—"you have no right to be here."

The light escaping Maura's bedroom shone on the man's grizzled face. His eyes, although glassy and unfocused, were dark with fury. "I told you I'd be back."

"I'll do whatever you want," she pleaded, the words bursting from her lips in a ragged breath as he sloppily finished emptying the contents of the can onto the carpet, paneling, and couch. "Please, just let my family go."

Water dripped from the strands of hair plastered to the man's forehead and slid down his tempered jaw. "Because of you, that schoolmarm of a bitch left me and took the shitload of money she'd inherited *with* her," he yelled, throwing the can on the floor. "So, let's just say I'm here to repay the favor."

As the gasoline fumes rose, House felt a tingling sensation behind its kitchen wall—yet kept its focus on what was happening in its living room.

"Please don't do this," Maura begged. "I'll call her and tell her I was wrong."

The man's lacquered gaze narrowed at Maura until they were just two uneven slits. "We're past you doing the right thing—"

"Get out."

House glanced to its left and found Shay standing beside the saloon doors, holding a large carving knife between her hands.

"Get out," she repeated, starting toward him.

"Don't come any closer, Shay," Maura warned, pointing at the floor.

Shay looked down at the dark, wet stain in front of her bare toes; adjusting her grip on the knife, she returned her attention to the intruder. "I've called the police. They're on their way."

A grunted laugh fell from the man's lips as he took a long draw off the half-smoked cigarette that was dangling between them. "I'll be long gone by the time they get here," he said, pulling a matchbook from his pocket, "...and so will all of you." With smoke rolling out of his nostrils, the corners of his mouth twisted into a grotesque smile as he lit a single match, set the entire pack on fire, and then tossed it onto the saturated carpet.

A fireball of blue erupted along the outer edges of the shag pile, devouring its fibers, as well as the varnished hardwood planks underneath it. The flames sprouted higher, climbing the fuel trails of the wood paneling beneath the staircase—and the lower right leg of the man's slacks.

The man didn't notice at first, but when he did, his actions to put it out were slow. Hunching over, he slapped at the fire consuming his leg with the palms of his hands, which only served to fan the flames.

House fought to breathe as thick black smoke and the smell of burning flesh filled the room.

The man removed his coat, and with a howl of slurred obscenities, began to beat it against his leg as he stumbled backward. Making his way outside, he staggered off the porch, then fell onto the wet grass, where he—between the pouring rain and his lurching half-rolls—managed to extinguish the flames.

House moaned in agony as the fire burned a hole through its wood flooring and dropped onto one of its joists.

The glass panes in the window beside the fireplace suddenly cracked and then shattered, sucking the oxygen out of the space with a thunderous boom.

Tendrils of smoke, laced with unbreathable fumes and gases, spread throughout the room, before ascending the stairs like an apparition—where Travis, his face frozen in terror, was squatting.

Letting the knife slip from her grasp, Shay held the crook of her arm across her nose and mouth as she looked through Maura's doorway that had become blocked with waist-high flames. Charlie was standing a few feet beyond the burning threshold with tears streaming down her cheeks as she held on to her grandmother, who was doubled over and coughing. "Take Grams out through the deck," she said, shouting to be heard over the deafening roar.

"What about Travis?" yelled Charlie.

A small flame leapt from the burning paneling and landed on the drapes that hung in the doorway. Fire began to dance across the velvet folds, igniting the fabric in a roaring blaze.

"Go!" Shay gestured at Charlie. "I'll get Travis!"

Dark smoke, shaped like angry fists, poured into House's vents, as the faux paneling disintegrated. There was a sharp hiss, and then the rubberized cloth that had been wrapped around its knob and tube wires for insulation burst into flames. House writhed in pain as its wooden laths and horsehair plaster were consumed by the blistering fire.

"Mom!" screamed Travis, clutching his teddy bear to his chest, as orange-tongued flames began to lick the wooden balusters on the staircase.

"I'm coming!" Dropping to her knees, Shay crawled around the smoldering couch and over to the carpeted landing, which House noticed had taken on a throbbing reddish glow. "Take my hand," she shouted, extending her arm.

Travis coughed and shook his head. "Billy's still upstairs!"

"I'll get Billy in a minute, but right now, I need you to take my hand!"

"I can't leave him!"

"Travis, come on," pleaded Shay, her fingers quivering as she stretched out her hand.

"Not without Billy!"

The balusters ignited, engulfing the banister within seconds.

Shay got to her feet and lunged for Travis. Wrapping him in her arms, she blindly carried him down the remaining steps before falling in front of the entryway.

As the wail of sirens sounded in the distance, the combination of the layered smoke and radiant heat raised House's temperature to an unbearable level. The glass shades on the wagon wheel exploded, followed by a brilliant flash of yellow—as every piece of furniture in the living room instantaneously erupted into flames.

Taking in a noxious breath, House's vision dimmed as the raging inferno swept over it.

Chapter 27

Rivulets of black water ran down the smoldering walls, feeding the ribbons of smoke still swirling out of the ten-foot diameter hole the firemen had made in the roof.

Listing heavily on its foundation, House watched as the men trudged through the soot-covered shell that used to be its living room, putting out hotspots along its charred floor. Furniture, pictures, lamps…everything its family owned…lay strewn about, having melted into unrecognizable pieces of debris. Most of its hand-carved oak trim, which surrounded its ceiling, windows, and doors looked like blackened alligator skin.

"Is she going to be all right?"

House shifted its weary gaze to the driveway, where just beyond Ed, who stood talking to the sheriff, was a red and white ambulance with the words, *Fire and Rescue* painted on its sides.

A dark-haired man, wearing navy slacks and a crisp white shirt with a fireman's badge pinned to it, turned to look at Maura as he knelt beside Shay in the grass. "The burns on her feet aren't too bad, but she inhaled a lot of smoke," he replied, hanging his stethoscope around his neck. "We need to take her to the hospital for—"

"I'm fine," said Shay in a hoarse voice.

The man glanced back at her. "I know it's hard for you to be the patient, Shay," he said, giving her a small smile, "but you need to let me do my job."

"What I *need* is to go back inside the house," she replied, trying to stand. "I have to get Tyler's things."

"Whoa," he said, holding her down, "just take it easy—"

"*You* take it easy," Shay said, raising her voice as she pushed his hands away. "I need his things."

"Shay…" Maura hurriedly knelt beside her. "We can't go in there right now."

"I just want his picture. I'm not going anywhere without it!" Shay's face—exhausted, grief-stricken, and covered in soot—flooded with tears. "I need it!" Clutching the sleeves of Maura's nightgown, Shay bowed her head and began to sob. "I need it…"

The paramedic exchanged a sympathetic glance with Maura. "I'll see what I can do," he murmured, getting to his feet.

"What's this button for?"

As Maura cradled Shay in her arms, House shifted its attention to its young masters. Travis was sitting behind the steering wheel of a pumper truck with a gray wool blanket wrapped around his smudged pajamas. A kind fireman sat next to him, explaining what all the switches and gages meant. Charlie sat on the other side of Travis, and even though she looked no worse for the wear, House could see her eyes reeling with devastation as she watched the smoke drifting across the gray sky.

"Maura?"

Returning its gaze to the driveway, House saw Ed walking away from the sheriff's patrol car.

"I'll be right back," she said to Shay in a reassuring voice, then pushing herself up, made her way over to where Ed was waiting. "What's wrong?"

"They caught the guy. He turned up at St. Mary's emergency room a few hours ago, smelling of gas, and seeking treatment for third-degree burns on his leg. He's handcuffed to a hospital bed as we speak."

A semblance of relief engulfed Maura's tired eyes. "Well, that's the first bit of good news I've heard in a long time."

Cupping her chin in his hand, Ed tilted it toward him. "You were damn lucky," he said, his lips flattening into a grim line. "This guy has a rap sheet a mile long, and is wanted in Bakersfield for two counts of aggravated assault and one count of murder."

"Luck had nothing to do with it," said Maura, drawing her head back.

Ed shifted his weight to his other foot and scowled.

"Well it *didn't*," she said.

"Excuse me, ma'am?" A man wearing a fireman's helmet and flame-retardant coat over a white shirt and tie came up behind her. "I've finished my investigation. It's pretty cut and dry, no surprises. I'll get the report written up and send a copy to the sheriff for you."

"How bad's the damage?" asked Ed, nodding at House.

The man took off his helmet and ran his hands through his thick brown hair. "About ninety percent of the fire was contained to the front room. There's extensive damage to it and the interior stairwell. It was a good thing we got here when we did. Old houses like this can go up like kindling."

Maura glanced at Shay. "When can we go inside and get a few things?"

"It's gonna be a while."

Ed reached out to shake his hand. "Thank you."

As the man walked away, Maura shivered beneath her blanket.

"Why don't you let me drive you and the kids back to my house?" Ed said, draping his coat over her shoulders. "We'll stop and pick up some breakfast along the way, and then you all can get a hot shower and some sleep."

"As tempting as all that sounds, I'm going to ride to the hospital with Shay. I don't think it's a good idea to leave her alone. Could you take the kids, thoug—"

"*Maura.*"

"*Ed,*" she said, mimicking his tone.

"You've been out of the hospital for all of three days, and—"

"Four."

"You're missing my point."

"Well, what *is* your point—because you don't seem to be doing a very good job of making it."

Ed sighed and rubbed his jaw. "I want you to come live with me. You, Shay, and the kids."

A gust of wind blew between them, making the collar of Ed's coat flap against Maura's cheeks as she stared up at him.

He shrugged. "Aren't you going to say anything?"

"Your house is a pigsty."

"Well, yeah—but it's got three bedrooms, and I can fix up the basement for Shay. I mean, it's not big by any stretch of the imagination, but it's comfortable."

Maura began shaking her head. "Edward Theodore Ratner, have you lost your ever-loving mind? Do you have any idea what you're sayi—"

Ed pressed his finger to her lips, silencing her. "I know *exactly* what I'm saying," he replied, looking into her eyes. "And the point I'm trying to get through that thick skull of yours, is that I love you, and I want you, and Shay, and those grand-rugrats of yours to come and live with me."

House felt the charred sill plate that its front floor joist was resting upon begin to move beneath the enormous weight it was under. Moments later, it slipped from the foundation, tilting House farther onto its side as Maura threw her arms around Ed.

Chapter 28

House stared curiously at the tall, wiry man with silver hair and dull gray eyes. Over the past three years, House had only seen the man who owned it on paper a handful of times, yet he'd been here twice in the last six days. He'd walked around the rooms with that petulant look of his that seemed to House to be permanently tattooed on his face, barking orders at the man who was with him, telling him the things he wanted repaired—and the things that could be covered up with new carpet and paint.

Today, however, he'd come to see Shay. "Sign here," he said, peering at her over the rim of his glasses.

They stood in the middle of the kitchen, and although it had not caught fire, the ceiling, cabinets, countertops, table, and appliances all looked as if they had been sprayed with black paint. The saloon doors—their wooden slats charred and blistered—now hung in a crooked manner above the threshold, while the linoleum beneath it lay scorched and bubbled.

"And don't expect your cleaning deposit to be refunded," he added.

Shay took the clipboard without speaking and scrawled her name at the bottom of the paper, then handing him the keys, turned around and, favoring her right foot, began walking away.

As she started across the living room floor, House saw her blue eyes struggling to stay afloat amidst the swells of profound grief that it knew was never going to leave her.

~

"This is the last of it," said Maura, handing a small lamp to Ed.

House's family had packed what hadn't been damaged by the fire and loaded it into a pickup truck Ed had borrowed from a friend. The smaller items had been divided between Shay's and Maura's vehicles. What they had left wasn't much, but House was glad that all of Tyler's belongings had gone unscathed.

Ed finished tying the rope around the luggage rack of Maura's station wagon and gave it a tug to make sure the cardboard boxes strapped beneath it were secure. "Are you sure you're okay to drive?"

"Of course I'm okay to drive," she snapped. "I'm not an invalid."

"I didn't say you were," said Ed, letting out a long-suffering sigh.

Maura shook her head. "I'm sorry…I just…" Her voice, overwhelmed with emotion, trailed off.

"I know," he said, wrapping his arms around her.

Tears began to slide down Maura's cheeks as she buried her face in his shirt.

Cradling the back of her head in his hand, Ed tenderly pressed his lips to her temple. "It's gonna be okay," he whispered.

~

"Yuck—even my underwear smells like smoke!"

"I know," said Charlie. "Just put them in the bag, and we'll wash everything at Mr. Ratner's."

Travis tossed them in the garbage bag that sat on the floor between them. As he reached inside the drawer for another pair, he glanced at the space beside his right shoulder and nodded. "I'll ask her."

"Ask me what?"

"Billy wants to know if you're enjoying having your own room?"

House had learned from Travis just this morning that Billy had miraculously survived the fire by climbing out the window, scaling the roof, and jumping down onto the deck.

"I guess," answered Charlie, folding her beloved jeans into a neat square, before placing them in the bag. "What about you?"

"It's different, because I've either shared a room with you, or slept in bunk beds with Tyler in our old house. I've never been alone, until now."

"You're not alone, though," she said distractedly. "You have Billy."

"Billy's not coming."

Charlie straightened. "What do you mean he's not coming?"

"Travis," Ed called, "if you're riding with me, you need to get down here."

Shoving the rest of his underwear into the bag, he turned and started for the door.

"What do you *mean* he's not coming?" Charlie repeated.

House's youngest master paused in the doorway. "Billy likes it here and wants to stay. And besides..." Travis shrugged. "This has always been his home."

Charlie stiffened as he gave a small wave to the empty space in front of the chest of drawers before making his way down the now-open staircase.

House's gaze shot to the chest, where it stared intently at the stationary shadow beside it, waiting for a flicker, or a shimmer of movement of any kind...but saw nothing.

After a moment, House shifted its attention to Charlie, and felt an overwhelming sense of sorrow beginning to stir inside its walls as she twisted the ends of the garbage bag around her fingers and started across the room.

As she neared the threshold, she stopped and looked back—then without warning, dropped the bag and placed her hand firmly against the wall.

No longer able to lift itself up, House's breath, saturated with ashes and soot, crackled through its vents as it shook with broken glee.

Charlie's chin began to quiver. "I'm going to miss you too." Wiping at her tears, she slowly lowered her hand. "Goodbye," she whispered.

Chapter 29

"Here's one, Daddy."

"Oh, good job, Rylee. Put it in here." The angry woman's husband extended a cardboard box to his daughter.

With a grin that covered most of her chubby face, the little girl placed the candy bar wrapper in it, and then resumed her task of searching for more trash — while House and its ever-growing resentment sullenly watched.

Although multiple stacks of concrete blocks had been placed under its scorched sill plate in order to lift it back onto its foundation, House's rooms, black as a raven's wing and stifling, pined in musty, undisturbed silence.

House did not know the exact number of years that had passed since Charlie and her family had left, but it did know that the string of occupants, as well as the landlords who'd come after, had been mostly unremarkable.

"Daddy?"

The man turned his attention to Harper, his oldest daughter, who looked to House to be about five.

"When can we go inside?" she asked, wisps of blonde hair fluttering across her rosy cheeks. "I'm cold."

Straightening, the man glanced at the large truck that was backed up to the Victorian's front porch. "Let's give Mommy a little while longer to tell the movers where to put everything."

Harper shifted her feet at his reply. "But I'm really cold."

"I'm *weally* cold too, Daddy," said Rylee.

The man set the box on the ground and took their tiny hands in his. "I know you are," he answered, pausing to warm their fingers with his breath. "How about if we finish picking up the trash on this side of the yard, and then I'll find a quiet place upstairs, where you guys will be out of Mommy's way and can watch cartoons on your tablets?"

"Deal," said Harper, scurrying past him.

"*Deawel*," Rylee repeated.

"All right, then...back to work, you." Leaning forward, he planted several kisses in rapid succession beneath her chin.

Rylee scrunched up her face and giggled.

A tender smile found its way onto the man's lips as he watched her turn and toddle across the uneven yard.

"Daddy?"

"What?" he asked, looking over his shoulder.

Harper was standing beside the wrought-iron fence, her eyes curiously fixated on House. "Do you think it's haunted?"

"There's no such thing," he said, walking toward her. "Remember the talk we had a few months ago? Those are just stories made up to scare you."

She wrapped her fingers around the rusty iron bars and wrinkled her nose. "Well, it sure is ugly."

"It's not ugly, Harper," he replied, kneeling in the grass beside her. "It's beautiful...and you want to know why?"

"Why?"

"Do you love Hoppy, your stuffed rabbit?"

"Uh-huh."

"And how many times has Mommy had to sew Hoppy's leg back on?"

"Lots."

"That's right, and besides that...his fur is all matted and dirty, and the tip of his ear is gone where you've chewed on it."

Harper cocked her head to the side in the same condescending manner House had seen her mother do it. "What does Hoppy have to do with that house being ugly?"

Her father pushed his glasses back up the bridge of his nose and sighed. "Well, Hoppy came to be in that condition because you loved on him so much. It's the same way with that house," he said, peering at it through the iron railing. "It's just been well-loved."

The man's words, although misspoken, caused a feeling of warmth to trickle through House—yet the sound of tires spinning on gravel made it dissipate before it had a chance to grasp hold of it.

"Look, Daddy…"

Following Harper's finger, the man's gaze shifted to House's driveway.

House did the same and saw two cars approaching. As they rolled to a stop, it recognized the first one as belonging to the real estate agent from the other day. Sliding out from behind his steering wheel, the man pulled his cell phone from his blazer and began typing on the screen with his thumbs as he waited for the driver of the other car to emerge.

After a few moments, the door to a metallic blue Honda swung open, and a tall woman, bearing porcelain skin and long coppery brown tresses, which had been pulled into a low ponytail between her shoulders, appeared.

"Well, this is it," said the agent.

House saw the woman look at its dilapidated exterior with an expression that bordered on indifference before retrieving a large suitcase and backpack from the trunk of her car.

"Do you need some help with that?"

"No," she answered, hooking her arm through the strap of the backpack, "I've got it."

The accommodating smile pushing against the agent's bearded cheeks evaporated. Turning around, he started down the weed-infested sidewalk. "This way."

As the woman followed at a distance, a fervor of excitement began to stir inside House, kicking up a layer of dust embedded in its carpet.

"Do you think she's moving in?"

"It kind of looks like it."

"Do you think she has kids?"

In the corner of its peripheral vision, House saw the little girls waving at the woman, their faces pressed up against the bars, as they fired one question after another at their father…who had his hand up as well.

Their incessant chatter and movements were hard to miss—yet House could tell by the way the woman abruptly shifted her gaze to the porch that she was pretending she had.

"Your new neighbors seem friendly," said the agent, removing the black security box from the handle around House's front door. "I'm surprised to see them moving in already, though. The last time I was here, the siding wasn't even finish—"

"Do you have the keys?"

"Uh, yeah…" Typing a four-digit code into his phone, the bottom of the box opened. "Here you go," he said, dumping a single key from it into her waiting palm.

House felt the grooves of the key begin to bump against the lock's worn pins.

"So, are you moving here for work or—"

"Are you sure this is the right key?"

"Uh…you just have to jiggle it."

House saw the woman purse her lips at his answer as she gripped the head of the key tighter. After several attempts, the grooves finally caught the lock and the cylinder turned, sending fresh air and sunlight spilling inside House's entryway as the door fell open.

"The water and gas have been turned on, but I was told the electric company wouldn't be able to get out here until later this afternoon. There's a coffee shop with WiFi two miles that way," said the agent, pointing in the direction of the ever-dwindling town, "if you want to wait—"

"I'll manage, thank you," she replied, setting her suitcase inside the door.

"Okay, well if you need anything or have any questions, here's your landlord's name and number. Oh, and he wanted me to remind you that if you should decide to buy the property, your rent would be applied toward your down paym—"

"Got it," she said, plucking the card from his sausage-like fingers. "You have a nice day now, Brad."

House was uncertain if the bulging knot that suddenly appeared beneath Brad's beard was due to the woman's patronizing tone, or the pithy look emanating from her whiskey-colored eyes; whatever the reason, it caused him to give her a curt nod in response. "You too," he said, then turning away, silently mouthed an unkind remark as he yanked the For Rent/Sale sign out of the ground and tossed it into the trunk of his car.

The woman watched him get in and start the engine, then—appearing unimpressed by the gunning of the accelerator and spray of gravel as he drove away—stepped inside and closed the door, locking it behind her.

A ringing sound began to echo throughout House's entryway, yet with its landline having been silent for years, it looked to its new occupant as she pulled her cell phone from her pocket.

Her eyebrows slanted downward as she stared at the picture of a dark-haired man smiling up at her from the screen. Dropping her backpack on the floor, she smashed her thumb against the red button beneath his face.

Moments later, a narrow beam of light shot out of the back of the phone. The woman held it in front of her as she moved from the darkened entryway into the living room, barely taking notice of the sparse furnishings that Eustace Powell, House's miserly and crotchety owner for the past two years, had provided, and into the kitchen, where she opened the curtains above the sink before picking up one of the mismatched chairs sitting beside the table.

House curiously watched her carry the chair back through the living room and into the entryway— which was no longer obstructed by a paneled wall— and wedge it underneath the doorknob.

Next, she stepped over to the window and slid her fingers between the vinyl blinds, parting them just enough to peer out. Her gaze swept in a methodic fashion across the drive, front yard, and as much of the side yard as it could—where it narrowed upon spotting her neighbors, who were walking the fence line, still searching for trash.

Seeming satisfied, the woman bent down to take off her shoes, but stopped upon noticing the condition of the carpet. Letting out a heavy sigh, she instead made her way into the small sunroom that had been set up as an office. As she shined the light from her cell phone along its barren walls and delaminating desk, the device rang again, causing the disenchantment on her lips to spread to her face as she looked at the screen.

House peered over her shoulder and saw that it was the same man as before.

She stabbed the red button once more with her thumb and slammed the phone down on the desk, creating a small fissure in the middle of the screen—which in turn sent a string of colorful profanities hurtling from her mouth.

The sky outside brightened as the low-hanging clouds drifted toward the open sea, bringing the woman's tirade to a swift end as a rectangular slit of light appeared beneath the gap in the door that led outside.

It took several grunts, pushes—and one well-placed kick—for the swollen door to finally relent, and as the woman stepped onto the deck, House heard her take in her breath as her indignant gaze fell upon the ocean. Stretched as far as the eye could see, the calm blue water sparkled in the sunlight, as if millions of tiny diamonds were dancing on the surface.

House gripped its pilings as she walked across its sponge-like boards. Last year, the stairs leading up to the deck from the side yard had fallen into such a state of disrepair, that Eustace Powell—in the name of saving money—had opted to tear them down and close off the entrance using a pair of warped two by fours.

Turning from the flimsy barricade, the woman looked out at the horizon and filled her lungs with the crisp ocean air, giving House the sense that she hadn't breathed in a long time. As the salty spray washed over her face and throat, she closed her eyes and rested her palms on top of the railing, sending a shudder coursing through House as it felt her smooth skin pressing into its weather-eaten wood.

A shadow drifted across the deck, making House absently glance up.

A young seagull was gliding on the wind. After flying past, it angled its gray wing down and circled back, landing on the peak of its roof. House could see a small fish wiggling in its beak. Making several sharp, jerky movements with its head, the bird opened its gullet and swallowed the fish whole, then letting out a noisy squawk, took off for the sky again.

As House watched the gull aim its still-hungry gaze at the ocean, it felt a tremor in its railing and saw that the woman's fingertips had curled around the splintered edge, turning her knuckles white—

while her eyes, now open and distant, were steeped in a glassy haze.

A sharp cry pierced the air, and as the seagull dove headfirst into the churning water, House felt the woman's hands slip from its rail as she turned and started back inside. Her footsteps were quick and sure as they found their way to her backpack, yet it took three attempts for her trembling fingers to latch onto the zipper and pull it open.

As she began rifling through the bag, the sun filtering through the kitchen window cast a dull light into the living room, enabling House to see her hands close around a bottle of tequila. Unscrewing the cap, she sat down on the sofa and pressed it to her lips.

A strong electrical current began to surge through House's knob and tube wiring, which increased in intensity as it jumped to the new wires in the uncovered junction box, making its walls and refrigerator hum with vengeful ferocity.

The noise, as well as the sudden illumination of the seashell-filled lamp sitting on the end table, caused the bottle to slip through the woman's fingers. She managed to catch it by the neck midway down, but not before spilling half of it onto herself and the cushion.

Swearing under her breath, she wiped at the fabric with her palm before hurrying into the kitchen and grabbing the dish towel that was hanging on the oven door. She pressed the towel into the cushion, letting the folds of it absorb the tequila, then straightened and stepped back.

House watched as her gaze panned from the wet spot in the middle of the sofa to the wide brown and green stripes running up and down it. Wadding the towel in her hand, she turned toward the fireplace — where her face flooded with disappointment as she took in her dimly lit surroundings.

Aside from the mismatched furniture, tongue and groove pine had been nailed into House's crumbling plaster walls in the living room. The thin boards, covered in knots, ran in a noticeable slant along the far wall and had been painted white — yet the oils in the wood had seeped through over time, causing large, elongated circles of yellowish-brown stains to form.

House's stone fireplace, which had been sealed off at the chimney, had separated from its hearth, leaving a three-inch gap that had been sloppily filled with mortar. The once beautiful rocks, dug out of the earth over two centuries ago, and carefully hewn by skilled hands — were now coated in visible brush marks of glossy black.

A shrill ring sounded again.

Throwing her head back, the woman stomped across the floor. "Oh my God!" she screamed at the cell phone as she grabbed it off the desk. "Stop calling m—" Her face paled as she looked at the number on the screen. Half-sitting, half-falling into the chair beside it, she hesitantly swiped her thumb over the glass.

"Wren?" said a man's voice. "This is Detective Lintz. I got your message that you left for me telling me that you'd moved. Are you okay?"

"Yes," she said in a raspy whisper.

"Listen, I know it's been a while since we last spoke, but I wanted to give you an update."

The tips of her fingers turned red as she pressed the phone to her ear, waiting.

"I'm sorry, but nothing new has turned up."

Wren squeezed her eyes shut, sending a stream of tears spilling down her cheeks.

"This doesn't necessarily mean we've reached a dead end," he continued, "it's just that without any leads, it's difficult to go forward. But I'm still looking at all the informat—"

She ended the call and dropped the phone on the desk, cracking its screen the rest of the way. Brushing the tears from her face with a set of rigid hands, she let go of the breath she'd been holding and slowly walked out.

As House's troubled new occupant stood in the middle of the living room, staring at everything and nothing at the same time, the sun began to set, waking the shadows. Drifting out of the corners, they slithered across the floor, consuming everything in their path, until the only light left was coming from the lamp on the end table.

Wren's chest suddenly rose and fell, sending a sharp, crackling sob rushing from her lips. Sinking back against the sofa, she took a long, quivering swallow from the bottle, followed by several more, and as dusk changed to night, House noticed that her eyes, which had grown still, no longer seemed to care about what was displayed in front of them…or the turmoil that was raging behind them.

Chapter 30

The hoarse bark of an elephant seal drew House's attention to the shore below, where a hungry pup was crying for its mother—who had abandoned it for the open sea this morning, after mating with a large bull male the day before. It wasn't alone, however. The narrow strip of beach was filled with pups; some were sleeping, some were playing…and some were starving. The latter had been on their own for close to a month, and the stored sustenance of their mother's rich, fattening milk had been spent. They floundered about in small tidal pools scavenging for shrimp, while others braved wading into the frigid surf a few feet from shore, lunging at anything unfortunate enough to be caught in the tide. Weighing in at just over three hundred pounds, they clumsily moved through the water like graceless blobs of silvery-gray flesh.

Of the two dozen females who had given birth, only one remained. House stared at her massive, but scarred body as she slept on the outcropping of rocks next to her pup. Perhaps her reluctance to leave had done more harm to the pup than good—for it would wallow in the surf during low tide with its one front flipper, then exhausted, return to the outcropping.

The sound of a shrieking cat began to bounce off House's walls. Blowing its breath out through its eaves, it turned its gaze inward and glared at the cell phone vibrating across the desk. This was the fifth time in ten minutes it had gone off, pushing the shrill cat screech it made every two seconds to beyond annoying.

House glanced at its new occupant, only to find her exactly where it had left her six hours ago: sprawled on the sofa with her arm slung over her face.

The noise stopped, but started up again, sending the phone plummeting over the front edge of the desk. It landed on the seat of the wooden chair with a clunk, causing the woman to bolt upright.

As the obnoxious ringtone continued, House watched her bleary eyes rapidly come into focus as they zeroed in on the noise. "Fuck!" she croaked in a loud whisper, then getting to her feet, stumbled into the office and grabbed her phone off the chair.

"Dr. Barnes," she said, leaning heavily against the desk as her breath fell out in jagged spurts, "I'm sorry, I'm running a bit late—"

"I don't want to hear any excuses, Wren." A man's stern voice came through the speaker. "You've already missed two appointments this morning, and my secretary has been fielding their angry calls on your behalf."

"I'm sorry," she repeated, squinting at the bright light coming from the screen.

"I *gave* you this job because I'm a firm believer in second chances, but you're trying my patience. If you want to destroy your career, go right ahead— but I'm not letting you take my practice down with you," he said in an unyielding tone. "I've worked too long and hard on securing..."

Holding the phone away from her ear, Wren rubbed her temple.

"...contract just to lose it because of your incompetence. Do we understand each other?"

"Perfectly," she answered, stifling a sigh.

"Well?"

Wren stopped rubbing her temple. "Well, what?"

"Get *going!*" he snapped. "Your eleven o'clock's been waiting for you for the past fifteen minutes."

"Oh—right, sorry. I'm logging on now. And, Dr. Barnes, thank you for giv—"

Three beeps sounded.

"*Twatwaffle,*" she muttered, staring at the blackened screen. Slipping the phone in her pocket, she grudgingly returned to the living room and pulled a battered laptop from her backpack.

After a few moments, a scowling, pale-skinned man with dark hair and spiked blond tips appeared.

"Hello, Milo. I'm sorry to have kept you waiting."

"It's okay, it's not like I have anything *important* to do."

"Again, I apologiz—"

"You're not in the same place." Milo's annoyed expression became distorted as he leaned closer, enabling House to see the pores on his nose. "The picture that's always hanging behind you is gone, and—*holy shit,*" he said, tilting his head, "you look like hell."

Wren adjusted the screen to where only her face was showing, then as an afterthought, straightened her ponytail. "Let's pick up where we left off on Friday."

"So, did you move?"

"You told me you had gotten a job at a restaurant," Wren continued, ignoring his question, "and that you were starting Saturday."

"Oh, yeah," he said, sitting back. "I was working at *Alonzo's Pizza Shack*."

"And how's that been goi—" Wren narrowed her eyes. "What do you mean *was* working?"

Milo's waxen pallor grew dark.

"What happened?"

"What *happened*?"

"Yes," said Wren in a tired voice, "what happened?"

"What happened was that I was busting my ass during the lunch rush, when this bitch accuses me of touching her pizza with my thumb as I'm placing it on the table in front of her. I assured her that I hadn't, but she called me a liar and insisted on getting a new pizza made."

"And what did you do?"

"What do you *think* I did?"

"I don't know, Milo," said Wren, sighing the words, "that's why I'm asking."

"I told her to go fuck her fat self, and then my manager—who'd had it in for me from the start—*fired* me for it!" Milo crossed his arms against his faded Nirvana t-shirt and shrugged. "I mean, can you believe that shit?"

"Prior to you saying those things, did you practice any of the anger management techniques we discussed? Like thinking before you speak...or taking a deep breath and counting to ten?"

Milo dropped his gaze. "No."

"What about your journal? Are you keeping up with it like I asked?"

"Oh, yeah," he answered, lifting his head. "I wrote about that day."

"Can you read that entry to me?"

"Just a sec." Getting to his feet, he disappeared from the screen.

Wren took the opportunity to yawn and dig the sleep from the corners of her eyes.

"Where the *fuck* is it?" House heard Milo say, followed by a drawer slamming.

As Wren waited, her newly un-encrusted eyes spied the bottle of tequila on the coffee table. Her gaze cut back to the screen. There was no Milo — only the sound of more drawers being opened and slammed. Curling her fingers around the bottle, she brought it to her lips, yet before its contents could wash over her tongue, Milo returned to his chair with notebook in hand. "Found it."

"Great," said Wren, feigning enthusiasm as she set the bottle down. "Let's hear it."

Milo flipped the cover of the small notebook open. "I got fired from my shitty job today all because I went off on a woman who called me a liar. Now that I've had time to think about it, I realize that I should've said much worse to her. She got off easy, and so did my asshole manager — who I would've throat-punched if he wasn't still in high school." He closed the notebook and looked up.

Wren stared blankly at him. "Thank you for sharing that."

"Did you like it?" he asked, flashing her a broad grin.

"So, what do you think it was about that woman that set your anger in motion?"

The corners of Milo's mouth reversed direction. "Because she called me a liar."

"And are you still angry with her?"

"Well, *duh*!"

"What do you think would have happened if you'd just walked away from her table and gotten your manager?"

"That dipshit would've taken her side and given her another pizza for free—which is what he ended up doing anyway."

"So, if you had walked away, the woman would have still gotten what she wanted."

Milo's shoulders drooped. "Yeah."

"And you'd still be angry over it."

"Yeah," he said, sliding farther down in his chair.

"But you'd still have…what?"

"My job," he mumbled.

"Yes, your job. A job that you desperately need as part of your agreement you made with the judge. And I'm going to remind you again that I have to write up an evaluation at the end of these sessions, stating whether or not I think you're fit for society." Wren leaned closer to the screen and shook her head. "We're more than halfway through—and I'm not getting a warm fuzzy here, Milo."

He raked his fingers through his pointy hair and sighed. "Do you think I could get my job back if I apologized?" he asked in a dejected voice.

"That's a decision you have to make on your own. But let's say, hypothetically, that you do, and your manager doesn't accept your apology." Wren paused and arched her brows in a hopeful manner. "You would…"

"I would…" Milo's thick unibrow aimlessly followed suit.

Wren nodded emphatically as if she were encouraging a baby to take its first steps. "Would…"

"Flip him the bird and walk away."

Her expression fell flat. "Well that's a start, I guess."

The feeling of footsteps on its porch sent House's gaze swerving outside in time to see a woman in a black puffy coat and green sock hat ring the doorbell.

House's new occupant suddenly stood, dumping the computer off her lap.

"Are you okay?" asked Milo, staring up at her from the floor.

Squatting beside the coffee table, Wren's hand shook as she grasped the corner of the monitor. "Our session's over."

"But what about—"

"I'll credit you for the full hour. Remember what we discussed," she said, rushing the words while peering at the door from behind the rolled arm of the sofa, "and I'll talk to you in a couple of days."

"Okay. Well, wish me luck on—"

With a click of her finger, Milo disappeared.

The doorbell rang again, followed by a series of impatient knocks.

Wren's breath began to quiver.

"Come and play with us...come and play with us."

Turning from the terrified expression plastered to Wren's face, House's baffled gaze began searching for two girls, whose creepy voices were now echoing off its living room walls.

"Come and play with us," they repeated in unison. "Come and play with us."

Reaching behind her, Wren grabbed her phone from her back pocket.

"Come and play with—"

"Zoe," she said in a strained whisper, "I can't talk right now. Somebody's at my door and I don't have a fucking clue who it is!"

House heard the person on the other end laugh. "It's me, dummy. *I'm* at your door."

Clutching her phone to her ear, Wren stood and ran into the foyer, then removing the chair that she'd wedged under the knob, unlocked the door and jerked it open.

The woman on the other side took off her sock hat, revealing a wave of thick reddish-brown hair that fell down around her shoulders. "Surprise!"

House's gaze flitted back and forth between the two women. After several seconds, it came to realize that—aside from Wren's painfully bloodshot eyes—they were mirror images of each other.

"Zoe," said Wren, shaking her head, "what are you doing here?"

"Well, you didn't sound so hot when I talked to you on the phone yesterday morning, so I thought a visit was in order. And..." Zoe pulled a black bottle with red foil wrapped around the cork from her coat. "I brought your favorite," she said, waving it in front of her. "So, what do you say we break in this new house of yours—"

Wren threw her arms around Zoe's neck.

"Aww, it's nice to see you too, sis," she said, hugging her back, yet her smile faded as Wren's shoulders began to shake beneath her hands.

Letting out a muffled sob, Wren buried her face in Zoe's coat.

"Shh..." Zoe whispered, holding her tight as she stroked the back of her head, "it's okay."

Chapter 31

Rolling clouds of steam infiltrated the cracks in House's plastered ceiling, leaving its trusses above it damp with sweat. As the moist vapors clung to the gold-veined mirror over the sink, the water in the shower shut off with a heavy clunk. After a moment, Wren drew back the mildewed curtain and stepped out.

House watched her begin to dry herself off with one of the thin, stiff towels left behind by a previous occupant, and couldn't help noticing that despite her face being free of tears, it was still plagued by sadness.

As Wren slid the towel down her neck and stomach, House caught a glimpse of several small scars on her chest—but before it could take a closer look, she covered them with a gray hoodie, then pulling on a pair of underwear and faded jeans, kicked the towel into the corner, along with her clothes from yesterday, and exited the bathroom.

Zoe glanced up from her phone when she heard her coming down the stairs. "You look better," she said, swiveling around in the overstuffed chair that sat beside the sofa.

"Thanks. I feel better."

As Wren stepped off the landing, House was again taken aback by their striking similarities to each other. Both had the same slender build, angular cheekbones, and flawless skin, while their voices—although identical in pitch—were also rooted in the same silky timbre.

"Where are all of your things from your apartment?"

"In storage," answered Wren, walking into the foyer.

House saw Zoe's lips stretch into a taut line as she watched her sister place the kitchen chair back under the doorknob before heading over to the window.

"Is that coffee I smell?" asked Wren, neutralizing the sun's welcoming rays with a flick of her wrist as she closed the blind.

Zoe rubbed her forehead. "It is," she said, forging a small smile as Wren turned around.

"From where?"

She stood and started into the kitchen. "I found a can in the cabinet."

"How old is it?"

"Well, it falls somewhere between expired and stale," Zoe answered, using her shirt tail to wipe the dust from the inside of the mugs, "but I don't think we should look a gift horse in the mouth."

Wren's damp hair clung to her face as she sat down at the kitchen table, which had a folded piece of cardboard under one of its legs.

"Here you go," said Zoe, taking the seat across from her.

"Thank you…and not just for the coffee."

"You're welcome. You know, this is going to be so much fun!"

"What is?" asked Wren, blowing the steam off of her mug.

"Us *living* together!"

Wren gave her a puzzled look. "You're moving in?"

"Yeah, it'll be just like when we were kids—except without all of Mom's drama."

"But what about your job? I thought you were working at *Jake's Bar and Grill* in Carmel."

"I was—but apparently hooking up with the hot delivery guy in the back storeroom is frowned upon."

Wren set her mug down and sighed.

"Did I mention that he was hot?" Zoe replied. "Anyway, I hated that job—nothing but drunks and college turds grabbing my ass every time I walked by."

"Sorry," said Wren, yet House got the sense that the hurt expression lurking on her face wasn't for Zoe.

"Don't be," she replied, giving her a dismissive wave. "Jake is the one you should feel sorry for."

"Why's that?"

"Because besides losing his *best* server ever," Zoe said, pausing to toss her long locks over her shoulder, "he also lost a whole case of Duckhorn that I took on my way out as compensation."

Wren shoved her tongue between her front teeth and upper lip and left it there for a few seconds. "Of course you did."

"But enough about me..." Clasping her hands together, Zoe leaned forward. "I completely get why you moved, but I'm dying to know why you chose this rundown house in the middle of fucking nowhere—that's at least a two-hour drive to your office—to live in."

Wren's reproachful gaze began backing away from her sister; it floundered across the table in rapid retreat before finding solace in her lap. "I was fired."

"Yeah, right..." Zoe picked up her mug and snorted. "For what? Stealing office supplies?"

A trace of red swarmed Wren's cheeks. "I got a DUI."

Zoe's toothy grin wavered as her gaze went from Wren to the bottle of tequila sitting on the coffee table in the living room. "When?"

"A couple of months ago." Wren shifted in her chair. "The attorney I hired got the charge reduced to something called wet reckless. I had to pay a thousand dollar fine and got sixty days probation."

"Well, that's better than the alternative," Zoe said after a long pause.

Wren shrugged her lips.

"Why did you get fired?"

"Because aside from the fact that my license to practice is now under review by the California Board," replied Wren, picking at the skin surrounding her cuticles, "my boss said it created potential liability issues."

"Why didn't you tell me any of this before now?"

Wren jerked her head up. "I tried calling you the night I was arrested. You didn't answer—and your voicemail was turned off."

"If I don't have voicemail, then Mom can't leave a message and expect me to call her back," Zoe replied in an unapologetic tone. "Why didn't you just text me?"

"You can't text from a pay phone, Zoe."

An awkward silence followed.

"You know..." Zoe said, giving her sister a playful kick under the table, "if I didn't know any better, I'd think you were trying to take my title of being the family screwup."

Wren moved her leg out of reach.

"Oh, come on, Wrennie...I was joking."

"Well, I'm sorry, but I lost my sense of humor four months ago—or have you forgotten already?"

"I haven't forgotten, Wren. That's why I'm here."

Wren's nostrils flared.

"*What?*"

"You and I both know that the only reason you're here is because you're broke and need a place to stay."

Zoe's eyes took on a wounded look.

The stale air circulating throughout the room grew rife with tension.

Letting out another sigh, Wren sank back against her chair. "I'm sorry," she said, shaking her head. "I didn't mean that."

"I'm pretty sure you did," Zoe replied in a curt tone. "But I forgive you...I guess."

Wren took a sip of the coffee and gave an audible shudder. "This is really bad," she said, coughing.

A lopsided smile crept between Zoe's cheeks, yet House could see that the tightness in her eyes remained. "Listen," she said, pushing her own mug to the side, "I think we could both do with something to eat. What do you say we go find a grocery store, grab some food, come back, have an early dinner—and get shit-faced off the bottle of wine I've got chillin' in your fridge?"

The corners of Wren's mouth began to lift, only to freeze midway up her face. "Crap—what time is it?"

"Almost two. Why?"

Wren's chair scraped across the linoleum. "I've got a session with a new patient," she said, hurrying into the living room. "Can you give me an hour?"

"I guess…" Zoe replied, leaning her shoulder against the kitchen doorway. "But I thought you said you were fired."

"My supervisor took pity on me and got me a job with *Mindful Shores Mental Health Services*."

"Sounds snooty."

"Yeah…well, aside from catering to the rich," said Wren, stooping to pick up her laptop and backpack from off the floor, "they do court-mandated therapy, which although is a cash cow—no one there seems to want to do. So you're looking at *Mindful Shores'* new Tele-health Anger Management Therapist for at-risk individuals."

"Cool," said Zoe, following her into the office. "So can I listen in—"

"No."

"I'll be quie—"

"No."

"Fine," she replied with a huff. "I guess I'll just unload my car then."

Wren pulled a folder from her backpack and sat down in the chair. "Be sure and close the doors on your way out."

House watched Zoe's brows come together as she yanked the set of French doors, which had been added a couple of years ago, shut.

Wren quickly scanned the top page stuffed inside the folder and opened her laptop. A few clicks later, a woman dressed in a bright yellow cardigan appeared. "Good afternoon, Stephanie."

House could see the woman's lips moving, yet her words were falling silent.

"Can't hear you," Wren sang under her breath as she tapped her right ear with her finger.

The ends of the woman's very black, very straight hair cascaded down the front of her shoulders as she began to randomly press buttons. "—hear me now?"

"There you go," said Wren, settling into her chair. "My name is—"

"So, how does this work? I mean, do we sit here and make small talk for a few minutes, or can I leave now?"

"Well, you have to stay for the entire session," explained Wren, "but you can talk to me about whatever you want. It's my job to listen, as well as go over some coping mechanisms that can help you."

"Oh...no, there's been a misunderstanding. You see, I'm only here because of my attorney."

"Most people are."

"No." The woman shook her head. "My attorney told me that he would speak to the person in charge of *Mindful Oceans*—or whatever it's called—and make sure they knew that I was to be marked down as attending each session."

"I hear what you're saying, Stephanie, but—"

"It's Steph."

"I hear what you're saying, *Steph*," said Wren, digging her bare toes into the carpet, "but your attorney is mistaken."

"Do you want me to get him on the phone?" she asked, the civil expression lodged behind her layers of heavy concealer becoming muddled with anger. "Or better yet, maybe you should talk to your supervisor…"

There was a soft knock, followed by the sound of the door opening.

"…because I'm guessing that you haven't been given all the…"

"*Psst!*"

House saw Wren's posture stiffen.

"Psst…*Wrennie!*"

"…regarding who I am."

"Steph, can you excuse me for just one, quick second?"

Steph opened her mouth. "Well, I—"

Tapping the mute button at the bottom of the screen, Wren's gaze shot across the room at Zoe. "*What?*"

"I'm sorry to interrupt you having your ass handed to you, but which bedroom is mine?"

"I don't care," she said, turning back to the woman.

"Okay—"

"Wait"—Wren twisted around in the chair—"take

the one on the right. I want the one with the bay window."

"Okay—"

"Now leave me alone."

Zoe twirled her hand through the air in a flourishing manner and gave an exaggerated bow. "Yes, my liege," she said in a poorly contrived British accent as she began backing out the door. "Sorry to have bothered you, my liege."

Biting down on her tongue, Wren returned her attention to the woman. "My apologies," she said, unmuting the call. "Now, where were we?"

"You were in the process of being ripped a new one," answered Zoe in a loud whisper.

"You're *here*, Steph," Wren said, giving Zoe a crude gesture with her finger out of the woman's line of sight, "because you agreed to court-mandated therapy in lieu of going to jail."

As Zoe closed the door and traipsed outside to her car, House heard a loud sniff and glanced back at the computer screen in time to see the woman's slender nostrils pinch shut. Reaching up, she touched the yellow barrette fastened to her hair, as if to make sure it was still in place, and then slowly let out her breath. "I'm going to explain this one more time. My attorney told me that these sessions were just a formality to show a paper trail. I don't *need* therapy."

"It says in your file that you were arrested for assaulting another mom at a PTA meeting and then keying her car."

"*That* was an unfortunate incident which got blown way out of proportion."

"How many children do you have, Steph?"

The woman crossed her arms. "Two. My son, Hunter, is in middle school…"

Something heavy hit the floor in the living room, drawing a subtle look from Wren. Through the smudged glass inserts in the French doors, she saw the crate of Duckhorn tipped on its side. Zoe cringed and mouthed an apology, then after performing a quick inspection of the bottles, gave her a thumbs up.

Flattening her lips, Wren turned back to Steph.

"…daughter, Rory, who's in third grade."

"They must keep you very busy."

"You have no idea. It's a full-time job driving them back and forth to soccer practice, dance recitals, and all the other extra-curricular activities they have."

"That sounds stressful."

"There have been days that I didn't know if I was coming or going," she replied, relaxing her jaw. "Take last week for example. I was driving to…"

Amazed at the sudden change in the woman's disposition, House watched Wren, who in spite of the commotion Zoe was making—between dropping things on the floor and tromping up and down the stairs—kept her focus on Steph and what she was saying.

"…then after all that, I had to pick up the dry cleaning, cook dinner, bake two-dozen cookies for Rory's Girl Scout meeting the next day, and then call all the moms in the PTA about volunteering for the Spring Festival—most of whom would rather talk behind my back about how I do things than lift a finger to help."

Wren paused to jot something down in the file. "It sounds like you are saying that you are overworked and underappreciated."

"Oh my God—yes," exclaimed Steph, throwing up her hands, "thank you!"

"How does it make you feel when your efforts go largely unrecognized, either by your family or the other moms?"

"Truthfully?"

Wren nodded. "This is a judgement free zone."

The woman eyed her carefully for a moment and then sat forward. "It pisses me off."

For the next forty-five minutes, Steph, sporting a triumphant look of validation, ranted about her fault-finding mother-in-law, apathetic husband, ungrateful kids…and the spiteful, backstabbing, venom-spewing, bored housewife-moms of the Lone Springs Elementary PTA.

Chapter 32

Dusk descended, shrouding the sky in a purplish gray, as angry waves, curling beneath hissing white foam, broke against the shore. A squadron of Brown pelicans, their long bills resting on their folded necks, circled silently above, searching for fish that had been caught up in the tide.

House's breath constricted as it watched the water rush over the golden sand. The past few days, it had noticed an alarming change in the depth of the tide. It had always covered half of the rocky beach below—but yesterday most of the inlet had been engulfed, creating a problem for the wildlife nesting in the lower crags of the cliff wall, and forcing the seal pups that remained on shore, whether ready or not, into the ocean.

In the distance, House could see the lone mother seal bobbing in the swells; with her flipper pressed against the outcropping, she fought to keep her head above the thrashing water as she called out with several high-pitched barks to her pup, who was frantically pacing back and forth on the ledge above her.

About thirty yards from shore, House noticed a large dark shape moving beneath the surface.

The tide suddenly surged, swallowing the narrow ledge and knocking the pup into the sea. As it began to cry and splash about, House saw the shape make a sharp turn toward the outcropping and then disappear into the depths below.

House instinctively leaned forward, making its floor joists groan as they struggled with the abrupt shift in weight. Sweeping its gaze across the tumultuous whitecaps in front of the outcropping, which was now all but submerged, it caught a glimpse of silver and saw the pup awkwardly maneuvering its three-hundred-pound body through the breakers with its one front flipper. As House searched for any sign of the shark, the mother seal surfaced beside her pup and began nudging it toward the east side of the inlet, where there were currently more rocks than sea.

House watched the pair draw closer to the mouth of it—only to notice the torpedo-shaped shadow moving beneath them.

Several pelicans, their beaks and necks outstretched, slammed into the water a few feet behind the pup.

The dark mass broke apart, and House let go of the breath it had been holding as dozens upon dozens of sheepshead leapt out of the water to avoid being the pelicans' next meal—yet the divebombing birds showed no mercy.

"What the hell is that noise?"

"It's just the house settling."

Upon hearing its name, House straightened, creating another series of creaks and groans, and turned its attention inward.

"It's like a thousand years old," said Zoe, plopping herself down on the bed. "How much more settling can it possibly do?"

A surge of heat rushed through House's dust-laden conduits, causing the section running above the bedroom ceiling to bang and pop as it expanded.

Wren glanced up as she pulled a pair of jeans from her suitcase.

"Maybe its haunted, ooh—or *maybe* a sexy ghost lives here. He can't cross over to the other side, so he's doomed to roam these empty halls looking for his lost love. But then one morning, I walk into my bedroom after taking a swim in the ocean, and as I'm peeling my very skimpy bathing suit off, I see him standing there, watching me with his smoldering blue eyes. Startled, I open my mouth to scream. He holds a finger to my lips as he looks at my perky, bare breasts, dripping with—"

"I swear to God, Zoe," said Wren, walking over to the dresser, "don't you ever think about anything other than sex?"

"Like what? Being a responsible grownup like you?" Zoe tossed her half-eaten pizza crust into the box at the foot of the bed and wiped her fingers on her t-shirt. "But while we're on the subject..." she said, watching her carefully, "have you seen Rick the dick lately?"

Wren shoved the drawer closed and turned around.

"*What*? It's an innocent question."

The cell phone on the nightstand began to ring.

Zoe squinted at the cracked screen. "Well, speak of the devil," she said, picking it up.

Wren snatched the phone out of her hand.

"I was just going to give him a friendly hello."

"No, you weren't," she said, tapping the red button before slipping it into her pocket.

"Why'd you hang up?"

Wren yanked a blouse from her suitcase. "Because I ended things with him."

"You ended things with Richard," Zoe repeated, drawing her head back in disbelief. "When?"

"A few days ago."

Wren's cell phone began to ring again.

"Does *he* know that?" asked Zoe, arching her brows.

"Yes, Zoe—he knows that! I didn't *ghost* him the way you've done every guy you've ever slept with! I had a very serious, very adult conversation with him and told him we were through."

House saw Zoe's eyes flash as if they'd been struck by a piece of flint. "Why's he calling you, then?"

"Because he doesn't want it to be over."

"I'm sure he doesn't," she muttered, leaning down to retrieve the bottle of wine from off the floor. "I mean, who else is he gonna find that'll drop everything they're doing and come running when he calls?"

"You know, I wasn't looking for—or even expecting—any sympathy from you," Wren snapped, the blouse she was holding crumpling between her fingers, "but a little understanding for what I'm going through would be nice, because there is a very big part of me that still loves him."

Zoe stared at her over the rim of her plastic cup. "Oh—no. I'm sorry you broke up with Rick the dick *again*. You must be absolutely devastated."

Wren's lips folded into a straight line. "I hate you."

"I hate you *more*," said Zoe, holding the bottle of wine out to her.

With a conceding sigh, Wren took it and sat down on the bed beside her.

"And for your information, I don't ghost *every* guy I've slept with. There were one or two that I actually liked."

"One or two…out of how many?"

"I know it seems like a lot when compared to *your* pathetic sex life, but I have a system that weeds out a ton of guys *before* we hook up."

"Oh, do tell."

"When men, who I deem to be assholes, losers—or make me think that I'd rather do it with one of the flying devil monkeys from The Wizard of Oz—ask me for my number, I give them a fake one."

"Wouldn't it be more humane to just tell them no?"

"Humane? They're not *dogs*, Wrennie. They're self-entitled pricks. Take this one guy from a few months ago that I met at a hotel bar. He was—"

"What were you doing at a hotel?"

"Stick with me," said Zoe, snapping her fingers.

Wren gave her a flat look. "Sorry."

"Anyway, this guy was wicked smart, funny, and handsome. Not rugged handsome, more like momma's boy handsome—you know clean-shaven, hair neatly combed—but I could work with it. So we were about ten minutes into our conversation, laughing and having a great time, when the dude standing next to me accidentally knocks my drink over."

"Ugh, I hate it when that happens," said Wren, letting out a dramatic sigh.

"Are you going to let me tell the story or not?"

"As long as it's the abridged version."

"Okay," said Zoe, scooting closer to her. "So the guy apologizes for spilling my drink, and tells the bartender to give me another one. I stop wiping my pants and look up to thank him—and we lock eyes. It was just for a split-second, but it felt like we had a real connection, you know?"

"Uh-huh." Wren lifted the bottle to her lips and took a long swallow.

"He places a twenty on the bar, gives me a wink, and walks away. So, I turn back to the momma's boy, and find him glaring at me. He asks me if I make a habit out of flirting with other men while on a date. I explain to him that—first, he and I weren't on a date, second, I was just being nice to the guy, and third, if he didn't like it, he could kiss my ass..."

A glazed look fell over Wren's face.

"...tells me he's sorry and starts twirling the ends of my hair around his fingers." Zoe paused and tilted her head. "You *know* how I am about my hair."

"I do," said Wren, sighing the words.

"The possessive way he was looking at me with those dark eyes of his was giving me the creeps, so when he asked me for my number, I gave him a fake one, along with a fake name. He then downed the drink the other guy had bought me and ordered two kamikaze shots. After we did those, he suggested we go back to his place. I told him I had to use the bathroom first—which I did, but then snuck out the rear entrance."

Wren set the bottle on her thigh and stretched. "Well, I'll give you that one," she said, crossing her ankles. "The guy was definitely a nut job."

"Hell *yeah*, he was. Oh, and did I tell you about the time a guy with a foot fetish brought his pet rat with him—" A buzzing sound began to resonate, prompting Zoe to reach behind her. Pulling her cell phone from her jeans, she glanced at the screen and rolled her eyes.

"Who is it?" asked Wren, adjusting the pillow behind her shoulders.

"Mom," she said, returning the phone to her pocket.

"Aren't you going to answer it?"

"Nope."

"What if Martin's gotten worse? She told me Monday that he was being moved to hospice."

"Well, she's got another daughter besides me that she can call."

As if on cue, Wren's phone began to ring, eliciting a nasally laugh from Zoe. Scowling, Wren handed the bottle back to her and swiped her thumb across the screen. "Hi, Mom."

House heard a woman's voice, low and frazzled, but couldn't make out what it was saying.

"Sorry, it was really late by the time I got here last night. I didn't want to call and risk waking Martin," she said, watching Zoe empty the last of the wine into her cup. "Yeah...the house is pretty nice."

Zoe looked around the cracked walls of the small bedroom and made a gagging gesture with her finger.

"No, I *haven't* talked to her today," said Wren, ramming her foot against Zoe's. "But I'm sure she's just busy."

Zoe gave an exaggerated nod before draining her cup.

"How's Martin? Uh-huh... Uh-huh... So, he's... Okay, but he's... Uh-huh... Listen, Mom, I need to let you go. I've got another call coming in... I know, but it could be a patient... Okay, talk to you soon. 'Bye." Tossing the phone on the bed, Wren sighed and rubbed her eyes.

"So, is he dead?"

Something flickered across Wren's face, leaving her cheeks scarlet. "No," she said, staring at the rumpled quilt beneath her. "They're just trying to keep him comfortable."

Zoe stood and started across the floor.

"Where are you going?"

"To bed."

"Wait..." The mattress creaked as Wren scrambled to her feet. "Don't go," she pleaded. "I promise, I won't say anything else about Mom or Martin. Tell me more about the guy and his pet rat."

"The wine's gone to my head," Zoe replied, clumsily edging past her, "and I'm tire—"

"I'm scared to be alone."

Zoe stopped and looked back. "I'm just down the hall."

"Please…" Wren reached for Zoe. "I don't want to sleep by myself."

House saw the hardened expression etched on Zoe's face begin to waver.

Seeming to notice it as well, Wren grabbed her suitcase and shoved it—along with the pizza box—onto the floor, then leaning over the bed, whipped the covers back and gave her sister a hopeful look.

"Fine," Zoe said, unbuttoning her jeans, "but no spooning."

Relief flooded Wren's eyes. "Thank y—"

"And first thing in the morning, we're washing these sheets because they smell like cat pee."

Turning away, Wren snatched a t-shirt from her suitcase. As she began to change into it, House saw Zoe watching her in the mirror above the dresser, before abruptly dropping her gaze.

"You know," said Wren, crawling into bed beside her, "this reminds me of when we were teenagers."

"Yeah…those were good times," Zoe said in a rigid voice as she propped her cheek on her fist. "Well, good night, shithead."

Wren's lips split into a wide grin. "Good night, fuckface." Rolling over, she turned out the light, drenching the room in darkness.

As the waves crashed against the bottom of the cliff, House heard Wren take in a small breath. "Zoe...I really am glad that you're here."

"Me too," she replied, yet her delayed and somewhat stilted response caused a deep disquiet to fill the room, further stirring House's apprehension in regard to its new family.

Chapter 33

"I don't understand. It was working fine last night." The filthy yellow water seeped through the towel on the floor and lapped at Wren's toes as she shoved the plunger into the toilet's throat over and over again. "How much toilet paper did you use?"

"I already told you," replied Zoe, holding her head in her hands as she sat slumped along the edge of the bathtub, "not a lot."

"Well something's making it overfl—" Wren stopped as her gaze absently shifted to the small wastebasket beside the vanity. "Fuck, Zoe!" Reaching into the bin, she held up a white plastic wrapper. "Please tell me you didn't flush a tampon down there!"

"Okay," she said, blinking her red-rimmed eyes at her, "I won't tell you."

"God—I can't believe you," muttered Wren, thrusting the plunger with such force that water splattered across her jeans.

"Don't you find it somewhat disturbing that there's a can of roach spray in here?" asked Zoe, turning the can over in her hand.

The doorbell rang, making House's shutters jerk as the small jolt crackled behind its walls.

Wren let go of the plunger and spun around.

"Who the hell could that be?" asked Zoe, pushing herself to her feet.

"Don't go down there," Wren ordered, latching onto her elbow. "You don't know who it is!"

Zoe pulled her arm out of her grasp. "That's *why* I'm going to open the door."

Wren shouldered past her, knocking her into the vanity. "But what if it's him?"

"He doesn't know where you live, Wren," replied Zoe, her hung-over expression morphing into frustration as she tried to go around her.

The bell rang twice more in rapid succession.

"It's *not* him," Zoe said in a weary voice.

Wren shook her head. "How do you know?"

"Because he wouldn't ring the goddamn bell!"

Giving little credence to her sister's words, Wren remained in the doorway with her arms and feet spread.

"Okay, look…" Setting the roach spray down, Zoe snatched the plunger from the toilet. "If it *is* him, I'll hit that fucker over the head so hard, he'll have to unzip his fly in order to see the light of day."

The doorbell went off again, its tinny chime sounding longer and more impatient.

"Let's go," said Zoe, prodding her with the rubber flange.

Wren took a step back. "Don't touch me with that thing!"

Zoe took advantage of the small opening and squeezed past her. "Come on," she said, grabbing her by the hand.

"Stop, Zoe—I mean it!"

"Nope, we're doing this." Making her way down the stairs with Wren in tow, Zoe removed the chair from underneath the doorknob, then taking a step to the left, jammed her shoulder against the hinges. "Ready," she whispered, raising the dripping plunger over her head.

House watched Wren's fingers fumble with the deadbolt before cracking the door open just wide enough to peer through. "Can I help you?" she asked, warily eyeing the woman, whom House recognized as the angry owner of the Victorian.

"Hi there, I'm your new neighbor—or I guess you're *my* new neighbor. I'm not really sure, seeing as how we both moved in on the same day." Her statement was followed by a short laugh that sounded to House to be as fake as the smile surrounding her brilliant white teeth looked.

Wren relaxed her grip on the door, causing Zoe to lower the plunger. "What can I do for you?"

"Well, when we purchased this land to build our home on, we had it surveyed and found that your fence," she said, pausing to point at the wrought iron barrier dividing the two properties, "is three feet over the line, so we're going to need you to either move it or take it down."

Wren's gaze cut to the fence and then back to the woman. "I'm only renting this house. You'll have to take the issue up with the owner."

"Oh...you're renting." The woman, wearing a white headband scarf and matching sleeveless coat, ran a flagrant gaze along Wren's unkempt hair and hoodie—which House noticed that aside from being on its second straight day, was baggy and stained with wine. "Well, I won't take up anymore of your time. If you'll just give me the owner's number, I'll be on my way."

"I'm in the middle of unpacking and am not sure where it is at the moment."

"You don't have it in your phone?"

House saw Wren tighten her grip on the door. "No."

"That's fine," said the woman, glancing at her smart watch, "I can wait for you to find it."

"Well, you can wait for me to find it at *your* house, because like I already told you, I'm in the middle of unpacking and don't have time to look for it right now."

The conceited smile affixed to the woman's face faded. "I don't think you fully understand the situation, here. Not only is that fence an eyesore, but my daughters could also accidentally fall while playing and cut themselves on one of the rusty bars, and then contract tetanus."

Wren's left eyebrow climbed her forehead. "That's not exactly how tetanus works, but if you're so worried about it, maybe it would be a good idea for you to keep your daughters away from that rusty ol' fence. Okay then..." she said, blinking her eyes in a sarcastic manner, "thanks for stopping by."

House watched the woman's mouth open and close as Wren slammed the door in her face.

"Wow," Zoe said, shaking her head, "who put a stick up *her* butt?"

"She was probably born with it," muttered Wren.

"Why didn't you just give it to her?"

"*What?*"

"The number," Zoe replied, gesturing at the card on the coffee table.

Wren snatched the plunger out of her grasp. "Why should I?"

"Where are you going?"

"To try and fix the toilet that someone clogged with their plug because they were too lazy to wrap it in toilet paper and toss it in the trash."

"I'll try and find some pliers," Zoe called after her.

"For what?"

"To try and remove the stick that crawled up *your* butt," she said under her breath.

Wren stopped in the middle of the staircase and turned around. "What was that?"

Zoe smiled innocently. "I said I'll start some coffee."

~

"...the same thing every single time. I'm so sick of her criticizing me in front of my boyfriend and kids. She doesn't like the way I dress, or the way I wear my hair, and she's told me more than once that I don't know how to cook, clean, or take care of my family..."

Suppressing a yawn, House shifted its weight to its other side as it listened to the woman prattling on to Wren through her laptop. For the past forty-five minutes, the woman had been talking nonstop — except for the handful of times she'd paused to dab at tears that were invisible to House.

"...last night, she complained that I brought her home the wrong kind of ice cream she *specifically* asked me for—and that I made a special trip to the store at ten o'clock to get. I swear, she makes me want to kick that walker right out from under her arms." Settling back against a cluttered sofa, the woman stuck a slender black pen between her lips and inhaled deeply, causing its plastic tip to glow a bright blue.

Wren lowered her fist she'd been using to prop her chin on and straightened. "Candace, last week when we talked...you agreed that the next time your mother said something like that you were going to tell her how much it hurts you. Did you do that?"

Thick white smoke poured out of the woman's pierced nostrils. "No."

"Why not?"

"Because it wouldn't have done any good. She'd just twist it around and make it all about her."

"Well—"

"That's what she does, you know." With a jerk of her head, the woman tossed her stringy jet-black hair over her shoulder, exposing a large tattoo embedded between the rolls of flesh on her neck. "Like, if she hears me complaining about my job, she'll launch into how she gave up her career to raise me and how I've never even once thanked her. I mean, what does she want me to do? Get down on my knees and grovel because she chose not to have me sucked out of her vagina as a fetus?"

Wren cleared her throat and reached for the bottle of tequila to the right of her laptop. "Candace," she said, pausing to pour a liberal amount of it into her coffee mug before taking an equally generous swallow, "we also discussed you just walking away from her when that happens. Did you try that?"

"I have a bad knee. It's extremely painful for me to walk anywhere."

"How about just going into another room, then?"

"There are five of us living in a two-bedroom apartment—there's nowhere to go."

"How about taking a relaxing bath?"

"So I can listen to my toddler bang on the door while screaming her head off?"

Wren shifted in her chair. "Candace, are you familiar with the term, displaced anger?"

The woman plucked a strand of hair off her face with a set of nails that were painted in alternating shades of black and white—and jutted an inch past her stubby fingers. "Should I be?"

Wren gave a slow blink and took another swallow from her mug. "It's when a person is harboring a great deal of hostility over a particular situation, and because they are unable to cope with it, lash out at someone completely unrelated to the source of their anger. In your case, I believe your sister is the—"

"Sister?" Candace scrunched her tattooed brows. "I don't *have* a sister."

Wren set her mug down and shook her head. "Sorry, I meant your mother. Your *mother*," she said, slapping her hand hard against her thigh as she repeated the word, "is the root of your rage, and the convenience store clerk you assaulted was the unfortunate recipitent…repicent…*recipient* of it."

The woman sat there wide-eyed, with lips slightly ajar, staring at Wren, and House didn't know if her befuddled expression was due to the sudden revelation—or the sloppy and somewhat slurred manner in which it had been delivered.

Heavy footsteps began to fall across the front yard, pulling House's attention outside, where it saw the angry woman's husband making his way toward the porch.

"I threw an energy drink at that clerk's bitch ass because she refused to give me a refund for a package of stale pretzels that I'd bought from there the day before..."

House began shuttering its gaze between Wren's office and the front porch as the man trotted up the steps and rang the bell.

Cutting her eyes toward the living room, Wren grimaced upon seeing Zoe get off the sofa and start into the foyer.

"...she rudely told me that I'd gotten them out of the clearance bin and all sales were final—"

"That's all the time we have for today," Wren interrupted, clenching her fists as Zoe opened the door.

"But we still have five minutes."

"I want you to think about what we discussed, and we'll pick up where we left off next week," said Wren, then tapped the screen with her finger.

"Sorry to bother you," said the man, dipping his head in Zoe's direction, who in spite of the cool weather was wearing a snug t-shirt and denim cut-offs, "but my name's Gary, and I live next door."

"Hi there," she replied, leaning against the doorjamb. "I'm Zoe."

"Uh...I think this is for you," he said, pushing his thin, wire-frame glasses back up his nose as if he were trying to keep his gaze from landing on the inviting space between her noticeably unfettered assets. "It was delivered to my house by mistake."

"Oh, you're so sweet," said Zoe, grazing the back of his hand with her fingertips as she took the package from him. "Thank you."

"You're welcom—"

"Why is it opened?"

Gary looked past Zoe to find an identical—albeit accusing—version of her standing in the entryway.

A frozen smile forged its way onto Zoe's lips as she turned around. "Wren, this is Gary—*our neighbor*," she said, arching her brows in a sharp manner as she spoke. "Wasn't it *nice* of him to bring this over?"

Swaying slightly, Wren responded by crossing her arms.

"I'm very sorry it's been opened," said Gary, pushing his glasses back up the bridge of his nose once more. "We had about half-a-dozen packages delivered a little while ago, and my wife opened this one right along with the others. It didn't occur to her to check the name and address on the box until she saw what was inside." He paused to shake his head. "She feels terrible about it."

"Having met your wife earlier, I highly doubt that."

House watched the man's face turn the color of a canned beet.

"Wren, don't you have a patient to call—or something?" asked Zoe.

"No," she said, keeping her eyes locked on their neighbor.

"Yeah, about this morning," said Gary, shifting his feet. "I want to apologize for my wife's behavior toward you. There are times when she can be a little..."

Wren tilted her head. "Rude? Condescending? Off-putting?"

"Uh, well I was going to say impatient," he replied, scratching the back of his neck, "but those work too."

House saw the corner of Wren's mouth twitch, while a sulking expression—bordering on jealousy—began to cloud Zoe's face.

"I'd like to make it up to you by installing your doorbell camera."

"Thank you, but I'm more than capable of doing it on my own."

"I'm sure you are, but I'd like to do this for you as a way of apologizing."

"That's not necess—"

"I brought my own tools and everything."

Wren looked at the screwdriver he'd pulled from his pocket.

"That would be wonderful," replied Zoe, stepping forward. "Wouldn't it, Wren?"

Wren glared at her sister. "No—"

"Here you go, Gary," said Zoe, her plump lips unfurling into a sensuous smile as she handed him back the box.

"Thanks," he answered, peering around her in order to acknowledge Wren. "I can do this in five minutes."

Wren glanced at her watch.

"Are you going to time me?"

"No," she said in a clipped tone, "I'm thinking you'd better get started."

"Oh—right, sorry." As House's overly friendly—and apparently masochistic—neighbor set about retrieving the doorbell camera from the box, Zoe turned on her heel and pushed past Wren, making her take an unsteady step to the left.

"Do you want it to replace your existing doorbell?" asked Gary, unaware of their exchange as he knelt on the porch.

"I probably shouldn't, since I'm renting."

"That's not a problem," he said, laying the pieces of the camera out in front of him. "That must be really cool…having a twin."

"I suppose it has its moments," said Wren, watching Zoe stalk into the living room, "but nothing comes to mind right now."

"What kind of doctor are you?"

Her gaze cut back to Gary. "A busy one."

House saw the pretty beet color return to his face as he screwed the baseplate for the camera into the brittle casing surrounding its door.

Leaning against the peeling jamb, Wren rubbed the throbbing vein behind her temple and sighed. "I'm a licensed therapist, not a doctor."

"A therapist," he said, pausing to tear the shrink-wrapped battery pack open with his teeth. "That must be rewarding, helping people through their problems."

Wren's face took on an unreadable expression. "It can be, I guess."

"So, what about your sister?"

"What *about* her?"

"What does she do?"

House saw Wren glance at Zoe, who was sitting in the living room with one foot on the floor and the other swung over the side of the chair as she scrolled through her phone. "She works in the alcohol distribution industry."

"Hmm…" Gary paused to spit out a piece of plastic. "That's different."

Wren's blank expression suddenly ignited. "Different how? You mean different from *me*?"

"Uh—"

"Just because we share the same face doesn't mean we share the same interests—and that's largely in part because of people like you. We spent our formative years trying *so* hard not to be viewed as a single entity by our friends, family, teachers, and complete strangers that today, we couldn't be more different. And just to save some time, I'll answer the question that nearly every single non-twin has asked: No, we can't read each other's minds, and when one of us gets hurt, the other *doesn't* feel it."

Keeping his eyes on the door casing, a crooked and somewhat insolent-looking grin spread over Gary's lips. "I meant that's a line of work I've never heard of."

The anger riding on Wren's face turned to embarrassment, leaving it crimson. "I'm sorry. It's just been one of those days."

"It's all right," he said, still grinning. "If you haven't noticed, I've got pretty thick skin."

Wren's humiliated gaze darted across the yard, searching for anything to light on—other than Gary—and eventually settled on the Victorian. "Your house is beautiful," she murmured, awkwardly tucking a strand of hair behind her ear.

"Thanks. We designed it ourselves. I've always wanted to live in a Victorian, but my wife wanted something new, so this was our compromise." Snapping the battery cover closed, Gary handed her the instructions. "All finished. Just download the app on your phone and you'll be in business."

Wren forced her gaze to return to him. "Thank you."

"It was the least I could do after what happened."

"So," she said, watching him pick up all the trash and stuff it inside the box, "what brought you all the way out here to Gosset Bay?"

"You mean Echo Point."

"*What*?"

Gary stood. "This place..." he replied, circling the air with his finger. "It's called Echo Point. Gosset Bay is the town adjacent to it."

House watched Wren's lower jaw jut forward.

The action prompted Gary to clear his throat and adjust his glasses for an annoying third time. "We built out here because we thought it would be a great place to raise our daughters, and it also made sense from a money standpoint because the land and property taxes are a lot cheaper here than in Monterey."

Wren stared at him for a moment, then placed her hands inside the pouch of her hoodie. "Are you an accountant?"

"An accountant? Ow!" said Gary, rubbing his chest as if her words had pierced his heart.

Wren cracked a smile; it was guarded, but genuine nonetheless — and lit up her entire face.

A harsh-sounding ping bounced between them.

Gary pulled his phone from his coat and frowned. "Sorry, I need to go. I promised my girls that we'd make s'mores and watch the tide roll in tonight. Rylee, my youngest has a bet with her sister on how high up the cliff it's going to come."

"It gets really high, doesn't it?" said Wren, appearing notably grateful that their conversation was about to end.

"It didn't used to, however, last month a jetty was constructed a few miles north of here to stop the nuisance flooding in town. It changed the direction of the incoming water, making the tide here higher than ever."

Wren tilted her head. "And you know this very unique piece of information because..."

"Oh — sorry. I'm a coastal engineer. I helped design the jetty."

Another ping sounded.

He glanced down at his phone and then swung his head toward the Victorian.

House looked as well and saw the man's wife standing on the porch, clutching her cell phone while glowering in his direction.

Gary gave her a brief nod and waved.

She responded by jerking open the door and disappearing inside.

A pinkish hue enveloped his face, causing him to drop his gaze to his feet. "Well, I guess I better get going. It was nice meeting you, Wren," he said, turning to go, "and if you should ever need anything, don't hesitate to give me a call. You know where I live."

"I will," she said, removing her hands from the pouch of her hoodie.

Stepping off the porch, Gary started across the yard. Upon reaching the wrought-iron fence, he paused to glance back at Wren and flash her a quick smile before slipping between a gap in the bars.

Wren turned and walked inside.

"Did you two have a nice *chat*?"

"Yeah," she answered, giving Zoe a sidelong look as she went past, "he seems nice enough."

"Well, he's definitely your type."

Wren stopped in the doorway of the kitchen and turned around. "What the hell are you saying?"

"You know exactly what I'm saying."

"No, I'm not sure I do," she replied, walking back into the living room.

"Oh my God"—Zoe slammed her feet onto the floor and stood up—"are you really going to play this game with me?"

Wren's eyes tapered, zeroing in on the disapproving pair staring back at her. A long moment of silence passed, prompting her to shake her head. "*What?*" she demanded, holding her arms out from her sides.

"You've been broken up with Rick the dick for all of what—seventy-two hours? And you've already got your sights set on your married neighbor."

"I don't know what planet you're living on, but here in the real world, me talking with a guy doesn't mean I want to sleep with him."

"You weren't *talking* to him, you were flirting—in that weird, little bitchy way of yours."

"I wasn't flirting with him, Zoe," replied Wren, stabbing the air in front of her face with her finger. "And you wouldn't be accusing me of that if you hadn't been so busy talking about *yourself* last night to hear me when I said that I was still in love with Richard!"

Zoe folded her arms against her chest. "So is his *wife.*"

Wren sucked in her breath, fueling her already reddened cheeks. "You know, I don't recall asking you for your opinion—or for you to even come here! And as far as what happened just now, you and I both know that the only reason you're upset is because my candy-ass neighbor paid more attention to me than you!"

House saw Zoe's prolonged expression of resentment begin to collapse under the weight of the hurt look that was now circling it. Turning away, she marched across the floor and grabbed her coat and purse off the grimy newel post at the bottom of the staircase.

"Where're you going?"

"Out."

"When will you be back?" asked Wren in a disinterested-sounding voice, yet House could see the panic building behind her eyes.

"I don't know." Zoe stopped in the entryway and turned around. "But if you don't want me ringing your fancy new doorbell in the middle of the night, you need to give me a fucking key."

Wren appeared to House to be mulling over her options, then picking up her keys from the coffee table, slowly walked into the foyer. A single tear caught on her eyelashes as she slid the key off the ring. "Zoe, I'm sorry."

"What are you sorry for?" she asked, taking the key from her. "What you said to me just now—because you're drunk in the middle of the fucking afternoon—or because you don't want to be alone?"

Guilt flooded Wren's face.

"That's what I thought," said Zoe in a bitter voice. "Don't wait up." Spinning on her heel, she jerked on the knob and looked back. "And don't you *dare* block this door with that damn chair."

"Zoe…" Wren stumbled forward. "Please don't go—"

The House on the Cliff

A loud boom ricocheted throughout House's entryway as the door slammed shut.

Chapter 34

Slivers of moonlight fell across Wren's face, highlighting her copper-colored hair as it curled around her pillow.

House shivered in the darkness, but could not feel the familiar movement of its shutters banging against its clapboards. Glancing outside, the comforting sight of the billowing ocean had been replaced by a busy street full of honking cars and angry people shouting.

"Do you like it?"

House's confused gaze shifted from the street to the man lying beside Wren.

"I love it," she said, holding up her hand as she admired the ring on her finger.

The splinters of light coming through the window reflected off the brilliant blue sapphire that was perched atop a band of silver and surrounded by a cluster of tiny diamonds.

"It belonged to my great-grandmother," the man said proudly.

Resting her head against his torso, Wren smiled and closed her eyes. "I've never been happier than I am right now."

"I feel the same way," he murmured, drawing her closer.

"And just think," she said, pausing to breathe in as he began kissing her neck, "we have the whole weekend together."

As House scanned the unfamiliar room, it saw the man hesitate, then pull away.

"What's wrong?" asked Wren, lifting her head.

"I'm sorry, but Kristy lit into me this morning when I told her I wasn't going to make Taylor's soccer game tomorrow."

"What time is her game?"

"Nine."

"Well, why can't you go see her play," said Wren, running her hand along his jaw, "and then come back to the hotel?"

Her suggestion extracted a deep sigh from the man. "It's not that simple," he replied, throwing his legs over the side of the bed.

"What? You mean you're leaving now?"

"I think Kristy suspects something," he said in what sounded to House like a very guilty voice as he looked over his shoulder at Wren. "So I'm not going to be able to see you for a while."

Wren's right arm jutted out from under the covers and hit the base of the lamp on the nightstand, flooding the room with light. "You told me you were going to tell her about us last week."

"I know what I told you, Wren," he said, pulling on his pants, "but her sister's been really sick with her chemo treatments, and this just isn't the right time to spring it on her."

Wren snatched his shirt from off the rumpled duvet and flung it at him. "It's never the right time, Richard."

"Come on, babe," he said, grabbing her around the waist from behind as she stood and began to dress, "don't be mad. I promise I'm going to tell her."

"When?"

Moving a lock of her hair out of his way, Richard tenderly kissed the top of her shoulder. "Soon," he whispered, "but for now, why don't you just kick back and enjoy yourself? The room's paid for through Sund —"

"That's not an answer," she said, spinning around.

Richard dropped his hands and took a step back. "I can't give you a definite date, Wren. You know the situation I'm in —"

"What I know is that we've been together for three years, and for the past two, I've been waiting for you to come clean with your wife and file for divorce, but you just keep coming up with excuses not to. I'm beginning to think this isn't an engagement ring at all. It's a shut-up ring."

"That is absolutely not true," he replied. "Now, come on. Tonight was really nice. Let's not ruin it by argu —"

"Do you love me?"

Richard's steel-gray eyes impatiently found their way to hers. "You know I do."

"Then prove it."

"Well, I thought I just did," he said with a smirk, "but if you want a repeat performance, I can —"

"Oh my God, Richard." Wren shoved against his chest. "Can you grow up for just one second?"

"Okay, okay," he said with a laugh, "I'm sorry." Folding his arms around her, his grin faded. "Listen to me. I love you and want us to be together. I'm as tired of sneaking around as you, and I promise I'm going to talk to Kristy...as soon as her sister gets better."

House watched the hopeful look perched precariously on Wren's face crumble to the floor. "Her condition is terminal, Richard."

He threw his head back and sighed. "Okay – after the bitch dies, then."

House saw Wren's expression darken. "You know what? I can't do this anymore."

"Wren…" Richard wearily ran his fingers through his salt-and-pepper hair.

With tears crowding her eyes, she gathered her purse and coat in her arms, and started for the door.

"Where are you going?"

"Home."

Richard followed her out into the wide corridor. "Will you please wait for just a minute?"

She stopped and whirled around. "Wait is all I've been doing for the past two years, Richard. I'm done."

"Goddamn it, Wren – you're acting like a child!"

The elevator behind her chimed and slid open, spilling several people out onto the bright paisley carpet. Some of them looked exhausted, some seemed wide awake, while others appeared inebriated; whatever their condition, it was plain to House that they were all very interested in the argument that was taking place a few feet from them.

Richard hurriedly motioned at Wren. "Please come back inside so we can talk," he said in a harsh whisper.

"The only talking that needs to take place," she replied, raising her voice, "is between you and your wife."

Murmurs and stifled laughter echoed down the corridor.

A swath of red cut across Richard's face, leaving it ruddy. Walking up to Wren, he leaned in close and clenched his fists. "Don't do anything you're going to regret."

"*The only regret I have is not breaking up with you sooner,*" *she said, holding back her tears. Taking a deep breath, she turned and began weaving her way through the crowd.*

House felt as though it were floating as it followed Wren into the elevator, and then across an enormous lobby, before exiting through a revolving glass door.

A dizzying rush of euphoria traveled through House as neon lights and bright reflective buildings went whizzing past the car window.

Twenty minutes, five stoplights, and three hard turns later, Wren pulled into a concrete structure and parked. The unnerving sounds of jackhammers, sirens, rumbling trucks, and chirping tires grew distant as House accompanied her into the dimly lit stairwell.

After climbing several flights, she traveled down a wide hallway and entered apartment 510. Locking the door behind her, Wren flipped on the lights and tossed her purse and shoes on the living room floor before heading to the bathroom.

As Wren turned on the shower and began to undress, House opted to take a look at its new surroundings — only to find that it couldn't leave the bathroom.

Stepping into the tiled enclosure, Wren pulled the curtain closed and tilted her head back, letting the water run down her face and neck.

As a cloud of steam rose toward the ceiling, House heard a sharp crack in the living room and instinctively shifted its gaze, but could not move past the bathroom wall.

The water suddenly shut off and House saw Wren peer around the curtain, her eyes wide.

A dull thud sounded, followed by another.

House saw Wren's heart begin to slam against her bare chest, causing the drops of water it was riddled with to tremble as she stepped out of the shower and reached for a towel.

House strained to see beyond the door, yet its efforts were useless.

With her hand shaking, Wren pressed down on the door's curved handle — only to stop upon seeing an elongated shadow fall across her feet. Sucking in her breath, she turned the thumb lock and began backing up until her thighs found the marbled vanity.

The sleek brushed-nickel handle on the door moved — and then began to jiggle violently, eliciting a whimper from Wren.

It ceased moments later, and in between the throes of Wren's convulsive breathing and roars of uneasy silence, the edge of the door splintered as it flew open and smashed into the wall beside the tub.

Wren screamed and held up her hands as a gloved fist slammed against the left side of her face. House helplessly watched the back of her head hit the toilet, and as her unconscious body crumpled to the floor, its gaze was swallowed by darkness.

"Wakey, wakey..."

Small patches of light infiltrated House's sight as its vision slowly returned, but its confusion as to where it was — combined with the foul stench of hot metal — abruptly gave way to fear upon seeing a man in dark clothing and black ski mask standing over Wren, whose hands and feet were bound to the bed. Opening her eyes, the left one of which was swollen and caked with blood, her naked body began to buck and thrash about as a muted cry fell from her lips.

The man's mask lifted slightly as if he were smiling. "Ah...there you are," he said, bending down to sweep a strand of hair from her cheek. "What I'm about to do wouldn't be any fun for me at all if you weren't awake."

House ceased to breathe as the man picked up a small soldering iron from off the nightstand and straddled her with his knees.

Half-formed sobs laced with garbled pleas filled the bedroom as Wren shook her head from side to side, coating the duct tape that was covering her mouth in tears and blood.

"After I'm done, you're going to remember me every time you look in the mirror." He cocked his masked head and let go of a low, measured laugh. "For a few months, anyway...and then I'll be back to put you out of your misery." Leaning forward, he pressed the metal tip of the soldering iron into the thin layer of skin above Wren's bare breasts.

As the smell of burning flesh filled the room, Wren arched her back and let out a muffled scream.

A piercing light jarred House awake. Straightening as much as it could, it fought to catch its breath, sending a whistling groan echoing through its vents—and although it was enormously relieved to be anchored inside itself again, its respite was short-lived when it saw Wren sitting up in bed, clutching her chest.

Flinging back the tangle of covers, she hurried down the hall and into the bathroom, where House felt her fingers grapple for the light switch.

As the bulb above the vanity lit up the small space, Wren turned on the faucet and leaned against the sink. With her body still trembling, she cupped her hands and splashed the water against her pale face, which was streaked with sweat and tears.

House watched her repeat the action over and over until her t-shirt and floor were soaked.

Wren removed her shirt and grabbed the towel off the bar beside her; gripping the green cloth between her fingertips, she took in a jagged breath as her eyes slowly rose to meet her reflection.

An involuntary shudder suddenly tore through House's rafters, causing the light above the sink to flicker, as its gaze went from the water dripping down her elbows to the raised pink scars embedded above her breasts.

Wren bowed her head as her chest began to heave with one inconsolable sob after another...confirming House's horrific realization that the marks on her skin were a concise string of letters that spelled out the word 'SLUT'.

Turning from the sink, Wren snatched a shirt of Zoe's that was lying on the floor beside the tub and hurried back to her bedroom, where she snatched her cell phone off the nightstand. As a distorted view of the front porch popped up on the cracked screen, Wren stepped back out into the hall and looked down the darkened staircase at the door — or more specifically — the chair sitting *beside* the door.

She glanced toward the bedroom at the end of the hall. "Zoe?" she called in a hopeful voice, yet could clearly see from where she was standing that her bed was as she'd left it: the freshly washed sheets, along with the rest of her laundry, lay in a pile on top of the bare mattress.

With her ragged breathing matching the labored rise and fall of her chest, she retreated to her bedroom, and then—with a sobbing grunt—pushed the dresser in front of the door, barricading herself inside.

Wren grabbed her purse from off the floor and emptied its contents onto the bed, where House watched her pick up, shake, and toss aside one prescription bottle after another—until one of them rattled. Placing two of the blue pills on her waiting tongue, she washed them down with whatever wine was left in her cup from last night, then trying in vain to draw a steadying breath, leaned back against the headboard...but did not close her eyes.

~

House listened to the waves crashing against the rocks below, but took no comfort in their sound. It hadn't been all that surprised to see Wren in its sleep, as it had possessed the cognizant ability to view Magnus' dreams and memories, yet its new occupant's nightmare had left it shaken to its foundation—not only on account of its content, but because for the first time in its life, House had left the confines of its walls.

The sudden feeling of tires turning onto the gravel drive sent House's attention swerving outside. Streaks of rain, resembling thin strands of spiderwebs, fell across the beam of the single headlight, which House recognized as Zoe's car. A second vehicle that sat higher and sounded as if it needed a muffler followed closely behind.

As water and asphalt slid down its roof and dropped into its gutters, House watched Zoe get out of her car and make her way back to the idling truck. After a moment, the engine shut off and a man appeared.

"Come on," she said, taking him by his hand.

The two of them weaved their way down the path before stumbling on the steps of the porch.

"Ow!"

"Shh..." Zoe whispered in a voice that caused several roosting birds to take flight from the tree above her, "you'll wake my sister."

"Sorry," he replied in an equally loud whisper.

As they neared the front door, House heard a click from the camera mounted beside it. Seconds later, a sharp pinging sound came from Wren's bedroom.

While Zoe struggled to insert the key inside the lock, House glanced back at Wren who, with the help of the pills she'd swallowed, had fallen asleep a short while ago. Still sitting upright, her head was slumped forward, and her chin was resting against her chest; her breathing was deep and unencumbered, and although her chiming cell phone remained in her hand, her fingers had grown lax.

The front door swung open, dumping Zoe inside. "This way," she said, motioning for the man to follow her.

As they started up the stairs, House noticed that it seemed to be as difficult for them as traversing the porch steps had been. Several more stumbles and giggles later, they reached the top of the landing, where their staggering silhouettes became lumbering shadows upon entering the darkened bedroom. Undressing each other between sloppy kisses and clumsy gropes, they fell backward onto the bed...and as their bodies intertwined, they slowly began writhing in unison.

Chapter 35

The mother seal stretched and gave her pup an affectionate nuzzle with her bulbous snout before diving beneath the swells. She reappeared moments later about two yards from the outcropping; bobbing amongst the waves, she barked twice and then waited.

The pup rose and waddled to the edge of the rock ledge. As the sun glinted off the malformed protrusion of skin where its right front flipper should have been, House felt its trusses stiffen—for even though it hadn't seen the great white in a few days, it knew better than to think it couldn't be lurking in the depths below.

Giving a single, high-pitched bark, the pup lifted its tail and, without hesitation, dove into the water, its shiny fur disappearing amidst the foamy spray. Seconds later, it surfaced next to its mother, and they began making their way toward the open sea, side by side.

House watched them until they vanished beneath the horizon, then sinking back against its foundation, found itself hoping that they wouldn't be ambushed by an orca as they neared the coast of Half Moon Bay—where entire pods were known to lie in wait for young pups as they swam out to sea.

Footsteps falling on tile pulled House's attention into its bathroom, where Zoe's guest, a man with light-brown hair, and colorful tattoos running up and down both arms, yawned and scratched his pale, dough-like midsection before lifting the seat of the toilet.

Hearing the rustle of covers, House shifted its gaze to the smaller of the two bedrooms in time to see Wren push the dresser away from the door and step out into the hall. Her face, although crusty from dried tears, was calm and stoic—until she entered the bathroom and found a strange man relieving himself in her toilet.

Letting out a blood-curdling scream, she danced backward as she grabbed the can of roach spray off the vanity and sent a steady stream of it into the startled man's eyes.

Shouts of pain mixed with profanities erupted from his mouth. He fell against the tub, pulling the shower curtain—and rod—away from the wall.

"Get out!"

Scrambling to his feet, the man blindly pushed his way past Wren and stumbled toward the stairs. He managed to make the first step, yet missed the next five—and rolled down the last seven, where the wall at the bottom of the landing brought him to a painful stop.

The man groaned and rubbed his eyes as he got to his knees.

Holding the bug spray in front of her as if it were a loaded gun, House could see Wren's heart pounding in her throat as she descended the steps. "I said get out!"

"Leave me alone, you crazy bitch!" he yelled, running toward the door. He leapt off the porch and started for his truck—only to stop in the middle of the yard and turn around. "I need my keys!"

"You can *walk*!"

With tears streaming down his splotchy face, the man held his hands in front of him as she pressed down on the nozzle again. "Wait!"

"Wren!" Zoe came running out and knocked the can out of her hand. "What the hell are you doing?"

Wren looked at her sister and blinked.

"Brian," said Zoe, reaching up to touch his face. "Are you okay?"

"Leave me the fuck alone!" he shouted, clawing at his blood-red eyes. "Just get me my keys and clothes!"

Zoe grabbed Wren by the arm and dragged her back inside. "What the hell's the matter with you?"

Wren shook her head. "I—"

"Never mind, I don't want to hear it!" said Zoe, gritting her teeth. "Go get him a bottle of water!"

As Zoe ran upstairs, Wren turned and looked through the open door at Brian, who was standing in the middle of the yard—wearing only a pair of navy briefs—as he cursed and dug the heels of his palms into his eyes.

With her shoulders curling over her chest, Wren dropped her gaze and started into the kitchen.

Zoe was already outside by the time she returned with the water. "Let me help you, Brian," she was saying, tenderly pushing a mop of hair from his forehead.

He snatched his jeans from her grasp. "I don't need your help!"

As Wren made her way down the steps and across the wet grass, she involuntarily glanced at the Victorian.

Gary, his two young daughters, and his wife were standing on their front porch, watching.

Wren's cheeks began to burn, and House didn't know if it was due to the commotion taking place in her front yard...or the fact that the t-shirt she was wearing barely covered the crotch of her underwear.

"Wren," Zoe yelled, "give him the water!"

Wren looked back at her sister, then held the bottle out to Brian. "I'm really sor—"

He grabbed it out of her hand and began rinsing his eyes.

"Is that helping?" asked Zoe, stooping to see.

Brian crumpled the empty bottle in his fist and lifted his head. Water poured from the inflamed slits of his eyes and trickled down his face. "When you told me you had a twin sister, you didn't tell me she was a fucking psycho!"

Throwing the bottle on the ground, he unlocked his truck and slammed himself into the driver's seat. Seconds later, the engine coughed and came to life with a sputter, sending dark gray smoke rolling out of the tailpipe.

As the rear tires began to spin, Wren stole another glance at her neighbors, this time locking eyes with Gary, who swiftly turned and herded his daughters inside, leaving his wife standing on the porch with her feet apart, arms crossed, and scornful gaze aimed directly at Wren.

"Thanks a lot, sis," Zoe muttered, purposefully bumping Wren's shoulder as she stomped past.

Wren turned and hurried up the porch steps. "I'm sorry, Zoe," she said, closing the door behind her. "I didn't mean—"

"I don't know what on earth I was thinking when I said that us living together was going to be fun—because you seem hellbent on ruining my life!"

"Oh, please..." said Wren, her contrite expression fading as she rolled her eyes.

Zoe reached the top of the stairs and whirled around. "Don't you dare try and minimize my feelings. I really liked that guy!"

"You mean Brian," she said flatly.

"*Yes*, Brian—the guy you blinded!"

Wren's hands found their way to her hips. "What's his last name?"

Zoe's face darkened. "You're missing the point!"

"No, *you're* missing the point," Wren shot back, her voice steadily rising as she trailed after her. "This is *my* house, and you should've asked my permission before bringing a complete stranger into it!"

Zoe's brows lifted in unison, creating an angry red line arcing across the middle of her forehead. "Your *permission*? Oh my God—do you hear yourself? You sound just like Mom!"

"You always do this!" said Wren, throwing up her hands as she followed her into her bedroom.

"What, Wren?" Zoe grabbed her shorts off the floor. "What is it that I always do?" she snapped, yanking them on.

"Try and derail my anger by changing the subject."

"I'm not changing the subject. I'm stating a fucking fact."

Standing in the doorway, Wren folded her arms as Zoe began shoving her clothes into her suitcase. "This was all your fault, not mine—and I'll be damned if I'm gonna feel guilty for defending myself."

"Whatever," Zoe mumbled, pulling her disheveled hair into a tight ponytail.

"Where're you even going? It's six-thirty in the morning."

"Wherever a quarter tank of gas will take me."

"Well, it's Sunday...so the bar in town is closed."

Zoe looked sharply at Wren. "Oh, that's rich coming from you." Dragging her suitcase off the bed, she walked up to her and stopped. "I'll stay," she said, the anger in her face wavering as her eyes subtly fell across the scars peeking out from the tattered neck of the t-shirt Wren was wearing, "if you promise to get some help—and I'm not talking about the kind that comes from the pharmacy or the bottom of a bottle. I'm talking about *real* professional help. Because you are spiraling out of control."

Silence, as uncomfortable as it was suffocating, filled the space between them, overwhelming House.

Uncrossing her arms, Wren took a rigid step to the right.

House saw Zoe's gaze flicker, returning her jaw to its clenched state. "See you around," she said, walking out.

"The only place you'll find open this time of day is church," Wren called after her. "But then, maybe that's what you need."

"There you go..." Zoe replied, holding up her middle finger as she started down the stairs, "being Mom again."

House watched Zoe throw her suitcase into the trunk of her Subaru, which was missing its rear bumper, and start the engine.

As she turned out onto the road, something glinted in the sunlight, pulling House's attention in the opposite direction. A white car, partially hidden behind the sprawling branches of a large pine, was parked along the side of the road, about two hundred feet from the driveway entrance. With the chaos that had taken place earlier, House was uncertain how long it had been there—and promptly looked to see if it was occupied, yet the dark tint on the car's windows made it difficult to determine.

A shaky breath, followed by a sob cut into House's concentration. Turning its attention inward, it found Wren sitting on the edge of Zoe's bed with her face buried in her hands.

House knew that Wren and Zoe's relationship was complicated at best, and felt it would be incredibly difficult for any outsider to see that beyond their constant bickering—and merciless, cruel judgement of each other—they possessed a rare bond. A love that was as loyal as it was fierce…and ran as deep as their shared secrets.

The sound of tires crunching on gravel drew House's gaze once more to the front yard, where it caught sight of the white car slowly coming up its drive. After rolling to a stop, the engine shut off, and a man dressed in dark jeans and a gray blazer got out and started down the sidewalk.

The doorbell camera clicked on, making Wren's phone ping.

Jerking her head up, she ducked into the hall, then staying low, tiptoed into her own bedroom, where she retrieved her phone from underneath the tangle of covers—only to drop it as the doorbell rang. She clumsily retrieved it from off the floor and clicked on the white bar at the top of her screen.

"Ms. Sutcliffe?" said the man, bending his tall frame to peer into the camera's open shutter.

Wren returned to her crouched position as she stared at the stranger standing on her porch.

Straightening, the man flipped the right side of his blazer back with his hand, revealing a gold badge that was clipped to the waistband of his jeans. "I'm Detective Gage Caldwell with the Monterey Police Department. I need to ask you a few questions. Your name and address were given to me by a Detective Lintz in Santa Cruz."

Wren placed her thumb on the bottom of the screen and brought it close to her mouth. "What do you want?" she asked in a harsh voice.

"I need to talk to you about what happened on the night of November second."

House watched Wren struggle to take in her breath. "I already told Detective Lintz everything I know."

The detective scratched the side of his head. "Yes, ma'am, I understand that...but there's been a new development in your case."

"What sort of development? Did you catch him?" she asked, the words jerking from her lips with hopeful trepidation.

"No, ma'am." The detective glanced at the Victorian before returning his gaze to the camera. "This is not something I care to discuss through the door. I understand how difficult this is for you, but I would appreciate it if you could just give me five minutes of your time."

His request was answered with silence.

House watched a scowl form along the detective's brow as he checked his watch.

Her hands shaking, Wren pulled on a pair of jeans, along with her trusty hoodie, and slowly made her way downstairs.

The detective impatiently rang the doorbell again. "Ms. Sutcl—"

The bottom of the door scraped across the floor as it swung open.

Detective Caldwell dropped his arm. "I'm sorry for calling on you at this hour, but when it comes to matters like this, time is of the—"

"You can have a seat over there," Wren said, pointing to the chair in the living room.

"Uh...yes, ma'am." He walked through the entryway and obediently sat down in the assigned chair.

Wren closed the door and followed, but went behind the sofa rather than in front of it, drawing a quizzical look from the detective. After skirting around the end table, she perched herself on the edge of the cushion that was the farthest from him and rested a clenched fist on her knee.

"I'll keep this brief, I promise." Detective Caldwell reached inside his wrinkled blazer and retrieved a small notepad. "You were attacked the night of November second," he said, flipping it open, "shortly after returning to your apartment on Laura Avenue, and—"

"*Laurel* Avenue."

The detective glanced at the scribbled writing on the page. "Laurel. Sorry, I read that wrong. You'll have to forgive me," he said, rubbing the corners of his eyes. "I've been up since three, and could really use a cup of coffee." The neatly trimmed—but half-grown—beard lining his jaw lifted slightly as he gave Wren a wistful smile.

"Well," said Wren, tilting her head, "maybe you should hurry up, so you can go get one."

House watched the detective's lips fold inward. Repositioning himself in the chair, he looked back down at his notes and cleared his throat. "What time did the assailant enter your apartment?"

"Don't you have that written down in your little pad?"

A tinge of darkness swept across the detective's face as he slowly raised his eyes to meet hers. "I do, but I'm checking my facts."

"It was a few minutes after eleven," she said in a clipped tone.

"And where were you before that?"

"Work."

"At work," he repeated, "and that was at…"

"The Crawford Building on Landis Avenue, where I worked as a therapist."

"Why were you there so late?" he asked, turning his hand over. "Were you with a patient?"

Wren's body, which had been poised on the edge of the cushion as if it were ready to take flight, stiffened. "I was catching up on my paperwork."

"Was anyone else in the building?"

"Probably. It's a big building."

"How about on the same floor as you? Maybe a janitor, or security guard?"

"Not that I saw."

"What time did you leave your office?"

"Around ten."

"Did you notice anyone in the parking lot, a strange car, or anything out of the ordinary?"

"No."

"What happened next?"

"I drove to my apartment."

"You didn't stop anywhere?"

"No."

"Not for gas, or a bite to eat…you just went straight to your apartment?"

Wren scratched her throat, drawing House's attention to the red blotches working their way up her neck. "That's correct."

The detective stared at her—his piercing brown eyes searching hers—as he tapped the tip of his pen against the pad resting on his leg. "Did you see the face of the man who attacked you?"

"No," she said, looking away, "he was wearing a ski mask."

"Was he tall, short…average?"

"I don't know."

"Did you notice if he had any tattoos or scars—"

"No."

"What was he wear—"

"I don't know!" she said, swerving her distraught gaze back to him. "I told Detective Lintz everything I could about that night. Why are you so insistent on asking me these things when my answers are in the goddamned file!"

The detective closed his notepad and sat forward. "I realize this is hard for you, Ms. Sutcliffe, and the last thing I want to do is upset you," he said in a soft voice, "but it's been my experience that after a few months, victims do sometimes recall a detail or two about their attackers they didn't initially remember."

"Well, that's not the case with me."

"What happened immediately after your assailant…" He paused and dipped his head in an apologetic manner, sending his dark hair falling across his furrowed brows. "…finished burning the word into your chest?"

Wren clenched the bottom of her hoodie between the folds of her fingers. "He left."

"Through the front door?"

"The fire escape outside my bedroom window."

"Did he—"

"I've answered all the questions I'm going to answer," she said. "Now, I want you to tell me why you're here."

The detective let out a weary sigh and scratched his jaw. "The body of a woman, bearing the same word on her chest as you, was found this morning in a wooded area near Quarry Park."

The blood drained from Wren's tear-stained cheeks, leaving them ashen.

"Her marks…the way the letters were burned into her skin…are identical to yours."

A shiver went down Wren's spine that made her shoulders convulse. "What are you saying?" she whispered.

House saw the detective give Wren a sympathetic look that bordered on pity. "I think it's very likely that the man who attacked you has followed you here."

Wren clasped her hands over her mouth and bowed her head as a stuttering sob tore itself from her throat. The sharp, tormented cry ricocheted off House's pine boards in the living room, making the glass panes of the window set inside them vibrate.

Getting to his feet, the detective forced his way into the narrow space between the coffee table and sofa, causing the empty bottle of tequila to wobble as his knee bumped against it. "I'm sorry."

Tears aggressively rose in Wren's tortured eyes like the tide, threatening to drown her in them.

"I know that isn't what you wanted to hear," he said, reaching out to place his hand on the top of her shoulder.

Wren visibly recoiled from his touch.

Detective Caldwell lowered his hand. "Let me get you a glass of water."

House felt movement on its porch steps, yet before it could look outside, Wren's phone pinged and the door swung open, causing the detective to turn sharply.

"What's going on?" Zoe demanded.

The detective's gaze darted from Zoe to Wren and then back to Zoe.

"Yeah—we're twins," she said in an icy tone as she stood in the doorway. "Who the fuck are you?"

Wren stood and let go of a ragged breath.

"Did something happen?" asked Zoe, rushing to her side.

Detective Caldwell, whom House noticed had suddenly become interested in his phone, absently looked up. "I'm sorry, I need to go." He started across the floor, his long stride matching his height, but stopped upon reaching the threshold of the foyer. "I've asked for a patrol car to keep an eye on your house," he said, glancing back at Wren, "but I don't know when or even if that's going to happen. In the meantime, you need to keep your doors and windows locked."

Wren remained by the sofa, clinging to Zoe like a child as he walked out the door.

Grabbing Wren by her upper arms, Zoe pushed her back in order to see her face. "What the fuck is going on?"

"Zoe..." Wren's chest began to heave, cutting off the words that were trying to form on her lips.

Chapter 36

House watched the white foam splash across the outcropping as the waves tirelessly broke against them. Other than the noisy seagulls flying overhead, the shore below was empty and void of life. As the sun rose higher into the sky, House found itself yearning for the winter day when the seals would return; however, with spring still a few weeks away, it knew it would be waiting a long time.

"Do you want something to eat?"

Sinking back against its cornerstone, House dismally turned its attention inside, where Zoe and Wren were sitting together on the faded sofa in its living room.

"I can warm up the pizza from the other night."

Wren sniffed and raised her head, which had been resting against Zoe's shoulder. "It's eight o'clock in the morning."

Zoe shrugged. "So?"

"I'm good," said Wren, wiping her nose with the sleeve of her hoodie.

"What all did this Detective Caldwell want to know?"

"He asked the same questions as the one in Santa Cruz."

"Which *were*?"

Wren sighed and dropped her hand into her lap. "Did I get a look at him? What was he wearing? Where was I before it happened? And blah, blah, blah."

"And did you tell *this* detective the truth?"

Wren's cheeks turned a vibrant shade of pink. "What the hell is that supposed to mean?"

"You know *exactly* what that means," said Zoe in a tired voice.

The sound of a phone ringing punctured the ensuing silence, which only elevated the tension between them.

Wren pulled her cell phone from the pouch of her hoodie—only to have Zoe snatch it from her grasp. "Why does he keep calling you?"

"None of your business. Give it to me."

"Why are you protecting him?" asked Zoe, holding it out of her reach.

Wren clenched her jaw. "I said, give it to me!" she yelled, then lunging across the cushion, pried the phone out of Zoe's fingers and stalked across the room.

"If I were you," Zoe called after her, "I'd be doing everything in my power to help the police catch this guy—which includes telling them that you were with Richard that night."

Wren stopped and whirled around. "But you're *not* me! And I don't owe *you*, or anyone else an explanation as to why I'm keeping him out of this!"

"Then I suggest you pack up all your shit and get the hell out of this house."

"I'm fine right where I'm at."

"*Are* you?" Zoe stood and pointed toward the foyer. "Do you really think that stupid doorbell camera is going to keep that guy from coming in here and—"

"Shut the fuck up, Zoe!" Wren shouted, the veins protruding from her neck looking to House as if they were about to burst. "This isn't helpi—" Unable to finish her sentence, Wren sat down at the bottom of the stairs, and as tears filled her eyes, bowed her face to her knees.

Letting out a small, exasperated-sounding sigh, Zoe made her way over to the landing and sat down beside her. "I'm sorry, Wrennie," she said, putting her arm across her shoulders. "I'm sorry for what I said just now, and I'm sorry for what happened to you, but most of all…I'm sorry that your head is so far up Richard's ass, that you can't see to do what's best for you."

Wren stopped mid-sob and looked up.

"And I'm not even going to try and pretend to understand why you ever took that pantywaist back the first time," she continued, meeting Wren's hardened expression with her own, "but two days ago, you told me it was over, so why not let the police know where you were that night?"

"Because…" said Wren, rolling her shoulder across her cheek.

"Because why? His wife? *Let* her find out. Richard's a big boy, and he knew what the consequences could be the *first* time he crawled into bed with you."

House watched Wren's lips spiral in a downward arc until they nearly touched her chin. "I don't give a damn about his wife. I'm worried about his daughter."

"A daughter that you've never even seen," Zoe said flatly. "It sounds to me like you're just making excuses."

Wren's face contorted. "I still love him, Zoe! Why is that so hard for you to understand? Richard sacrificed a lot to come to the hospital, and he never left my side! I've thought about what happened that night every second of every day for the past four months—and the only reason I'm still here is because Richard was there for me!"

As Wren's words, filled with rage and torment, reverberated through the room, House saw Zoe look away. "I'm sorry, Wren," she said in a voice crackling with guilt. "I'll never forgive myself for not being there for you…and although I can't change the past, I can change the here and now." Taking in a small breath, she turned her steely—albeit wet—gaze back to Wren. "Now that you've broken up with Richard for good, why not let the police know you were with—"

"I didn't break up with him," she blurted. "He broke up with *me*."

"Why?"

Wren paused to lick the tears from her lips. "It was over my surgery."

"What surgery?" asked Zoe, yet House saw her steal a sideways glance at the top of her hoodie.

"After my burns had healed, Richard talked me into having plastic surgery, saying it would help me to forget what happened and bolster my confidence. So I met with a surgeon, and after several consultations, she scheduled the operation for this coming week…but then I got the DUI and lost my job. I had to cancel the surgery because I'd given every cent to my attorney. It was then that Richard told me he thought it would be best if we just went our separate ways."

Zoe balled the fingers of her right hand into a fist. "Fucking prick," she muttered. "He doesn't deserve you."

"I know," she said, giving her a tearful nod, "but that doesn't make it hurt any less."

The sun disappeared behind a cluster of dark clouds, casting a long shadow across the staircase as Wren's phone rang again.

"Why is he still calling you?"

"Because he wants the engagement ring back."

"Tell him to piss off."

"I have, but the other day he told me that he'd lied about the ring belonging to his great-grandmother. It's actually his *wife's* great-grandmother's—and she's been looking for it."

"You know," said Zoe, shaking her head, "my hate for him just keeps growing. Don't you ever give it back to him."

"I couldn't if I wanted to, because after he told me the truth, I went and pawned it."

Zoe let out a stiff laugh. "Well, that's fucking karma if I've ever heard of it."

The clouds opened up and rain began hitting the roof, drawing Wren's mournful expression to the ceiling.

"Listen to me," said Zoe, her rigid smile fading, "you need to think about the very real possibility that there's a connection between Richard and the guy who did this to you. Maybe he's a jealous co-worker, or some guy Richard crossed in a business deal, or maybe...his wife found out and hired someone to fuck you up."

Deep pockmarks appeared on Wren's chin as it flattened.

"That's why I think you need to let the police know. If I'm wrong, I'm wrong, but at least you will have done everything in your power to catch this creep—"

A booming roar suddenly shook through House, making Wren jump.

"It's okay," said Zoe, pulling her tighter against her. "It's just thunder."

House watched Wren's embarrassed gaze drift aimlessly around the room, eventually settling on the empty bottle of tequila on the coffee table. "You know," she said bitterly, "five months ago, I was perfectly happy. I had a nice life, lots of friends, my practice was thriving, and I was in love with a man who I thought loved me back. But now..." Wren shook her head and knotted her fingers together. "I can't even make it through the day without having a drink...or bursting into tears."

A flash of lightning lit up the window, enabling House to see that Wren's reflection had grown dark.

She dug her fingernails into the back of her hand, drawing blood. "He took everything from me."

Zoe removed her arm from around Wren's shoulder and straightened. "Not everything. You still have me...and this time I'm not going anywhere. I promise I'm going to help you get through this."

Wren's eyes, sunken, red, and skeptical locked with Zoe's. "How?"

"One step at a time, sis." Leaning over, Zoe tenderly kissed the side of her head. "One fucking step at a time."

The wind changed direction, and the rain began to pelt the front windows.

Zoe listened to the drops of water plinking against the glass panes for a moment, then nudged Wren with her shoulder. "I'm sorry for getting so upset with you this morning. I should've asked or, at the very least, texted you last night to let you know I was bringing a guy home."

"I'm sorry too," said Wren, running her hand through her hair. "I overreacted."

Zoe pinched her thumb and forefinger together. "Maybe just a little."

The seashell lamp on the table in the living room flickered as another clap of thunder rolled through House.

"Is that why you came back?" asked Wren. "To tell me you were sorry?"

"Well, *that*..." said Zoe, tilting her head, "and I remembered that I'd left my case of Duckhorn behind."

The startled silence that followed was quickly succeeded by a hiccupping giggle...and snorts of laughter.

Chapter 37

House stared at the darkening horizon, watching the small silhouette of a trawler drift past the setting sun; with its nets hauled in for the day, it was headed for the wharf to sell its catch to the only fish market left in Gosset Bay. The cannery, having closed long ago, was now a half-deserted mall that peddled antiques and crafts to tourists; some of whom were in search of a good deal, while others had stopped to walk the new pier and had meandered in—still most, it seemed, were just plain lost and looking to get back on the main highway.

"What did Lintz say?"

House shifted its gaze inside and found Zoe in the upstairs hallway, steam rising off her bare shoulders like pillars of smoke, as she peered down at Wren, who had walked out of the office.

Wren stopped and looked up. "Were you listening?"

"No."

"Then how did you know who I called?" she asked, placing her hands on her hips.

"Lucky guess," Zoe replied innocently, leaning over the rail.

Stepping around the sofa, Wren began making her way up the stairs. "All I got was his voicemail, but I left him a detailed message explaining what Detective Caldwell had told me."

"Did you tell—"

"*And* that I had something more to tell him regarding that night."

Zoe finished drying the ends of her hair and smiled. "I'm proud of you, sis," she said, tossing the towel on the bathroom floor. "What do you say we celebrate by getting out of here for a while?"

"What did you have in mind?"

"I don't know. How about we drive up the coast, have a nice dinner somewhere, and then get a room? I know the manager at the *Ocean Safari Inn*, and am pretty sure I can get him to give us a discount."

The wall sconce in the hall cast a dim light across Wren's face, enabling House to see the dark circles lining her eyes. "And how do you suggest we pay for all that?" she asked, folding her arms against her hoodie.

Zoe gave her sister a dry look. "I know you keep a credit card with a zero balance to use for emergencies."

"Okay, first of all, how do you know that? And second—"

"Details aren't important," said Zoe, rushing the words as she pulled a navy halter top over her head and zipped up her jeans. "What's important is knowing that in less than an hour, we could be sitting in a fancy restaurant enjoying a nice big lobster, with a side of fantail shrimp that have been deep fried to perfection, or…" She paused to make a sweeping gesture with her arm. "You could just stay here and stare at the walls in *this* dump."

House's left front shutter drooped.

Wren cast a hesitant glance toward the front door, which had the chair wedged under it once again. "Give me ten minutes to change."

"Mm...and maybe brush your teeth."

"You're one to talk," Wren grumbled, pushing past her. "Miss Halitosis three years running."

"Screw you. How was I to know that eating grapefruit would give me bad breath?"

Fifteen and a half minutes later, two of which were wasted trading barbs, they were both dressed and headed downstairs.

As they started into the foyer, Wren's phone began to ring.

"Is it him?"

Wren frowned as she glanced at the screen. "No, it's one of my patients."

"Well, tell them to call back during office hours."

"It might be an emergency," she said, pressing the phone to her ear. "Milo? Is everything okay?"

Zoe let out a groan-filled sigh. "If we get there too late, all the good lobsters will have been taken."

Acknowledging Zoe with a slight nod, Wren closed the French doors behind her and opened her laptop. Moments later, a distressed-looking Milo appeared. "What's going on?"

"I went to *Alonzo's* and apologized like we talked about."

"And?"

"I told the manager that I was extremely—not very, but *extremely*—sorry for talking to that lady customer in such a rude manner."

"Did he accept your apology?"

"Yeah."

"That's great—"

"But when I asked him if I could have my job back, he laughed and told me to get out, or he was going to call the police and have me trespassed." Milo slammed his shoulders against the back of his chair, making it creak. "Can you believe that dickhead?"

Wren's eyes swarmed with empathy. "How did that make you feel?"

"It made me want to beat the shit out of him."

"And did you?" she asked in a voice filled with apprehension.

Resting his elbow on his knee, Milo put his left thumb over each of his knuckles and cracked them one by one as he stared at Wren. "No," he finally said. "I counted to ten like you taught me and walked out."

The feeling of spinning tires sent half of House's attention swerving outside, where it saw the white car belonging to Detective Caldwell coming up the drive.

"I'm very proud of you, Milo."

Giving her an incredulous look, Milo narrowed his eyes and leaned forward. "Did you not *hear* what I just said?"

"Yes, I heard you," Wren answered, "but you went against your thoughts and walked away. That is a huge step forward for you."

The darkness in Milo's eyes faded. "Yeah…" he said, the right side of his mouth lifting into a crooked smile. "I guess it is."

A pinging sound echoed between them.

Wren glanced at her phone—and got to her feet.

Moments later, House felt its walls tingle as the doorbell rang.

Zoe hurried into the foyer and after cautiously peering out the window, shoved the chair out of the way and unlocked the door. "Come in," she said, taking a step back. "Wren's on the phone with a patient, but she'll be out shortly."

"Thank you," he replied, smoothing his hair with his fingers as he walked inside. "And I'm sorry, I didn't get your name this morning."

"It's Zo—"

"Did you catch the guy?"

The detective's gaze shot past Zoe to find Wren standing in the living room. "No, I'm sorry. I just came by to…" He paused as his warm brown eyes subtly took in the red top and white capris she was wearing. "Are you two going out?"

"We were just about to go to dinner," Zoe replied, stepping back into his line of sight.

"Dinner can wait," snapped Wren. "Why are you here?"

"The department can't spare a patrol car at the moment. So until we bring this guy in, I'd feel better if you had some sort of protection." Reaching inside his blazer, he pulled out a black rectangular device; it resembled a flashlight, yet its edges were slightly curved at the end, and had two small metal prongs sitting on either side of a tiny bulb.

"Is that a stun gun?" asked Zoe, leaning closer to the detective than she needed to.

"It is."

Zoe placed her hand on his arm. "So, how does this bad boy work?"

"I'll show you," Caldwell said, his bearded lips taking a slight upturn as he handed her the stun gun. "You turn it over and flip the safety switch on."

"Like this?"

"Perfect," he replied.

"Now what?"

"Do you see the red light?"

Zoe nodded, sending her hair spilling across her bare shoulders. "Uh-huh."

"That means it's on."

"What do I do now?" she asked in a helpless-sounding voice.

House saw Wren scowl at her sister — which went unnoticed — as she continued to shamelessly flirt with the detective.

"You want to press the button above it."

A faint ring began to filter into the living room, causing Wren's hand to fly to her back pocket — only to find it empty. "Excuse me. I need to get that."

"This button?" asked Zoe, holding it in front of the detective's face as he watched Wren make her way across the living room.

Returning his attention to Zoe, he nodded. "Yes, that activates it."

Seconds later, a blue light began to arc between the metal prongs.

Wren grabbed her phone off the desk. "Detective Lintz, thank you for calling me back."

"Is it ready to use now?"

"It is. So, if someone's coming at you, you grip the edges of it like this," Detective Caldwell said, wrapping his fingers around Zoe's as she held the stun gun.

Zoe playfully bit her lip as she stared into his eyes. "Then what?"

Sighing, Wren closed the door and turned her back on the two of them. "I have some more information to give you about that night."

"Now you want to press it into their upper shoulder, or hip, but the most effective hit is just below the rib cage."

"Wait" — Zoe's enamored gaze suddenly widened in horror — "you're the guy from the hotel bar — "

A silent gasp fell from her lips as Caldwell jammed the stun gun into her exposed abdomen. "That's right, bitch," he said, his upper lip curling beneath his flared nostrils. "Did you think you could just ditch me like that and get away with it?"

House felt its own breath leaving it as Zoe's arms and legs violently shook. Her knees began to buckle, and she fell backward, striking her head against the corner of the chair sitting beside the door.

Stepping over her lifeless body, Caldwell jerked open the front door and, with one swift kick, tore the doorbell camera from the wooden casing, then crushed it with the heel of his shoe.

"...should have told you this months ago," Wren continued, "but I just—"

"Wren, listen to me very carefully," Lintz's voice boomed. "I never spoke to a Detective Caldwell, and Monterey PD said they don't have anyone by that name."

Wren's face went pale.

"They also told me that no body of a woman has been found anywhere within a hundred miles of their vicinity in the past forty-eight hour—"

Splinters of glass and wood flew across the room as the left door exploded against the wall.

Wren screamed as Caldwell yanked the phone out of her grasp and smashed it against the corner of the desk.

"Where's Zoe?" she whimpered, trying to peer around him as she began backing up.

"Her whereabouts are the least of your problems," he said in a low voice, walking toward her.

Wren held her hands out in front of her. "Why are you doing this?"

"Because you have the poor misfortune," he said, grabbing her by the arms, "of looking exactly like your sister. You see, one night after leading me on to the point of no return, she told me she'd be right back—only to leave me hanging. So you know what I did?" Grinding his jaw, he jerked her closer. "I sat in the parking lot of that damn hotel and waited for her to come out...but it was *you* I followed home."

Wren's terrified expression went from confusion—to a panicked understanding that caused her breath to catch in her throat.

"You know," said Caldwell, his eyes narrowing, "I was moments away from putting you out of your misery this morning, just like I promised I would four months ago, but then your sister—your obnoxious, foul-mouthed, *twin* sister—comes barging in, and I realized at that moment that I'd made a grave mistake. I had to abandon my plan and go for a drive to work things out in my head."

Turning loose of her right arm, he began to run the backs of his knuckles along her chest. "But then, as I was chastising myself for hurting such a beautiful, innocent person as yourself," he continued in a contrite tone, "it suddenly occurred to me that you were *also* at that hotel." He gathered the folds of her top between his fingers. "Is that a sick game the two of you like to play?"

"No, you don't understan—"

Giving a forceful jerk, he ripped the fabric down to her navel.

Wren closed her eyes and let out a restrained sob.

"Aww now, it's not so bad," he said, touching the jagged scars snaking across her chest. "Not bad at all. In fact, I'd say it's a work of art."

As he traced the outline of each letter with his fingertips, House noticed a small bulge in his pants.

"Please…" Wren begged. "Let me go."

"It's just so beautiful," he murmured, then with his pants growing tighter, bent down and slid his tongue over her raised pink flesh.

Wren's free hand suddenly jutted out from her side. Grabbing the laptop, she swung it hard at Caldwell's head, slicing open the skin above his left temple.

"Fuck!" he yelled, stumbling backward.

Seizing the opportunity, Wren unlocked the door that led to the deck and ran outside. In the encroaching darkness, she could see Gary standing on his own deck, holding Rylee. "Gary!" she screamed, frantically waving her arms. She called his name over and over, but the howling wind devoured her shouts before it could reach him.

Gary set Rylee down, then taking her by the hand, disappeared inside the Victorian.

"You know, I was going to make this easy on you!"

Wren turned to find Caldwell coming up behind her.

Blood streamed down the side of his face as he held a long, serrated knife against his leg. "I can't say the same for your sister, though. As soon as she comes to, she's going to wish she'd never laid eyes on me."

A pair of bright headlights swept across House's wooden clapboards. Glancing to its left, House saw the black sports car belonging to the man who lived in the glass and steel structure pulling into his circle driveway. After shutting off the engine, the man slid out from behind the wheel and started ambling toward his front door.

"Help me!" shrieked Wren.

The man stopped and looked at House.

"Help m—"

"Shut the fuck up," Caldwell said in a hiss-filled whisper as he held the knife to her throat.

The man listened intently for another moment, then turned away.

As the man walked through his front door, Wren's tearful gaze began to flail helplessly about—only to abruptly stop. Before House could follow where it had settled, however, Wren swung her right foot between Caldwell's legs, connecting the top of her sandal to the waning bulge in his crotch.

Caldwell let out a yelp and doubled over.

Wren sprinted across the deck to where the stairs used to be and climbed on top of the rail, then crouching to steady herself, slowly stood.

House began to tremble, for it knew it was at least a ten-foot jump to reach the hard-packed earth, with nothing in between to break her fall but pounding surf and jagged rocks.

Caldwell limped toward her, his face red. "What the fuck are you doing?" he said, his words coming out in a pig-like grunt.

Keeping her eyes on the dark, unforgiving landscape in front of her, Wren swung her arms back and—there was a snap as the board gave way beneath her feet.

House felt its pilings that were dug into the cliff begin to slide as it strained to catch her, but without anything to extend, it could only watch her plunge into the churning abyss below.

A blind fury tore through House, shaking every square inch of its foundation—which caused the left piling underneath its deck to slip the rest of the way off its berth.

The deck pitched and tilted, knocking Caldwell backward and throwing him against the broken edge. With his legs dangling over the side, his eyes filled with panic as he clawed at the crumbling boards in front of him.

There was a thunderous boom as the century-old beam, unable to hold the weight bearing down on it, snapped in half and tumbled down the cliff, taking huge chunks of rock, most of the deck—and Caldwell—with it.

The plummeting wood smashed against the cliff wall and exploded, sending debris flying in every direction before being swallowed by the raging sea.

Listing heavily on its side, House desperately searched the dark water for Wren. A giant swell crashed against the rock facing, sending plumes of spray high into the air. It was there, amidst the swirling white foam, that something red appeared.

House could see Wren's arms barely moving as she struggled to stay afloat. The rising tide had carried her toward the cliff wall, and House noticed a small tree jutting out from the rocks about twenty yards from where she was. Wave after giant wave washed over her, pushing her closer to the tree.

The wind suddenly changed direction, whipping the sea into a frenzy; the waves thrashed violently about as their malevolent fingers pulled Wren beneath the black water.

House's breath pumped rapidly in and out of its flue, sending chunks of creosote flying onto its roof, as it scoured the churning sea for any sign of its occupant.

As the moonlight glinted off the water, Wren breached the surface; coughing and sputtering, she began paddling toward the tree, dragging her right leg behind her.

A large swell crashed over her head, slamming her into the crag wall. Lifting her arm, Wren managed to grab hold of one of the tree's small limbs as the pounding surf repeatedly flung her against the razor-sharp rocks.

Shouts of profanity mixed with incoherent raving drew House's attention to the gaping hole where its deck used to be. Detective Caldwell, half-bobbing, half-drowning amidst the swells, seemed to be intact—yet the powerful current had carried him far beyond the outcropping of rocks, which were still submerged beneath the tide.

As sirens wailed in the distance, he slowly turned himself around and started swimming toward shore—but was suddenly dragged under. Seconds later, he burst above the surface and let out a garbled, high-pitched scream. House watched in both awe and horror as a long white belly rolled over onto its side and began to thrash about, while the enormous snout attached to it shook Caldwell like a rag doll, turning the water red.

Chapter 38

Under the heat of the midday sun, House repeatedly threw its weight against its north side in an effort to right itself, yet after a dozen failed attempts, gave in to exhaustion and despair. Falling back against its lopsided cornerstone with an almost paralyzing fatigue, House watched the Coast Guard slowly circle the mouth of the inlet. As the men on board used grappling hooks to retrieve planks of wood and debris that were bobbing in the waves, divers below searched for Caldwell's remains — because they had naively assumed he'd drowned.

Taking satisfaction in knowing that only pieces of him would be found, however, House fastened its gaze to the side of the boat, hoping that the water lapping softly against it would be enough to lull it to sleep, yet the police officers and detectives milling about its property made it impossible to do so.

Letting out a weary sigh, House turned its attention inward, and as it stared at its bloodstained entryway, it slowly came to the realization that no family was ever going to find happiness within its walls.

~

"Fuck!"

House despondently watched the billowing smoke pour out of the oven as Zoe yanked her burning lasagna from the lower rack. The sudden feeling of footsteps on its porch caused House to shift its gaze from the pungent gray swirls circling its kitchen ceiling to the front door, where it found the Victorian's owner standing on its tattered welcome mat with one box stuffed under his arm, and a second one balanced in the palm of his hand. Using the index finger on his free hand to push his glasses back up the bridge of his nose, Gary rang the bell and nervously cleared his throat.

Zoe dropped the blackened pan on the counter and marched into the living room. "What?" she yelled, jerking open the front door—both of which made Gary flinch.

"Uh, is this a bad time?"

"Would it matter if I said yes?"

"Oh...sorry." Lowering his gaze, he turned away.

"Gary, I'm kidding," she said, waving him in. "It's fine."

"Are you sure?"

Her lips flattened into an impatient smile. "I'm sure."

As he walked inside, House watched him abruptly draw his head back as his nostrils flared. "Is something on fire?"

"Not anymore," Zoe replied, closing the door behind him.

"Uh, I won't stay long," he said, suppressing a cough as smoke drifted out of the kitchen. "I just wanted to drop off this pie as a sort of welcome home—"

"Zoe!" Wren's voice bellowed from upstairs, followed by an angry clopping sound. "What the hell's burn—" She fell silent as her disgruntled expression landed on Gary.

"How are you?" he asked, the slender box on his palm wobbling slightly as he looked up at her.

"Well...I've been better."

"I'm sorry," said Gary, shaking his head. "That was a stupid questi—"

"Look, Wrennie..." Zoe paused to point at the box. "Gary brought us pie!"

Wren leaned heavily against the crutch that was tucked under her right armpit. "Did your wife make it?"

"Huh? Oh—God no," he said, letting go of a small laugh as he pushed his glasses back up his nose. "It's from the coffee shop in town."

"Even better," replied Zoe, eagerly taking it from him. "Do you wanna stay and have a piece?"

"Sorry, I can't. I just wanted to drop that off and see if there's anything the two of you needed," he said, yet House noticed he kept his focus on Wren as he spoke. "And I also wanted to give you this."

Wren stared at the other box he'd slid out from underneath his arm through the swollen purple slits serving as her eyes.

"It's a new doorbell camera," he said, holding it up higher for her to see. "I'd be happy to put it on for you."

"That won't be necessary."

The enthusiasm in Gary's face crumbled.

House saw Wren wince as she took in a small breath. "It's not necessary, because I'm not staying," she said, rushing the words as if she wanted to undo the hurt forming behind those puppy dog eyes of his. "I'll be moving out as soon as I'm well enough to drive."

Clutching the pie between her fingers, Zoe turned and made her way into the kitchen—which still hung thick with smoke.

"I understand," said Gary, seeming oblivious to Zoe's sudden departure. "I'll just leave this here…" He paused to place the doorbell camera on the arm of the sofa. "You can take it with you."

Wren nodded, but didn't say anything.

"Okay…well," he said, turning toward the door, "take care."

"Gary?"

He stopped and glanced back.

A single tear slid down Wren's bruised cheek as she looked down at him. "Thank you for calling the police. One of the detectives at the hospital told me it was you."

"No thanks are necessary," he said, reaching for the knob, "not *all* men are assholes."

Wren's tightly pursed lips widened into a painful grin.

Gary opened the door and gave her a small nod. "'Bye, now."

"'Bye," said Wren.

Out of the corner of its peripheral vision, House saw Zoe stab the pie with the knife she'd been using to cut it.

~

The afternoon dragged over into the evening as House, unable to right itself, dismally watched its surroundings from its new vantage point.

Blaring music laced with vulgarity, loud shouting, and occasional screeches of laughter could be heard coming from the glass residence, making House grimace as its upstairs windows buzzed and vibrated to the booming beat.

The noise must have drawn Wren's attention as well, because House saw her slowly sit up and grit her teeth as she set her right leg, which was stuffed inside a boot-like contraption with Velcro straps, down on the floor, then reaching for her metal crutch, pushed herself to a standing position and hobbled across the room.

Parting the curtains with her left hand, which was covered in cuts, scrapes, and deep purplish-yellow bruises that extended all the way up to her neck, Wren peered out the bay window. The bright lights emanating from the glass house greeted her, making her drop her restricted gaze to what was left of the deck below.

House listened to her labored breath begin to tremble as she gripped the panel of the curtain.

"That's some party next door, huh?"

Wren lifted her head, but did not turn around. "Sounds like they're having a good time," she replied in a soft voice, then licking her cracked lips, added, "you should go over and introduce yourself."

"Yeah," Zoe replied, leaning her shoulder against the doorjamb, "I bet he's got a lot of good shit to steal."

"I'm being serious."

"So am I. Have you seen that guy's car? It's a lambor-fucking-ghini!"

Wren answered her with a sigh.

The volume of the music suddenly increased, escalating the awkward silence that had drifted between them.

"Did I hear you talking to someone on the phone earlier?"

"It was Detective Lintz."

"Did they find Caldwell's body?"

"No," said Wren, keeping her eyes on the window. "He called to tell me that the car he was driving came back registered to a Duncan Hensley. He's going to text me his driver's license pic in the morning so you and I can make a positive identification, but he told me this guy did time for assaulting his ex-girlfriend by holding a soldering iron to her face, and he also has charges pending for assaulting a woman outside of a bar in Rio del Mar last year."

"I don't know why they're waiting on an ID from us," grumbled Zoe. "I mean, how many assholes do they have running around that use soldering irons on people?"

Closing her eyes, Wren took in a stilted breath. "He also said that the police found a tracker under the fender of my car, and that his trunk was filled with…"

"Filled with *what*?"

Wren tightened her grip around the handle of her crutch. "Lots of things they suspect he was going to use."

House saw Zoe's lips stretch into a grim line. Pushing herself away from the doorjamb, she rigidly walked into the bedroom and came to stand behind Wren, allowing House to see the two dark bruises embedded in her pale skin; straddling the bridge of her nose, they angled sharply downward before curving under her eyes, which bore a somber expression. "Do you want some lasagna?" she asked in a quiet voice. "I scraped off the burnt parts."

"No thanks."

"How about some pie, then?"

"I'm not really hungry."

A look of frustration tinged with anger surged across Zoe's face. "Well, let me know when you are," she snapped. "In the meantime, maybe you could tell me when you were planning on letting me know that you were moving out."

House saw Wren's shoulders stiffen—an action that did not go unnoticed by Zoe.

Using her crutch to turn herself around, Wren held her left arm tight against her ribs as she eased herself down onto the window seat. "I just assumed you knew," she said, avoiding her sister's penetrating gaze.

"What"—Zoe shrugged—"do you think I'm all of a sudden fucking telepathic?"

The muscle beneath Wren's blackened jaw flexed. "There's no reason for me to stay here anymore."

"You mean there's no reason for you to stay here with *me* anymore."

Wren looked up at Zoe. "Well, unless you're planning on paying the rent—which is unlikely, seeing as how you have no money and no job," she said, a knotted thread angrily poking out of the closed wound on her right eyebrow as she raised it, "you're going to have to leave here too."

"Where the hell are you going?" asked Zoe, crossing her arms. "Back to Santa Cruz?"

"No."

"Where, then?"

"A place that has room for both of us."

"Once again," said Zoe, giving her an impatient sigh, "where would that be?"

Wren hesitated, seeming to weigh the words on her tongue. "Mom's—"

"No"—Zoe began shaking her head—"absolutely not!"

"You know, neither one of us is exactly in a position to choose," Wren said pointedly.

"I would rather sleep in my *car* than set foot inside that house!"

"Zoe, I know you think I hate you for what happened," Wren called after her as she started out of the room.

Zoe's footsteps faltered.

"But I don't."

Looking to House as if she were on the verge of tears, Zoe slowly turned back to Wren. "Well...you should."

"What happened was a crazy, stupid thing, but it wasn't your fault, and if this had to happen to one of us...I'm glad it was me."

"Nobody likes a martyr," Zoe replied in a rough voice, yet House heard the sorrow beneath it.

"I'm not claiming to be one." The contusions on Wren's throat expanded as she swallowed. "What happened was penance for my sins."

Zoe walked back across the floor. "Hooking up with Richard wasn't a sin," she said, sitting down beside her. "It was just a reflection of your poor judgement." Bumping Wren's shoulder with her own, she forged a small smile.

The edges of the bruise lining Wren's jaw turned red as tears began to roll down her cheek. "It's not that."

"It's okay," said Zoe, sweeping Wren's matted hair off her face. "Just tell me."

Wiping at her tears, Wren's mouth twisted open in anguish. "Do you remember that day when we were eleven, and I convinced you to pretend that you were me...and go fishing with Marvin?"

Zoe's forehead creased—then tightened as her breath seized in her throat. A powerful shudder ripped across her shoulders and traveled down her legs, leaving them trembling. "What are you saying?"

"I'm sorry," Wren whispered through her tears. "I was afraid of what he was going to do to me. That's why I asked you to pretend that you were me."

Zoe's eyes filled with so much hurt that House had to look away.

Wren threw her arms around Zoe's neck as an unintelligible apology, mixed with violent sobs, rushed from her lips.

Chapter 39

The yellow and black police tape stretched across House's deck flapped in the breeze as the surf pounded against the shore below. With a loud squawk, a young gull swooped down and perched itself on one of the remaining deck posts and began preening its feathers with its tiny beak.

"Are you going to be okay to drive?"

"I'll be fine."

House reluctantly turned its gaze to its driveway, where Zoe and Wren were preparing to leave. The past week had consisted of long periods of silence, lots of tears...and copious amounts of alcohol.

"Are you sure?" Zoe closed the trunk of Wren's car and walked around to the driver's side. "It wouldn't hurt you to rest here for another few days, you know."

"I'm perfectly capable of driving myself to Mom's," Wren said, tossing her purse and backpack into the front seat. "Besides, tomorrow's the end of the month, and I can't afford to put any more money toward rent."

"How long do you think you're going to stay?"

"At least until Marvin—" Wren swallowed the rest of what she was going to say.

"At least until Marvin what?" Zoe prodded, her tortoise-shell sunglasses dropping slightly as she arched her brows. "Croaks? Takes a dirt nap? Meets his demonic maker?"

Wren's lips folded inward. "I'll probably stay until after the funeral."

"You can hasten that by holding a pillow over his face—or you know, just stand on his oxygen hose."

Wren placed her hands on Zoe's shoulders and pulled her closer. "It may not be in a court of law...but I swear to God he's going to have his day of reckoning," she said, pressing her forehead to hers. "And after he and I are done, I'm going to tell Mom what he did to you."

Zoe drew back with a scowl. "Have you ever even *met* our mom?"

"I know," replied Wren, wiping at the corners of her eyes, "but that's not going to stop me. Not this time."

"Have I told you that you're my favorite sister?" asked Zoe, her face filling with gratitude.

"You can still come with me. I know it's not an ideal situation, but at least it would be free room and board."

"Thanks, but I'm going back to my old bartending job."

Wren narrowed her eyes. "Really?"

"Yeah, Jake told me that the new guy was stealing him blind, something about there being a missing case of Duckhorn."

"Zoe—"

"I'm kidding. The guy was skimming from the till."

"What about a place to live?"

"There's a small apartment above the bar that he's going to rent to me. And speaking of Duckhorn...here. You'll need it where you're going."

Wren looked at the bottle Zoe was holding out to her and slowly shook her head. "Thanks, but I think I'm going to try being sober for a while."

Setting the Duckhorn on the hood of her car, Zoe cupped Wren's face in her hands and gave her a cheerless smile. "Are you going to be okay?"

Wren cleared her throat. "I promise...if *you* promise."

"It's a deal," said Zoe, nodding.

"And I'm going to be staying on with *Mindful Shores*, but starting tomorrow, I have a standing appointment three times a week with my old supervisor in Santa Cruz."

"Good for you." With her eyes growing moist, Zoe held her arms open wide. As Wren fell into them, House saw Zoe's gaze shift to the Victorian as if doing so would keep her impending tears at bay. "Uh-oh..."

"What?"

"Don't look now, but your lovesick neighbor's looking this way."

Gravel crunched beneath Wren's boot as she took an uneven step backward and glanced to her right.

"'Byeeee, Gary!" Zoe called, giving him an enthusiastic wave.

"Stop it," Wren said, swatting at her arm with a giggle.

Turning its attention to the Victorian, House watched a perplexed Gary give a hesitant wave back.

"Are they leaving?"

Gary's fingers went limp at the sound of his wife's voice. "Yeah," he answered, resuming his task of pulling the garbage tote down the drive.

"Well, the second that For Rent sign goes back up," she said, marching along beside him, "I want you to call the number on it and ask them how much the owner wants for it."

"Why?"

"So we can buy it and tear it down."

Gary stopped and placed his hands on his hips. "What on earth for?"

"God, Gary!" The woman rolled her eyes. "Do I have to spell it out for you? The only kind of people that house is going to attract are degenerate lowlifes. What if the next one's a crackhead? Do you really want someone like that living next door—with our daughters playing in the front yard?"

"Jillian," he said in a weary voice, as he pushed his glasses up his nose, "I think you're overreactin—"

The shrill honk of a car horn diverted his attention. Looking toward the road, Gary watched Wren drive slowly past, her long red hair blowing in the breeze as she gave him a radiant smile and wave.

Crossing her arms, the woman cleared her throat—loudly.

Gary turned back, his cheeks red.

"Make the call the *second* you see that sign."

As she started up the drive with her fists clenched, the vile determination on her face—combined with the fear in Gary's—filled House with utter trepidation as it watched the taillights of Wren's car vanish from its slanted line of sight.

Chapter 40

Dawn broke over the horizon, streaking the sky in muted shades of pink and orange. House, listing heavily on its side, turned its gaze to the Victorian; standing straight and tall, dapples of color fell across its new neighbor's sparkling windows as the faint aroma of coffee drifted from its kitchen.

House took in a shallow breath and shoved its flue open as far as it could. "Hello?" it called out in a feeble voice crackling with dust and debris. As it anxiously awaited a response, the sudden rumbling of a truck sent its attention swerving to the road.

Fearfully digging its sill plate deeper into its crumbling foundation, House watched and waited.

Moments later, a semi-truck carrying a load of steel pipes drove past.

House relaxed its grip on the sill, yet its feelings of apprehension remained. A few weeks ago, Brad the real estate agent had stopped by and put the For Sale/Rent sign back up, prompting Gary to begrudgingly walk over and take a picture of the number printed on it.

Shifting its gaze to the sign, House stared darkly at the four red letters that had been prominently attached to the top of the post yesterday afternoon.

As the pungent smell of mouse droppings intensified in the stifling heat, House felt as though it were about to suffocate as it began to wonder what would happen to it after it was torn down. Would whatever it was that made it alive slide into the sea and be drowned amongst the rocks, or would it be free to roam the earth the way it did that night with Wren in her dream? Would it float away with the clouds, or stay right where it was, bound forever to the top of this forsaken cliff…or would it just simply cease to be?

House's vision dimmed and its breath grew shallow, for despite having existed over two centuries, with years of loneliness—spanning decades—stretched between, it took no solace in dying.

As the sun ascended into the sky, House turned its gaze inward and receded into the darkness.

~

A faint sound woke House with a start. Rousing its right side from its cornerstone, it cast a fumbling glance into each of its rooms…but found nothing. As a wretched and miserable silence loomed inside it, the sudden sensation of gravel being displaced sent its attention veering outside, where it saw a burnished-orange Lexus coming up the drive.

Plumes of dirt and smoke rose from underneath the car's tires as it skirted around a large pothole before coming to a stop. Seconds later, the driver's side door opened, and a woman with long dark hair got out.

As House intently watched her walk around the front of the car, the rear doors flung open, expelling a young boy and girl.

"Wow, this place is cool!" said the boy, running across the front yard.

The girl, who looked to House to be about six, followed, but stopped upon reaching the broken sidewalk and turned. "Mom? Are we really going to live here?"

House began to tremble with excitement, sending an eerie whistle coursing through its vents as its breath rushed out of it.

"We certainly are," she answered, sweeping a pensive gaze along House as she opened the passenger side door, "but your daddy has to make a few repairs to it first."

An older woman with silver hair slid out of the seat and slowly stood.

"Well, Mom?" asked the younger woman, locking arms with her. "Is it just like the pictures?"

The lines embedded in the woman's face crinkled as her lips curled upwards. "No," she said in a soft voice as she clasped a hand over her chest, which was adorned with a black beaded necklace, "it's better."

House fought to keep still as its new family climbed the steps to its porch.

"Mom," said the girl, watching her unlock the front door, "are there ghosts in this house?"

Slipping the key in her pocket, the woman looked down. "Nope," she answered, giving her daughter a reassuring smile as she took her by the hand. "No ghosts in here."

As they walked inside, House noticed that the older woman remained behind. Dressed in black pants and a gray cardigan, her silky hair followed the curve of her slender face as her seasoned gaze roamed across the porch. After several moments, she raised her hand and pressed her palm against the peeling column.

House was suddenly jarred by a familiar heat surging from her fingertips, causing the glass panes in the light hanging above her to rattle.

"Grandma Charlie," the boy called to her excitedly as he poked his head out the door, "come and show us yours and Uncle Travis' room!"

She turned and gave a small laugh. "I'll be right there."

"Can't you come now?" he begged, his curly locks falling across his forehead as he motioned for her to follow him inside.

"Tyler?"

"What?"

His mother appeared in the entryway. "I want to show you something."

"What is it?"

"Well, you'll have to come with me to find out," she said, pointing him in the direction of the stairs. As he galloped toward them, the woman glanced apologetically at her mother. "Take your time."

Giving her a nod of thanks, Charlie waited until the door had closed, then taking in a small breath, rested her cheek against the column. "Hi, House," she whispered.

Long buried feelings, tangled in forgotten memories, began to swirl inside House like a tempest, making it feel as though it were going to drown in its ecstasy.

"It's all right…" Tears slid down Charlie's face as she closed her eyes and smiled. "I'm home."

~ ~ ~

THANK YOU, READERS!

Thank you for taking the time to read *The House on the Cliff*. If you enjoyed it, please consider telling your friends or posting a short review. Word of mouth is an author's best friend and is very much appreciated.

~ Belinda G. Buchanan

More Books By Belinda G. Buchanan

Mysteries
The Monster of Silver Creek
Tragedy at Silver Creek
Winter's Malice

Women's Fiction
After All Is Said And Done
Seasons of Darkness

www.belindagbuchanan.com

Printed in Great Britain
by Amazon

d88ce767-6641-4af1-acca-a8b36516a8e7R01